JACOBUS
A Eunuch's Faith

INDIA CONNECTION
Book 2

Paul Trittin

ISBN 978-1-956001-31-0 (paperback)
ISBN 978-1-956001-32-7 (eBook)

Printed in the United States of America

CONTENTS

ASSYRIA
Babylon
PARTHIA
PERSIA
Jerusalem
Gaza
NABATAEA
SINUS PERSICUS
ARABIA
Koptos
AEGEYPTUS
Berenike
SINUS ARABICUS
OMAN
AETHEOPIA
MA
Aden
SOCOTRA
Pano
MARE

BALUCHIA
GEDROSIA
A
mmana
Oraea
Barbaricum
ARIACA
Barigaza
RE ARABICUS
PANDYAN
TAMALA
Paravur
Mylapor
Muziris
CHERA
ERYTHRAEA

MARCH 23, AD2018

Since the decision by the United States Supreme Court which declared same-sex marriage legal, there has been a more intensive bombardment of gays and issues related to their rights within the public debate. Emotionally, the USSC decision did little to extinguish the flames of the firestorm ignited by the Stonewall Uprising in New York City in 1969.

Those of us who . . . through no fault of our own . . . have been ridiculed, shunned, and even told we were unwanted in our home churches, have become incognito believers in exile. We have had no choice regarding our sexual identity. We were born gay. Even Jesus recognized this biological phenomenon. He declared to his disciples that it would be better if 'born eunuchs' do not marry women (Matthew. 19:12). In the history of the United States it was only during slavery and the Civil Rights Movement that one minority of our population has been so targeted as homosexuals have been targeted recently.

For 4200 years eunuchs, including 'born eunuchs' (homosexuals) have been a troublesome minority to a powerful and demanding majority. Opposition has often included threats to their very lives, both legally and illegally. Regardless of what they have been called, they have been misunderstood, maligned, and murdered. Even so, "born eunuchs" have held some of history's most prestigious positions and provided society with limitless creative geniuses. Even that has not made them acceptable among many traditional societies, especially ecclesiastic organizations and Faith Communities.

The chasm between gays and the Faith Communities gained broad public attention after the Stonewall Uprising. The conflict recently increased because of the emotional and divisive issue of same-sex marriage. That decision has not resolved the problem within the traditional religious communities. We are continually reminded that the conflict over eunuchs is not new to either this generation or to this nation.

There is value in noting the diversity of this global minority in the first century, for historically that was the mid-point between the first legal trial involving eunuchs in the twenty-first century BC and our trials in the twenty-first century AD. What have we learned in the last twenty-one hundred years that influenced our treatment of this minority? It will be the work of other researchers to do such a comparative study between our present population and the 'homosexual eunuch' population in the first century.

Jacobus, A Eunuch's Faith is a historical fiction which considers the interaction of three great events in the western world during the first century, which still affect us today. They were like siren calls that Paul Trittin, the author of *Jacobus*, could not resist.

The first great event was the consolidation of scores of small, individual kingdoms into the vast Roman Empire.

The second great event paralleled the growth of the Roman Empire, which was in part the result of Rome's military conquests. It was fostered by the rapid expansion of a newly established 'global' trading network created through the efforts of artisans and businessmen and their growing 'world' consciousness. In *Jacobus*, Aetna Shipping is a prominent maritime business headquartered in Syracuse, Sicily, which was eager to become a major player in the Mediterranean world and beyond. It was owned by a group of very successful Jewish businessmen comprised of one extended family.

Those two events required an immense labor force which would be made up primarily of slaves, which often included man-made eunuchs. Integrated with the general population were also what the Greeks referred to as 'born eunuchs.' Members of these two groups of men were often considered society's losers.

The third stimulus was the impact a new religious teacher, Jesus of Nazareth, and his Jewish followers, who would have an unimagined impact on the future political and moral climate of the region. The Jews had always been a thorn in the flesh of the Romans, so the Jewish leadership fearfully kept close watch on their new prophet.

Trittin's narrator of his tale set in this period is Jacobus Didymus BarSirach, a young, precocious, Jewish boy from a non-religious family. After a somewhat traumatic but privileged childhood, he presents an account of his efforts to successfully combine love, trade, faith, and an immense work force in an era of rapid change. All brought together by the interaction of the three dynamic forces mentioned above.

At the male adult legal age of fourteen, his father apprenticed him and his brother to the family-owned shipping company's labor force. Josephus, Jacobus' twin, was interested in math, science, and engineering and was assigned to work at the local shipyard of Aetna Shipping located in Valencia, Spain. Jacobus was sold as an apprentice to the head of the family, at Aetna's headquarters in ancient Greek city of Syracuse on the island Sicily. He soon began his training on the *Dolphin,* a trading ship calling on ports throughout the

Mediterranean. His exceptionally mature judgment often made him suspect by members of the crew and fellow maritime traders, but his success record was undeniable.

Growing up as homosexual eunuchs there were moments of high drama like when as children, the BarAbraham twins were 'caught' enjoying their penises together. Like many children, their father's unrealistic shock and response made a lasting impression on them. The one positive result of this early experience is that later it enabled Jacobus to be more keenly aware of the physical and emotional needs of the slaves and crews on his family's ships. The twins were motherless from birth and grew up in a home devoid of nurturing and affection from their father. Consequently, when Jacobus observed the love and trust among their eunuch slaves, which was often underestimated and misunderstood, he was amazed. His father's choice to ignore their family's Jewish religion did little to prepare him for the Jewish faith as it was lived out by his relatives in Aetna Shipping's leadership in Sicily. Some of the family even became involved in the new movement within Judaism often referred to as 'The Way.'

From five to seven million men, one-fourth of the estimated male population of the Roman Empire during the first century, were slaves at the bottom of society with no rights or personal identity. Many lost all semblance of individuality and endured greater indignity when they were intentionally castrated, made eunuchs, to assure greater security for their owners, but gave them no value for breeding. This created an immeasurable degree of suffering.

Using conservative numbers, there were three to five million castrated and born eunuch slaves who were physically or psychologically unable to parent children. There was also a minority of female slaves used to bear children who would grow up as slaves, and also lose all semblance of their own individuality, especially when sold off at very early ages.

Why would an author choose this as the environment for a precocious, sheltered, sexually struggling, rich kid to learn how to become a man? Trittin has an answer. Since eunuchs were first legally identified in 2100 BC, they have often been treated as less than human or at least half-males without moral regard. Trittin wanted us to see eunuchs . . . all three kinds which Jesus recognized in Matthew 19:10-12 of the Christian Bible . . . presented as 'different' but equally valuable human beings. He believes they should be recognized for their unique spiritual insights, human sensitivity, and creativity and perceived to be as valuable as are heterosexuals, even though they should not be expected to marry a person of the opposite gender. It is his desire that all eunuchs be recognized as possessors of God given possibilities instead of being viewed and treated as subhuman or moral derelicts. Trittin's goal is to help correct the problem of misidentification and false inferiority of eunuchs of all types.

Through a story that is first centered on the love between twin brothers, Trittin discreetly reveals sexual experiences of a 'normal' young eunuch or any maturing male youth might experience. Too often the typical negative reactions by parents and some contemporaries have had frightening and intimidating results. Without explanation or discussion, the negative reaction is often interpreted to mean anything sexual is dirty and off-limits. Jacobus, made an interesting observation regarding those experiences. "It was a learning I carried through much of my adult life. What I'm doing or want to do might not be wrong, but if other people who don't like it, learn what I'm doing or want to do, I'm in trouble." Therefore, the tension caused by the conflict between the twins and their father, is never resolved, just tolerated.

Life expectancy in the Empire during that century averaged little more than thirty years, causing adult responsibilities to begin at a young age. At fourteen boys were considered men and could get married and begin to procreate. Jacobus often questioned his father's inability to understand him and his brother, and his unwillingness to discuss sexual issues with them. This has been a common problem for fathers and sons of every generation. A few issues might have been unique during the Roman Empire, but most of them have been on-going throughout our 4200-year history of trying to understand and deal with eunuchs.

It may appear that Jacobus' life meets few problems, and he usually receives immediate acceptance. However, memories from a mother-less childhood and the emotional rejection by his father caused much pain and may have moderated his personality and yielded a greater compassion than one might normally expect in a youth. Coping with three murders occurring during his early manhood, certainly would be challenging for any teenager.

The struggles with his own sexuality gave him insight into many of the emotional and physical needs of the slaves and eunuchs living in shipboard isolation. Jacobus' recognition of the power of and need for intimacy was evident in his youthful ability to cope with the problems of the men on board ship or on land.

Trittin, through his characters, artfully shared how Jacobus was on point almost every time. He, like eunuchs/gays in every generation, learned that they cannot be sure how they will be treated outside of the closet. Throughout the book there is no concerted effort to encourage romantic love, but love of any description wins almost every time by example without sermons or explanations.

Frustration and uncertainty are strong incentives for change. Adulthood at fourteen and the prospect of a life aboard ship with slaves and eunuchs was a future he faced with fearful acceptance. Will his future years be more satisfying than what he experienced as a child?

Paul Trittin can control the future of Jacobus and his friends. However, it is the sad reality that today there continues to be too many murders, rapes, suicides, and family and church splits because we have not yet learned to walk together on a road to reconciliation through forgiveness and respect. Gay Christian Fellowship, an organization Trittin and I started, has as its mission "to strive for a reconciliation between the LGBT and FAITH Communities, seeking a culture of forgiveness and respect." May every reader join us on the walk to recognition and acceptance of each person's right to be themselves as God created them . . . straight or gay, religious or non-religious, progressive or traditional.

Reverend Dr. Marvin G. Baker
Gay Christian Fellowship, Carson City, Nevada

PROLOGUE

After arriving at our destination in Jerusalem, Sadhu descended from our horse cart and pulled the bell chain and within a minute a servant appeared to welcome us. Descending from our carts to enter the grand home, we waited to be greeted by our influential host. As he entered the antechamber where we were waiting, he called to have his house servants to take our baggage and servants to the guest wing of the house, so our rooms could be prepared for us.

Our host was truly curious about the pilgrims he had agreed to house during the celebration of the Jewish Seder and the following Festival. He looked carefully at his seven guests who were a strange group of pilgrims indeed. Before him stood three wealthy Indians, three fabulously wealthy Greco-Judeans, and one rather common but true Judean. On the surface they were four men, one woman, one teenager, and one child. What else were they?

Detecting his curiosity, Stephen went around the room and introduced each of us and we shared our reasons for the difficult journey, finally ending with me, his younger brother. Swallowing hard, I began to share with our host the deeper reason why our family made the trip to Jerusalem.

"I can only speak for my own family, which does not include the rabbi from India. Our family has representatives in every major port of the Mare Internum and deals significantly with Jewish merchants.

Over the last year or so there have been stories from clients and rabbis alike about the Prophet from up in Galilee named Jesus. What we have heard of him rings with how we see God's hand in our world beyond Judea. I spoke with one of his disciples during a recent trip to Caesarea, and what he told me lit a fire in my soul and in the souls of many of my family. Simon, my brother's brother-in-law, has even had a vision of walking with the Prophet through the streets of Jerusalem, so we are expecting to see him here."

After a quiet moment, Nicodemus, our host, gave us a strange response, "I know Jesus personally and will verify that he is sent by God. However, he has never come to Jerusalem during Seder. At this point I have no reason to believe he will be here this year, but if he does come I will be honored to introduce you all to him at the appropriate time. In fact, if he comes, we will all know it immediately and you may be able to hear him speak."

Following a moment's silence Sadhu raised his head to speak. "We too have heard of him in Alexandria, but as foreigners we have had a difficult time trying to verify the many reports we have heard from servants and slaves. As you know, Alexandria is a city of orthodoxy devoid of political intrigue like Judea, and my fellow rabbis have refused to discuss him with me. To be honest, we are surprised to hear this from Jacobus. We have never spoken of this or any other deep spiritual issues with our colleagues. Sir, we are also here to meet the Prophet."

Looking at Yacobsa, he nodded and gave me the biggest smile ever.

What was God doing by putting us all together at one time with only one purpose . . . to meet the Prophet? It was beyond my ability to comprehend. How did we end up in the home of a man who personally knows Jesus? I was becoming very sure that the next two weeks would be a period of my life I would never forget.

CHAPTER 33

NICODEMUS – APRIL 5, AD29

With sunlight pouring into our room through the large, high, atrium window, we awoke with an eerie feeling . . . missing the usual fresh smell of the sea. We were discovering it truly was more than a legend that the often-pungent smells of a massive landlocked city, without the flow of water to drain away its urban wastes, and in Jerusalem, drying blood from temple sacrifices was sometimes nauseously revolting. Even so, it was a comfortable spring morning with doves cooing on the rooftop and songbirds singing in the atrium's fruit trees, just as they did at home in Syracuse. All of this was accompanied by the sound of trickling water from the atrium's fountains fed by a large manually circulating cistern on the roof of the servant quarters.

Opening my eyes, I realized Stephen was holding me tightly against him, while his contented son lay asleep on the other side of him in our large bed. Nicodemus only had four available guest rooms, one for us, another for Sadhu and Rahelani, and two smaller rooms for Yacobsa and Simon. However, before we had adjourned for the evening Hanno informed me that Yacobsa had invited him to escape the servant quarters and sleep with him. If I had need of him I could find him there. Smiling, I wished him a good night. Once a eunuch, always a eunuch!

The house was still quiet, so I closed my eyes and reveled in Stephen's warm breath on my shoulder. Eventually voices could be heard on the other side of the house, signaling it was time to begin stirring and awaken my man. Of course, once I made the slightest noise, Aaron popped his head up over his father's shoulder to ask if I had a good night. Chuckling, "Yes, your father kept me very warm." Satisfied, he asked when we were getting up. Before I could answer, his father opened one eye and shot back that it would be a few minutes yet, but that he could go ahead and get dressed and play in the atrium if he chose. He thought a minute after trying to tickle his father, he decided the atrium would be a good idea. As he put on his tunic and closed the door behind him. I rolled over into Stephen's arms, and we had a wonderful time sharing our love, even if for only a few minutes.

Hearing Aaron laughing with someone in the atrium, we both jumped up and donned our tunics as a knock came on our door. I hurried to open it and was quite surprised to see Sadhu wrapped in a brightly woven fabric reaching mid-calf. Excusing himself, he asked if we had heard anything about breakfast. Nicodemus had served us a light supper before we retired, but I understood where Sadhu was coming from. We had had a sparsely nourished day and I, too, was famished. While we were speaking, one of the house staff came to tell us that breakfast was ready. I hurried to Yacobsa's room to reach him before his father. I rapped on the door and shouted, "Breakfast."

Since I had alerted his son, Sadhu returned to his room to see if Rahelani was ready to go on to breakfast just as Yacobsa stuck his bare torso out the door. I told him we were gathering to eat so they needed to move quickly. Stephen and I went on to the dining area where the floor was covered with beautiful carpets of all sizes and at least a score of large, fat cushions to lean on as we ate the sumptuous spread laid out on large brass platters. Naturally, Hanno and Yacobsa were the last to arrive and it was after Sadhu had already said the blessing. They obviously had had a great evening judging by their laughter as they walked through the doorway. Rahelani shook her head, of course, and frowned briefly until she noticed that no one paid the slightest attention to them.

As we completed our meal, Nicodemus's steward appeared to inform us that in thirty minutes our guide who would show us the city would be arriving. Getting ready for our first exposure to the Holy City was exciting. When our guide arrived, he asked if our servants would like to join us. I knew Aaron BarHanno would, and I asked Sadhu about his servants. He said he would join me as we went to the servant quarters to inquire. We arrived just as our servants and Nicodemus' were finishing their breakfast. I was right. Aaron desperately hoped he could see the city. However, Rashvi, Sadhu's valet, was the only Indian servant who wanted to go with us. We just joined the group when Stephen came to inform me that he had business with Nicodemus and that I should tour the city with the others. Within minutes we met our guide in the antechamber, and immediately struck out, excited as school children.

We only walked past two houses before our guide identified our first point of interest. It was the porticoed courtyard in front of King Herod's Western Palace which was built against the heavily fortified western wall and now served as the Jerusalem residence of Roma's provincial governor. Then we walked back down past Nicodemus' house, and at the other end of the street we entered the towering Greek Theater which was also used for all types of public events. From there we followed the tall wall which separated the palaces and mansions of the aristocratic upper city from the hovels of the lower city.

We eventually reached the Hasmonean Palace built by the descendants of Judas Maccabeus who led the revolt against the Greek Empire. It was built in honor of that victory and the reinstatement of Jewish worship in the Temple. It is because of that victory that we celebrate the Festival of Lights during Hanukkah. Proceeding on, we walked through a gate in the second high wall which separated the upper city from the working class neighborhoods and the military barracks of the northern city. We were instantly in a typical oriental environment with shops and bazars everywhere.

As we walked further into that part of the city, we followed a great wall to our east that was built of giant stones larger than horses. I couldn't help but wonder how they stacked up each giant stone, to say nothing about how they cut each one so perfectly. We soon came to a massive staircase which cut up through the wall and led to an enormous colonnaded courtyard. When we reached the court, we were amazed that it was the size of an average village or small town, but what stunned us all was the magnificent Temple near its center. Staring up at such a magnificent structure, designed like nothing we had ever seen before, it seemed as tall as the Pharos and four times as massive. Unfortunately, we only had time to walk around the Temple before we were required to move on.

Back down in the city, we sought out an open-air market where we purchased our lunch which was comprised of lamb, chicken, grapes, bread, dates, and sweet pastries. We were pressed to eat on the run and washed it down with warm tea. Before our lunch could be completed, we found ourselves at the south side of the Temple and were surprised by the sight of a massive Greek-styled Hippodrome built for high stakes chariot races held inside of Jerusalem. It extended a third of the way to the gate in the southern city wall. At the upper end of the Hippodrome was its entrance which opened onto a spacious, formal square with trees and fountains and framed on three sides by porticoes of Greek columns. The columns continued south on each side of a perfectly straight avenue also going nearly to the southern gate. Shortly before reaching the gate we arrived at the famous, Greek-styled Pool of Siloam which reportedly contained healing waters.

Once again, to avoid the poorer section of the city, we walked back up the avenue past the Hippodrome, and up into the Temple Court where the priests were beginning to slaughter the day's sacrifices. Eventually we reached Nicodemus' home with time to recover from our exhausting tour before dinner.

Later that afternoon I joined Hanno, Aaron BarHanno, and Sadhu in Yacobsa's room. They were vivaciously animated by what they had seen, especially the spectacular Temple which had been totally restored sixty years earlier by King Herod. The striking varieties of marble, the gigantic objects of cast bronze, and massive amounts of gold leaf were scattered everywhere. In fact, while we were speaking of the Temple, Sadhu mentioned that he would like to return the next day, dressed as a rabbi, and visit with some of the theologians. Each of us agreed it would be exciting to go with him and try to learn more about our faith.

Surprisingly, it was at dinner that we learned more about theology than we ever expected. We knew that the Sanhedrin was the governing assembly of Judea, but we were unaware that they were also a theological body judging theology and doctrine as well. With Nicodemus as a member of that assembly we had our own theologian present at dinner. We all thought of the sadhu as the person qualified to discuss these matters with our host, but Nicodemus saw things otherwise.

Before we were five minutes into our meal, Nicodemus turned to Simon and asked him why he thought God gave him his vision and if he was certain it was not the result of too much garlic and wine. Simon was caught completely off guard, but he swallowed hard and for some strange reason he felt comfortable telling his entire vision to all of us.

"What I will tell you I have never told in its entirety to any one, not even my wife. About four months ago, I went to bed very tired. In the middle of the night I awoke with a start to a gentle male voice calling me to meet him in Jerusalem. I got up and looked throughout the house, but my wife and I were the only ones not in the servants' quarters, and she was asleep. All I could do was lie down and try to go back to sleep too, which is what I did. It was then that someone began shaking me, but I wasn't in bed. I suddenly realized I was standing on a crowded street holding onto the hand of a young boy."

Suddenly, Simon froze and became as pale as a ghost. He looked across to Little Aaron and began to choke up for a minute before continuing. "I . . . I was holding my nephew Aaron's hand, so we wouldn't be separated in all the pushing and shoving of the crowd around us. Then the man shaking me pulled me away from Aaron and commanded me to help another man who had just fallen in the street near me. As I helped him up, the man who had grabbed me said that I also needed to carry what the man had dropped when he fell. So I did. I put what he dropped on my right shoulder, and I helped hold him up with my left arm. As we walked together, he thanked me and said his name was Jesus. He was very tired as we continued walking together through the crowd to somewhere beyond the congestion of the narrow streets. Finally, someone told me that I could put down what I was carrying for Jesus.

"As I looked into Jesus' eyes he thanked me for my help and told me he would see me again soon. Then everything got dark and I heard a man's voice calling for his father. At first, I thought it was the little boy that I lost, but then I knew it was Jesus calling. I looked everywhere but I couldn't see him. It was too dark, so I shouted back, 'I can't find you.' Then I felt an earth quake, but it was just my wife trying to awaken me because I was still shouting, 'What happened? I can't find you!' I persisted to shout for several minutes. 'I can't find you!'"

Simon looked at each of us in turn and stated, "I know the vision was real because I was in Jerusalem holding Aaron's hand, and here I am in Jerusalem where I have never been before. I'm here because my brother-in-law came with his ship to bring me. On the ship was my nephew, Aaron, whom I had never seen before, but who looked so familiar when I first saw him. He was the boy I had lost in the crowd."

We all sat quietly for several minutes in awe of something none of us understood. The silence was finally broken as Simon looked at Nicodemus and asked if he could tell him what it meant. Before Nicodemus could say a word, Simon looked over to Aaron and smiled, then suddenly began to wail in terror.

We were all afraid that his 'dream' was too much for him. Before long he settled down and apologized to Nicodemus. "When I looked at Aaron just now I remembered the last part of my vision. When I finally found Aaron right where I had left him, he asked me, 'Uncle Simon, why are your clothes all covered with blood?'" Simon broke down again.

Since he could not complete his meal, Nicodemus advised Simon to feel free to retire to his room until he felt better. Waiting for our host to moderate our discussion, I said what we were all thinking, "What if Jesus does come to Jerusalem from Galilee?" No one would speak, and no one moved.

After a few minutes a very disturbed Nicodemus made an unexpected statement. He shared, "Several members of the Sanhedrin are frightened of Jesus. Every fifty or hundred years the people rise up against their subjugating governments and a bloody war ensues which we seldom win. If one happens now, we will be wiped off the face of the earth by the Romans. They almost did that to Galilee a few decades ago, and they can do it here. The Jesus I know is definitely not a man of violence but one of peace and love. But that also frightens some members of the Sanhedrin.

"The Sanhedrin will do absolutely anything to prevent those who might manipulate Jesus to influence the people to drive out pagan Roma. If they try, it will bring down Roma's wrath instead. Some militants will try to use anything or anyone . . . like a gentle Jesus . . . to drive out Roma. Even if they use a man as passive and defenseless as Jesus against a revolting army of inflamed citizens, we are doomed. They want freedom from foreign governments, religions, or philosophies at any cost. The Sanhedrin cannot allow such violence, even if it is the peaceful Jesus they fear as the one to spark it. Yes, my dear friends, I also am frightened. For this reason I didn't expect Jesus at Seder. Now I'm not so sure."

We spent the rest of the evening picking at olives and smoked tilapia from Galilee, while exhausting ourselves discussing unknown fears based on Simon's mystical vision. We all did our best to doubt Simon's tale, but Sadhu . . . very familiar with the supernatural in India . . . knew by the terror on Simon's face that the vision was real. He was now more determined than ever to meet with as many rabbis as he could in the five days before Seder.

After breakfast the next morning, Sadhu, Stephen, Simon, Yacobsa, Hanno, and I left for the Temple. Nicodemus gave us the names of several scholarly rabbis whose theology was totally devoid of any political influence. When we arrived at the Temple, we began the frustrating process of trying to find the rabbis on our list. The first available rabbi we found studying in one of the alcoves of the

Temple was not on Nicodemus' list, but he was not teaching any students either, so we approached him. He was very traditional to the point of rejecting God's actual participation in our contemporary world of Roman technology and Greek philosophy. The next rabbi was not much better. He believed that because of the violent world in which we lived, God had become a spectator to our self-centered folly toward self-destruction. The third rabbi we approached called himself a Sadducee and stated his belief that our primary duty on earth was to do what is good as human beings. In his opinion, he also saw God as a spectator who had no real intention to accept any of us into his heavenly kingdom after we die. We live for today only.

In total frustration, we finally saw an official looking man dressed in robes like Nicodemus. The sadhu introduced us and shared our quest to find a rabbi we could speak with about the power of God in the contemporary world. He was surprised that we, as pilgrims traveling so far, were looking for such a rabbi. He told us that he had visited with one such rabbi who was on our list earlier in the morning and he would be honored to take us to him.

Following him to an alcove in the portico at the far corner of the courtyard, we found a young rabbi studying some of the recent Greek translations of the Torah created by rabbis at the Library of Alexandria. Aside from the Aramaic translation in Babylon, which is also used in India, there had never been a serious or scholarly translation of the Torah into any other language. That was never needed because Jews, unlike my father, rarely assimilated into their host cultures. Now, as western cultures became more influential, it was decided such a translation would soon be needed in the nearly universal Greek language of the Roman Empire.

As our guide introduced us to Ephraim, he appeared pleased that Nicodemus referred us to him. He commented that his work, writing commentaries on the Torah and other great books written by our forefathers, keeps him so busy that he seldom has the time to visit with his own patron, Joseph. His estate in Arimathea was only fifteen miles north of Jerusalem. In a tone of jest, he claimed Joseph had to bring him foreign seekers to get me to appreciate him. Then laughing, he claimed, "The life of a scholar is always dull . . . to everyone but the scholar."

As Joseph shared our story and our purpose, Ephraim lit up like a torch to think that news of Israel's newest prophet had reached across the empire and had even brought another scholar from the Jewish remnant in India.

Leaving us in Ephraim's care, Joseph asked our pardon as he continued on to a previous commitment. Now that we had met someone who appeared free to discuss Jesus in a positive context, we were hard-pressed to know the proper questions to ask. What was his background? Where did he come from? Who is his sponsor? What Jewish sect is he a part of?

As it turned out, we asked all the typical questions for which Ephraim had none of the typical answers. It appeared as if Jesus was operating completely outside the Jewish establishment. In fact, so much so that he had accumulated many influential enemies. Ephraim was sure of one thing . . . Jesus knew the Torah, the Prophets, and the religious books better than the Pharisees themselves, as well as other religious leaders who have tried to use our holy writings against him. That brought him to the most revealing point we had heard from anyone.

"This new Prophet speaks with the voice of absolute authority . . . absolute! That has made him many enemies among the powerful who think they are the only ones who wield absolute authority, except with the Romans, of course. For centuries these men have controlled all existing religious and secular authority and have given no hope to the rest of us."

Looking intently at us all, Ephraim declared, "Judaism's greatest spiritual dilemma is this . . . what will we do with Jesus? Either we accept him and change our ways, especially in how we relate to God and how we relate to each other. Or we reject him and face a cataclysmic cultural and spiritual crises. It must be one or the other. My fear is that, like in other societies, we could very easily make the choice which goes against history. Israel . . . Judea, Galilee, and even Samaria . . . will cease to be a spiritual force in our world. What will take our place? I have no idea. One thing I am positive of is that it will not be the elite in the Temple."

Completely rattled, we got our answer, but not the answer we sought. Could we really be on the threshold of a drastic shift in history? We thanked Ephraim for both his insight and his honesty. We decided it was time to return to Nicodemus' home and perhaps speak with him tonight about what he thinks all this could actually mean.

We arrived home an hour before Shabbat, which gave us adequate time to prepare. At five minutes before sundown we heard the gong calling us all to the dining room. The smells coming from the kitchen area were richer than any I had smelled anywhere else except Rahelani's kitchen. Wow! Was Rahelani in the kitchen with her servants fixing us a Shabbat we would never forget?

When we got to the dining carpet and our individual cushions, Nicodemus' wife stood at the end of the room waiting. After we were all seated, she announced that the evening's Shabbat came straight from the hands of our Indian sisters. She then sat next to her husband and the candles were lit, the prayers recited, and a song of praise sung. Seated with us was our servant, Aaron BarHanno, and Sadhu's valet, Rashvi. We were all dazzled as the two Indian servant women in spectacular saris paraded in with platter after platter of tantalizing dishes and placed them on the carpets in front of us. Then the two of them came in carrying a huge brass platter with a roasted young goat laying peacefully on a bed of bright yellow rice. They placed it on the medallion woven into the center of the carpet. If this was Shabbat, what would Seder be like?

In spite of the festive atmosphere, dinner that evening began on a contemplative note until Nicodemus asked, "Sadhu, how did your day at the Temple fare? Were you able to locate any of the rabbis on my list?"

Swallowing his most recent bite of pulled roast goat, Sadhu looked up with a stressed expression upon his face and replied, "At first we could find none of the rabbis on your list, so we looked for rabbis who were not busy with students. We were stunned with the vast diversity of theological perspectives, most of which left us feeling that in Jerusalem, God was distant and unconcerned about humanity. We began to ask ourselves why we had ever come to Jerusalem in the first place. There is more orthodoxy in Alexandria. However, all was not in vain for we soon met a friend of yours, Joseph, from the town of Arimathea. When we showed him your list, he said he had just left one of the rabbis, Ephraim, at his labors over a portion of the Torah recently translated into Greek. He took us to him and introduced us as friends of yours.

"Asking us to sit and join him, we immediately asked what he knew of the Prophet, Jesus. He didn't speak of Jesus himself, but of what he represented to Judaism and mankind in general. He felt we were at a crossroad in history, and if we as a people make the wrong choice, our nation of Israel would cease to exist as God's light to the world. He felt we could even be nearly destroyed like my ancestors six hundred years ago, only this time it would be much worse. He fears deep within his spirit that we will reject God's prophet and find ourselves in a world of severe chaos. Nothing will ever be the same again . . . but he still had hope . . . he shocked us when he said the Prophet will not die in vain. Also, he was sure a remnant will survive, as in the past, who will carry this message of God's love to worlds we now know nothing about.

"My dear Nicodemus, Ephraim is expecting the worst, but he revealed no fear or distress to us. He only revealed his faith that God would be with us forever. We must ask you if these are the words of a scholar detached from reality, or from a delusional mystic?"

With tears welling in his eyes, he replied, "Neither. He is a holy man of great faith. He does not seem like a mystic, but a prayerful man of God. I see the same things as he does. I cannot see things continuing as they are much longer. With the Pax Romana now in place, those who survive the calamity ahead will be able to spread the love of God to every country within the Empire and beyond. All will not be lost, but our world as we have known it, very well may be."

Silence! . . . We sat together in deep thought, not knowing what to expect. It was a delicious drawn-out dinner we had that evening, punctuated with Nicodemus' anecdotal stories of Jesus' ministry in the Jewish territories of Galilee and beyond into the Greek City States of Decapolis, the Phoenician cities, and down into Judea where his opposition has been intense.

The next morning each of us took our servants with us to visit some of the exciting places we had visited earlier. Because it was Shabbat, the only truly busy place in the city was the Temple. The crowd was a devout one. Men were wearing their prayer shawls praying for God's mercy and deliverance. From there, Nicodemus led us up the Mount of Olives to appreciate the best view of the Holy City. From there he took us down to the City's most popular garden,

Gethsemane. We walked the hill to the Golden Gate which took us back up to the Temple Court and then out the other side to the Upper City and home.

Almost every one of us had heard of these places all of our lives, but most of us never dreamed we would actually be there some day. We all returned home determined to see more the next day, when the city would be teeming with pilgrims, shoppers, children, and animals. Then we would also begin our search for Simon's sons, Alexander and Rufus.

CHAPTER 34

THE VISION – APRIL 9, AD29

Now that the 'Day of Rest' had passed, we decided to spend much of the following day in the bazars of the northern city. When we were there a few days earlier, we noticed an energy they permeated throughout that area which existed nowhere else in Jerusalem. Like most pilgrims, each of us desired to purchase mementoes of Jerusalem, reminding us of the time we spent there. So we were off to the bazars. Unlike the day before Shabbat, all the servants wanted to join us. I suppose we all had a bit of a holiday spirit about us, because Seder was only three days away, followed by the week-long Festival of Unleavened Bread. That is when the city goes crazy as everyone celebrates our people's deliverance from nearly four hundred years of slavery in Aegyptus over twelve hundred years ago. It's the remembering and celebrating of our peoples' last meal in Aegyptus that we commemorate at Seder.

Leaving our hosts to themselves for the day, the twelve of us left the house in a buzz of excitement. Passing the Hasmonean Palace, we walked through the gate into the northern city, passed the stairs to the Temple, and on toward the bazars in the heart of the quarter. We spent a quiet morning making our purchases and stood in the shade of the closely packed buildings to eat our lunches.

After an hour of just walking and looking, we heard people shouting in the distance. The people around us began running through the streets toward the northern gate shouting that Jesus was coming. Frantically, Stephen rounded up all of our group to prevent anyone from being swept into the rush of people running to see Jesus. Finally, he got us all together and we quickly began to walk as a group, holding onto one another, following the direction of those who ran ahead.

Walking about four streets further, we began to hear people shouting "Hosanna" in unison, which Stephen translated from idiomatic Hebrew as *'God, save us.'* That only confused us more until the crowd began backing up the street as though they were being pushed. Feeling unsafe in these narrow, winding streets Stephen confirmed that we were all together. Then we entered an alley where we could watch what was going on without getting separated. Once we stopped, Hanno immediately put Aaron on his shoulders, so he could see, too. Fortunately, the alley we slipped into had an uphill grade going the direction of the Temple. Looking over the heads in front of us, we saw the street packed with people walking in our direction singing, "Blessed is he who comes in the name of the Lord!" followed by, "Blessed is the coming kingdom of our father David!" That was exactly what Rabbi Ephraim and Nicodemus feared most . . . religious agitators!

We continued to watch as the crowd in front of us began to move a little quicker, pushed up the hill by those who were singing, and waiving palm branches they had cut along the road coming into the city. Soon the singers and palm waivers were right in front of us, marching like they were in a parade. Within five minutes we saw Jesus riding a young donkey like a peasant. Could that unassuming man really be Jesus? He was nothing like any of us expected. He just sat there staring straight ahead with a strange intensity, as a young disciple led the donkey toward the Temple. What was happening? It made no sense. Walking behind him were his other disciples, including Thomas Didymus who I recognized from Caesarea. Eventually the crowd thinned out and we were immediately in a now quiet street again. After another hour we began to make our way back toward the gate to the upper city. When we got to the Temple staircase, we saw only normal traffic, with the exception of Jesus' young disciple holding the donkey's rope . . . waiting.

That was all Stephen needed to see. He assured us he would return in a few minutes and then walked over to the young disciple. Greeting the young disciple by identifying himself as Stephen BarSirach, a pilgrim from near Roma and leading a delegation from India, he asked if Jesus was going to be in the city through Seder. The young disciple, John, thought he would be there throughout the Festival, but he would only be in the city during daylight hours. After the completion of the Festival, they would be returning to Galilee. As Stephen turned to leave, John hastily added that most of his master's time in Jerusalem is usually spent in the Temple complex. Thanking John for his help, he returned to us and we continued to Nicodemus' home.

At dinner, Nicodemus became very agitated when he heard what had happened with Jesus. He knew this would call for an emergency meeting of the Sanhedrin soon after Seder, hopefully after the Feast of the Unleavened Bread. His frustration was that these people are not helping Jesus but setting him up for destruction. Intermittently throughout the meal, his own agitation would flare up as he claimed the people in the street were playing directly into the hands of those who would eventually destroy Jesus. Each time Nicodemus said things which evidenced threats against Jesus, Simon became more and more despondent, almost to the point of melancholy.

After dinner, Simon confided with Stephen that he needed to get in touch with Alexander, find out where he lives, and move to his home as quickly as possible. Stephen went straight to Nicodemus and explained the situation. Simon needed an emotional sanctuary rather than the atmosphere of doomed supposition he sees us fostering here. He did not feel ill towards any of us, but we were seeing something he feared yet felt he could not avoid.

Nicodemus had sensed the same problem and understood his fears. He said he would begin a search for Alexander BarSimon in the morning. Then asking what his other son's name was, he vowed he would also begin a search for Rufus BarSimon as well. However, Nicodemus needed to speak with Simon before we all retired for the night. He stressed the need for as many clues as Simon could share with him.

The next morning, immediately after breakfast, Nicodemus left for the Temple tax office, and the more comprehensive Roman tax office. The senior tax agent in both offices assured him that if he returned midafternoon the clerks should be able to share the reports on each of the men. Something within him urged Nicodemus to remain in the Temple and the Sanhedrin precincts for a few hours to take the pulse of the men in power.

Later, as Nicodemus entered the meeting chamber, he immediately knew there was trouble. There were animated clusters of black robed men everywhere. The basic tone was, "We need to stop it before it's too late." Worse yet, it seemed someone on the inside also saw the danger the nation faced, but that person saw the Sanhedrin as the solution and offered to help them fix it . . . for the right price. Nicodemus was disappointed that Joseph wasn't in the chamber picking up on this latest news, but he had probably returned home to Arimathea until after the Holy Days.

Returning to the tax offices at the hour appointed, both agents gave Nicodemus identical information. The brothers live in a house they own together in the village of Bethphage up on a ridge just an hour away, on the far side of the Mount of Olives. Nicodemus verified their probable location and he was confident his man servant could take Simon there without a problem immediately upon his return home.

Walking through the door on his arrival, the atmosphere was somber, at best. Asking for Simon, he shared with him what he had learned about his sons and that his manservant would take him to their home immediately. Getting his things together, Simon met Nicodemus' manservant in the atrium where we all said good-bye. Before he left he promised to send word about Seder the following day. When he was gone, Nicodemus called us back to the atrium and shared what he learned at the council chamber. We were all devastated by Nicodemus' report of the possibility of an arrest after the week of celebration and feasting following Seder. We all wondered what type of inside informant had offered to help the governing council. Our thankfulness to Nicodemus for removing Simon from that hotbed of intrigue in Jerusalem could not be expressed with more sincerity.

Then Nicodemus told us something which explained the urgency of the Sanhedrin discussions. "By midmorning, the venders of sacrificial animals for the Seder sacrifices had brought their livestock into the Temple court to sell to foreign pilgrims and city dwellers who had no livestock of their own. Within an hour after they began selling and changing Roman coinage for the acceptable old Judean "Temple" coinage at outrageous exchange rates. It was then that Jesus entered the Temple court. He became furious with what he saw, picked up a cattle herder's whip, and drove all of the sellers and money changers out of the Temple court. When I arrived at the council chamber, he was still releasing sacrificial doves and vendors were still trying to pick up their coins which were scattered everywhere. The animal tenders were running throughout the northern quarter of the city in the attempt to locate their animals and drive them into the large square below the Temple.

"As he completed his deed of cleansing the Temple, which many of us thought should have been done years ago, he continued to shout, 'God's house will be called a house of prayer for all nations, but you have made it a den of thieves.'

"It wasn't until I left for home that the chaos finally subsided, and everyone was relocated. This irritated the council beyond words. Most of the council who were there this afternoon agreed that something needed to be done about the Temple abuse, but Jesus doing it alone, as if he owned the Temple, had pushed many over the edge."

At dinner we were all very sober. We were unable to understand what and why these things were happening. Halfway through the meal we had a break when Nicodemus's manservant returned from Bethphage. To change the tone around the meal, Nicodemus asked him to eat with us and share what he learned. Once he began, we knew this would be pleasant and maybe exciting.

Un-coached he began, "First, Simon is truly a man of God and wants more than anything to learn if God has something new and fresh for his people. We avoided any discussion of his vision, but I could tell it was constantly on his mind. He has a difficult time, however, with the stubbornness and sometimes belligerence of his Jewish religion toward non-Jews. He sees no need to set ourselves so far apart from everyone else that other people cannot relate to us and see God's love through us.

"When we got to Bethphage, we were surprised to find the home of his sons to be large and well-appointed in a significant olive grove and vineyard on the far side of the village. The home is spacious and half empty, so Simon's eldest son, Alexander, is excited about all of you joining them for Seder. You don't need to bring anything . . . only your change of clothes. They don't seem to have wives or children yet, but they have adequate servants to meet your needs. He suggested you come a day early to simply enjoy the beauty of the hills and be away from the craziness of the city during this time of year."

Hearing this, Stephen suddenly remembered that Leah's grandfather had groves east of Jerusalem. They must have been passed on to Simon and his sons. He felt derelict for not inquiring more in depth about his wife's family. Simon's grandfather must have left Judea for mysterious, perhaps political reasons, like so many in those years when Herod the Great, with the help of Caesar Augustus, was consolidating his power following the collapse of the Hasmonean Dynasty.

Stephen felt much better knowing that the twelve extra guests would not be an imposition. Besides, he was sure that Rahelani and her servants would also see to it that the feast would be more than moderately special.

As the evening progressed Rahelani and Nicodemus's wife went into the atrium's garden to relish the fragrances of the roses and miniature orange trees in the peaceful night air. All of the men including both Sadhu's and our manservants continued to recline with Nicodemus on lush overstuffed cushions around his beautiful dining room carpet. Rather than speaking of Roma or Judea we asked Sadhu to share some information about our people living in India. He agreed but told us it may not make very much sense, as history seldom does.

"After Jerusalem's protective walls were destroyed in Judea's total conquest by Babylon's armies, six hundred years ago, four young Judean princes, Daniel (Belteshazzar), Hananiah (Shadrach), Mishael (Meshach), and Azariah (Abednego) were taken as personal tribute to the Babylonian King, Nebuchadnezzar. They were "given" as a valuable human tribute of high born, well-educated, freshly castrated eunuchs. The historical books of scripture tell us of their courage and memorable deeds for God's glory. Naturally, as royal eunuchs they were prevented from carrying on their family names, which is why Nebuchadnezzar changed their Hebrew names to Babylonian ones. However, they still inspired many young Judean men to live godly lives and teach the generations after them to be faithful to the one true God.

"A few decades later, another pagan king, Cyrus of Persia, swept out of the eastern mountains to conquer Babylon without shedding one drop of blood. In the next few decades the Jewish population had to make one of three difficult choices . . . stay within the Persian Empire, follow God's new prophet, Nehemiah, and return to the home of their ancestors in Judea, or migrate to new opportunities in lands to the east called India. The majority decided to stay where they had lived all their lives and made their homes. A significant minority chose to return to Judea and rebuild Jerusalem and the Temple and strive for a more faithful Judaism. That left a small minority who decided to follow God's leading to the rich and vast land of India.

"After centuries of relative peace and prosperity, our number in India has grown significantly and we reside in several kingdoms that appreciate our ability to trade with our Persian counterparts. In recent decades the same admiration has come to us because of our Jewish counterparts in the Roman Empire. My family was very successful in the gem and gold trade in the far northern kingdoms conquered by the Greeks nearly four hundred years ago. Now many cousins are specialists in cutting precious gem stones of every description.

"Rahelani's family is totally different. They were scholars and strategists rather than merchants. To this day they can be found in the courts of three kingdoms. In fact, her mother was a princess given to her Jewish father for services he rendered in preventing a potentially disastrous war with a far more powerful neighboring kingdom. Her father was a mighty man of God and taught his daughter the truth about God. She became an ardent testimony to God's power and love in the court of her father. They had three sons and two daughters.

Rahelani is the oldest sibling, and all, including her eldest brother are royal councilors. One is even personal councilor to the present king, his cousin. All are also devout believers like their parents and siblings. I also worked for the present king's father for many years as trade attaché for all non-Indian overseas trade, including the HanChin, the Spice Islands, Arabia, and the lands of the Elephant Kings. This prepared me for the Roman traders who replaced the previous Greeks as they began appearing in our port city of Muziris, near the southern tip of India.

Turning to Stephen he added, "When we first met your brother, Jacobus, we knew he was searching for a fuller truth. Not just for himself, but for his family, and possible descendants. This truth is what we have sought all our lives in India, then in Alexandria, and now in Jerusalem. God has miraculously brought us all together, not to be disappointed but inspired. I do not fear this week. I believe this week is to become the beginning of God's outpouring to all the earth, even India."

It was an eloquent lesson I have never forgotten, for Sadhu was right.

Retiring that night was very contemplative. Those of us who had partners cherished them all the more. Those who did not, prayed all the harder that God would bring one to them. Simon's room remained empty as Hanno and Yacobsa became more enamored of one another. Was God's spirit a key part of their affection? I prayed it was. They could do twice as much for God together than they ever could apart.

The next morning was Tuesday, and we only had two more days until Seder. I wanted to take our little family, Stephen and Little Aaron on a casual walk of discovery through the city and the countryside around it. Nicodemus told us at breakfast that by nightfall the city would reach its maximum population level as the last of the pilgrims arrived in time for the sacrifices. The meat of these sacrificed animals, now dedicated to God, would then be taken home and prepared for the feasts ahead. If they couldn't use all the meat, that which they left at the altar would be given to the poor.

Nicodemus was right, Jerusalem was like an ant hill. Everywhere we turned there were even more people than the day before. When we walked out the northern gate, we were in shock at the number of tents, people, horses, donkeys, sheep, and camels appearing as though they were stacked on top of one another, stretching up the hillside. The crowds were so intense that shortly after lunch we headed back to Nicodemus' home in frustration.

Wednesday was going to be a not so quick and easy walk as we were earlier lead to believe, but a formidable and tedious trip to Bethphage. Making our way out of Jerusalem took over an hour, always being very careful not to lose anyone, especially Little Aaron. It would have been more difficult if Hanno had not put him on his shoulders again, so he could see. It took nearly four hours to reach the village but only five minutes to locate the house.

It was a fabulous country estate, near the top of a hill on the far edge of town, overlooking a pastoral vista of olive orchards, vineyards, and pastures. Rapping on the door, a servant had it open before Stephen finished his last knock. We were extravagantly welcomed by servants and hosts alike. The brothers were excited to meet their two cousins, Aaron and myself. Then there was their legendary uncle Stephen who they made over like dogs with a bone. But the most awesome guests were the ones who came all the way from India . . . the sadhu, his elegant wife, and their charming son Yacobsa. To avoid some confusion, Stephen then introduced "his" manservant, Hanno, who only spoke Greek and Carthaginian, then "my" manservant, Aaron who only spoke Latin and Carthaginian, then the sadhu's servants who only spoke Malayalam and Aramaic. Alexander began to laugh hysterically when he asked, "Am I the one who was supposed to have hired the interpreter.

We had a great afternoon and evening, just getting to know the brothers. The later it became, the surer my suspicions were that Simon's sons could be uncut eunuchs. I asked Stephen what he thought about two wealthy Jewish men in their late twenties or early thirties who were still unmarried and without heirs. He concurred with my suspicions. It took me half an hour to find Yacobsa and when I asked him, he feigned surprise, but then replied with firm conviction that he was very sure of it, at least Rufus. When we stopped laughing I had to ask the only unasked question of the last few days, "Why is God pulling so many eunuchs together from all over the world?" As we shared that question among the others, we all sensed that there was more to our saga than any of us first suspected.

The next morning after a quick breakfast, everything and everyone was busy cleaning the house to perfection and preparing food for the Seder. By an hour after midday and another quick lunch the house was declared clean. Fortunately, we had several extra servants and the brothers had started the day before we arrived, or we would have been cleaning and polishing that nest of unmarried men, until the end of the Feast in another week.

By sundown the feast was ready and so were we. As the only rabbi among us, the sadhu was asked to officiate. It was a beautiful service in both Hebrew and Aramaic. Little Aaron was perfect as the young questioner asking why God did what he did fourteen-hundred years ago. But the most beautiful part of our Seder service was when Yacobsa began playing a pair of tablas, small Indian talking drums, which he had hidden somewhere in his baggage. After about twenty seconds, the Indian servant girls lifted up finger cymbals and played a counter rhythm to the drums. No sooner had we captured the counter rhythm than Sadhu's manservant, Rashvi, began playing a haunting melody on what looked like a small lute with a long finger board to increase the number of possible tones and pitches, innumerably more than a simple lute.

As our ears finally adjusted to the exotic melody, we were all stunned as Rahelani began singing in deep mellow tones of sorrow. She had us captivated as she accompanied her song with the most phenomenal movements of her hands. As she went from sorrow to the tragic sounds of a death dirge, the instruments softened to a drone. Suddenly, the instruments burst into boisterous joy, as her voice reached a fevered pitch, and the rhythm of her hands and head began going in all directions for at least five minutes. Without warning everything stopped, until on the count of four, the music began again in a gentle melody Rahelani held her hands up in a gesture of prayer and sang the sweetest melody like a bird, and then it stopped. What Rahelani was singing about was not lost on any of us, even the two Aarons. It was the most beautiful story of our slavery, the death of the

Egyptian first born, the joy of freedom, and our thanks to God as a people. It was more beautiful than anything we had ever heard. Until the day I die I will remember being carried away as a participant in our ancient story of deliverance as expressed by our Indian family.

When the long ceremonial portion of the Seder was completed, with its multiple symbols to reinforce our memories and the memories of our children, the servants of Alexander and Rufus brought out a massive feast. In the center of the carpet was placed a huge platter of lentils and rice topped by a roasted lamb curled up as if asleep. That is not what took our breaths away. It was the tips of peacock feathers extending beyond the platter's edge, coming out from under the huge mound of lentils and rice which was meticulously covered with pure gold leaf. It seemed like forever before any of us could speak. Softly, the sadhu announced, "This meal is Rahelani's and my small offering to God for his goodness to us, not only for his material and spiritual blessings, but for the most wonderful son any parent could ever ask for, and the many new children of His who have been brought into our lives. So, as I ask God to bless our feast together, remember in eating as in life, too much gold is never good for you. Let's pray! He went on to offer a most sacred prayer in his musically accented Aramaic.

The next morning after ingesting all the food, the wine, and the gold, we had a torturous time getting up to make our midmorning departure for Nicodemus's on the far side of the city. Simon had decided to rejoin us for the festivities in the city and the final planning of our departure. At times like that, I am so thankful that time is never truly exact, but a generous approximation for our intentions.

By an hour before midday, the crowds in the northern quarter were getting far too jostling for Hanno to continue to carry Aaron on his shoulder. It was becoming too difficult, and he needed a break and began looking for a safe place to pass him to his father as planned.

When we reached a corner where the crowed seemed less boisterous, he lowered Aaron to the ground and passed him to Simon, to pass on to his father.

Before Simon could change hands with Aaron, a Roman soldier in full uniform grabbed his free arm and told him to pick up the cross which none of us saw laying in the middle of the street, beyond the people in front of us. Simon was totally disoriented and didn't comprehend what was happening. The soldier shoved him and shouted a second time to pick up the cross. Bending down he picked it up as best he could and supported it on his shoulder. Not knowing what to do next, he just stood there turning back to look at us. Seeing our horror, the sudden shock in his eyes registered his instant awareness. Looking down in the other direction, he saw a dreadfully bloodied and swollen faced man, wearing terribly bloody clothes. He was sitting on the ground with his shoulder supporting him against a wall.

As each second seemed like an eternity, the Roman soldier whipped the almost faceless man twice, then grabbed his nearest forearm and jerked him to his feet and threw him against Simon so he could keep his balance as they walked into the crowd together. From behind me I heard the loudest most haunting scream of my life. There stood Rahelani almost fainting in her son's arms. Sadhu turned to me and said that God just showed her what was happening, and it almost made her heart stop. We all gathered around her as we tried to follow in the direction Simon was going. We could only walk at the pace of a drifting jellyfish. It took us an hour to even get through the unfamiliar city gate. We were a short distance beyond the gate when Simon came staggering out of the crowd weeping heavily as he reached his brother-in-law and threw his arms weakly around his neck. As he tried to pull himself together, he rubbed the snot from his running nose onto the sleeve of his soiled robe.

Before he could replace his arm around Stephen's neck, his young nephew grabbed it and asked in panic, *"Uncle Simon, why are your clothes all covered with blood?"*

CHAPTER 35

DEATH – APRIL 14, AD29

Each one of us was exhausted and emotionally stressed knowing that we had just lived out Simon's vision. When Stephen asked if we should head back to Nicodemus', Simon . . . in iron willed determination . . . blurted between his sobs, "No! No! I must go back. They're preparing to kill him. I can't leave him now. He appreciated my coming to help him and told me that God's blessing is on my family."

Looking to each of us, we all nodded yes.

Hanno put Little Aaron on his shoulders again, and the servants picked up the bags containing the things Rahelani took to the Seder. Following Simon, we slowly walked to a small hill nearby which was crowded with people. As we arrived at its base, over the heads of the people we saw a cross being pulled by ropes until it stood nearly upright. Then it began to slide and dropped upright into a hole cut into the rock. Its thud was punctuated by a horrendous scream. When the cross fell into place, people cheered and ridiculed its naked victim. But that wasn't Jesus!

As the crowd quieted, we heard another shrieking scream as the sound of hammers pounding heavy spikes into bone and wood filled the silence between the screams. Suddenly all was silent, other than a grown man crying. Then we saw a second cross being lifted up and dropped into its hole, also punctuated by a horrendous scream from its naked victim. But that wasn't Jesus!

Then the crowd became as quiet as death itself. Once again, we heard the hammers striking the nails, one after another . . . haunting silence. Then we saw a third cross being lifted up and dropped into its hole . . . still silence. It was Jesus, naked, with only his own blood to cover the shame that crucifixion places on its victims, looking out on the world before him, hanging between two thieves. Even the crowd was silent and in awe. A few from the Sanhedrin tried to ridicule him but the crowd neither jeered nor scoffed. The silence was disturbed only by the sobs from broken hearts. Following Simon, we began our slow journey up the rocky hill toward the terror before us.

As Simon pushed his way into the crowd, people saw his bloody appearance, made way, and told others to do the same. When the soldiers recognized Simon, they made a place for us by a group of crying women and the young disciple, John, who Stephen had spoken to at the Temple steps a few days earlier. People revealed their curiosity as they backed away from Simon, wondering what the blood-stained man was doing among them with his strange international delegation and their heavily burdened servants. The greatest surprise was how elegantly dressed the Indians were . . . even their exotic servants.

As the brown skinned lady who appeared so regal, almost like a queen in her gold and jewels, knelt near the other women, she gazed up into the eyes of Jesus. In a voice more beautiful than the night before, she began to sing a song of praise to God in Malayalam. Once again she used her hands to first express her soul's praise and then her pain. Again, her servant women pulled out their finger cymbals and followed her lead. At that moment I saw Rahelani for who she really was . . . a princess who was accustomed to taking control of any situation . . . even death. When she finished, she bent down, touched her head to the ground, and sobbed. Then I remembered what the sadhu told us back in the alley. She had screamed when she saw Jesus collapsed on the street, "God revealed to her what was happening, and it almost made her heart stop."

I had to wonder if this is what she saw.

We stood there for hours. We watched. We listened. Even the thieves on either side of Jesus changed their tone, especially the one to his left who we heard calling him Lord. During this time, Stephen and I were able to share with John our beliefs that God revealed to us. Something amazing was preparing to happen. Immediately, he looked at us in disbelief. How could we know what Jesus had shared with him and the other disciples just the day before? We couldn't explain it. We just knew.

For some reason, God had brought the twelve of us together from across the empire and beyond to be there with Jesus . . . and John . . . on this day of Jesus' death. Such a miraculous happening proved a great comfort to John. Then catching us off guard he asked where we were from. After we told him, he pointed to the six Indians. Stephen said it the only way he could think of at the time, "The elderly man is an Indian rabbi, his wife is a royal princess . . . the daughter and sister of kings . . . the young man is their son, and the others are servants." We were amazed when he put his arms around our shoulders and kissed each of us on the neck. He then turned to the elderly woman who he had identified as the mother of Jesus and concentrated on comforting her. Had she walked the long distance from Galilee for this, the murder of her son?

At noon, darkness spread rapidly across the sky to the west, and the horizon quickly filled with ominously black clouds. The wind began to blow as the heavy dark storm clouds rolled in from the Mare Internum, the wrong direction for a storm this time of year. The sky continued to darken when Jesus shouted, "Eloi, Eloi, lema sabachthani?" It was a strange blending of Hebrew and Aramaic, spoken from a partially toothless mouth with terribly swollen lips. As close as the sadhu could understand it near the foot of the cross, Jesus said "My God, My God, why have you forsaken me?"

After making a few more personal statements he looked down and spoke to his mother and then to John. It was later that we learned he referred to John as "My Beloved." It was a term of great endearment which none of his disciples, even John, would ever explain to us, in the days and years to come.

Then Jesus gasped, "It is finished," and took in his final breath.

Abruptly the earth began to tremble and roar from deep below its surface, as a crack opened in the stone, running through the hole which held His cross upright. At the same time the sky began to clear. This was not a murderous execution as we had first thought. It was obvious that God had his hand in this from the night of Simon's vision, and probably long before. Again, I had to ask, "Why did God bring us here?"

Within half an hour after the earthquake, while John and Jesus' mother went to the cross to hug Jesus' feet and legs in his death, someone put his hand on Stephen's shoulder. Turning abruptly, he saw Nicodemus, our now good friend. He told us that he and Joseph had been watching from a distance, and that Joseph had just left to ask the Roman Governor for Jesus' body for burial before Shabbat arrives at sun-down. Stephen offered to help in any way possible. "Our servants are here, and they would want to do any of the labor for which they might be needed, especially our two former cargo slaves."

Nicodemus smiled and took one last look up to Jesus before heading to the governor's palace just around the corner from his home.

As Nicodemus walked toward the city gate, Stephen and I joined John at the base of the cross. He was weeping quietly as he hugged Jesus' legs closely to his chest as they became soiled in death. I placed my arm over John's shoulder as Stephen shared softly, "I have just spoken with Nicodemus and he informed me that as we speak, Joseph of Arimathea is negotiating for Jesus' body, so that we can remove it from the cross immediately, rather than leaving it here to rot for weeks. Joseph feels that God is definitely with them and that he will receive permission to take Jesus down and bury him in a tomb that he had recently completed for himself. Our servants will do everything for you. Nicodemus will stop by his home to obtain a large linen sheet for a burial wrapping and a linen towel for his head covering. Let Jesus' mother know everything is being taken care of for her. Oh, by the way, would it be permissible for Princess Rahelani to join the women in their mourning? She had a vision of this earlier this morning. She feels God has brought her here from India for this moment."

In her mourning, Jesus' mother overheard Stephen. She lifted her head from her son's mutilated feet, and motioned for Rahelani to join them as a few other friends were coming forward. Rahelani knelt beside her and prayed God's peace upon her as the others gathered around them. Stephen went back and told the others in our group what Nicodemus and Joseph were doing and that our services would be needed. I remained with John as he continued to weep while hugging and kissing the bloody legs of his dead master.

An hour later, the two members of the Sanhedrin returned with everything that was needed, even a large iron clamp with handles which Nicodemus thought would make it easier to remove the spikes from Jesus' hands and feet without mangling them more than they already were. The mere thought of Roman soldiers doing that task was frightening.

The soldiers always maintained a ladder at the execution sight for removing bodies, both fresh or decomposed, and for hanging signs like they had done over the head of Jesus. Since Hanno spent most of his life as a sex slave he had no experience with heights, but farmer Aaron was perfect for the task. Before Aaron set up the ladder, we asked everyone to stand back as he gently worked to loosen each spike and then extract it from each heal bone. As first one foot and then the other were freed, Jesus' legs stretched full length as his body now hung only from the spikes in his wrists which were now his total support.

When Aaron placed the ladder against the cross beside Jesus' head, and then climbed up, he was face to face with Jesus' piercing eyes, unaltered by his death. The life hardened slave began to sob as he worked. First, he removed the thorns from his head. Hanno then threw one of the soldiers' long ropes up to him which he wrapped around Jesus' chest to his back and then up behind each shoulder and over the beam, letting each end drop to the ground behind the cross. Immediately Hanno and Sadhu's manservant, Rashvi, picked up the rope ends and held them secure, pulling Jesus' body firmly against the cross. Arron scrambled down, still sobbing, and moved the ladder to Jesus' left forearm.

John quickly returned to hold the free-swinging legs, crying, hugging, and kissing the man who had done so much for him. I walked up to him again to embrace his sorrow. Suddenly, before I knew what happened, he pulled me to the cross with him. I couldn't help but recall the death of Mago and how he had died for me. Seeing Hanno holding Jesus upright with his rope caused an instant vision of he and I holding Mago in death while we shared one another's sorrow. A minute later I placed my cheek against Jesus' limp thigh, looking across to John, his eyes filled with tears and once again he kissed Jesus' leg as though his heart was being ripped out. I could do no less for John, or for Jesus, as I pressed my lips to his other cooling, bloody leg and kissed it as well. Instantly my view of God totally changed. He was now very personal. He really did care about me, and he truly did LOVE ME. I knew it beyond the shadow of a doubt. I felt like a new person. John also felt what had happened to me and tenderly put an arm across my shoulder and smiled for the first time that awful day.

As we worshiped God at the feet of Jesus, we both felt true hope. By that time Aaron had worked the spike out of Jesus' wrist and his body slid down a few inches more and twisted toward me. With Hanno and Rashvi holding each end of the rope steady, which allowed John and I to hold him tightly as Aaron moved the ladder to his other arm, and gently worked on the last spike that held Jesus to the cross. We heard the spike fall to the ground, as Jesus' mutilated body began to slide into our arms, as Hanno and Rashvi began letting the rope out a few inches at a time. Eventually he was almost level in our arms, so John and I could face each other across his chest and hold him in our joined and locked arms.

That was the moment his mother rushed up and kissed his bloody body and his swollen lips with the tenderness only a mother can share with a dead child. Stephen saw how frail she was and guided her to sit down on a nearby rock with a level top designed like a mourning seat. Soon he led John and me over, so we could lay her son out on her lap and in her arms. Backing away, John walked up to me, and without the slightest discomfort or shame, kissed me and thanked God that he had brought our unusual family to him. It was then I noticed Little Aaron, again holding his Uncle Simon's hand. He was quietly weeping in his own confusion and personal terror.

The sun would set in an hour and a half and Shabbat would begin. We were therefore not in much of a rush, as Joseph's new tomb was not far away. Joseph was not a frail old man, but perhaps a decade younger than the sadhu. He had many years ahead of him before he would need his tomb. Within a year or two John would come and remove Jesus' bones, clean them meticulously as he would mourn one last time. Then he would place all the bones into a traditional stone ossuary box and seal it. Before leaving with the box, he would clean the tomb like new, and remove all decayed matter whether grave clothes, clumps of hair, or dried flakes of flesh. He would then take the dry waste out to an open field and burn it . . . probably below the ancient tombs in the Kidron Valley. When that would be completed, he could place the ossuary box in a small permanent tomb, bury it in a favored field or even under the floor in his house to always sense Jesus' presence with him.

The time had come to roll the body into the linen sheet Nicodemus had brought, and then carry Jesus in a procession of over twenty of us to Joseph's new tomb at the upper reaches of the Kidron Valley near the Garden of Gethsemane. As we arrived at the tomb with Joseph, we opened the linen sheet and John thoroughly washed Jesus' body, removing all traces of the drying blood and other fluids. Then after John washed his bloody hair, Hanno and Aaron placed the body on the large sheet laid out on the decomposing slab. Placing his feet near one corner, they folded the sheet over them as tightly as possible, then began to roll the body as firmly as a butterfly's cocoon, tucking the sheet in securely at both neck and feet to hold it intact. Positioning the fully wrapped body in the final position on the decomposing slab, they covered his face and wrapped his head with the linen towel. Everything was complete but the perfumes and funerary spices and oils which would be poured over the wrapped body, to the point of saturation, sometime after the Shabbat sun sets, perhaps first thing Sunday morning.

Being our senior rabbi, Joseph performed the funeral liturgy and we joined in a traditional Hebrew hymn for the dead and prepared to help close the tomb with the Roman guards who were stationed at the tomb, due to the fear of possible trouble after Shabbat.

With the sun slowly setting behind the city, it was so different than what we had expected that day to be like when we kissed Alexander and Rufus goodbye after our delicious breakfast. Now, in the twilight, we sorrowfully bid farewell to Jesus's mother and all the women who traveled with her, but first Rahelani held onto his mother as they wept in each-other's arms. The most difficult for me was the embrace and kiss from John. It screamed out for help and for the love he would never be blessed with again. It was a help and love no one could ever replace. As far as I could see into my future, the two of us would never meet again. Those hours we had spent together at the foot of the cross, holding the legs of Jesus, had bonded our souls for life. While the sky darkened, we prepared to go our separate ways.

Arriving at Nicodemus' house, we relived it all over again as we shared the details with his broken-hearted wife. She knew all about the meeting of the Sanhedrin and the ridicule her husband and Joseph endured. She had heard Jesus speak several times and knew he was sent by God, but in what capacity? She could never comprehend. To kill him out-right, in the Roman fashion, was beyond her comprehension. We all needed to share what we felt, emotionally, intellectually, intuitively, and spiritually. The more we shared, the more the hiding places of our emotions became exposed. After we shared all we experienced, from Simon carrying the cross to the closing of the tomb, we each needed *our* Shabbat meal, which actually became little more than a midnight snack laced with a few prayers.

CHAPTER 36

RISEN – APRIL 16, AD29

It was Shabbat, but each of us was physically and emotionally exhausted. We were in the Holy City, so what? We were still emotionally drained. What had we just lived through?

Our journey to Jerusalem was meant to bring a spiritual high point to our lives that had otherwise become mediocre or worse. We wanted more in our faith than words and prayers which carried our people through over twelve hundred years of obstacles since Moses founded Judaism in the desolation of the Sinai Desert. We had suffered and died at the hands of our enemies and were continually punished by the God we worshipped. We needed our Seder to prove to us that we can and will survive whatever comes against us. We knew that we didn't look like much, but we also knew that we would survive.

Then this! A prophet who many people thought was sent by God to teach us compassion, love, and a desire for peace and generosity was brutally murdered under the blessing of our own spiritual leaders. How could our faith survive such trauma? How could we survive our own humanity? The world was changing as fast as Roma could roll over us like a giant boulder. Now, how could we survive when it was our own faith that betrayed us?

Without Nicodemus and Sadhu, our rabbi's, I don't know how I would have survived to say nothing of the other eleven. We returned to Nicodemus' home Friday night almost wanting to die . . . not to celebrate Shabbat. In fact, we didn't celebrate anything but our personal misery. We sat against the cushions and nibbled on scraps while fighting the temptation to drink too much.

How must John and Thomas have felt that night? Thomas, like the others, was afraid for his life. He was sure he would be arrested and killed like Jesus, so he hid. Amazingly John's love for Jesus was much greater than any fear he had for his personal safety.

By the end of the day, as the Romans soldiers began to understand that Jesus was someone special, John knew he had nothing to fear from them. I doubt if he ever feared them anyway. John, just a few years older than myself, had the spiritual strength I wanted when I returned to Nicodemus' home. What will tomorrow hold . . . and the next day . . . and the next? I wanted to know but could have never imagined how the forces of history would stand our tomorrows on their heads. The inventions of Ctesibius and Archimedes would continue to count away the minutes as they disappeared never to return, but the meanings of those days were changed forever.

That Shabbat morning, none of us were up with the sparrows. We may have been awake, but we found a sense of security in the arms of those who loved us. Most of us stayed in bed until noon, especially those of us who had someone to hold, or one with whom to share the true value of love. The only one to sleep soundly that night was Little Aaron whose faith and trust was so perfectly childlike that he slept like the proverbial baby with dry diapers. He laid on the other side of Stephen, exhausted but content even though he witnessed three bloody executions. I was sure he would have nightmares, but he never did . . . never.

Naturally, we ended up spending the entire day with Little Aaron whose experiences the day before would travel with him through his entire life. For some mysterious reason he didn't seem to be impacted by the horror or injustice of what he saw and experienced. He seemed to see it as a tragic story full of wonderful people who loved him and loved Jesus. The only time the bloodiness of it all seemed to affect him was when Uncle Simon returned to us with blood all over his clothes. That shock seemed to have prepared Little Aaron for what he would see throughout the remainder of the day. We were certain he was the youngest person at the crucifixion and the only things that seemed to irritate . . . not traumatize . . . him was why didn't anybody take down the bodies of the other two men who he saw the soldiers kill prior to our leaving. He also couldn't understand why the soldiers took all of the clothes off of each man before they nailed them to their cross. For some strange reason, or reasons, he saw everything else through a mystical or spiritual lens bestowed on him by God.

Much of the day was devoid of any significant conversation, except that relating to God's love and why he brought each one of the twelve of us to Jerusalem that day, under the protection and hospitality of Nicodemus and his wife. It was not well-developed plans that brought us here. We all saw it as the finger of God. Hanno persistently continued to remind us that God was putting something together that was bigger than we could imagine. He understood Jesus' need to die before God's plan could be set into motion. At first that seemed so much like a barbarous Carthaginian concept, but the more we talked about what brought us here on that one specific day, the more we were certain it truly was the finger of God.

All we could do, as we faced the day after such horror was to ask for God's strength and his peace within our spirits. We all knew the day would go on, as we must also. We were in no rush to head back to

Caesarea, and Nicodemus advised against it until we knew the political situation on Monday or Tuesday. That being our circumstance, Simon really wanted to spend more time with his sons in Bethphage. He was sure he could find their home without a guide, but Hanno, Yacobsa, and Aaron BarHanno decided to go with him, and they knew the way. They would stay until Tuesday, then return and check on our revised plans. If we had a date for departure established which was quite soon, then one or all of us would return to Bethphage for Simon.

Everyone agreed that it was a reasonable plan which could be modified as needed. The servants laid out a late lunch for everyone before the men left. I knew why Hanno and Yacobsa wanted to go, but I was a little puzzled about Aaron, maybe he just wanted to be with his hero Hanno. Slave or not, Stephen gave him permission to go and enjoy himself. If he needed anything or developed a problem, he was to let Hanno know immediately. After all, he only spoke Carthaginian and Latin, but we were sure he would be fine. Since we were all famished, when lunch was spread on the Carpet, the platters were picked clean within fifteen minutes. Kissing the four men goodbye at the door, we gave them a final warning to avoid all crowds.

Just after sunset we heard a great racket of yelling, screaming, and even clashing metal coming from east of the wall which separated us from the lower city. Shabbat was over and we feared some residual from the crucifixion might be flowing over among the poor and desperate elements of the city, who had finally found their voice through Jesus. Now they lost it since Jesus was killed and buried. If that was what we heard, it would prove a disaster for them and for us both. Roma was prepared for any hint of insurrection and they saw no distinction between the poor and the rest of us.

By midnight the disturbance ceased. All that remained was the wailing of women, which indicated there had been more than an incidental loss of life. Fortunately, John had told us that Jesus' disciples were staying in a village outside of town which assured us that probably none of his disciples were in that altercation. All we could do was pray. The rest of the night was calm other than the usual sounds of barking dogs and the typical minor domestic violence.

Soon after sunrise, we were all up and hungry and ready to face the day. Our priority was to see if John needed any help opening the tomb, anointing the body, or reclosing the tomb for Joseph. The servants were wonderful. Because of our diminished appetite over the last twenty-four hours they put out a wonderful spread of chilled fruit, pastries, cheese, yogurt, eggs, fresh baked bread, and sliced meats. I doubt if any of us realized how hungry we really were until we smelled the food being prepared, then it was too late. We were as ravenous as Hispanic wolves.

By midmorning, we took what servants we had and walked to the district of tombs in the Kidron Valley across from the Garden of Gethsemane. It was our intention to mourn with those who would be gathered there, and to help them saturate Jesus' body and wrappings with perfumes, spices, and oils before closing up the tomb for a year or two, after which John would collect his bones for their final burial.

When we arrived at Joseph's tomb, we were struck with a fear bordering on panic. The tomb had been opened but the women weren't there, nor were any of the men, including the Roman guards. Then we noticed a shadowy figure sitting on the decomposition bench inside the dark tomb and holding the linen burial sheet close to his chest. As Stephen and Nicodemus slowly approached the tomb and entered it, I heard them speaking to the man in very soft tones.

In just a few minutes Stephen motioned for us to come to the entrance. As my eyes adjusted to the gloom, I recognized John, once again in tears, holding the sheet in which we had wrapped Jesus. My heart screamed out to him as I stepped between the two men and sat down next to John. Once again, we met in a mixture of fear and sorrow as I wrapped my arm around his shoulder and held him tightly, not saying a word. We waited silently until John had the strength to speak. What he told us was both amazing and very frightening.

"Last night we all stayed at a home which a friend loaned to us in the city. We thought it would be an easier place to hide where no one expected us. The women got up early this morning to go and purchase whatever was needed to complete Jesus' entombment. When they completed their purchases, we expected them to return and get us to open the tomb for them as we had agreed. but they never came, and we began to fear for their safety.

"After waiting nearly an hour longer than we expected, Mary Magdalen finally arrived totally out of breath. What she told us caused us to doubt her mental faculties. She explained that in their distracted state they had forgotten about getting us and continued straight to the tomb. When they arrived here, the tomb had already been opened and the soldiers were gone, but there was a bright white light glowing inside, like the cool light of a full moon on a clear winter night. Approaching to obtain a better view of the interior and the source of the light, they saw the linen wrapping folded neatly on the bench next to the linen head towel we used to cover his face. But what truly frightened them was the source of the light. There was a man sitting on the bench next to the burial clothes all dressed in white. The source of the light was not a lamp, which burns yellow or golden, but the actual clothes of the man, well actually she said it was the man himself and his light shined through the clothes, but that's not possible! But is any of this possible?

"Here she began to get a little hysterical, claiming that the man asked them why they were looking for the living among the dead.

Stunned by such a strange question they just stood there wondering what to say in reply. When the man spoke to them again, he said that he knew they were looking for Jesus who was crucified. Then he forcefully stated that he was not there. Standing he pointed out into the garden and said with assurance, 'He is risen!'

"In pure confusion and fear of a politically based hoax, the women fled. Something pulled Mary Magdalene back into the garden to walk and pray among the tombs and try to understand what she had just seen and heard. Up the hill a short distance she saw who she thought was the caretaker of the tombs and the garden around them. As she approached him, she asked him if he knew what they had done with the body that we placed in the new tomb, just two nights ago.

"It was a simple question from a troubled, grieving woman and she waited for a simple response, but there was no answer. The silence was broken when all the caretaker said was, 'Mary.' It was the sound of her name that changed her world. She recognized his voice, and her future was forever altered. She looked . . . loved . . . listened . . . and then ran to tell us, his disciples.

"She ran to our hiding place and told us why she was late and what had happened. Instantly, I bolted out of the room with two other disciples, running as fast as we could as they followed me to the tomb. We found it empty, just as she said we would, but there was no man in bright clothes, and no gardener who looked like Jesus walking among the tombs. Nothing! The others went back to our hidden location with heavy hearts, but I had to stay in here with all that remained of the man I love so dearly."

Just to be on the safe side, Nicodemus suggested that John return to hiding immediately, and we would follow him a safe distance behind in case someone was watching for him, or any other disciples. Once we knew he was safe, we would check to find out what we could about what had been going on. All agreeing to the plan, Rahelani began to fold up the linens and wrapped them in her bright green silk head covering, like a luxurious gift, and presented it to John. As he left to reenter the city, we broke into groups of two to be less obvious and followed one another as Stephen and Nicodemus followed John. He eventually reached an unpretentious door, knocked in a code, then as he stepped in, he turned and waved goodbye, with Jesus' shroud clutched tightly to his chest.

Reaching Nicodemus' home, our anxiety level was higher than ever. Also, we had no idea how this was going to affect our departure to Caesarea.

CHAPTER 37

CONFUSION – APRIL 18, AD29

The days passed excruciatingly slow until Tuesday afternoon when the men were to return from Alexander's. Then we would determine our departure date for Caesarea. We continued to wonder if the disciples of Jesus had learned anything more. On Sunday, Nicodemus had discovered and confirmed that the High Priest sent messages to all the rabbis that the body of Jesus had been stolen by his disciples. He did this because he believed the disciples would claim that the Temple guards were the ones who stole the body. Both Nicodemus and Joseph knew the truth but seeing the political direction everything about Jesus was going, they decided to keep quiet until they learned more specific facts.

Stephen sent a message to the warehouse sergeant in Caesarea early Monday morning after learning of the "official report" on Sunday evening. He received a reply on Tuesday after lunch. There was a ship due in port in about ten days with three days scheduled for cargo activity before its departure to Athens and then on to Syracuse. If we were to leave on that ship, the sergeant would need to know within nine days to prepare for our return home. Otherwise, Stephen should let him know his preferred later schedule. Sadhu decided they would also stay in Jerusalem until we left, then he would travel with his family to Alexandria by way of camel caravan routed through Gaza.

After lunch, I suggested that I go to the disciples' hiding place to speak with John and possibly Thomas before Simon and the others returned from Alexander's later in the afternoon. Sadhu didn't want me to go alone and asked me to take Rashvi along. Rashvi was ready in seconds and we were out the door. Fortunately, we were both certain of the hiding place's location, and after reaching the neighborhood we spotted the house about fifty paces away. Standing at the door, I tried to imitate the knock I watched John give from a distance on Sunday. It worked and someone cracked the door open and looked at us briefly. Seeing the Indian he opened the door and welcomed us. I asked for Thomas or John. Thomas wasn't there, but John was called. Rushing to see me, he put his arms around me and kissed my neck. I asked them if they had heard anything and he smiled excitedly as he told us Jesus had visited them by appearing in the room without entering through the door. He talked to them and taught them several new things about God and what he wanted them to do for his children.

I asked if he knew of the stories about them that were being spread through the synagogues. He said he did and added that now they knew Jesus wasn't really dead and that helped all of them have courage for the future . . . all except Thomas. He hadn't been here to speak with Jesus personally.

I explained that we would be leaving for Athens soon, then home to Syracuse, so Stephen and I would like to meet with all of them before we left. I also mentioned how very concerned Nicodemus and Joseph were for their safety. Assuring us that they would be fine, John approached Rashvi, gave him a strong hug, and asked him to convey his appreciation to his masters. Then he hurried to get Rahelani's head covering for us to return to her because it was a very valuable gold-embroidered silk fabric. Rashvi called him back and said to John, "She would be embarrassed if you return it to her. She gave it as a gift, a wrapping for the shroud. It belongs with the shroud forever."

After John thanked Rashvi, I asked him to give greetings to Thomas from me, Jacobus BarSirach, who had met him in Caesarea about eight months ago between the fishing boats on the north beach. Startled that I knew Thomas, John asked me to come again before our departure from Jerusalem and maybe I could greet Thomas myself. Before we left, I asked if he would give Jesus a message from Simon of Cyrene, the man who carried his cross out of the city. He wanted him to know that he believes Jesus is God's son and he knows that he is always walking beside him. Surprised when I told him that Simon was my sister-in-law's brother, tears began running down his cheeks for joy. John silently nodded his head, and then he gave me a long kiss farewell . . . on the cheek. Before he closed the door behind us, he reminded me to return again soon.

Rashvi and I arrived home minutes before Hanno, Yacobsa, and Aaron. They had a wonderful time with Alexander and Rufus. The brothers were stunned to learn what had happened to their father, and especially to Jesus. They told us that just prior to Seder, Jesus had been staying with a neighbor just inside the village where they lived. They took their father and the three of them to meet 'Simon the Leper' who was still in a state of shock. He was very happy to meet them and thanked them for all they had done for Jesus. They ended up spending all day Monday with him and his family.

Wednesday morning at breakfast, Hanno asked if I could take Alexander's little cousin to join them for a few days in the country. Stephen had just decided to spend a day or two with our sergeant and some of our agents in Caesarea. That would leave Yacobsa's family and servants with Nicodemus. Hearing that plan, Yacobsa ran to his parent's room to tell them what we were doing. He found them more than willing to spend some time walking in the olive groves. By midafternoon we were all packed and ready to leave. Stephen assured us that if he felt any need for us to return to the city when he finished his work in Caesarea he would come to Alexander's and retrieve us. Since Nicodemus was in another Council meeting at the Temple, we thanked his wife for their hospitality, and added that Stephen would retrieve us in Bethphage when it was necessary.

In a little over an hour we were in Bethphage sipping cool, well water flavored with sweet wine from their own vineyard. Alexander and Rufus were fantastic hosts and made us feel a part of their family, even though some of us really were, we were also strangers. The next five days proved to be close to idyllic, with the brothers doing all they could to make us comfortable, especially Sadhu and Rahelani who had taken to the brothers like their own sons.

Just before noon on the fifth day, Stephen arrived from Jerusalem to give a report on the state of things in both Caesarea and Jerusalem. If we were all agreed, the ship would be ready in six days, providing all was on schedule. It turned out that the ship taking us to Athens and on to Syracuse would be the *Dolphin* under Captain Lucius Paulus. I, for one, was eager to be on my old ship again . . . as a passenger heading home.

Suddenly each of us were set upon by our own indecision and confusion.

Should we stay at least a month longer? The indecision slowly became determination. Unanimously, we chose to remain as long as necessary to see our involvement with the disciples through to a spiritual resolution for each of us.

When Stephen returned to Caesarea, he gave a letter to Captain Paulus for Leah stating that we would not be home for at least eight weeks, but considering all that had happened we were no longer certain of anything. He told her of all the horrors and victories they had encountered, and that our greatest concern was what was happening in Jerusalem, and more specifically, what was happening with John and the other followers of Jesus. Also, we would be spending some time up in Syrian Alexandria with our carpet partners there.

Nicodemus had been lavishly hospitable, and we knew he would not mind if we stayed longer with them, but no one ever wants to ruin a good thing. Not that he would tire of us, but because of his position on the Council. Our residing with him, as believers in what was being referred to as "The Way," which may soon be woven within the theological tapestry that has become Judean Judaism, might prove dangerous for Nicodemus and his family. However, if we did decide to stay in Jerusalem longer, Alexander may be willing to house some of us, and draw less attention to Nicodemus. There were many things to consider. Perhaps Sadhu and Rahelani would like Stephen to take them to Aegyptus, Alexandria with him on the next ship he sails to do business there. So many things needed to be sorted out, but one thing for sure was that we needed to visit with the disciples several more times to learn what Jesus was planning to do, or maybe even see him ourselves.

The next morning, when Stephen was leaving for Caesarea with Leah's letter, Simon, Sadhu, Hanno, Rufus, and I decided to go as far as Jerusalem with him. We could then spend a few hours learning from the disciples what Jesus had taught that was so different from our ancient prophets.

We packed a great deal of food and wine for the midday meal and headed for their hiding place. As I knocked on the door, it was Thomas who opened it and shouted gleefully when he saw us. In fact, he greeted me with a kiss on my cheek which I learned was their new way of greeting one another.

Welcoming us in, everyone was delighted the Indian rabbi was in our group. They had heard so much about him and his wife who sang so beautifully at the cross. Then there was the Carthaginian slave who helped lower the body of Jesus down from the cross. When they learned from John that Stephen was the man who joined with Nicodemus and Joseph of Arimathea in arranging for the final events at the cross, they were overjoyed. There was not a dry eye among us after I introduced Simon, the man who carried the cross and walked beside Jesus as he struggled to the top of the hill. Before the crucifixion, most of us meeting that day had been strangers, unconnected. Now it was a moment for remembering. Those God had gathered from different regions of the world had stayed at the cross to help until the end . . . the disciples who had known Jesus from the beginning had scattered and fled. It was true, they all mourned the death of Jesus, but it was also true they all celebrated his resurrection. They were definitely united . . . they were one!

Stephen, being the sort of man he was, got right to the point. We needed to learn all the disciples could teach us of Jesus' many lessons that had changed so many people's lives during the past three years. They excitedly agreed and recommended that we use the same room upstairs that Jesus and the disciples had used earlier. However, before going up we gave the food we had brought for our noon meal to the women.

We climbed the stairs and in the large open room we sat in a circle ready for the sharing to begin. As we assembled, a large burly disciple named Peter was getting ready to speak. The first thing out of his mouth was a confession of his own cowardice in denying any knowledge of Jesus on the night of his trial before the Sanhedrin.

With the confession off his chest he began sharing practical lessons of proper Jewish behavior, first with our families, then our friends, and finally our enemies. Then he surprised each of us, as he emphasized that the Laws of Moses were now to be used as guidelines. The new law was very simple: "Love God with all your heart, mind, and spirit, and love your neighbor as you love yourself." He told us there were no greater commandments than these. That was exactly how Jesus lived. It was also how the BarSirach family began living in Syracuse when we first heard of him.

Mary Magdalene soon came upstairs to invite us down to eat. She looked past Peter and instantly realized that we were the men from the cross and the tomb. She raised her arms in praise and came to kneel in front of each of us to thank us for what we had done for her master. Hearing the racket above their heads, the other women came rushing up the stairs. They were thrilled to see us again as well. But it was Mary, the mother of Jesus, who wept with a mixture of joy and grief as she saw Rahelani's husband, the rabbi. She fell at his feet thanking him for all his wife did for her in her abyss of grief. This spirit of thankfulness continued as she recognized Hanno and me as the ones who joined John as we laid her son's body in her lap. Next, she recognized Simon, who had been covered with her son's blood after helping him out of the city to his place of execution, all while carrying the cross for him. All she could do was praise God for the mysterious ways in which he works. Acknowledging her thanks, we were all on our feet and on our way down to a feast.

As the sun was beginning to set on a wonderful afternoon of learning, inspiration, and praise, they kissed us all goodbye before we walked out the door. It was then, I truly realized there was an honest and pure bond growing between John and me. He wrapped both arms around me and kissed me. As he released me, tears ran down his cheeks. When we stepped apart, he said in a manner of fact tone that he would never forget me regardless of what happened in our world. Then as he let go, he told me that he loved me. I, too, began to tear up. Everyone knew there was something special happening between us and they waited patiently for us to say our goodbyes. I recalled, as I walked out the door of the hiding place, that I felt the love of all of them. I also felt we were on the threshold of a new world. It would still be a world of violence and destruction, but it would also be a world in possession of a hope it never had before. It was a hope based on our knowledge of God's divine love for all humanity. Kissing Stephen goodbye as he left to spend the night with Nicodemus, I was probably more excited about my own life and future than ever before.

Arriving at Alexander's shortly after twilight, we were welcomed by our fantastic family which was impatient to learn what had happened. After sharing for an hour, the servants left and began to prepare dinner. It had been an unreal day, and our next four days were spent in near idyllic serenity in both contemplative prayer and times of corporate prayer each morning. The brothers were superb hosts, sensitive to traditional propriety balanced with the need for love felt by both types of eunuchs.

This was first revealed when Alexander's manservant, Eli, declared his undying love for our mutilated slave, shy and withdrawn Aaron BarHanno. Almost everyone knew of his sexual mutilation and that he thought he could never be loved by anyone. From the day the Romans cut him up during his castration in a hot African wheat field as punishment for some insignificant infraction, he had seen himself as sub-human. Suddenly there was a man, a real man with all his masculine beauty, who had declared his love for him.

Eli tried from the first day they met to get the Latin speaking cargo slave to understand that he saw his eternal and external beauty as a single whole. Having to use Alexander as his Latin interpreter made his courtship nearly impossible. Aaron's scars were a part of what made him as gentle and sensitive as he was. His basic plumbing still worked, but that was not the issue. Eli had fallen madly in love with Aaron, and he couldn't be discouraged by any of the cruel ugliness that was hid beneath his clothes. The Carthaginian cargo slave was beginning to realize that love was not based on what he had or didn't have between his legs or what it looked like. It was what he had in his heart that mattered. Humorously, Stephen was already thinking that he might need to transfer Aaron's ownership to Alexander in payment for all of our housing and food expenses during our indefinite stay in his home. We all celebrated their growing love, for Eli even had the courage to ask our rabbi to perform a celebration of union before our small congregation . . . and he agreed.

However, Alexander's declared love for Yacobsa was another matter. They lived five days hard journey apart by camel caravan, which made their union nearly impossible. A long-distance relationship would be doomed, so they had to deal with this like rational men. Yacobsa wasn't really the problem because he realized his entire future and the future of his family hinged on his position in Alexandria and with us as we traded with India through Aetna Shipping. He knew this and was willing to consider Alexander as a steppingstone to his perfect mate . . . whomever, wherever, and whenever that may be. We were all praying for the two of them. Alexander knew his love was doomed, but he continued to pray that a miracle would develop. He eventually understood the facts were what he needed to face. Realizing this, be began to lessen his pressure on Yacobsa and learned to be happy having him in his home and in his arms for as long as he could.

With so much romance in the air, Simon soon realized his sons were definitely not freaks because they were uncut eunuchs with no interest in women, but he was still saddened that they would never give him grandchildren. Thankfully, Stephen had married his sister, even though he also was a eunuch and had no interest in women. At least he tried and gave Leah three and possibly four beautiful children. If Stephen could force himself to do it, why couldn't Alexander and Rufus? Why did this curse fall upon him? Strangely, he had noticed weeks ago that everyone God seemed to use since he arrived in Jerusalem appeared to be just like them. What was God saying? He even stopped fearing them and found himself loving these men in a brotherly and spiritual sort of way. Then there was the slave Aaron, who was sexually butchered like a lamb at Seder, yet someone still loved him enough to devote his life to him. Where would this end? What was God teaching him? Why did Jesus include him here through his vision? These were questions for which Simon had thought he needed answers for, but he was slowly discovering they truly didn't need answers. WHY NOT? They only needed compassion and love. When he looked beyond who they fell in love with, they were like everyone else. Perhaps we were all normal if God did the creating of each of us.

With that new compassion in his heart, Simon too began enjoying the budding romances around him, but his eldest son, Alexander was getting himself into a real emotional mess. Would Alexander even listen to him after all the cruel things he had said to him in the past? Only if he apologized for his former mean spirit. This had been a long journey, but Simon was reaching his ultimate destination, both for his sons' love and their trust.

It had been five days since anyone of them visited the disciples and I was itching to be with John again, so at breakfast I asked if anyone would like to spend the day with me and the disciples. Sadhu and Rahelani were the first to answer in the affirmative. Yacobsa and naturally Alexander wanted to join us, and both Aarons decided to go also. We left right after breakfast putting us at their door in less than an hour. Once again Thomas came to the door to welcome us. I think I got their secret code mixed up because they were beginning to detect in advance when we were the ones at the door. This time there were several other men among them who we had never met. The first person I saw at the far end of the room, however, was John who jumped to his feet and ran over to me and greeted me in his uninhibited way with a sincere kiss and the warmest of hugs. Immediately, he began to introduce us to everyone in the room and what we did at the crucifixion and burial.

Then he came to Alexander and Aaron BarHanno. Seeing the look on John's face, I introduced Alexander as Simon's son with the large olive grove and vineyard in Bethphage. Everyone knew about him, but no one actually knew him. That left Alexander a little unsettled. But he felt less conspicuous when Aaron was introduced as the one who delicately removed Jesus from the cross, avoiding any further Roman brutality. Of course, Little Aaron was a smashing success and he loved the attention.

When all formalities were fulfilled, we were told that Jesus had been there the day before and was now in Galilee. They would be leaving in the morning to meet him there. Naturally, Alexander asked how he could be in Galilee now when he was in Jerusalem yesterday. Peter walked up to him and placed an arm across his shoulder and began to explain. "Since Jesus rose from the dead sixteen days ago, he is not chained to this world like we are. That does not mean he is a ghost . . . because he isn't. When he is here, he eats and drinks with us. The first time he came to meet Thomas he had Thomas stick a finger in the nail hole in one of his wrists. It was moist and warm. Where a soldier had stabbed him in his side with a spear to verify he was actually dead, Jesus asked Thomas to place his hand in that deep wound. It, too, was warm and moist. He was real and alive!" Peter continued, "When he visits us, he does not walk through the doorway for the door is usually locked. He simply appears among us sometimes sitting here or sometimes standing over there. It makes no difference. When he leaves here, he is somewhere else instantly. We were all frightened at first, but after eating a meal with him we became certain he was alive. He exists in two worlds at once, if that makes any sense. No, we don't understand how God does it. Our only concern is that it is him, our Lord and Master.

"In fact, you came just in time for we will leave tomorrow to go to Galilee. We will be staying there until the week before The Festival of First Fruits, which we will now call Pentecost in Greek. It is the celebration of the beginning of the summer wheat harvest, or forty-nine days following the day after Seder. This year, that's seven weeks after the day Jesus died. We hope to be back here in Jerusalem the week before that, for Jesus wants us to celebrate the festival with our friends here in the city of his execution."

With that long explanation, Peter revealed to us why they believed Jesus was much more than a prophet and actually the Messiah, God's Son, Israel's Deliverer.

Our presence with them that day had a sense of sacredness. I sat with John the entire time, often with him holding my hand. I began to see in him as a true man of God in spite of his youth. He had lost someone very dear to him, but he was reconciled to the fact that without Jesus' death there could be no true life for anyone. For John there was no longer the question, "Why did he have to die?" Now it was only gratitude, "He died for me!"

I saw a faith in John that I wanted to see in myself. I knew I would miss him while he was gone. In fact, there was a very strong probability I wouldn't be here when he returned. In truth, I may never see him again. As I often looked at him that day, I realized that he faced and understood the same probability. When we left late that afternoon, I was resigned to the fact that God brought the two of us together in a deep, pure love not for ourselves but so that we might understand it and share it with others on both a human and a spiritual level.

Standing by the door, with arms around each other, I knew our love and friendship for each other was to last forever and was turned over to God. As he kissed me goodbye, I knew I would see him again . . . whether it be in this world or the next.

The walk back to Bethphage was lonely but blessed. I had learned so much about faith and love. I was sure for the first time that God loved me, and I loved him. It was all because of Jesus' death and resurrection.

Now, my next question seemed so shallow. Would we depart for Syracuse tomorrow or would we wait until the disciples returned?

That evening we weighed all the reasons for leaving and the reasons for staying. After an hour-long discussion Stephen decided we would stay until the first ship departing for Syracuse after the Festival. If anyone needed to leave sooner, for any reason, Stephen would arrange passage from Caesarea as quickly as possible. We were all satisfied with the decision, especially Aaron BarHanno who by now was deeply in love with Eli and could not picture life without him.

The next few weeks were busy as we set about going back and forth to Caesarea and even a trip to Alexandria to verify that our first annual order from India was placed through the proper channels and the gold was sent to Berenike on the Sinus Arabicus for its departure for India at the beginning of the monsoon winds. Fortunately, we had Sadhu's people and one of ours traveling all the way to India and back insuring the best possible results. We also made a quick trip to

Alexandria in Syria to visit with the Jewish carpet merchants from Persia and establish a strong relationship.

Previously, Stephen had bonded with them as a Jew so that our orders could be placed there with certainty that the carpets would be on their way from Persia within two months and on their way to Syracuse within a month later. This required our purchase of a small warehouse in Alexandria, Syria, and staffing it with some of our people from other ports. By so doing, we were able to put it on our regular route from Caesarea to Athens.

All of this required major investments on our part, but the last year had proven to be an exceptional generator of profits. After share distributions to all family owners were deducted, there were adequate funds to proceed with these expansions. Stephen, Sadhu, Hanno, and I did most of the traveling. On our trip to Alexandria, Aegyptus we also took Rahelani, Yacobsa, and their three servants. We brought only Yacobsa and Rashvi back to Caesarea with Sadhu.

During these weeks before the Festival of First Fruits, Stephen was able to maintain contact with Leah and other family directors in Syracuse via ship mail. Nearly every five to ten days a letter also arrived from Leah. She was stunned at the news of the Prophet's death and even more so with his resurrection. She was truly thankful that Aaron had gone with his father and Uncle Jacobus on this trip to experience such history-making events in the Jewish world. She always assured Stephen that she and the baby were doing well. It had become obvious that she was eagerly awaiting our return.

CHAPTER 38

THE WAY – MAY 27, AD29

It was six days before the Feast of Weeks or of the First Fruits of the Spring Wheat Harvest which is celebrated Forty-nine days after the Seder. We knew the disciples of Jesus would be returning to Jerusalem soon. Stephen, his son Aaron, Sadhu, Yacobsa, Hanno, Rashvi, and I had just returned to Caesarea from Alexandria and planned on stopping in Jerusalem on our way to Alexander's home in Bethphage to rejoin Simon. Stephen decided to use our warehouse horse cart to transport us as far as Jerusalem with plans to walk to Bethphage later. When we arrived at the Northern Gate we thanked the driver and walked through the city gate. It was evident that people were preparing for a holiday in five days. The streets were crowded, and merchants were selling greater quantities of food to more customers than before we left.

Walking to the disciples' hiding place we noticed the door was ajar, meaning that either they had just arrived home from Galilee or their safe space had been raided. We all said a prayer and stayed back as Stephen walked to the door and knocked loudly. Soon we heard him speaking to someone inside who we couldn't see. Then smiling, he turned to waive us in.

While Stephen waited for us to collect our baggage, I saw him reach into his money pouch and pull out some silver coins to help with the disciples' travel expenses and the cost of provisions. Dragging our things to the door I saw that it was Mary of Magdalen who Stephen had been talking with. He informed us that several of the men had not yet returned from shopping, but the rest were upstairs. As we entered, Mary Magdalen had us place our baggage in a small alcove just inside the door and invited us to go up and speak with whomever was in the meeting room.

The disciples had arrived the previous morning. Jesus had appeared to them and told them to meet him in a secluded grove of trees on the back side of the Mount of Olives in an hour. They returned to Jerusalem at twilight, but for some reason the disciples couldn't share with the women why Jesus wanted to meet with them so suddenly. That night they didn't get much sleep as they were talking until almost daylight. In the morning, about an hour before we arrived they were still running in and out stocking up on supplies in preparation for the feast.

After my eyes adjusted to the dim light, I saw Thomas, Bartholomew, Philip, Andrew, and Thaddaeus, but no John. I didn't realize how disappointed I would feel if John wasn't there. I was definitely looking forward to seeing him again. I had just realized that when someone grabbed me from behind and spun around with me a couple of times as he laughed in my ear. Letting me down, John turned me around and kissed and hugged me. He was as excited to see me as I was to see him. We laughed and went on and on without realizing we had disrupted everyone else's conversations. We were both embarrassed when we discovered what we had done. I caught Peter's eye as he was soberly shaking his head. When he noticed everyone else thought it was funny, he finally cracked a sincere smile.

Once it quieted down and we each found a cushion to sit on, Peter began to brief us on the days they were able to spend with Jesus in Galilee. What startled us was the details Peter had shared. "Jesus was teaching us that more and more non-Jews would be attracted to The Way. Those of us who are Jews will need to teach them the Ways of God and his people. Presently this is not a major issue, but he stressed that the Kingdom of Heaven is now open to the non-Jews and that means we will be needed to take the place of the teachers in the Temple because its use would soon be taken from us. All mankind must be brought into God's family, not Jews alone. That meant that he wants us to share God's love with anybody who will listen. Then we will need to teach the ways of God which will become very important as more pagans begin to follow the teachings of Jesus.

"Since none of us are learned men, we need to see more rabbis, like the sadhu, among our number who are capable of teaching the Greeks, Romans, Persians, Indians, and more about how to follow the ways of God through faith in the teachings of the Messiah, Jesus. We were also faced with a true shock, having never considered the possibility of being driven out of the Temple and out of the synagogues. Jesus insisted that we would be, and it would happen sooner than we think. When we asked if every follower of The Way must first become Jews or become like Jews, he seemed strangely vague. He told us the Spirit of God would show each person the right way to go. The weaker would probably need to become like Jews, whereas those with greater spiritual strength might not. That is what God's spirit would soon reveal to us. As of now, we still don't understand completely what he meant by that statement.

"Even though we had always thought of Jesus as teaching and ministering primarily among the Jews, he warned us that within a year we would be cast out and persecuted because of him. This was difficult to believe. We had never thought of ourselves as anything but good Jews. Now he tells us we will be removed from the Temple and the synagogues and persecuted because of him. Soon some of us would even be killed by the Jews . . . our own people."

As the other disciples began arriving back from their various chores across the city, each one resolved to continue the work which Jesus had begun throughout the entire empire. Sadhu asked, "Is Jesus to continue being the Spirit of God throughout the earth as we reach out to a pagan word? Is he the one who will tell us which person is strong and which is weak?"

This time we were surprised to hear Thomas respond. "Jesus told us that the Spirit of God will guide us from within us. It took us a few days to understand this concept of a more inclusive God. Jesus told us that the Spirit of God would be coming to us and that we would then learn more about God and his love. He assured us that the true Spirit of God has not visited us yet. Up until his death, Jesus guided us in times of need as the physical voice of God, but he is no longer with us, so God's spirit will reveal himself directly to each of us in a personal way. This will enable us to truly love one another as God the Father loves us. People will know we are brothers in Jesus by our love for one another and all mankind, no matter how different they are from us. Then and only then will the world turn to God. The Spirit of God will enable us to do this nearly impossible task."

That explanation helped, but Hanno in his own simple, pure faith way of understanding, still needed help, "Is Jesus to be that Spirit of God, or is there really to be a third person beside God the Father and Jesus?"

Peter stepped in to explain the impossible one more time. "Hanno, it will not be Jesus. While we were still with him in Galilee, Jesus began to speak with us about this. Then yesterday near Bethany as he finished sharing with us about these things he began to float up into the air and then he suddenly disappeared into the clouds. I know it sounds like we are making this up . . . but we're not! He really did disappear into the clouds. We didn't believe it either, and we watched it happen! He really disappeared into the clouds in the sky. We don't know what to think of it either, but we know this time he is gone, and we won't see him again. It is like Moses crossing the Red Sea with our ancestors. We don't understand it, but our ancestors claimed it happened. That has always been the pillar of our faith. Now this, another pillar, is to be added to our faith. Today we don't understand, and tomorrow we won't understand, but we know what we saw. Before he left he said he would return at the end of time. He simply said that we were to watch, wait, and pray. The Spirit of God would come upon us at the appointed time."

Then John, who still had an arm around my shoulder, summed it up, "We decided to do what he told us to do. Wait. Just wait! . . .wait! . . . wait!"

After another hour of discussion, questions, and answers, Mary Magdalen came upstairs and said dinner was ready. Going down to the large eating area where they served their meals, we asked what the women thought about all of this. They didn't seem to have as much difficulty in accepting what the men had seen, because they had seen the glowing man in the empty tomb who told them that Jesus was alive. Mary Magdalen went on to say, "When we told the disciples about what we had seen, they wouldn't believe it. Now they know better than to make the same mistake a second time."

The afternoon was spent listening to other reports about Jesus and the stories Jesus had told them during their weeks with him in Galilee. He warned them of many terrible things ahead but assured them that he would always be with them. Some of his predictions were frightening. Others were encouraging. Things were going to change forever, and it would be up to us to make a positive difference.

In the evening as we prepared to return to Alexander's, John told me repeatedly how much it meant to him for us to be so concerned about them and the mysterious things that were ahead for them. This time, as we carried our baggage out the door, instead of a boisterous kiss from John there were only tears. We both knew of the other's love, but we also knew we would never be together as lovers. I was so fortunate that I had Stephen through those difficult days of young love. He knew my love for John was pure and would never stand between us, but he also knew there was a reason for it. Both John and I matured emotionally because we had each other to talk to about deep spiritual and personal things. We had someone to hold who cared and understood. Our love came about while holding the legs of Jesus when he died. The next time we would be together our lives would change forever.

Arriving at Alexander's an hour before dark, we had a wonderful reunion and an unexpected evening of sharing about the disciples and their last day with Jesus. Simon was completely beside himself with anticipation for what was ahead, but he was also a little saddened by the reality of our soon departure for home. Through the many weeks with his sons he learned to love them for who they were and also to accept the fact that they would never give him grandchildren. The greatest expectation in a Jewish family was to be fruitful and multiply. Without a multitude of children, Israel would never have survived through the centuries. Having children was inseparable from who we have been. The Torah even forbids a man from spilling his seed upon the ground instead of in his wife's, or concubine's, womb. Its author, Moses, had no place for men who could not or would not impregnate a woman. But Jesus loved John even though he knew he would never produce children. Was our world beginning to change already? Was it allowing us to be eunuchs without feeling guilty for not helping to populate the earth with God's children? Only time would tell, but this was a beginning.

A few days later, the disciples sent us a message asking us to join them and many of their fellow believers in two days for the Feast of Weeks, or the Feast of Pentecost as the Greek speaking Jews called the celebration. We knew that with the crowds in the city, the inflated cost of providing such a feast would be astronomical. We sent word back to John with their messenger that we would bring enough food and wine to feed at least fifty guests. Immediately we set about slaughtering two sheep and ten chickens. The cook began baking stacks of bread and even some honey pastries. All of the agricultural workers began collecting dates and small melons. Fortunately, there were still some oranges on the trees and sacks of dried grapes in the cellar and enough fish in the pond below the house to net at least twenty without affecting their population. Rufus located two water jugs with their lids in tack, which we could fill at the spring in Bethphage. Alexander figured we would need two donkey carts to get it all to Jerusalem in one trip. In fact, we realized there might even be enough food to feed a hundred. We knew the disciples invited a large crowd, and now they would have plenty left over to last for days.

The night before we were to leave, the staff began loading the donkey carts with the heavier items like wine and water. All the chickens were roasted and packed in baskets along with some cooked garden vegetables. The sheep would slow roast through the night, over the cooking fire behind the house. By sunrise we were ready to start loading everything else as it was packaged.

By midmorning the donkeys were hitched, and we all marched in procession to the heart of Jerusalem's northern quarter. By the time we arrived at the house there were already at least thirty guests upstairs visiting with the disciples. We assisted Alexander's servants, and our own, and we had the carts emptied in no time. We depended on Mary Magdalen to show us where to put everything. She must have been some business woman in her day because she surely knew how to organize things and tell people what to do. She and the other women were ecstatic over all the food and drink, for they could now spend most of their time taking care of the other needs of the guests without any concern for the food. In fact, Rufus sent the donkey carts back to the house and then took over in the kitchen himself. Our servants saw to it that everything would be ready in two hours.

Little did we know that this feast would mark through the decades, the issue which initiated our eventual separation from Judaism. Looking back, I can see that we worshipped the same God, often in the same ways. However, it was becoming very clear that the Temple priests were making us less welcome every day. Following the teaching of Jesus was becoming more difficult, but the question was, "If we could no longer be Jews, what were we?" That question had not been seriously asked until now, and the disciples needed to figure this out before our Jewish feast day was over. Most of the disciples were using the term, followers of The Way of the Messiah, and discontinued their use of followers of Moses.

Only time would tell, but within a matter of weeks, most of us began referring to ourselves simply as followers of The Way.

CHAPTER 39

PENTECOST – JUNE 3, AD29

As it approached midday, Rufus was busy with the servants in the kitchen as the last guests for the Feast had arrived, totaling about one hundred and twenty men and women. We were a meeting of "believers" from all over Judea and Galilee, with a few from Phoenicia, Syria and even a woman from Samaria. It was an amazing group of men and women who had gathered to celebrate our Jewish traditions of thanksgiving, and also to learn what had actually happened with Jesus on his last days on earth. They all wanted to learn firsthand if Jesus really was more than a teacher of God's love. Rumors had spread like wild fire the last few weeks, and most seemed too fantastic to be true. Most of the guests had been disciples of Jesus for more than a year, and they had known him well. Many had been healed by him, and Lazarus had even been raised from the dead after three days in his tomb. They all had grown to love and trust Jesus.

The big question on everyone's mind was, "What next? Where do we go from here?" The most difficult question was still, "Why did he have to die such a horrible death?" This Jewish celebration of thanksgiving was tainted with a sorrow that would not dissipate from the hearts of each guest. They had all heard that Jesus had risen from the dead, but few had actually seen him. Peter had already heard some rumors on the street that the disciples had claimed Jesus had finally disappeared from earth and would soon come back. This last rumor was what was troubling most of them. None of them were sure that the authorities might not still hunt them down and exterminate them to destroy the memory of Jesus in the hearts of the people. They wanted to be sure that he was now completely out of the picture. Especially concerned were Mary, the mother of Jesus, and his brothers who were with her on that dreadful day.

Peter had developed an agenda for the afternoon which he had hoped would answer many of these questions and calm many fears, but first we needed to celebrate the Feast of Weeks together. He sent Mary Magdalen downstairs to check on Rufus' schedule. She returned immediately calling out that the feast was on its way. What a feast it was, too! People ate their fill of numerous dishes, some they had never tasted before, but there was not a single complaint heard from anyone.

Once the leftovers were cleared away, most of the kitchen help joined us upstairs. Before addressing the group, Peter informed us that the disciples met and filled the spot Judas left empty with Matthias who we would now refer to as an apostle, meaning missionary in Greek. That term more accurately described their function now that Jesus was no longer present.

After those discussions, Peter then called us back to a time of prayer and praise to God. In the middle of our praise time there was a strange sound like a powerful wind blowing through the room, but there was no wind, just the sound of a great wind. Shortly after, first one, then a second, then a third guest began to loudly praise God in languages they never learned. There were those in our trading family whose native languages were Carthaginian, Cyrenese, Tamil, Malayalam, Farsi, Aegyptian and Syriac, all of which we heard clearly and accurately coming from the mouths of untutored Galilean peasants who were speaking these languages with perfect accents as they praised God for his goodness and love. There were many others in the room who also heard God's praises being extoled in other languages spoken by untaught Galileans and Judeans.

How many of these miraculous events were to happen to the followers of Jesus and why? As each one spoke in a language they didn't know, a warm light seemed to glow from their heads. Then as the person next to them turned to ask where they learned to speak so perfectly in their own mother tongue, the one who spoke claimed they knew nothing of that language. Mysteriously, even though they denied knowing the language their neighbor claimed they heard him speak, they could not deny what they had said in their praise to God in their own language. We were all perplexed and very confused.

Many who heard it downstairs in the street where they were spying on the disciples tried to find a believable explanation. They agreed God was powerful, but not that powerful that he would work outside of the natural order of things. Their explanation was that Alexander's wine had made everyone too drunk to understand what was happening. In the meantime, those of us who were there began searching for its deeper meaning.

As the afternoon progressed more people learned of what happened. It seemed that each time someone left to visit a public latrine five more people heard of what happened, until hundreds were struggling to get inside the now unhidden hiding place to hear Peter and some of the others speak, and of course hoping to hear another foreign language outburst.

It became urgent that Peter make a statement to those who were not among the invited guests, many of whom were not even followers of The Way, but critics. "Let me explain this to you. These people are not drunk as you might suppose for it is still early in the day.

"Our patriarch, King David, spoke of the resurrection of the Messiah, that he would be neither abandoned to the realm of the dead, nor would his body see decay. God has raised this same Jesus to life, and many of us here are witnesses of it. Therefore, let all Israel be assured of this one thing, God has made this Jesus, whom you crucified, both Lord and Messiah over all."

When the people who came in after the feast that afternoon, heard of these declarations they were cut to the heart and said to Peter and the other apostles, "Brothers, we are sorry for our evil ways. What shall we do?"

Peter replied, "Repent for what you have done and be publicly baptized, like you have privately done many times in the mikvah, to make yourselves ceremonially clean. Every one of you should do this publicly in the name of Jesus the Messiah for the public declaration of the forgiveness of your sins. In so doing, your repentance will draw you closer to God, who will grant you the gift of this Holy Spirit. The promise is for you and your children . . . for all whom the Lord our God will call."

It was an amazing day and as we returned to Alexander's about an hour after dark, we reclined in the fountain atrium and talked openly and prayed together until midnight asking for God's guidance. We all knew that we needed to go on with our lives and plan for our trips home. But when? It was approaching mid- summer and the sea breezes were almost non-existent in the eastern Mare Internum. It was decided the most prudent thing to do was to hire passage with a camel caravan to Alexandria where we could attend to much needed business issues until the winds began to blow out of the desert to the south.

CHAPTER 40

UNITED – JUNE 10, AD29

Eli had determined it was time to celebrate his union with Aaron before we all left and took "his" Aaron home to Syracuse with us, which was originally our intention to do. Through the years Eli had saved up a little money and he had already spoken to Alexander about borrowing the balance for a Bride Price. His intention was for it to enable him to pay Stephen for Aaron BarHanno's freedom. But since Aaron was a castrated eunuch and could never produce children, Sadhu and I advised Eli that all he needed to do was promise to take care of him and approach Stephen about giving Aaron to himself as a wedding present. He looked at Sadhu and me like we were crazy, but we encouraged him to try, then they could keep the Bride Price money.

Unknown to any of us, Stephen had already agreed to pay Alexander for the expenses incurred by our long stay with him and Rufus by giving the slave, Aaron, to Alexander as payment in full. When Eli learned of this agreement, he was as proud as any groom with a new bride . . . as well he should be. What they didn't know was that after Aaron's slave deed was signed over to Alexander, he was planning to give Aaron's Certificate of Emancipation to the couple as a wedding present, eliminating any fear of them ever leaving his household.

Aaron was a very handsome man, if you never had to see how his loins were mutilated in his brutal castration. In fact, it was a miracle he lived through it. Someone must have put a lot of love and hard work into keeping him alive. One day I went for a swim with him and he allowed me to examine him and to see if the rest of his manhood worked properly. I was startled to discover that his manhood was like a superior pearl inside of the ugliest of oysters. That coupled with his tenderness and love for God truly did make him a priceless catch.

Since Eli was really chomping at the bit to finalize his union with Aaron, we decided to set the date of their union at the seventh day after Pentecost. They were already treated like a family by everyone and would always be secure and protected in the home of Alexander and Rufus.

Because neither of the brothers would ever have a wife, Eli and Aaron were also secure from their own fear of women. Of course, after he was castrated, Aaron had lost all hope of ever having a mate who really loved him. The unique thing about both men was that they were also born eunuchs and had no desire for women anyway. That attribute made them both valuable as trusted household servants. With a born eunuch the women of the household would not only be safe from sexual advances from their protectors, but also have the freedom to develop friendships with them without fear of any suspicion of impropriety. Of course, all of those issues would never arise in the all-male household of Alexander and Rufus.

The strange thing about this wedding was that even though it was a rare union between a house servant and a slave, everyone was looking forward to celebrating it. The most obvious was the elder of us all, Sadhu the rabbi. Since reconciling with his own son's identification as a eunuch, he was able to deal with his own pain of never having descendants beyond Yacobsa. In a strong patriarchal society like India, to not have heirs was often considered shameful. He finally reached his reconciliation with this dilemma through witnessing Stephen's and my love. Of course, Stephen's children, which his wife was able to give him, helped as well, especially Little Aaron who went with us everywhere. Sadhu had accepted the medicine of love and discovered his son was quite a fantastic man after all. In fact, he had actually grown to deeply love and respect his son, even though he spent every night in Alexander's bed.

As Sadhu worked out the plans for the ceremony, both men encouraged him to make all the decisions. That meant the ceremony would be part Judean and part Indian but definitely Jewish in structure, with the exception of its solemnization which would be in the name of Jesus, the Messiah. His greatest regret was that his princess, Rahelani, could not be there to help with the details, but she and her women were greatly needed in Alexandria. The second surprise was Sadhu's son, Yacobsa, whose excitement was beyond containment because of his father's expressions of joy and goodwill toward the male couple. He began to realize that someday his father really would be willing to solemnize his union, too. He had no illusions about the fact that one of the partners in the upcoming union was castrated and therefore could never produce children anyway. The case could be made that the demand for a traditional wedding was irrelevant. However, what if his chosen mate was not a castrated eunuch? That would rest in God's hands.

Through all the excitement, my only sorrow was for Hanno. Yes, Stephen was away on one of his constant trips to Caesarea for at least three days out of every five. It was always his intention that Hanno would sleep with me whenever he was gone, but I was beginning to realize that such an arrangement prevented him from finding a man of his own who he could spend his life with. Of course, another part of the problem was that he always promised he would definitely go with me wherever I went, as my servant and my companion. He saw us as inseparable no matter what the circumstances might be. I understood the reality that I was just a teenager and he was a man who needed someone at his side. To make things even more difficult was the honest fact that I could not stand the thought of losing him. I freed him because I loved him, but I also knew I couldn't let go of him because I loved him. All I could do was pray that he finds someone he could love more than me.

Thinking of Eli's and Aaron's permanent union was forcing me to think of all the countless other eunuchs who are forced to be emotionally and physically alone for their entire lives. Worse yet, were some who are pressured to pretend to be like other men and marry a woman, as did Grandfather Sirach and Stephen, for the sole purpose of keeping the family line intact. If they refuse to marry, they are cut off from everything and everyone they hold dear. I suppose it must always be that way. But why? What I find amazing was that Jesus's parents knew he was different, and they never forced him to marry. They loved him and allowed God to use him as he chose. If all parents were like that, this world would have much less suffering.

It was only three days before our great wedding feast in Bethphage. I was sure most people thought it was socially wrong that we were making a big affair out of it. Some of Alexander's neighbors thought it was scandalous to throw a wedding feast for servants and slaves, because it was against the accepted social order and religious precedence. But Jesus taught that in God's eyes there were no slave or free, we were all one. Also, he taught that there were no male or female, but we were all equal . . . now that was radical, and he was a suspect to many religious leaders because of that position. Since the beginning of recorded history, men took, or bought, women to give them children, cook their meals, and satisfy their sexual needs. Now, Jesus has begun to turn all those traditions on their heads. Slaves can now be given the same respect as freemen in our households. The world will never be the same . . . I thought. Old laws and traditions die hard, even if the reasons we use to hold onto them no longer make sense. Will people ever really change? I surely prayed they would.

At the time we were too busy to worry about it. If people from the village decided not to honor us with their presence, that was their problem. As followers of the Messiah, we must return love for scorn. We knew that many of Alexander's neighbors would shun us anyway because many discovered we were followers of The Way, but that could not be changed either. I knew that most of the apostles and the women who were followers of Jesus would be here to celebrate with their spiritual brothers. The day before, when I was in Jerusalem to see how they were doing, Thomas told me that because of Temple opposition they were going to use a Greek term for Messiah. This would also enable the non-Jews to see Jesus as relevant to them. Therefore, we were encouraged to begin using the Greek title, Christ. For those of us who are Jews, that might prove a bit difficult, but we would learn.

That night as I returned to Bethphage with John and Thomas, twelve chickens and a sheep had already been slaughtered and were being dressed by Hanno and Rashvi. If no one came we would have enough meat for several weeks. At breakfast, I thought it rather strange that Hanno and Rashvi were serving and having a great time doing so even though they didn't share a language between them. Even Stephen and John noticed a difference in their demeanor, and they didn't seem to mind that we noticed. Were my prayers being answered? But I never suspected that Rashvi was a eunuch. He always stayed apart from everyone else socially and did his job impeccably, staying in the background whenever possible. He was the ultimate servant to Sadhu.

Later that morning I cornered Yacobsa about his father's valet. Smiling broadly, he shared what he knew, "About sixteen years ago our king, my uncle, had a small territorial skirmish with a neighboring king. Each side lost a few dozen men, and my uncle also captured some noncombatants as well as some military personnel which he refused to return. They included four men who were staff slaves to the military commanders. Each had unique qualities and my uncle decided to keep them for himself since they were all cut eunuchs. Rashvi was one of them. These were highly educated men who had many talents, and there were several positions in the palace and the government for which these men would be perfect. He also needed to find out which of the four he could trust to work within his palace household. This man had to be trusted and preferably a eunuch at birth because he would be responsible for the welfare of the palace women among other important duties.

"He tested each eunuch with a prostitute several times, and then with several prostitutes. The eunuchs naturally knew these were tests, so they all resisted the female temptations. But sometimes it is impossible to hide our lust when an erection gets in the way. Rashvi stayed as limp as a hanging rope. Even after the other three were eliminated, my uncle decided to test Rashvi two more times, each time with another born eunuch. The first was a young and very handsome man. Rashvi passed with very high marks. The naked young man was hardly in the room before Rashvi began to mount him. Then, a few days later, a masculine soldier built like a god came to Rashvi totally nude. Rashvi immediately turned on all his charms to seduce that powerful man. Naturally the soldier responded with great passion as Rashvi hoped he would. He found Rashvi irresistible and mounted him as quickly as possible. It was obvious to the king that neither wanted to stop. It went on for an hour. My uncle was assured that he found his true eunuch. Please Jacobus, don't share any of this. The king, you, and I are the only ones who know any of this.

"Rashvi worked in the palace as the perfect servant to the king for five years. Then as my father needed help with his business, he gave Rashvi to his sister, my mother. That was nearly six years ago, and he has been the perfect manservant and assistant to father. Soon, Rashvi discovered that I might be a eunuch also, and he asked to work part time as my tutor. It was then I discovered he was the most discreet man I have ever met, and he taught me many things. To this day I am sure my parents never guessed he came to my room after midnight on a different night each week. He taught me how to make love to a man, and he taught me well. Rashvi has always thought of my parents before himself and would never hurt them, for they have become his family, and I his son.

"Yes, my precious Jacobus, I see what you see. Our servants have fallen in love with each other. It's perfect because they are both cut. They are the eunuchs which have the most difficult time finding love. They often accept a status of shame which is frequently used to discredit their value as men and lovers. Shall we encourage them? After all, they may be working together for the remainder of their natural lives?"

Instinctively, I jumped into his arms and kissed him in a burst of pure joy. We decided to approach them with our blessings the next day just before the wedding. I was walking on a cloud and had to let someone in on our scheme. The first person I could think of was John for he had wisdom beyond his years. I knew I could trust him, and he might be able to advise us as to how to go about it. In speaking with John, he became as excited as if it were to be his own wedding. In fact, that is what he suggested . . . not that "he" get married but that we suggest they get married right after Eli and Aaron. In speaking with Yacobsa he didn't think his father would object, even though he was sure his father never dreamed Rashvi was a born eunuch like his own son. Besides, this would unite our two families in yet another way. He promised to talk to his father and if he agreed, he would need to keep it as a surprise until the last minute.

Then, about fifteen minutes later, Yacobsa approached the two apostles and me to let us know his father actually wept when he found out that Rashvi had felt he needed to hide his true identity for all those years. And yes, he would be honored to perform a double ceremony. The Apostle Peter was caught totally off guard but caught up soon enough. He thought it was one of the most loving things ever. Men who never thought they could find love in their lifetimes have found it. "What a beautiful week it has been!"

I didn't have time to discuss this with Stephen for he was spending the day in Jerusalem sharing with Nicodemus and checking on caravan schedules to Alexandria. We would not have a ship from Caesarea to Alexandria for at least a month when the winds would pick up again. Stephen arrived shortly after dinner, exhausted but satisfied. "The caravan leaves in three days and we will need to leave at sunrise to get there in time to load the camels and be ready for our departure. The only problem is that the caravan assembles at the west end of the city, where we normally depart for Caesarea. That will add about twenty minutes to our trip to the camel grounds, but if we can use the donkey carts again for our baggage we should do just fine. Everyone's excitement level was building, knowing that the day after the wedding would be a crazy one.

That night in bed after a wonderful time of sharing our love, I told Stephen we were going to have a double wedding the next day and that it was going to be a surprise for the second couple, Hanno and Rashvi.

Being the perfect strategist, he asked if Hanno knew about this. When I told him "no," he advised that I get up and go to him tonight and check it out with him. I had never dreamed of a problem with our plan, but as Stephen pointed out, surprises often surprise the wrong people. Jumping out of bed, I wrapped a towel around myself and rushed upstairs to Hanno's room. Knocking softly on the door I waited fearing Rashvi might be with him and I would spoil their time together. In a minute Hanno appeared at the door in the nude. Embarrassed, he said he was expecting someone else. When I asked if it was Rashvi, he blushed and nodded, surprised that I suspected,

I got right to the point, "Are you in love with Rashvi?" "Yes, very much."

"Does he love you?"

"Well . . . yes, very much."

"Do you want to spend the rest of your life with him?"

"Well . . . yes, but more importantly I also want to spend my life with you?"

"If you could do both would you?"

"Of course I would!"

"That's all I needed to know. Tomorrow you and Rashvi are being united right after Eli and Aaron . . . but don't tell Rashvi unless you really feel you need to."

Instantly, he pulled me to himself and gave me one of those wonderful kisses for which I will always remember him. It took me another fifteen minutes to return to the door and back to Stephen. When he asked how it went, I told him . . . everything. When he broke into laughter, I almost pushed him out of bed.

The next morning was a beehive of activity as flowers were picked and finishing touches put on the food as it was placed in a warm brick oven to hold until noon. Then we all had to get dressed and ready to receive the guests. For the sake of the men, we were praying for at least fifty, but we had over ninety. Many of the villagers came, probably more for curiosity sake. Most of the women and even Jesus' mother and brothers came to honor the men who helped at the cross and burial, and all the disciples, now apostles, were able to make it, too. It was probably the largest double wedding for servants and eunuchs in local history . . . forget the probably.

Rufus even hired some musicians from Jerusalem who added the perfect touch. Alexander was greeting everyone like it was his daughter who was getting married. All the guests were in the highest spirits as we gathered on a large sandy area behind the house overlooking the orchards, vineyards, and the large spring fed pond. The canopy was up, and the rabbi was in place. As planned, Eli asked Hanno and Rashvi to stand up with them acting as family witnesses. It was the perfect image of family and everyone who knew was holding their breath wondering how the rabbi would pull it off. Then we all gasped as the sadhu entered in an elegant robe followed by Peter. Were these to be the first weddings performed after The Way was forcibly separated from Judaism? Probably! Why not? These men had been the most downtrodden of all men and we were excited to celebrate their happiness and love.

Sadhu could not have been more right in his plans. The ceremony was part Indian and part Judean, but it was also part of something entirely new, the blessing was asked from "Jesus the Christ," the Savior of the oppressed. As soon as Peter blessed Eli and Aaron, they turned to face their guests and instead of walking to greet them, they stepped aside as Hanno took Rashvi's hand and lead him to stand with him under the canopy. For the first time as a couple, in front of Sadhu and Peter, the very proper Rashvi broke down in tears as Sadhu spoke to him softly in Malayalam, his mother tongue. As Rashvi regained his composure, Sadhu announced in Aramaic, "We are now going to celebrate a second wedding between two more castrated men who speak multiple different languages, none of which are common between them. They are both working on Aramaic, so help them all you can. The one language they do speak is love, and they do speak that one very well. Shall we begin?"

The first part of the ceremony was in Malayalam, beautifully presented by Sadhu, while a second was delivered in Aramaic by Peter who ended it in another benediction in the name of Jesus, the Christ. By the time they kissed one another they were both in tears again. One had been a child sex slave, the other a former guardian of women. They were now united as powerful men of God. They are looked down on by the "righteous" because their ability to father children was taken from them and the desire to father children was never given to them. On that note the local Judean musicians broke out into music as we all began to dance uniquely different dances. Eventually, some of the dancers began to peel off and headed to the tables covered with food.

That night there were four less men searching for another man's room.

CHAPTER 41

CAMELS – JUNE 12, AD29

Before the sun broke over the horizon, Stephen was knocking on doors to get us ready for a quick trip to Jerusalem's Western Gate and the caravan grounds. After the two donkey carts were loaded and Little Aaron was seated in his place atop the lead cart's baggage, we assembled in front of the house for our farewells and two important presentations.

The first, was our payment for over six week's room and board from Stephen. Very ceremoniously he handed over to Alexander in lieu of payment, the document which made him the sole owner of the slave, Aaron BarHanno, with all the rights and privileges of ownership.

Then, in front of a startled Aaron, Alexander pulled a document of his own out of his robe, which Stephen wrote up the night before. He held it up over his head and proclaimed, "This document, hereby signed by me, declares all bonds of servitude of Aaron BarHanno are satisfied and redeemed by his current owner, Alexander BarSimon. Therefore, I hereby declare Aaron BarHanno a free man." As we all gathered around Aaron and his new husband, he almost passed out with disbelief. Only a few short months earlier he was an unknown cargo slave in the hold of a ship, brutally castrated, and doomed to a life of hard labor. Suddenly, he was a free man, united to a man who loved him more than life itself, all because he asked a stranger a question about the living creator God.

Once the congratulations were completed, we all needed to say goodbye again before our donkey drivers, Eli and Aaron, could get our carts rolling. Our carts began moving out at a fairly good pace, enabling us to reach the caravan staging area in adequate time. Immediately, Stephen found the captain in charge, who led us to our fourteen camels where our three camel drivers were waiting. After the carts were unloaded, we were clustered around Eli and Aaron for the last time. Tears flowed freely, and kisses were lavishly shared, even from Simon who had grown to have a great appreciation for Aaron's faith and strength. It was very difficult for me to see the two faithful men of God drive their carts away, not knowing if I would ever see them again. I hoped that if I did, they would at least have a common language between them. But it was Hanno, Aaron's spiritual father, who shed the greater tears at their departure. We all respected the beauty and the pain those tears revealed.

With the carts disappearing into the distance Stephen introduced us to the captain of the caravan, Ascalon BarEphraim, who had been leading his camels back and forth to Alexandria for nearly twenty years. He was a native Judean, but his wife was an Alexandrian Jew, so he used the caravan business to keep a home in both locations because his wife feared the constant instability of Jerusalem. Ascalon introduced us to the three camel drivers who would be working with us, two young Aegyptian boys about my age, and one Judean a little older. Immediately after the introductions, they began loading our pack camels. The first thing the boys did was to assure us that we would get used to the strong "fragrance" of the camels, and their sometimes-nasty dispositions. They added that they loved each camel because they gave the boys some very good work.

Our departure was scheduled for midmorning, so when the camels were loaded we spent the rest of our time letting the camels become familiar with us, their new riders. Each person had his own camel and had to learn its name and how to get on and off their camel. Aaron was experiencing the event of his life, having never been up close to an animal as large as the one he would be sitting on for the next eight days. There was no need to worry about guiding the camels like we would a horse. They would be tied together in two groups of five and move as a single unit. There would also be one driver leading the three baggage camels. Because of the recent holiday, there were many other travelers that day, and we needed to be observant when we dismounted during our toilet breaks and remember to return to the camel which was assigned to us.

Abruptly, we were told to climb onto our camels for departure, get comfortable; and be ready to leave. What a shock! If camels look funny, they ride even funnier. Each saddle had a high narrow back on it to help us stay steady, otherwise we had to hold onto anything we could grab in order to keep from falling off. Instantly I understood why camels are called the ships of the desert, for I had only sailed through two major storms which were rougher than a ride on these creatures. We were fortunate to have our drivers walking beside us until we stopped for lunch.

We discovered the next morning that coming down out of the Judean hills on camel back would be one of the most difficult parts of our trip. With every step-down each hill we felt as though we were being thrown forward onto the camel's neck, and then thrown to the ground where we were sure to be stomped on by their giant feet.

At lunch everyone was given dates, bread, an orange, and water. Resting our backs against our camels as we ate, we got a strong, up-close, appreciation for their fragrance. Aside from the slight discomfort, it was wonderful to be sitting on solid ground and not rocking as high as a rooftop, while in fear for our lives. During those breaks we also had about twenty minutes to get to know our camel drivers a little better.

During the intermittent breaks each day, and again when we pitched our night camps, were great social times for all of us. But on our first night we became suspicious of the sacks of camel dung which had been collected by the pack drivers and laid out on the ground at the end of our caravan. We had noticed that they had been collecting dung throughout the day as our beasts walked merrily on their way. There were over a hundred camels and as soon as we dismounted for the night, sacks of fried dung were run back forward to be used for the fires to cook our evening meals of rice and lintels provided by the caravan. Seeing this for the first time, created a cautious feeling among some of us, but after a tiring day our hunger overpowered the sight of burning dung under the cooking pots.

With each stop we got to know our group's lead driver a little better. He was also the Judean driver who looked after Aaron. He had commented that the eight of us seemed very close to one another and began to share some of his own life history in hopes of learning more about his interesting passengers. He told us that his nick name was Timnah, after his home village at the foot of the Judean hills about a fifteen-minute walk from where we were camped for the night. He spent his life watching the caravans going by and they sometimes stopped in this open area to camp and eat.

He always enjoyed working with his father's camel, so two years ago he came down to the camp one evening and met with Captain

BarEphraim. He asked for a job after telling him how he worked with his father's camel. The captain agreed to take him on a three-day round trip to Jerusalem. When they returned in three days, they sat down to dinner together and decided what to do next. Excitedly Timnah ran home to inform his father and rejoined the captain before they left in the morning. Ever since that morning he was called Timnah after the name that had been given to the rest stop generations earlier.

His method worked well, and we began sharing our own stories. He claimed we were the most interesting group he had ever led on this route. He noted some of the obvious relationships among us and tried to learn more. Stephen nodded and began telling him that he was from Sicilia and was traveling with his eight-year-old son, Aaron, and his young husband, Jacobus, from Hispania. Taking that as a cue, Simon introduced himself as Stephen's brother-in-law from Cyrene. Then Sadhu introduced himself simply as Sadhu, which means rabbi, and also as Stephen's business partner from southern India. Yacobsa introduced himself as the rabbi's son, now from Alexandria. Hanno had his first chance to say what he had wanted to say (in Greek) for weeks. "I am Hanno from Carthage and this is my husband, Rashvi from India."

By the time we had finished, Timnah realized how correct his estimation was. We really were the strangest group he had ever traveled with. He was engrossed by the fact that several of us were married to each other, and when he asked if that wasn't very unusual, Stephen replied that Sadhu was our rabbi and had performed the marriage of two others of our number who couldn't join us on this journey. When he told Timnah that they were just married three days before, along with Hanno and Rashvi, Timnah shook his head in amazement that men were able to be romantic partners for life. In his village of Timnah such a thing could never happen.

Stephen clearly understood the deeper meaning of what Timnah said and took the bait immediately. "Couldn't happen? Why not? Are there no young men there who could love you?"

Realizing he was discovered he dropped his head and mumbled, "No."

Then my heart broke for what I saw on his face was pain, not embarrassment. Rubbing Stephen's bare leg for emphasis, I spoke as tenderly as I could. "Timnah, you are a handsome young man, and I can tell you are great with people. Have you never had a boyfriend who really cared for you?"

"Never. I have always been afraid they would call me a eunuch and there is nothing more degrading than that. To be a eunuch is worse than anything because they don't see you as a man. They think of you as almost a woman."

Pondering what to say next, I asked him if he spoke Greek. When he nodded yes, I turned to Hanno and explained what was going on. Speaking in Carthaginian I asked if he would do something special for our young friend.

Then in Greek I asked Hanno to stand and remove his clothes. As he did so, I told Timnah that Hanno was proud of his masculine body and killer good looks. When he was totally naked, I asked him to hold his manhood to one side. As he did, he smiled tenderly to Timnah.

Seeing the expression on Timnah's face I asked him, "What do you see hanging between Hanno's legs?"

"Nothing. I don't see anything."

Suddenly understanding what was going on, with the help of Sadhu's translation, Rashvi stood and stripped like Hanno. He then reached for Hanno with one hand and held his manhood aside with the other hand. I then asked, "What do you see now?"

"Nothing. There is nothing there either."

Then I stood up and took my clothes off and pulled my manhood aside and asked, "What do you see now?"

"Balls. Balls like mine."

Not to be outdone, Stephen stood up and dropped his clothes. "To that, what do you see?"

"Wow. The biggest balls I have ever seen."

Then one at a time Simon stood in tears looking into Stephen's eyes as he smiled back and nodded. Again, I asked, "What do you see?"

"A man just like my father."

Then Yacobsa stood and did the same. Again, I asked, "What do you see?" "Aside from his dark color he looks just like me."

Then we were all surprised when Sadhu stood and dropped his clothes, as I asked, "What do you see here?"

Beginning to cry, Timnah replied, "He looks just like my grandfather used to look."

As I began to ask him what the differences were that he saw between us. Aaron interrupted and looking at his father he boldly said, "Don't forget about me!"

As he stood and took his clothes off, he proudly displayed his small erection. Then he boldly said, "I am a eunuch, too! I have always been a eunuch, but I have balls. I am so thankful that all the men in my family are eunuchs, except Uncle Simon and Grandfather Sadhu, of course. But they are special, and I love them anyway." The giant heart of that eight-year-old had broken any tension.

Finding myself at a complete loss for words, I could only stand there looking at Aaron with tears running down my cheeks. I was so proud of his courage and honesty.

Breaking the silence, Stephen said what we all felt, "My son, Aaron, has demonstrated courage, knowing that we are a misjudged minority, open to persecution and ridicule if we don't hide ourselves from everyone in the larger world and sometimes even from each other. On occasion we even grow to hate ourselves because that is how others feel about us. But when you strip us down you see the real man, whether he is the product of Man's cruelty or of God's love or both, we can be blessed if we choose to be. Among us today there are only two who are not eunuchs. One is a respected rabbi. The other carried Jesus' cross as he helped Jesus reach the point of his crucifixion and death. Others here lowered Jesus from his cross, handed him to his mother, and then placed him in his temporary tomb. You see, Timnah, we love you. We have been honored by God even if we are eunuchs. We believe God placed us here to encourage you on our trip to Alexandria."

As Timnah sat there before us and cried his heart out with thankfulness, we all scrambled to get dressed before someone walked by and thought we were more than a little strange. As Timnah regained his composure and we regained our clothes, it was obvious he wanted to stay with us rather than join his colleagues at the back of the caravan. It was also obvious he wanted to talk about something else, but he seemed reticent to mention it. I couldn't comprehend what could be tougher for a teenager to talk about than their own despised sexuality. As I hoped, he responded to a few of our previous statements. His first question was, "Did you really know Jesus?"

Stephen picked that one up immediately by stating we only knew him for a few hours before he died. Then he referred to Simon who shared how he had met him in a vision months ago and that it was because of that vision we all joined him on this year's Seder pilgrimage. Turning to Simon, Stephen asked that he share his vision with Timnah and then the events that happened five months later. As he spoke, Simon not only shared what happened but how he felt about the vision and then of walking with Jesus while carrying his cross to where they crucified him. From there Stephen took over and told of his death. He shared what we did to comfort and aid his family because they came down from Galilee and there was no one there to help them. Then I mentioned how I comforted his beloved disciple, John, as we both held Jesus' legs as our eunuch slave pried the spikes out of Jesus' hands and feet. He explained how Hanno and Rashvi lowered him to the ground with ropes so John and I could place him in his mother's lap, and then Hanno helped carry him to his tomb. We also became friends with his close disciples. In fact, we were with them at the Feast of Pentecost, and they all came to Hanno and Rashvi's wedding along with Jesus' mother and brothers, just three days ago.

Timnah was nearly in shock and asked Stephen bluntly, "You expect me to believe that God would use eunuchs in such ways as those things you claim you did? What happened when you were with the Disciples for the feast of Pentecost? Did they welcome eunuchs to this holy feast?"

With tears in his eyes and a cracking voice Stephen replied, "Yes, they did, and after the feast Rashvi heard a Galilean farmer praising God and glorifying Jesus in his Malayalam language from India. The rabbi here heard a Galilean fisherman speaking in Tamil, another Indian language. Hanno heard a woman praising God in Carthaginian. And Simon heard the same from a Syrian speaking a dialect of Cyrenese from the other side of Aegyptus. It was a miraculous day and God showed us he would reach out to both eunuchs and women in the same way as he does to the most pious of men. All he asks is that they believe and obey."

Timnah sat there in awe of the concept that God would love him the same way, even if he was a eunuch and could not create children for Israel. But stranger still, each of us eunuchs also found ourselves praising God in a language we never learned.

Later when Aaron fell asleep in Hanno's arms, it became evident that Timnah had no desire to join his friends around their campfire that night. It appeared that he just wanted to be held close and assured that he was not an evil person because he was not attracted to women and would never create a child. I looked around our group. I could spot no one who would really fit what he needed that night.

Then Simon tapped me on the shoulder and asked if Stephen and I thought he should ask Timnah to sleep with him that night. I was stunned. When I looked at Stephen I saw that he was stunned as well. However, we soon realized the young man needed a strong, positive father figure that night more than he needed a handsome eunuch. Going back to Simon I suggested he ask Timnah and see how he responds. Before I knew what was happening, Timnah was in Simon's arms in tears. It wasn't long before they stretched out next to Simon's camel covered in a blanket suitable for two.

The next morning Timnah didn't want to leave Simon's side until it was time to prepare the camels for the day's march. While he was doing his job, I asked Simon how it went for Timnah during the night and if he seemed to sleep well. In response, Simon surprised me again when he haltingly said, "Maybe I shouldn't have asked him to sleep with me. Don't get me wrong. He was fine. It was me. I enjoyed holding him in my arms, comforting him in my sleep. When I awoke in the middle of the night, there he was, still backed up to me as though it was totally natural. Every time I awoke during the night, there he was. When I would hold him, it gave me a very good feeling. This morning when he got up to go to work, he couldn't hide his modest erection, no matter how much he tried. What should I do about that?"

Immediately, I told him that was too much for me to call. I suggested he speak to the Rabbi before we mounted up, and that way he could think about it during the day. Quickly he ran over to Sadhu and spoke in a very animated fashion, shaking his head in the negative several times. As soon as they quit talking, Sadhu placed his hand on Simon's head and offered a very somber prayer. With the "Amen" they hugged one another, and Simon walked to his camel with a smile. Sadhu stood motionless with a huge grin on his face shaking his head.

Each time we stopped that day, Timnah was with us as quickly as his chores were completed. We all knew the proof would be if he rejoined his fellows at the end of the caravan when we stopped for the night. Just as I hoped, when his chores were completed at the end of the day he was with us again, like he was a part of our extended family. What surprised us most was that instead of sitting with some of the younger guys, he went straight to Simon and sat next to him. He did or said nothing overt or even spoke with him that much, but he obviously felt secure with that older father figure. Of course, Simon was expecting the worst, but it never came. As I look back, I think both Timnah and Simon simply wanted someone with a sexual attraction opposite from their own to affirm themselves as acceptable. I will admit, however, that Simon was a bit confused and at one point even a little defensive, but Timnah was as upbeat as any small-town eunuch could ever be.

Continuing down the Coastal Highway toward Heliopolis, we were within two hours of the city when we entered a tropical paradise of palm trees, orange orchards, and many other exotic sites nourished by the great river. Once we reached the massive Nile west of the city, we were stalled for nearly a day as we waited in line for the large barge like ferries to carry us and our camels across the vast river to Surd. Once again, as we waited, we were constantly accompanied by Timnah. It was as if he bought passage with us and was not an employee. However, when work needed to be done, he was the first to go do it. Finally, it was our turn to cross the Nile and get back on our way. Each barge could handle about twenty camels and maybe fifty people. Of course, the local people had priority, so we had to split our group and take several separate barges about twenty minutes apart.

I almost made a bet with Hanno that Timnah would try every way possible to get on the same barge with Simon. It seemed the odds were stacked in my favor and I suppose they were. When the barge left the bank, there was Timnah and Simon standing together up front, so Simon could get the best views of the ancient city as Timnah explained everything to him. An hour later, on a sandy plain we were formed up and ready to head northwest toward Alexandria for at least four more hours before we needed to camp one last time. We stayed as far as possible from the lush Nile estuaries for fear of hippopotamuses, crocodiles, or cobras, all of which terrify camels, to say nothing of people.

The next day, continuing along the western most estuary, we reached the eastern gate to Alexandria several hours after our noon meal. We estimated that we had five hours of daylight left to get our baggage to Sadhu's home. Timnah asked us to wait before untying anything. He needed to check with Captain BarEphraim about the camels, and he would return in a few minutes. While he was gone, Rashvi ran to the house to let everyone know we were home. A few minutes later Timnah returned with two different camel drivers and a smile too big for his face. He told us to lead the way and they would follow with our baggage camels.

Fifteen minutes later we reached Sadhu's home as Rahelani was walking out the door with Rashvi and a group of servants. It was suddenly a babel of languages until Sadhu clapped his hands and shouted, "Aramaic please!" Everyone began to laugh but switched over immediately. Each of us went to Rahelani and greeted her personally. She was like a mother whose many children just arrived from everywhere for Seder. I thought it was appropriate to introduce Timnah to the "princess" . . . of course she would send me to my room without my dinner if I called her that in public. After I introduced Timnah, I told her that Mary, the mother of Jesus, sent her special greetings and instructed me to thank her for all she did to help her through her son's murder. With that, Rahelani began to weep and asked how she was holding up. I told her that she was doing terrific ten days ago at Rashvi's wedding feast at Alexander's home.

Hearing that, she screamed at the top of her voice for Rashvi to get over to her immediately. In seconds he was bowing before Rahelani. During this whole exchange Timnah's eyes were as big as hen's eggs and his jaw fell open and wouldn't close.

Yes, the camels did get offloaded, Rashvi was forgiven, and we all got washed including Timnah, as best he could, and then sent off the camels with the two boys while he remained behind . . . . as we all expected.

CHAPTER 42

TIMNAH – JUNE 21, AD29

Rashvi knew he was in a tough situation. Not only was he old enough to be Hanno's father, but he had been gifted to Rahelani by her brother, the King of Chera in south India. In finding the love of his life he had defied the intensions of that gift. How could he resist? Hanno had much in common with Rashvi. They both had been castrated, had been a slave and then a freeman. Both had been unquestionably loyal to their masters, and they had faith in God through the Christ. There it ended! Hanno was disturbingly handsome and built like a warrior. His hairless body was covered with rippled muscles and topped off with the most beautiful eyes and the warmest smile this side of India. And oh, what a lover! His castration as a child didn't hurt him in that department. Perhaps his being a child sex slave for fourteen years didn't scar him as much as a person might think.

Rashvi's question was, "How can he love me, an older man nearly twice his age? I surly don't possess the assets he has, nor do I have his stamina, but he loves me. He really does love me!"

I knew Hanno better than anyone, and yes, he really did love Rashvi. For months I had watched him light up every time Rashvi entered the room, as graceful as a swan floating down a river in the moonlight. It was only a matter of time before these complete opposites would collide, never to be pulled apart. As difficult a time as Eli had courting Aaron with only the linguistic help of Alexander, so Hanno courted Rashvi. Ever since that morning, watching the power of their eyes and smiles as they served breakfast just one day before Eli's and Aaron's wedding feast, I knew what they had was real. Unfortunately, they also needed a translator to share the words they needed to say to one another. It turned out I was that someone they both trusted with their emotions and dreams. No one else ever knew that it was through my mouth that they shared their love with each other that night I sat in the corner whispering sweet nothings into the darkness as they embraced each other. Understanding each other's words for the first time, they kissed passionately as they wept for joy. Soon words were no longer needed, and I left to rejoin Stephen with some vague excuse for my absence which I think he saw through completely.

On the morning of their wedding, I saw beyond any doubt that those two unbelievable men were bound together for life, and I was happy for them. The problem was that I wouldn't be with them every morning when they awoke nor every evening when they laid down together. The perfect answer was nine days crossing the desert with their camels side by side. At night sleeping between those two camels, who fortunately seemed to like each other as well, was the perfect wedding bed. Whenever those two camels were resting side by side, we knew they were watching over their charges.

Abruptly, their wedding retreat from reality was over. It was back to normal, whatever that would be. But first Rashvi, with Hanno holding his hand, had to face Rahelani who didn't have a clue of what was happening. As I watched the drama unfold, I was relieved to see no anger only disappointment that they couldn't wait until they got to Alexandria, so she could be the proud mother of the bride. When I overheard Rashvi's translation, I had to join in the laughter with everyone else within earshot. Even Timnah, who stayed glued to my side, enjoyed watching the happiness of Rashvi's master.

In the meantime, I was beginning to detect a small problem developing with Timnah. Simon had become his father image whom he loved beyond words and who loved him like a son, but his attraction for me, only three years his junior, was beginning to make itself obvious. I spoke with Stephen about it the night before as we cuddled between our camels with Aaron pressed against my back. I had a fear that Timnah would ask Captain BarEphraim for his separation pay when we reached Alexandria. When he sent his fellows back to the caravan without him, I was sure he wanted to adopt us as his family. As I mentioned it to Stephen again later that evening, all he said was, "Well, we just lost Aaron." I understood. What he meant was we needed to let God work it out like he had done every other time.

That evening's meal was fabulous, and I got the impression that Timnah had never eaten like that in his entire life. When he didn't leave as we began to head for our sleeping mats, I knew I had to say something. I asked him to join me in the home's small garden in the rear of the house. As we sat down on a bench in the moonlight, I decided to hit the question straight on.

"Timnah, why don't you want to return to the caravan? Aren't they going to look for you?"

In response he also became very direct and stated, "The captain won't miss me. I am like a slave, but I am free. That is no life. My best friends are the camels. They understand me like my father's camel does. No one else cares, not even my father. My mother died when I was young, so I have no one. Jacobus, I always wanted a brother like you who understands who I am and doesn't beat me up if I look at you the wrong way."

As tears began to well up within my eyes, I looked into his tearing eyes and surprised myself when I said, "Timnah, if you need a home . . . really need a home, . . . you can have one wherever Stephen, Aaron, Hanno, and I are. If you need a family, we are also here for that. Even Simon adores you like a son."

"I have felt that in you . . . all of you."

I assured him he was safe with us, and Stephen would see that he grows and matures into a great man. We would teach him and pray with him as one of our own.

Then he dropped the roof on me that I should have expected. "Jacobus, I have never been kissed since I was three when my mother kissed me the night she died. I will understand, if you refuse, but could you kiss me? It would mean so much to me."

At that point he began to sob. I pulled him to his feet and wrapped my arms around him for I understood the courage revealed by that wounded young man. I lifted his chin with my finger and looked into his eyes as I leaned forward to kiss his trembling lips. As I held him tightly, running my tongue across his tender lips, he broke down and lost all control. After that short initial kiss, he threw his arms around me and hugged me like he would never let me go. It felt right to be in his arms to comfort him and, yes, love him. He needed me, and I discovered that I needed his childlike trust like I also need Aaron's. Timnah did not need a friend, or even a lover. He needed a family, and I knew God had chosen us to give it to him.

After another twenty minutes of kissing and hugging Timnah, I felt like I had shared a cup of cold water to a man who was at deaths' door, dying from thirst in the desert. Gently pulling myself away from his desperate arms, I wiped the tears from his eyes with my fingers, kissed each eye, and told him to follow me. As I reached the room that Stephen and I shared with Aaron, I took his hand and led him into the dimly lit room. Stephen was already laying naked on our mat waiting for me. He smiled broadly and pointed to the floor next to my side of our mat. Stephen knew me better than I knew myself for he knew I would not send Timnah back to the caravan. He obtained a third sleeping mat so Timnah could lay next to me, allowing us to talk more if we needed.

As I undressed and laid down next to my husband, I looked at Timnah and pointed to his mat. Almost ashamed, he began to disrobe until I saw the cause of his shame. He was only as developed as an eleven-year-old adolescent. Stephen saw it too. He leaned up on one arm and asked Timnah if he would rather sleep between me and him. At first, he had a horrified look on his face, but then he agreed as both Stephen and I made room between us. Lying on his side with his back to Stephen he laid his head on my shoulder and began to sob again. I realized that he had never in his entire life been so openly accepted.

Awakening the next morning, before anyone else, I found him still on his side with his arm across my chest. I was surprised to see Stephen also lying on his side snoring gently with his arm around Timnah's stomach. It was a strange situation, but I knew it was the right thing for us to do. He had never been accepted in his entire life because of his own fears of rejection. Somehow, he sensed our acceptance of his underdeveloped organ and I was sure it all began with Simon who accepted his loneliness and gave him security in its place.

Lying on my back, I turned my head to face him straight on and look at his face. I realized how handsome this camel driver really was, and as I got a better whiff, I realized I would have to bathe him as soon as we got up. First, I had a more pressing problem. Aaron had just awoken and peaked over his father's shoulder to see who was laying in his normal place between us. With a grin he saw me looking back at him. Placing my finger over my lips he understood and got up and came around and laid down on the mat we had unrolled for Timnah. He slid it up against my own and cuddled up next to me and went back to sleep. I awoke a while later as the increasing morning light began to filter into our room and I noticed that no one had moved. The only thing different was that Timnah's hardness was pressed against my hip. I decided the best thing I could do was to totally ignore it even after he awakes. He needed to feel that we considered him completely normal and deficient in no way whatsoever.

Soon he stirred slightly, feeling Stephen behind him. It took no imagination to know what he felt behind him. His eyes shot open when he realized that he was pressed against me as well. I looked into his panic-stricken eyes and leaned toward him and gave him the sincerest kiss I could muster in my groggy state. As I rolled on my side facing him, I allowed him to feel my hardness against his own. Again, I smiled and wished him a great morning. Slowly his tension began to subside as he realized that he was totally accepted. Then he raised his hand to the back of my head and kissed me like I knew he wanted to the night before but couldn't. As I accepted his efforts at being manly and self-accepting, Stephen stirred and startled the poor man with an anatomy he never dreamed existed.

I chuckled and assured Timnah that Stephen accepted him exactly like he was. After all, Stephen was a eunuch, too! He finally grinned and stated that if he knew eunuchs could be built like that, he would have never cringed when the kids called him a eunuch. As he said that, Stephen squeezed him tightly as he rolled over on his back, taking Timnah with him, totally powerless to respond, as Stephen's power stood up between Timnah's own legs. Then we all began laughing at the ridiculousness of the situation. Of course, the ruckus awoke Aaron and he gleefully piled onto the laughing pile of masculinity. Finally, we caught our breath as I told Timnah that he smelled like a camel and he needed to get up and follow me for a good scrub down.

Fortunately, Timnah knew I wasn't kidding, and stood up proudly without the slightest evidence of past shame. Even though he couldn't take his eyes off Stephen's sheer power and beauty, this was beginning to embarrass Stephen in a role reversal which I actually found amusing. As I took a towel, I handed one to Timnah and told him to try and conceal his stimulation before he shocked the other men. Laughing we left the room to scrub the camel smell off each of us. Finding that the small room with the wash tub was not in use, we picked up the buckets and took them out to the well in the back garden. When the tub was full, we both dropped our towels on a bench, found the soap, and stepped into the tub together. With us both still stimulated we accepted that for what it was . . . our own lack of fear or disgrace. I scrubbed him down first as he relished every touch of my hand, the scrubbing rag, or even the soap. Then I realized once again that this was probably the first time anyone had ever gently touched his body. He was beautiful as he closed his eyes and let me almost scrape that caked dirt off him.

He suddenly caught me totally unawares as I was scrubbing under his arms. He began to shake all over as he threw his head back and his eyes fluttered while he began to pant. His manhood had been touching my hip and he became over stimulated. His embarrassment was immediate, and he almost jumped out of the tub. I quickly dropped the soap and held him tightly as he began to descend from his first sexual high in the presence of another human being. He was embarrassed beyond his ability to speak, so I continued to hold him and kiss his neck until he totally descended. Then I kissed him on his lips and told him what a man he was. Looking straight into my eyes he replied, "That was no joke! I don't understand what happened." Smiling one last time as I began to fish for the soap, I began to rinse him down as he prepared to scrub the grime off me. That proved to be a startling experience for both of us.

After we finished drying each other, and we wrapped ourselves in our towels to head back to our room, we first dumped the filthy water in the garden. Arriving back at our room Stephen and Aaron were both ready to head for the tub. In the meantime, I had to find clothes in our baggage for both of us as well as Stephen and Aaron. As we completed dressing, we threw our soiled clothes into a basket to be washed, but when I held Timnah's tunic over the basket I told him I was throwing it away because it was beyond help. I didn't mean to embarrass him, but I did. He thought I was putting him down because he was poor. I kissed him again . . . it seems I had to kiss him constantly . . . and told him he had just worn them out and it was time to find something else.

Timnah was definitely not a dumb peasant, and once he got through the next few months, he proved to be a very cleaver man. He only needed people who would believe in him and take the time to teach him. The thing that showed me his quick mind more than anything else was his mastering of Greek and his nearly fluent skill with Aegyptian, the language of Aegyptus' peasants. After nearly three hundred years of rule by the Ptolemaic Pharaohs, Cleopatra was the first ruler to learn to speak the ancient Aegyptian language, but Timnah learned to converse in it by spending two years tending camels with Aegyptian peasant boys. I couldn't help but wonder what else that young man could do, given a little time and encouragement.

We had a late breakfast that morning because I was evidently not the only one who had many stories to share. Naturally Hanno and Rashvi were the last to sit at the wonderful spread of fresh chilled melons, sweet cakes, dried sardines, and sweet Nile delta dates. It was beautiful to watch those two lovebirds find ways to communicate. The adoration in Rashvi's eyes even made Rahelani smile. Because Rashvi was castrated as an adult and Hanno as a young child, their contrast was more than just that of color, but a difference of hair. Rashvi's dark black wiry hair all over his chest, legs, and perfectly trimmed beard, compared to Hanno's hairless and smoothly polished caramel skin was astonishing. I suppose the word to use for them was exotic. Add to that their constant efforts to read one another's mind made them a delight to watch.

By days end Stephan and Sadhu had made a preliminary plan for reaching India by the end of the year. We would take a reasonable portion of the gold on deposit in Berenike and purchase a stable open trans-ocean ship with two strong masts. It would need to be about 75 feet long by 24 feet across the beam with cabin space for a full crew and ten archers to fight off pirates with sleeping space in the hold for four cargo slaves, and storage space in the stern of the hold for enough food and water to last at least sixty days for thirty people. The ship should be no older than ten years and be fitted for monsoon sailing. We needed possession of it no later than the last of July, so it can be loaded and sailing down the center of the Sinus Arabicus by August fifth. We also needed to procure an experienced Greek captain of Aegyptian lineage with at least twenty years' experience with the India trade. We should offer him two percent of the purchase price of the goods, with an additional percent if we incur no losses of men or cargo. When we returned, we would need to have on deposit with our agent, enough gold equal to twenty-five percent of our Indian purchases to cover the Roman import tax.

We had less than six weeks to pull this entire venture together. Our agent in Berenike was prepared, and letters had been sent on an earlier ship to Sadhu's family in Muziris, asking them to begin preparations for our significant purchase of the most popular items in the Roman trade. We would be making payment to the Chera King in Roman gold, Aethiopian emeralds, red Italian coral beads, fine Italian wine, plus exquisite Roman glass. All the components were in place. Now the gears needed to begin to turn! But how?

Probably the best way to begin was to send a correspondence to our agent in Berenike via a three-day ride by horse to Myos Hormos at the head of the Sinus Arabicus, and then another five days south by horse to Berenike. A government rider was hired and sent out immediately with those orders.

We would also need to send our front men, Hanno and Rashvi. After a short discussion, Sadhu suggested we also send Timnah as a test of his zeal and thirst for truth and adventure. We all agreed without reservations. I would then leave with Sadhu, Rahelani, and most of their staff. Two female servants would be left behind to care for Yacobsa for a year as he consolidates the Persian Carpets from Alexandria, Syria, and other trade goods of specific importance to his king in India. To accomplish that he would also spend part of his time in Syracuse and Ostia with Stephen. I would leave with the Indians in three weeks, with our cargo, heading up the Nile to Kopios and then the twelve-night camel caravan across the desert to Berenike. We would spend each day sleeping once again between our camels, or perhaps in tents around a well. Everyone assured that it would be too hot to travel by day.

We all needed to rendezvous at our agent's office in Berenike in five weeks. It was a complicated and expensive plan, but if done correctly, we would be well placed in the center of the lucrative India trade within four years. One of our ships in the harbor was sailing for Cyrene and then on to Syracuse in two days and Stephen, Aaron, and Simon needed to be aboard. Stephen's new child would be due within three months and he had a lot of work to do in Syracuse before he sent for Yacobsa to shop with him in Roma.

CHAPTER 43

BERENIKE – JULY 26, AD29

It was two days since our plans were established and the clock of the universe began to mark every minute of each of those two days which I had left with my beloved Stephen. Everyone in the house knew how painful this was to be for us, with that in mind, everyone's consideration toward us was extremely gracious, even Aaron's. Every time we had a break in our day for even an hour, we spent every minute of that time together. Because we only had two nights left, Aaron and Timnah slept in the small room down the hall. It was a precious time. These memories we would keep alive in our minds and hearts for nearly a year, or maybe more. We knew our strength would enable us to survive the separation until God brought us together again. Yet, there was no denying that our emptiness would still be with us.

On the last morning, it was dreadful to leave our sleeping mat. I had to kiss Stephen over and over. I needed to remember every inch of him until I returned from India. I had never met anyone so loving and gentle in my life. For many months, I would have only these memories.

The inevitable arrived and Simon knocked on our door to tell us it was time to leave. Stephen gave our acknowledgement as he lifted me from our mat and held me against his heart. He began to dress me as tears ran down his cheeks. Then as I dressed him my tears turned to sobs.

Ten minutes later we were at the front door with Simon and Aaron ready to leave for Aetna's Alexandria warehouse and docks, escorted of by a dozen members of our family. When we reached the ship, the captain was at the foot of the loading planks to greet us. Suddenly I found it very hard to say farewell to my stepson. I knew Aaron would remember me, but would he remember how much I loved him? I lost it as I kissed him for the last time knowing he could be four inches taller when I would see him next.

Stephen stood with his son and brother-in-law on the deck in front of their tent. Looking up at them, I reflected on how much I had grown to love and respect Simon since that bloody morning in Jerusalem. His new love and understanding for his eunuch sons had grown beyond anyone's expectations. It was his expression of love and compassion toward Timnah which surprised everyone. I was so fortunate to be a part of such a family who not only loved each other but also our Lord God and the Son he sent to us. Hearing heavy sobbing behind me, I turned to see Timnah waiving frantically . . . to Simon . . . who was waiving back.

As the ship was pushed away from the dock, we knew they would have a slow journey without the proper wind behind them, but at least they had some breeze to carry them on their way. In six or seven days they would be in Cyrene, and then about ten days later Stephen and Aaron would be in Syracuse with Leah and the girls. Life will go on. In nineteen days, we will begin our journey up the Nile to Kopios with our modest cargo, and then there will be twelve days across the desert hill country by camel to Berenike and our rendezvous with the others. Fortunately, most of our trade goods destined for Rahelani's brother were searched out by her in Alexandria while we were still in Jerusalem. If our three horsemen, who will be leaving in three days, are successful we will have our new ship at the docks and be ready to sail on schedule.

That night as we prepared to go to our separate rooms, Timnah came to me and asked if it would be permissible for him to sleep with me the next three nights before they left for Berenike. Hesitating to give an abrupt answer I asked him to check back with me in ten minutes. I knew we both needed companionship, I would need it because I have lost mine for the following year, and he because he had never had companionship. As tears filled my eyes, I removed my clothes and laid down on Stephen's sleeping mat. I waited for what seemed like forever. Eventually there was a soft knocking at my door, and I told Timnah to come in. The lamp was still lit, and I saw a handsome young man standing at the foot of my mat, smiling nervously. As I patted the spot next to me, he dropped his towel and laid down beside me. When he spoke, I knew I had not misjudged him. "My dear Jacobus, I did not come to your bed tonight for sex, but only to be with you and learn how to care for you before I can properly care for myself. I love you, Jacobus, for you have charted the course of my life." We began to tear up as usual. Soon, we wrapped our arms and legs around each other, and I quickly fell asleep from exhaustion as he held me tightly against his warm body. His compassion enabled me to feel secure in spite of my loss.

The sun had climbed high into the bright blue sky before I finally awoke. The first thing I saw were Timnah's hazel eyes looking back into mine. His face was still covered with tears. I doubt if he could have moved an inch all night. Our legs and arms were still locked together, and much of that time he probably just watched me, experiencing feelings he had never known before in his entire life . . . complete acceptance and love. We worked hard with the other two men for the next three days, procuring the extra gold, packing their personal items, and contracting with a cavalry platoon to allow our three horsemen to travel with them to Berenike.

The next two nights with Timnah were far more casual as I set about to teach him a few things he never had the chance to learn previously. Once he overcame his huge insecurities, and even a few fears, he trusted me completely as we did more talking than anything else. His tenderness truly amazed me, but he had already shown me that earlier. Working with our camels . . . talking gently with them and referring to each by name . . . was intrinsic to his personality. That last night he wanted to put all that theory into practice and have me make love to him and later allow him to make love to me. I explained why that would not be possible, but I assured him he had no reason at all to ever be ashamed of his body. It was perfect for him. That morning, after we dressed, we decided to kiss goodbye in our room and prevent any unnecessary confusion.

Going to the military staging area to the south of the caravan field, we found the cavalry platoon they would be riding with to Berenike. We were immediately shown their three mounts and packhorse, for the platoon captain wanted to leave within the hour. After loading their horses with food and water, they hid small pouches of gold in inconspicuous places on their persons, their horse's gear, and in their food and water. Before they mounted up, we all stood around them and prayed God's protection on them and their journey. Then they joined the platoon heading southeast to Memphis and then straight east to Myos Hormos at the northern tip of the Sinus Arabicus. There they would change to fresh mounts and proceed south to Berenike. They would not be going at a full gallop that time of year, but they would be moving much faster than a camel caravan would.

Back at the house I began the weeks-long task of procuring as much as we could of those items Rahelani's king would take in trade in place of gold. Yacobsa and I began visiting many of the warehouses which knew of him, and as we finalized each purchase, it was delivered directly to the Aetna warehouse at the east end of the docks. The warehouse sergeant was as excited as we were about this new venture with India. The shipment we sent to Syracuse about seven months earlier was the most luxurious cargo he had ever seen. He knew that if all went well, next year we would be loading three of our ships with the same quality cargo. He already knew that a load of carpets would be arriving from Alexandria, Syria, before we sailed up the Nile and that it would be trans-shipped to Syracuse with Yacobsa on board to prepare them for distribution in Roma. Stephen had been able to negotiate a twenty percent volume discount over our last shipment which meant that this time the hold could be nearly half full of fine carpets alone. If this venture went well, Aetna Shipping could become one of the top five maritime traders on the Mare Internum.

As mid-July approached, we hired a moderately sized Nile river barge and moored it at the end of the warehouse dock next to the gate to the Jewish Quarter. The warehouse hands began loading all of our Berenike bound cargo, and two of them slept on the barge every night because of its vulnerability with an open hull. Before long, it was time to ferry it through the city canals to the western estuary of the Nile where it would be secured as we continued to load our baggage, small chests of cut emeralds, Italian red coral beads, and a little more gold, just in case. Once it was moored to the sea wall, the three-man crew mounted its mast and massive cotton sail.

The last two days were sad for all of us as we began to feel the pain of more goodbyes. I was even surprised when Yacobsa asked if he could sleep with me those last nights. The sweet man had no one since he and Alexander broke up nearly two months earlier, and he and I had always been close. I almost felt like his request was a trap which would confuse one or both of us. Then it hit me, if he just wanted the sex, he had that with his friends in the other trading houses of the city. What was this all about?

Half an hour before bed time I asked him to join me at the Nile barge. As we sat on the stern and watched the beauty of the stars and avoided the ears of our warehouse guards, I asked why he wanted to sleep with me. After all, he knew the depth of my love for Stephen, but he also knew Timnah had slept with me for some unknown reason. His answer was as simple and direct as it was surprising.

He was embarrassed as he began talking. "I have not had an erection in years. I really don't know if I ever will again. Do you realize that this plague is worse than being castrated? I just hold it in my hand and beg it to wake up, but that one eye just looks at me and continues to ignore my needs. A cut eunuch is more of a man than I am. I need your help. I have watched you for nearly a year and you seem to be able to help everyone. The men I am with are very nice and they love making love to me, but when I find the right man, I want to make love to him, too, and not just lay there like a woman! Jacobus please, at least try to help me. I am way too young for this,"

I guess I did make a practice of helping other men, but this? I'm not a doctor, I'm just a romantic teenager. Putting my arm around him I promised to do what I could, but the problem was his, not mine. I could only be the cheering section at his chariot race, not much more. For some bazar reason, I decided to approach it like he was not having a physical problem but an emotional problem. I agreed to do everything I could and still be honest with him. I stood up and placed both of his hands at my waist and then put my arms around his neck and kissed him before I tilted my head up and nibbled on his ear and neck. I told him he would be wonderful in bed, then I reminded him that I belonged to Stephen.

We slowly and gradually walked back to the house. Arriving at my room I stopped and held him in my arms. We stripped and in the dark room without an oil lamp, his dark body basically disappeared from sight. My fingers saw more and made up for what my eyes missed. Everything about him was beautiful. He didn't have the wiry hair on his chest as thick as Rashvi, but what he had was like threads of fine Chinese silk. I caressed his hair and licked it like a cat with a kitten. From that point on I made over his manly beauty and his strength. Removing my tunic, I continued to tell him how magnificent he was. We laid down in one another's arms and feel asleep with my praises being whispered into his ear.

Each time we awoke during the night I told him he was my handsome warrior, my gladiator, and my prince. He also responded with complete abandonment to my every touch. I did not want to make him feel like a woman. He had experienced too much of that already. He had to be my champion, but there was a line we both knew could not be crossed.

As the sun came up and I could see him in all his glory, I really had the chance to appreciate his beauty. I could see why Alexander wanted him, but I also knew why Yacobsa could never accept him, or anyone else, as a lover. Unfortunately, I only had one more night to prove to him that he was still a man . . . or did I?

The next day I took Sadhu for a walk to our Nile barge. I felt foolish talking about his grown son the way I felt I needed to, but it was important that he knew what his son had faced for nearly a decade. He really didn't want to be another man's woman. He wanted to be more than a stereotyped eunuch. He wanted to be a man like every other man who could make love to the person he loved. As I spoke, I felt foolish as a young teenager speaking to a senior rabbi like Sadhu, but I didn't know what else to do.

After a while I told him what I did with Yacobsa that night and that I needed to do it again, and maybe again and again, until he overcame his fear of failure. I didn't know if I was doing the right thing, but I had to try something. Sadhu had no knowledge of his son's problem and he needed to know his son was one of my best friends and it hurt me to see him suffer so. Somehow, I needed to show Yacobsa that he already was a sexually powerful man, he just needed to realize that power. I told Sadhu I had no idea what made him crawl into such a passive shell, but I wanted to find a way to pull him out of it.

Sadhu remained silent for a few minutes and then he thanked me for loving his son so much, but he wanted to know what all of this pretend loving and passion was going to do to me. I told him that it was because of that very fear that I was speaking to him. I loved Yacobsa very much, and I have since the day I first met him, but I never touched him, even though at times I wanted to. I was going to be separated from Stephen for nearly a year. I needed someone to help and love while we were apart, not someone to have sex with or to take Stephen's place in that way. No one could take his place. I really felt that I was supposed to help his son, or at least let him know I loved him enough to try.

Sadhu admitted that he knew Yacobsa had been deeply troubled for years, but he could never get him to talk about it. He thought he was beginning to understand, but it was so foreign to anything he understood about God's plan for our sexual lives. He claimed I had already shown him so much with all our beautiful eunuchs. Then he confessed that he never could do what he thought I could. He also assured me that he would be wrestling with God over this as he asked him for his love and mercy for his wonderful son.

There was one other thing I needed to ask him, "Sadhu, how much time can Yacobsa spend away from Alexandria knowing that the carpets from Persia may come in tomorrow, or even today."

"Jacobus, that is for you to tell me. How prepared are they at the warehouse? Is Yacobsa really the only one capable of filling your shoes, or can the sergeant do that for you as easily as Yacobsa?"

"Sadhu, you are right. I guess I have already answered my own question. I am going to tell Yacobsa that he is taking a month off before he heads to Syracuse. They can hold the carpets until he returns. I will talk to the sergeant immediately and then I will talk with Yacobsa. Oh, if Rahelani hears some strange noises coming from my room tell her it is her son's doctor treating him." Within the hour I found Yacobsa at the dock with the captain of one of our recently arrived ships. It turned out not to be the ship from Syria or from Caesarea. Our carpets were evidently still on the water. Leaving him with the ship's captain I went to the Sergeant and told him our slight change of plans. He saw no problem and he was even grateful for the opportunity to take care of the situation until Yacobsa's return. During that time, he could ship both the Indian and his standard cargo to Syracuse for Stephen. Thanking him I gave him a gold coin I had been saving for an emergency, and if that wasn't an emergency, I didn't know what was.

I ran out of the warehouse door and grabbed Yacobsa away from his casual conversation with the captain and yelled at him as we ran through the gate of the Jewish Quarter, "I can't take another minute of watching you standing there with another man. You are so handsome I need to get home with you."

After an hour of holding and caressing Yacobsa as I told him what a catch he would be for some lucky man, I left him alone as I went to bring Sadhu and Rahelani up to date. I found them finishing their packing for India in the center room of the house. Sitting down I told them that the carpets did not arrive yet, but that the sergeant would take care of them when they did arrive. Therefore, Yacobsa would be able to travel with us at least as far as Kopios and possibly as far as Berenike. Which one would it be? That would depend completely on Yacobsa.

When I heard Sadhu beginning to explain our dilemma to Rahelani, I dashed back to my room. Opening the door, I whispered to Yacobsa how I couldn't live without such a magnificent man and jumped on him one more time with my clothes still on. The thing I may have feared was already beginning to happen. I really was allowing myself to fall in love with him. We had three weeks to work that one out . . . somehow. There was no way I could let him get between me and Stephen.

After that half hour of talking and caressing I needed to get Yacobsa ready for his vacation because once he got back, he would learn how much of a slave driver Stephen could be. We were all packed and loaded onto the Nile barge by midmorning. Within minutes our sail was up, and we began to enter the west Nile estuary heading for Memphis. The Nile was at the beginning of its annual flood and the water would continue to rise until mid-September when the river would remain stable until October. We would be at least two months ahead of its peak flow. We should still reach Kopios by the thirteenth or fourteenth of July, which would still keep us on schedule to catch the monsoon on the south Arabian coast which would carry us to India's Malabar Coast in forty-five days. The race was on and we knew we were cutting it very close.

Sailing up the Nile gave Yacobsa and me a lot of time to just be together and say some very sexy and romantic things whenever we were out of everyone's earshot. Most of our time was spent in awe as we passed the pyramids and the many ancient cities and temples at the river's edge. Since the boat men only spoke Aegyptian and Greek we knew they couldn't stretch their ears to hear anything juicy. The others we needed to be more careful with. Even though they spent most of their time at the bow of the boat, Sadhu and Rahelani did what they could to keep everyone away from the stern. We could then talk and play together during the day, and cuddle under a blanket or lounge under the stars at night. We left the delta under a waning moon and it would be a new moon in a week, giving us maximum privacy at night until we reached Kopios. That therapy was keeping me busy at night, causing me to wonder how realistic it was for me to try and keep that routine going at such a pace. On our last night before Kopios, I almost failed in my last attempt to show Yacobsa how much he excited me. I nearly panicked!

Much of the next day was spent unloading the barge and loading thirty-seven camels, twenty of which were loaded with forty amphorae of the finest northern Italian wine and seven with fourteen amphorae of the finest Hispanic olive oil. Each of those camels also carried smaller containers and bails of less bulky trade goods. Many of the remaining pack camels were blessed with our personal baggage.

That evening, just before sunset we were saddled up and ready to head to the first of twelve wells which we should reach shortly after sunrise. We would travel like this until after the thirteenth day when we should reach Berenike at about mid-morning. Because we slept during the day, which was the only time I had with Yacobsa, we tethered our fragrant camels about three feet apart and draped our two goat-hair tents over them to give us more room and privacy. After the third day we discovered that my energy level was shot, and all I wanted to do was sleep through the unbearable heat like the more intelligent camels.

Halfway to Berenike, in the middle of the day when everyone was asleep, I was awakened with a start. Yacobsa awoke wanting me so badly that his body came alive and he was rubbing his manhood against me. He kept at it for at least twenty minutes and had two massive releases in the process. When he finally collapsed, his manhood refused to join him. I was so exhausted I actually slept through his victory. When the sun began to set, the camel drivers awoke each of us, and Yacobsa sheepishly backed away from me as I turned over to face him to give him the wildest kiss of his life. After ten years he awoke in the middle of a deep sleep ready to perform like a man. He had received a fabulous gift from God, and we took a few minutes to stop and thank him for it. That evening even his parents noticed a difference in him. He had proven himself to himself, that he really was a man again and capable of being a great lover, too, In the dark, as we were loading up and untethering our camels, I couldn't keep my hands off him. I really was happy for him. And in ten days I would need to say goodbye to another person I had loved for nearly a year.

In the meantime, we both shared our affection during each of the next six days, giving him greater confidence with each new success, even though he was banned from having sex with me. His tenderness and sense of romance was off the charts and I knew he would make any man a great life partner. Then it dawned on me. I thought of the answer for him. Timnah! He would be in Berenike when we arrived. I knew he already had a great fascination for Yacobsa, and maybe Yacobsa could be fascinated with him, too! We had been thinking of sending him back to Alexandria anyway to work with Yacobsa but had never taken the discussion any further. I may have to play the Roman cupid here and see what would happen next.

On the early dawn of our thirteenth day, we crossed over our last hill. Below us was a moderate sized, but primitive, city with an expansive blue shoreline lapping up against its white sand beach. There were several ships still at the docks waiting to leave for India, and one of them should be ours.

CHAPTER 44

CUPID – AUGUST 4, AD29

Our caravan picked up its pace as it came down the well-worn road, through the ravine, and into the small shoddy city. Keeping the homesick camels under control, we proceeded toward the docks in the effort to find our ship, and hopefully a crew. Or at least that was what we thought we were doing. After going through town and reaching the docks we discovered that the camel drivers had an established meeting place. It was a large staging area where caravans, crews, and prostitutes congregated. There was only a small string of camels there when we arrived and a few dozen sailors probably looking to be hired. Then I saw him. Beautiful Hanno, charging like a bull elephant through the small crowd, yelling my name at the top of his lungs.

He reached me as I was still astride my camel, and he could hardly wait until the camel groaned and complained its way to the ground, allowing me to dismount. The second I did, Hanno had me in his arms, twirling me around and kissing me like a long-lost lover, which I suppose is what I was. Once he settled down, he directed us to our new ship which was moored nearby. It looked exactly like Stephen's specifications, and he beamed happily as we all praised him for his selection. He proudly told us that it was the best one on the market that season, and he only had to pay twenty gold pieces more than Stephen had budgeted. I told him not to worry because we brought some extra gold beyond what we will need in India just in case we had such an emergency. Then he assured me not to worry, as our agent had taken care of it from the money for an extra crewman that Stephen had on deposit.

While everyone else was still on their camels, he asked the drivers to follow him. About five ships up the dock he stopped at a beautiful ship that looked brand new. Proudly Hanno exclaimed, "This will only be her second voyage. Her owner died of a mysterious illness on the voyage back from India last spring. We had the winning bid on her, thanks to the help of or agent's cousin who was the agent of the previous owner. We got it for fifteen percent less than it cost to build seventeen months ago!"

He was definitely proud of the success of his first independent assignment we had given him. Walking through the ship I had to admit it was much better than any of us connected with Aetna Shipping had ever expected. As I inquired about the crew, he glowed like the Pharos lighthouse. He had originally contracted with seven crewmen, but our agent recommended two more in case the monsoon got a little rough.

In his excitement he had to share his unexpected success concerning the crew. "Six of the seven crewmen thus far were former galley slaves who were getting too old at forty and were sold by the Roman Navy in the Alexandrian market. Rashvi was familiar with these sales and knew that these slaves were not criminals sentenced to the galleys for life. Actually, they are military captives, like Rashvi, who had proved their metal but now needed something a little less physical. These men had been purchased as cargo slaves by a local trading company in Alexandria. That was much easier than their past jobs. Each of them had worked off their servitude for the same company until it was shut down by the Roman government for some sort of fraud. These six were freed so as not to encumber the government with six more things to take care of in an auction. They are Britons and only speak Latin so Timnah has been dealing with them. He likes them very much because all six chose castrated slavery over death, and as it turns out four were born eunuchs anyway. The other two are satisfied with their lives enlivened with an occasional prostitute. The seventh crewman was a disenchanted Alexandrian fisherman who ran away from his wife, whatever that means. I doubt if that will affect his performance with us. By the way, he's a great cook. I was heading down to find another two or three sailors when I saw your caravan coming onto the beach. You and I can shop for sailors tomorrow."

"By the way. Why is Yacobsa with you? Is he traveling with us, too?"

"Oh, no. He only came this far to take Timnah back to Alexandria. Also, his coming here served two purposes."

"All right, what's the second?"

"He has been having some serious sexual problems which I'll explain later. He needed the extra three weeks with me that this trip gave him.

"Ah, uh huh, right," was his final response with a deep throated laugh.

As we approached the ship, Timnah was the first to spot us and nearly broke his leg jumping off the ship to greet me. There was no doubt in anyone's eyes that he was a young man who really loved me. I was gratified by the boost in his male self-confidence which he seemed to attribute to me. If only he and Yacobsa could generate the same chemistry! At that moment, while he was still prostate on the ground, Yacobsa dismounted his camel and rushed to Timnah's side to be sure he didn't break anything. To feel assured that he was all in one piece, he felt compelled to rub his thigh until the pain began to subside. That was definitely a good sign. When he lifted Timnah to his feet, Yacobsa insisted he keep his arm around his neck and exercise his leg. For some reason it took until our noon meal to relieve the pain.

As Rashvi showed us about the ship, Hanno assisted the camel drivers unpack their beasts. He didn't understand camels like Timnah did, but he did an excellent job. Unfortunately, Timnah seemed to need every bit of Yacobsa's attention which was actually fine with me. It seemed Yacobsa knew he was spending the next three weeks and probably much more with Timnah and was set on making a great first impression.

Soon I had our seven sailors called out of the shaded hold and back into the unbearable sun to get the cargo on board as rapidly as possible. As quickly as the camel drivers unloaded and tethered a camel a crewman was there to get the cargo aboard. Within two hours we had all thirty-seven pack camels unloaded and the cargo safely aboard ship. After tipping our drivers I asked the sergeant of the team when they were planning to head back to Kopios. Learning that they and the animals would need to rest a few days, I made arrangements for Yacobsa and Timnah to return with them.

After getting Sadhu and his Indian retinue aboard, the next order of business was to get some food in our stomachs. Fortunately, the fisherman really was a good cook, so we had a great meal spread out on the deck within thirty minutes. By that time Timnah affirmed that his thigh was much better, so he had to join us with Yacobsa at his side. In the middle of our wonderful meal I brought up Yacobsa's return trip to Alexandria in three days and the fact that he required a great deal of help with the shipment of Persian carpets in preparation for their trans-shipment to Syracuse and on to Roma. Looking at Timnah with a generous smile, I asked him if he felt he could handle that amount of detail and hard labor. I told him that Yacobsa already had servants to take care of them, and the two men only needed to do the paper work at the warehouse. It was then I saw Yacobsa squeeze his thigh as they both smiled and agreed that would be a great solution to the problem. I couldn't help but wonder which problem they were referring to. I couldn't help but wonder how long Yacobsa had his eye on Timnah, and if that young man was the real reason he needed a sudden "cure."

It was settled and both Sadhu and Rahelani seemed pleased. This was also going to require us to keep the two men busy on the same projects for the next three days. I had already assured them that the placement of the amphorae of wine and olive oil would create a perfect private space in our large hold for the two of them to sleep. My next concern was that we needed ten archers, probably Aegyptian, who could protect the ship in case of an attack from Arab pirates. There Hanno beat me to it again. He apologized for not procuring all ten, but he did hire nine great Aegyptian and Nubian hunters. As of that day those nine were the only ones available in Berenike. I agreed to go meet them with Sadhu first thing in the morning.

After lunch Hanno took me down to inspect our stores. He was sure he had enough, especially if we had three less people to feed, the tenth archer, the eighth crewman, and Timnah. Then he remembered he had already purchased three Galatian cargo slaves. We would take possession of them the day before we were scheduled to depart. With that he felt that he and Rashvi had covered everything on Stephen's list and perhaps a little more. Suddenly I remembered that when the *Dolphin* first pulled into Valentia, she had a torn mainsail. Urgently I asked if we had two spare mainsails. Hanno groaned, and I wondered where we could possibly find two spare sails in the middle of nowhere.

Then he grinned and retorted that there were already two spares left in the hold by the previous owner.

Standing up, I walked over to him and threw my arms around his neck and kissed him like I always kissed Hanno. Then I froze, remembering Rashvi had been sitting with us, watching. In an apologetic demeanor I turned to him and saw not a frown of jealousy but a giant smile of pride. He had finally found a man as efficient as himself, and what a man he proved to be.

Having been up for over twenty hours, we were all starting to run down and many of us had already started to nod off to sleep. Yacobsa was exhausted. He had spent three weeks with a very deficient sleep pattern. I took him down into the very dim hold where the crew had created their private space. Without a second thought he removed his clothes and laid down. Looking at him longingly, Timnah glanced at me in resignation and began to walk by me to go back on deck. Holding my hand against his beautiful chest, I whispered to him that Yacobsa had endured a difficult month and he really needed to have Timnah lay down beside him. I assured him that no one would bother them before dawn. He knew exactly what I meant and kissed me while removing his clothes.

It was two hours after dawn when the two men extricated themselves from their hidden lair and climbed on deck for breakfast. They both looked totally refreshed and happy, even though I was sure they only got half the sleep everyone thought they got. Looking directly at Yacobsa I knew he was smitten by the perfect man for him. Immediately after breakfast they announced they were going to take a warm Sinus Arabicus bath just a short way up the beach past the last ship.

As we watched them walk down the docks together, Sadhu and Rahelani thanked me with tears in their eyes. I wanted to tell them how much I loved their son, but I simply replied that he was a special man and that Timnah adores him. Then I chuckled as I thought to make a mental note to remind Yacobsa to ask Thomas, or one of the other disciples, to perform their union next time any of them were in Alexandria.

Speaking with Hanno, I mentioned that I noticed there was no name on the ship. Acknowledging my observation, he led me to the cabin and picked a beautiful seashell off of the table. He handed it to me and asked what I thought. I agreed that it was a very beautiful sea shell, but I thought that in real life it moved much too slowly to name a ship after. Shaking his head in disagreement, he reminded me that pearls exist in ugly, unmoving oysters, but the triton moves gracefully along the bottom of the sea oblivious of any storms that are blowing above. I agreed to think about it, for we needed it painted on the ship in the next two days. By late afternoon I agreed. One of our Briton eunuchs who had a steady hand immediately began to paint the new name on the stern and each side of the ship's bow.

The next morning Hanno and I went to collect our Aegyptian and Nubian archers. These were strong men and would be able to help with the ship in many ways even if we never came under attack by pirates. As soon as they were settled into their quarters, I joined Hanno and Rashvi as they walked to a large windowless stone building about half a mile on the other side of town. There we collected our three Galatian slaves, one of which was a stunningly beautiful blond with skin like milk. Hanno led them by their rope around their necks to the *Triton*. Once aboard, Hanno removed the rope and untied their hands and told them that as long as they were owned by Aetna Shipping, they would never wear ropes or chains again.

Later that afternoon the whole family joined Yacobsa and Timnah as they went to the caravan grounds to meet their camels. Yacobsa was given the same one he had a few days earlier, and she seemed pleased to see him again. Actually, I think she just knew he was lighter than a load of baggage. It was Timnah who was amazing. Within minutes his camel was keeping a constant eye on him to be sure he was going to be her rider, and when he did climb on, she was ready to go without a single roar of complaint.

The farewells were difficult for all of us, but the camel driver finally called everyone to their camel to prepare for departure. They needed to reach the first well shortly after sunrise. As we watched them go through the city and up the ravine on the far side, we saw them disappear. Each of us felt an emptiness deep within our hearts and a full share of sorrow.

At sunrise the next morning, a small ship appeared from the north and in three hours pulled into the last dock to the north of us. Hanno came to me immediately and told me that this was going to be my big surprise, and was he ever on the mark with that prediction. As they were still tying up to their moorings Hanno and I headed to greet them. When we arrived at the foot of the loading planks, Hanno was right. There looking down at me was Lucius Paulus the finest captain in our fleet. He ran down the plank and into our arms as we laughed, and everyone tried to talk at once. I knew Stephen was taking responsibility for the captain, but Lucius Paulus was a total surprise. The two cargo slaves who walked behind us instantly ran up the plank to retrieve the captain's baggage and a few incidentals sent by Stephen.

Walking back to the *Triton*, we shared a few things that had happened during the past eight months. It was great to see him again and prove to him that he did well when he taught me the ways of the sea. We only had one more day to prepare for departure and I was sure we would be riding the tide in thirty hours, now that we had Captain Paulus aboard.

CHAPTER 45

SOCOTRA – AUGUST 17, AD29

Our sailing date was upon us. We had our crew, our archers, our family, and our captain ready to sail within an hour after sunrise. Since I was really a peg up on him in the structure of Aetna Shipping, the captain asked that I no longer refer to him as Captain Paulus when not in public, but rather captain or simply Lucius. Even though I was still a teenager he saw us as colleagues or even equals. More specifically I was sure he wanted us to truly be friends.

He had spent the majority of the last thirty-six hours going over the entire ship like a Roman tax collector, learning more about her and becoming more excited with every step. Finally, he had to ask where we found such a vessel at such an amazing price.

As proud as I could be, I said to him, "Stephen and I agreed that none among us could be in Berenike to select and buy our new ship, so we felt there could be no one better at that daunting task than Hanno. He is a man you helped train and who knew ships inside and out. In fact, he was physically considered an integral part of a ship for five years, even though he had never been on a ship this large."

Shaking his head in disbelief, Lucius simply replied, "Less than a year ago he was a cargo slave in the hold of my ship and now he is purchasing large ocean-going ships like a Roman senator . . . Unbelievable!"

Then I gave him another point to ponder. "It is also true that his financial and negotiating advisor was a former Indian slave who married him two months ago while we were in Jerusalem. Oh yes, they don't yet speak a common language."

With that, Lucius began to feel like the world had just turned upside down and that he was reaping the benefits of it. "None of this makes any sense in the real world. To top it off, I was pulled from the *Dolphin* and out of nowhere sent to the end of the earth to captain a great treasure-ship like the *Triton*. Now I am sailing to India with a teenager who was thrust upon me a year and a half ago . . . and now we are colleagues!" It seemed the Fates were with him.

With all sails open, we left Berenike and began the dangerous voyage down the center of the Sinus Arabicus on our way to the Roman outpost in Aden, where we would stock up on fresh water and catch the monsoon winds blowing toward India. Looking at his new charts, the Captain expected us to reach Aden in about ten days. Hearing this, Sadhu lit up like a candle. Calling Rahelani to join us, they spoke in Malayalam for about five minutes. The longer they spoke the more excited they became. Then they turned to us and flatly stated that we must sail past Aden and go directly to Socotra, a large island off Cape Elephant and due east of Aden. When I asked Lucius if he could recall hearing of such a place, he opened one of his Aegyptian charts and tried to locate the island. Failing, he suddenly spotted a large island the Greek sailors from Aegyptus called Dioscoridus. Could that be it? Sadhu perked up and asked if there were any notes about the island. When Lucius read the word "incense," the Indians clapped excitedly. That was it!

Looking at both of them for an explanation, Rahelani spoke up in Aramaic, "When I was a child my father, the King of Chera, traded with a Greek who came to Muziris directly from an Incense Island about which I remember very little. What I do remember is that the frankincense the Greeks brought from there was the sweetest and most powerful we had ever encountered, much better than that from the Arabs in Aden or Dhofar. In fact, my brother still has some left which is now only used for state funerals."

After I finished translating Rahelani's demanding and descriptive statement, Lucius reacted like most often happens with Rahelani. His eyes about popped out of their sockets when he understood she was more than a passenger on his ship, but a royal princess too. As Rahelani looked directly at Lucius, she asked, "How many days longer would it take to get to Socotra? Is there a harbor noted that we can pull into?

Looking at me for some type of understanding as to what was going on, I smiled and replied, "Princess Rahelani and her husband are financial partners with Aetna Shipping in the development of our new India Trade Division, and you are now an official part of it, too! By the way, Hanno's husband, Rashvi, whom you have met, was a eunuch in the royal palace of Rahelani's brother. My dear Lucius, you are a part of something very big. No one in Roma has these kinds of connections. Even the Emperor's cousin is excited about the possibilities here, and yes, we have some of the most influential and richest eunuchs in the Empire in our camp.

"One more thing you need to know, the princess' husband is a much-respected rabbi in not just India but also Persia where he went to Rabbinical School. Because of that, he is also a friend of many Jewish rug merchants throughout Persia and the entire Parthian Empire, which is crossed by the Han emperor's Silk Road"

Shaking his head and with his famous grin, Lucius slammed his hands down on the open charts spread out on the deck, and shouted, "Let's do it! Socotra it is," and he was determined to find out where the old Greek port was located . . . one way or another.

On the fifth day out of Berenike, our watch caught sight of an Arab dhow approaching from the southeast. All of its sails were open, and it was moving toward us at a worry-some speed. Hanno surprised us again when he and his cargo slaves brought up on deck about twenty tall Roman infantry shields. His purpose was to give everyone, including Rahelani and her servant girls, a shield to stand behind at the railing to look like we had a full platoon of soldiers on board. Hanno then explained his plan, "As soon as they get ten minutes from us, move closely together and form a metal wall. If they continue, on my signal, reach over and also hold the shield of the archer to your right. At that time, I will signal to have a volley of arrows fired at the dhow. If they persist, I have arrows wrapped in cotton and dipped in oil ready to be lit. When all are burning, I will signal for nine flaming arrows to be shot at their sails. If they persist, the archers will continue to shoot flaming arrows at the men themselves and directly into the dhow. May God be with us!"

At that point, Lucius stood in shock as he realized his former cargo slave had just instantaneously taken over command of his ship, and everyone was obeying his orders.

The Arabs evidently thought we were bluffing, but when their sails caught fire and burning shreds began to fall to the deck, not only did they become immobile as we sailed past them, but we saw a few men with burning clothes jump into the sea. The expense of hiring archers was worth it, and so was Lucius's training and belief in Hanno through the years. Five days later we passed the Roman outpost of

Aden and sailed into the Mare Arabicus heading straight east to Cape Elephant and the islands beyond.

Traditionally, frankincense resins had been harvested in Aden, Dhofar north of Cana, Ethiopia, and the mountainous desert southwest of Cape Elephant.

According to Rahelani's father the best they had ever purchased came from the mysterious island which separated the Mare Arabicus from the Mare Erythraean. Unfortunately, Socotra's variety of frankincense was more difficult to reach and had become very rare over the millennium as Aegyptian and Greeks both found it easier to trade with the Socotrans than with the Arabs or Aethiopians with their inferior varieties. We knew we were taking a chance, but Lucius discovered there was a statement on the back of the chart identifying a beautiful rivulet of sweet water flowing out of the mountains on the far eastern tip of the Island. The chart also indicated we should find a small port, Erhor, which had traded frankincense with the Ptolemaic Greeks from Aegyptus for hundreds of years.

Six days beyond Aden, we sighted the tall mountains of Socotra rising from the sea. Sailing along its northern coast we saw the strangest landscape. There were the most bizarre trees scattered across a barren and rocky desert landscape. A day later, we reached the eastern end of the island and the old trading town of Erhor. Pulling into the bay, we dropped anchor and rowed ashore in the ship's long boat. We immediately spotted the rivulet flowing into the bay. After beaching the boat there, for the oarsmen to fill our barrels with fresh water, Hanno and I walked into the town. There we met a man who spoke a distorted form of Greek who said there was a sheep herder up in the hills above the town who still had several old boswellia trees which continued to produce frankincense. Giving him two silver coins, he eagerly agreed to take us to meet him and serve as our translator. Two hours later, we were in the mountains standing in front of an old stone house with about thirty goats inside of its walled courtyard. When our guide called out, a very old man stepped through the doorway and welcomed us.

With a sudden burst of excitement, our translator told him what we wanted to buy. The old man also became excited beyond words. It seemed that the trade out of Aden had almost ruined his cash business. When I asked what we could buy for one silver coin, he answered one ball of frankincense resin. Obviously, he thought the teenager he was negotiating with was just a joke or worse . . . stupid. Laughing at him loudly, I put my pouch full of silver away and told him that now I understood why Aden was taking all his business away. Bowing my head in respect, I apologized for wasting his time and turned for the door.

He protested loudly, so I slowly turned back in response to his loud protest. I offered him one silver coin for ten balls. Ten minutes later we both felt quite satisfied with one silver coin for eight balls of resin. I opened my large money pouch and counted out twenty coins for one hundred-sixty balls. As we turned to leave, he called me back again. Seeing my money pouch was full of silver, he asked if I could purchase one hundred-sixty more balls for a total of twelve silver coins. He had a deal! He counted out one hundred-sixty balls and then gave me four more as a bonus and I gave him twelve coins. Immediately he asked if we were planning to return. I told him I would if he would start giving me his best prices, otherwise I would go back to Aden and buy where the Romans don't allow cheating. With that incentive he swore he wasn't cheating me, and to prove it he would sell me on the spot twenty balls per silver coin. With that I asked him how many "high quality" balls he had left. He looked into his treasure box, and after a few minutes he said that he could sell me four hundred balls for twenty coins. I agreed and we closed the deal. I am sure he wondered who that teenager was with all that money and influence. Walking down the mountain I began to wonder that myself!

We returned to the *Triton* with seven hundred-twenty-four balls of top-grade frankincense for a price of about fourteen balls per silver coin. It seemed like a fair trade for both of us. While we were gone the oarsmen had filled up four wooden casks with cool, fresh water. Boarding the ship, I shared with Sadhu what we paid, and he responded that it was about half the price they were asking in Aden for a much poorer quality.

Since leaving the Sinus Arabicus, the monsoon winds were blowing northeast out of the African heat, similar to what they did this time of year in the Mare Internum. Once on the open ocean, our sails filled to full capacity as we sailed strait east toward India at what seemed to us a very good speed.

CHAPTER 46

MARE ERYTHRAEAN – OCTOBER 2, AD29

Our stop on the long-forgotten desert island of Socotra had proven to be fortuitous. With a very minor investment we had obtained what we hoped was a small fortune in high quality frankincense. With the island still in our wake we shaved off a small sliver from one of the balls and set it in the middle of a silver coin. Hanno brought up an oil lamp from the hold, lit a sliver of wood. and touched it to the sliver of dried resin. Slowly a slight trail of smoke rose off the coin. The resulting fragrance was undeniably one of the most aromatic experiences any of us had ever experienced. Immediately, we all knew we would be visiting Erhor in the future.

As the sun set directly behind us leaving the shadow of a distant mountain on the horizon, we began the longest leg of our journey to India and a new way of life. We then had somewhere near forty days at sea ahead of us. We needed to reach Muziris before October or risk drifting on the open ocean without the proper wind. Only Sadhu's family had taken this trip before, and they had tried to prepare us by making us aware of the trials which could lie ahead for us, not the least of which were terrible monsoon storms as we drew closer to India.

The next morning at breakfast, Captain Lucius was a cavalcade of questions about India in general. He was sailing across the Mare Erythraean, what we knew to be the largest body of water in existence, and he felt the need to understand what type of world he would encounter on the other side. Both Sadhu and his wife Rahelani were highly educated people, and were Aetna Shipping's Indian partners, so who better to teach him. There were several others who were eager to learn of this new land including myself, Hanno, two of our Briton crewmen, and one cargo slave by the name of Tectos, whose interest seemed very unusual to all of us except Hanno. That also meant that everything Sadhu shared in Aramaic I would need to translate into Greek and Latin. These would definitely be long and tiring sessions every morning after breakfast, especially for me as translator.

The first thing we learned was that the climate was much like the Nile Delta, hot but much more humid. The big difference would be all the rain and the very dense forests unlike anything else in the Roman world. One other thing India and the Nile had in common was cobras, only the Indian cobra was much larger and very aggressive. Of course, we would also find elephants, both domestic and wild. The domestic elephants were often treated like family, even to the point of being pampered. The wild elephants were mostly in the forests where the rhinoceros, lions, tigers, and leopards also lived. There were also monkeys everywhere and some of the most beautiful birds on earth.

We were warned to never drink water out of a stream without boiling it first, because some of that water carried sickness. If we are out of the city and become thirsty, there are palm trees everywhere, like those in Aegyptus, only growing much closer to the coast. In the part of India around the trading center of Muziris we will be able to find these elegant palm trees along all the rivers and streams. These amazing palms have a fruit as large as a child's head which contains a large nut full of delicious water. The trick is getting into the nut without losing the sweet water.

These types of discussions continued every morning for a little more than an hour after breakfast. It seemed as though every discussion only created more questions. There was one thing that Lucius needed to prepare himself for that Hanno and I had already learned. The food was sometimes so hot and spicy that it might be too intense to swallow without a cup of milk or yogurt in your other hand.

The great thing about Sadhu's discussions was that everyone participated, even the brilliant Galatian slave, Tectos. Since he was close to my age, often after the discussion sessions when everyone broke up and scattered to different parts of the ship, I would ask Tectos to engage in private discussions with me, to help improve my Latin accent and vocabulary which was actually pretty good. I think he knew it, too. It was obvious that he wasn't going to say so . . . and neither was I. Slowly I noticed a fresh element of trust in the way he spoke to me. In many ways he was like my wonderful liberated slave, Hanno. I suppose that was the suppressed reason why I looked forward to our brief times together.

After our first week out from Socotra, we were pounded by our first truly fierce monsoon storm. The wind was not as violent as in many storms we encountered in the northwest quarter of the Mare Internum, but the quantity of rain was unbelievable. Fortunately, the two hatches to our cargo hold had solid wooden panels which could quickly be secured to shut out the water from entering through the hatches' otherwise open grates.

As the weeks progressed, these storms increased in frequency and intensity. Two of our Nubian archers and one of the Aegyptians became terribly seasick during each storm, but as the weeks passed the severity of their sickness seemed to moderate. Lucius began a tradition during these storms which we all appreciated. As soon as the storm subsided, he tapped into an amphora of fine Italian wine he had set aside, and everyone enjoyed a cup of undiluted sweet wine to celebrate the fact that our world had once again become horizontal.

About half way through our crossing we encountered a significant family of the largest whales any of us had ever seen. The largest ones Lucius had seen were about as large as our large ocean-going ship, but these whales were perhaps a third larger than that. They were magnificent creatures which treated the *Triton* as though it was one of their own kind. After swimming around us for about an hour they decided we weren't so much fun after all and on some signal, they all turned and headed south. We watched their great geysers of water for at least another half hour until they disappeared. The mysteries of such creatures were immense. Would we ever be able to understand them or the vast world they considered their personal domain?

One interesting phenomenon Lucius pointed out to me as we left Socotra and headed into the open ocean, were the stars. The North Star was now much lower in the sky than we had ever seen it in the past. What seemed even more amazing was that there were completely new constellations of stars to our south which seemed to rise out of the ocean from nowhere. He pointed out that amazingly, it was about two hundred fifty years earlier that a Greek astronomer, Eratosthenes from the city of Cyrene, had calculated the circumference of the giant ball we call earth. He also claimed the stars at the bottom of the earth would be different than the stars we see at the top. I slowly began to realize how great God's world was. It was so much more than what we knew of in the Roman world, or even in the Indian. How many more wonderful places had he created which we have no understanding of in our little corner of the earth?

On our fifth week out, we witnessed the stars in action like few of us had ever seen prior to that night. It so shocked the night watch that he sounded the alarm to get everyone up on deck to see the show. Every few minutes stars were flying overhead like swallows. On two occasions we even watched two fly overhead at the same time, going in separate directions. What confused me was this, if stars were stable and permanent, why were they flying all over the sky that night? We noticed three unusual things: First, the North Star was closer to the horizon than any of us had ever seen before. Second, new stars began to appear to the south. Then, on one night the stars were moving all over the sky. It would take another Greek to figure it all out.

Fifteen days after the night of flying stars we noticed a narrow strip of land on the eastern horizon. Calling Sadhu, we needed him to confirm where we were. After a few hours we noticed the narrow strip of land begin to turn into the vague shadows of mountains appearing in the far distance. Sadhu continued to study them until sunset when he became quite sure that Muziris was just a little further to the south of where we were headed. The captain altered our course to the southeast so that at sunrise Sadhu could obtain a better calculation of our position.

That morning, we were all at the rail watching the sun rise over the ghats, as Sadhu referred to these mountains. Shortly after noon, he called Rahelani to his side and pointed. They both excitedly identified two mountain peaks and claimed we would be at the mouth of the Periyar River leading to Muziris shortly after dawn the following day.

The next morning, in the early light, we saw nine Roman freighters anchored an hour's distance down the coast at the mouth of the Periyar River. For some reason we never considered that with all the sea ports on the Indian coast why so many Romans ships would want to be trading here. Finding the best anchorage possible, we dropped anchor just before sunset and consulted with Sadhu to determine our next steps.

We were about a twenty-minute row from the mouth of the Periyar when we dropped anchor. After speaking with Sadhu, the obvious next step was to lower our longboat into the water very early the next morning and have Sadhu, Rahelani, their servants, Lucius, Rashvi, Hanno, and myself, along with two rowers make their way down the rope ladder into the boat and go to Sadhu's home where he could begin making contacts with the king and his people.

It rained again that night. Before our landing party left the *Triton*, the humidity was already causing our rowers to perspire excessively. At least it wasn't raining that morning, but the sky was heavy and definitely not looking friendly.

Almost immediately we found ourselves returning greetings in both Latin and Greek to men aboard the ships we passed. Our excitement reached a fevered pitch as we entered the mouth of the river. We had only gone up river for about twenty minutes when Sadhu directed us to turn south out of the river and up into a muddy, saltwater estuary.

The glamor and excitement of our adventure dissipated as we continued south for about an hour, past two very poor fishing villages. The only excitement we had was inspired by the dozens of beautiful flowering plants all around us, both in the trees and on the ground. Eventually we reached a very modest, long wooden wharf on the east bank of the estuary. Surprised that we were approaching our final destination, I tried to suppress my disappointment when we stopped at the south end of the sagging wharf and cautiously went ashore. Before we left, Lucius instructed the sailors to return for us before dark while bringing as much of the baggage as possible belonging to the princess' party.

From the south end of the wharf there was a well-worn but muddy road leading directly into the dense and gloomy forest. At the end of a fifteen-minute walk we reached the first of many Muziris warehouses. Because Sadhu knew the sergeants, we were given a warm welcome and a quick tour of the buildings and their contents. The first building was packed with huge baskets full of India's black gold and Roma's spice of choice, black pepper. We walked through four other warehouses which contained other spices from lands to the east of India, and luxurious HanChin silks, carvings of beautiful jade stone, and graceful pottery which was smooth as Roman glass and green as forest moss.

The variety of products was endless until we arrived at the last warehouse which was exclusively packed with natural, uncarved, Ivory tusks of every shade and size. Surprised by the amount of Ivory, I asked Sadhu why they consisted of so many shades, from soft yellow to white, and where it all came from. He explained. "The oldest ivory was the darkest and a third of the ivory came from cutting the ends off the long tusks of living old or retired timber and war elephants. Some came from wild rogue bull elephants which came out of the forests and destroyed crops, homes, and sometimes even people. These old bulls needed to be destroyed. The rest came from dead elephants, killed in wars or by other circumstances. There are some tusks which are taken from skeletons found in the wild elephant graveyards hidden deep in the forests. Elephants would periodically go to touch the bones of their ancestors and then, in their last days of old age, without food or water, they eventually laid down by their ancestors and died.

"Elephants are the most intelligent and valuable animal we have in India other than the cow. They work hard and earn good money for their owners who love them very dearly. When they eventually die they are sometimes cremated as though they were members of the family, leaving their severed tusks behind for their masters to sell so they can buy a new elephant. You will also find that in India many people worship Ganesh, the elephant god, who is loved very much as the god of wisdom and the remover of obstacles.

After walking through a few more warehouses, Sadhu thanked the sergeant and led us on a thirty-minute walk to the region's main city of Paravur. Learning that this small city was where Sadhu and his family lived we eagerly accepted his invitation for a meal in his home. As we continued our walk, with every minute the number of people and ox carts on the road seemed to increase until we finally reached the city center which was a mass of humanity and full of some of the strangest and foulest smells this side of Roma.

I soon noticed that at least one hundred people stopped and bowed in greeting to Sadhu and Rahelani, with their hands in the gesture of prayer. Finally stopping in front of Sadhu's synagogue, he asked if we would like to see its interior. The Indians are so polite . . . of course we wanted to go inside! It was a beautiful synagogue which would hold at least two hundred worshipers, about a hundred-twenty men and boys on the ground floor and about eighty women above, in the second story gallery. In many ways it reminded me of the synagogue in Syracuse.

Leaving the synagogue, within three blocks we arrived at a large walled compound surrounding a beautiful multi-storied mansion built around a multi-storied atrium, while the home's walls were shaded by a columned veranda and gardens full of exotic plants and trees. Upon entering the compound people surrounded us and made a tremendous fuss . . .servants and family alike. Eventually a woman a little younger than Yacobsa threw her arms around Sadhu and gave him a very familiar looking kiss. We soon learned that she was Yacobsa's sister, Merrayum. She and her family approached Rahelani and bowed properly before kissing her. Immediately she asked about Yacobsa and she seemed surprised to learn that he stayed behind in Alexandria. She was even more surprised to learn that Rashvi would return with the captain and myself to Alexandria and then on to Roma. After all, he was given to her mother by the former king. Why would he be going to Roma?

When those chaotic and boisterous introductions eventually quieted, we were led into the dining room of Rahelani's beautiful home where we sat down and were formally introduced. It was then that Rashvi proudly introduced his husband, Hanno, the powerful looking Carthaginian sitting next to him. In shock Merrayum asked Rashvi when they were married. When Rashvi told her that it was after the Feast of Weeks in a small village just outside of Jerusalem, she naturally needed to know what he was doing in Jerusalem. There Sadhu picked up the conversation and shared the story of the vision which took all of us to the year's Seder in Jerusalem. He naturally shared our unusual involvement with Jesus the prophet and how he entered the picture, along with the circumstances of his death and resurrection.

Shaking her head, she declared that all of this was far too much for her to absorb and that it would take time to figure it all out. But the fact that Rashvi had married a man was what she really had problems with. She even wanted to know if he was *hijra* or some kind of beggar eunuch dressing like a woman. That question irritated Rahelani to the extent that she ended the conversation very abruptly.

Fortunately, the staff soon began to bring out some wonderfully prepared dishes which quickly introduced Lucius to the spicy foods of India which he seemed to heartily enjoy. By the end of the meal it was late afternoon and Sadhu offered to escort all of us back to our rendezvous with the longboat, allowing us a couple days rest while he began his work at the Royal Palace. As we bid a good evening to everyone, Sadhu sent five male servants ahead to retrieve everyone's baggage.

On our way back to the wharf, Sadhu took us by three Indian temples which were very different from those in the Empire. Even in a small city like Paravur the temples were as many as four stories high and were completely covered from top to bottom with deep relief sculptures of ancient legends which depicted many of India's thousands of gods and her ancient kings engaged in their many wars and loves. The artistic skill and imagination of Indian architects, sculptors, and colorful painters were beyond anything I had ever imagined possible . . . and this was not a major city by any means. Just as in the Greek and Roman worlds, the fine stone temples were painted in fantastic colors which were created all over the Empire and beyond. What made them so different were the hundreds of relief sculptures which were painted in scores of various vibrant colors.

Those few hours we spent ashore were invaluable. As I was beginning to understand what we were actually doing in India, it began to take on a different affect then I had assumed it would. The flow of Roman gold continued to fill the treasuries of India's many kingdoms, the personal coffers of their kings, and the pockets of Roma's trading merchants like Aetna. I could only foresee the wealth of Roma's gentry eventually begin to decline. After looking through some of Muziris' warehouses I felt sure that they were really getting the best of our trading arrangement, even as Aetna Shipping was becoming very rich.

CHAPTER 47

MUZIRIS – NOVEMBER 8, AD29

Our second night anchored off Muziris was also rainy, hot, and humid. It occurred to me the next morning that it was because of these discomforts that the grass was tall and green, and the trees were lush and still budding new leaves and colorful blossoms in October. Looking across to the shore that evening, I could see many banks of flowering shrubs and small plants dressed in a stunning array of colors. When I looked closely into some of the trees, I could see what looked like long stems of colorful flowers hanging from huge tree branches as though they were using the wet barked limbs as their garden soil. I vowed to take a much closer look at them when I went ashore in the morning.

Excited about going ashore, I also took a closer look at those ships anchored near us and was puzzled that there were few if any crewmen on board. Some ships actually looked deserted and I wanted to know why. Calling to Rashvi I asked him if he knew the reason and was surprised by his answer. "There are at least two major reasons why there are so many ships at anchor here at one time. First, it takes so long to negotiate a full hold of cargo. The second is because the ships have nowhere to go until their sails can be filled with the early monsoon winds of winter. That is when the snows begin to fall in the far north and the monsoon winds reverse themselves as that part of India and the HanChin Empire begin to cool. Only then can any of us pull anchor and head back to Aegyptus."

The issue of weather made sense. I never really understood weather dynamics, but it took less than three months to get here, and it will take only three months to return to Alexandria. The rest of the time we just wait for the winds, like we were doing in Aegyptus and often do on the Mare Internum. So, what the sailors do in the meantime became my bigger question. Rashvi simply answered, "Because of this delay, His Royal Highness has built a village with ample housing for the foreign sailors to live in until the monsoon winds begin again."

Seeing the look of surprise on my face, Rashvi smiled and said, "Many sailors don't mind the dead time. They use their pay and rent young women or boys from the Avarna people who live primarily on the edge of the forests and are outside of the Indian cast or social economic system. The women and boys get to choose who they wish to reside with as personal servants for as long as the foreign sailors are here in Muziris. The sailors and archers pay the families more than they could earn in two years doing their usual work. It is a great source of income for the Avarna people, or who we Indians often call the Untouchables. They are a primitive and simple people who have lived in the forests since long before we Indians came down out of the snowy north and conquered them. Also, His Royal Highness allows the foreign sailors to live in Muziris rent free.

A young woman or a boy not only keeps the sailors and archers satisfied at night, but they cook and do all of the household chores as well. It is good work for them because they are taken care of, well fed, and even cherished by the light skinned men from the west who kiss and make love to them. The Avarna are the same people we Indians are forbidden to even touch. They live much better than they would at home with their own families. Their parents often compete for who they see as a good man for their children to live with. It is a valuable experience for those young people who can now earn a bride price or a small dowry. In this system everybody wins . . . the sailors, the young women, the boys, and their families. No Indian would dare to touch them, but these sailors love them. Actually, the Avarna are very similar to the camp followers who travel with the Roman army, except the Avarna stay in one place, and they have their families nearby if things don't work out."

Like everything else, this brought up another question. "Where is this village?" Rashvi then presented another proof of the system's value when he explained why the warehouses were located in the heart of the forest and not on the river's edge or in a town.

"The sailors and their servants needed a place to live and have a degree of privacy. Therefore, many years ago Rahelani's father set aside several acres of land located close to a secluded stream and hidden among the forest trees to be used for our trader's village which he called Muziris. Only the sailors from Roma and the locals know the village by that name and where it is located. He then built his warehouses in the forest just a few paces south, behind Muziris. It is there, that during most of the year the warehouses enjoy the protection of the foreign archers and the occasional foreign soldier who lives beyond the trees and out of sight. So, you see, even the king wins!

"His Royal Highness also had a small room built by the door of each warehouse where the king has four guards stationed at all times. As you noticed yesterday, it is a difficult place to find or even get to if you don't know exactly where it is. You can be sure the sailors and archers love the privacy of their one room huts and their little family they have while living as guests among us. If they have the money, they can even rent their servant's siblings for the duration of their stay. There is only one absolute law the sailors must follow. If they kill their Avarna companion, they are exiled to their ship and never allowed to enter Muziris, or even come ashore again. After all, the Avarna live by the king's favor and they technically belong to him.

"If you like, the next time we are out we can walk through Muziris and you can see for yourself how the sailor's live while ashore. Oh yes, I almost forgot, it is up to each individual captain to maintain order with his own men living in Muziris, or he and his ship will be banned from trading with our kingdom ever again."

It was a brilliant system. No invading Arab pirates from Dhofar or Oman would ever find Muziris between trading seasons when the ships are not anchored off shore as obvious beacons. It would be forbiddingly difficult if they were to ever try to invade during the rainy season. Their only escape route through the streams and canals could be completely cut off by the army in a matter of hours.

The more I spoke with Rashvi the more I realized what a treasure Hanno had found in him. Not only is he handsome, but his intelligence and spiritual depth are beyond that of any slave I had ever met. Of course, I had never met a 'royal' slave before.

The next morning, I asked if Rashvi and Hanno would be willing to give me a more comprehensive tour of the warehouses and the village. They eagerly agreed. Lowering the longboat into the water and climbing down the rope ladder to find our seats, our oarsmen shoved off and we began our personal guided tour of Muziris. Several times I had the sailors stop the boat because I needed more time to observe the environment and the birds. I enjoyed the time this gave me to ask questions and learn more about this amazing new world. Rashvi identified the plants growing in the trees as being in two groups, the air plants and the orchids, both of which produced magnificent flowers of many different colors. He also pointed out several beautiful birds, some of which he claimed could be taught to repeat words. I had heard of such birds, but they were supposedly only from south of the great desert and I was eager to see one up close while here in India.

As we reached the north end of the sagging wharf, Rashvi asked if I would like to spend the night with the sadhu and his family. It sounded like a wonderful opportunity, so I told the sailors to go back to the ship and inform the Captain we would find a way to return in a day or two. As they rowed out of sight, Hanno took Rashvi's hand and mine as he walked between us on our way to Muziris. He said he was deliriously happy because he was with the two most important people in his life. Even though Rashvi couldn't understand everything Hanno said, I was concerned about the possibility of him having feelings of jealousy. However, as I looked across at him I saw a giant smile on his face even before hearing my translation of Hanno's comment into Aramaic. For the first time, I realized that Hanno had somehow, in spite of an immense language barrier, informed him of our great love for one another. With that realization, I immediately felt deeply loved and comfortable with the two of them together.

It was still a little strange, however, because Rashvi was nearly three times my age. I am sure that if I pressed him, he would probably admit that being with younger men made him feel younger, too! Still, I was sure we made quite a sight for the locals, two short men, one much taller or one older and the other two much younger. The shorter were holding the hands of a very tall and powerful man who looked like a Roman gladiator. It was obvious to each of us that we were family, even if it may not have been so obvious to others because we were also of three different colors.

Following a narrow path through a dense grove of trees and brush we suddenly stepped into the open clearing and there it was . . .

Muziris . . . the wealthy Indian city known all over the Empire. Laid out in rows before us were at least one hundred small huts, many with cooking fires burning in the front of them. Rashvi was correct in his statement that the Avarnas were definitely different from the Indians. Upon a casual glance they appeared to be a more primitive race. Yet, for the most part, each one seemed happy, or at least content with their status in the village and the men they were caring for. Most of the girls appeared to be between fourteen and perhaps twenty, and the less prevalent boys I saw were between thirteen and seventeen. We also saw many sailors as well. They seemed very content with the arrangement and the opportunity to spend several months on dry land and still get paid.

Rashvi then informed me, as I translated, that each ship had its own allotment of huts. As the huts first become occupied, the Avarnas will go to each new occupant and ask for the job. The king keeps a Greek speaking agent in Paravur who establishes the rent prices for the servants and insures that each transaction is fair and honest. This avoids a lot of fights and general misunderstandings. One thing that surprised me was that some of the sailors kept their Avarnas naked, as if they were slaves. Everyone seemed to treat that as a natural course of things in this sweltering heat. Both Hanno and I became quite interested, simply because we had never seen a naked woman or girl in our lives. When we discussed it later, we agreed that there appeared to be nothing physically interesting about them.

As we continued to walk through the village, we greeted one of our own Britons, with copper colored hair all over him, who was sitting in front of his recently acquired hut playing with his new servants, a naked boy sitting on his lap, and a girl kneeling beside a cooking fire. He responded with a happy tone in his voice, revealing that he preferred his state in Muziris to what he had on the *Triton*.

Leaving him to enjoy his new pets, we followed a break in the south edge of the forest and soon reached the first warehouse. We immediately released our clutched hands as Rashvi greeted the sergeant by name. When Rashvi reintroduced me to the sergeant and told him that I was the buyer, he looked at me and then at Rashvi as though we were trying to pull something over on him. As the constantly translated discussion continued among the three of us about my desire to evaluate the tusks he had in stock, it seemed that would be the best way to once again be alone together. When the sergeant offered to lead us to that warehouse, I knew that Rashvi was planning to use me as a translator between him and the love of his life when he declined the sergeant's offer. This was going to be a fun experience, if not truly quite awkward. I had served a real purpose in this relationship. I had helped them frequently aboard ship but there were over twenty people cramped on that ship who could listen in. Now we were going to be alone, if we could convince the sergeant that we needed to get some work done.

After convincing the sergeant that Rashvi could find what he needed to show us, he finally left us to locate the ivory warehouse ourselves. Rashvi hastily led us to the warehouse where he turned to Hanno and became very affectionate while speaking to him in Aramaic. I knew my purpose was to translate into Greek for Hanno, so that is what I did. It was beautiful to hear, and then, speak their most intimate thoughts to each other. It was inevitable, but Hanno became so amorous he needed to make love to his husband immediately. At that point I didn't need to tell Rashvi anything, for they each knew what the other was thinking. As they gracefully performed the dance of love, they still needed me to lay next to them as they whispered beautiful words of love and endearment to one another. I was so intently participating verbally that I became very amorous myself, which I was gratefully able to relieve without missing a word between them, or letting them know that anything else was happening.

When they finished, and caught their breath, they desperately wanted to stay wrapped in the other's arms and whisper their words of love over and over again. I was actually surprised at the number of Greek words that Rashvi had picked up and also the number of Aramaic words that Hanno had already begun responding to. It was obvious that I had two very bright and motivated students.

After ten more minutes of romantic play which Hanno asked me to join, we finally left the warehouse and went to tell the sergeant that we would see him again in a couple of days, when I had decided how much in the warehouse I would purchase.

Departing the warehouses, we proceeded toward the road into town to see a few more sights before arriving at Sadhu's for lunch. This time, Rashvi pointed out the number of cows wandering about everywhere. He explained that the cow was a sacred animal to the Indian Hindus and, technically, nobody owned them. If one looked undernourished, it was fed. If one was preparing to calve, someone would assist, and if a family needed milk, they would milk a nearby cow. It was then that I noticed what appeared to be Avarna men in brief loincloths walking the streets picking up cow manure like the camel drivers did in the desert, and obviously for the same reason . . . fuel.

Reaching the center of the city, Rashvi asked if we would care to see the inside of a very unique temple before we reached Sadhu's home. I eagerly agreed as I translated to Hanno. For some reason Rashvi passed two beautifully sculpted and painted temples and finally stopped at a smaller one not far from where Sadhu lived. As we prepared to enter its open porticoes, I detected the faint smell of frankincense. I was pleased to note that It was not even close to the strength and the sweetness of the frankincense we brought from Socotra.

Walking into the building I totally forgot about frankincense. Jarring my senses I couldn't believe what I saw. My eyes were immediately drawn to the entry walls and I realized that all of the painted human sculptures were totally naked! The men were all in sexual arousal, and they all portrayed countless sexual positions with their partners. Each scene had from one to five very erotic participants and in all gender combinations. This was not a temple dedicated to fertility or love like in Greece or Roma. It was joyfully illustrating the hundreds of ways we could show our gratitude to the gods for giving us sexual pleasure. The participants might be in a chariot, on horseback, or even riding an elephant, but out of the hundreds we saw, there were no two alike. Indian artists are not only immensely skilled, they also have limitless imaginations.

After half an hour of over stimulation, Hanno and I walked out of the temple in utter amazement and headed directly to Sadhu's beautiful home, hoping to be there in time for their midday meal. Pulling the heavy door chain which rang the loud bell inside the massive wooden gate, we soon heard someone on the other side fumbling to open the small door in the middle of the gate. It was just like at our home in Syracuse. Soon the door swung open to the excited chatter of one of Rahelani's servant women. She tenderly hugged each one of us forgoing the normal more formal Indian greetings we had learned in Alexandria. Running into the house she began calling someone and soon Rahelani stepped out on the colonnaded veranda and joyfully welcomed us. It appeared that we timed it perfectly as they were just putting the midday meal onto the low tables in the dining room. It smelled wonderful, but I was concerned there wouldn't be enough.

As we sat down on our designated cushions, I was delighted to see Yacobsa's sister, Merrayum, and her husband sitting next to me. Rahelani assured us that Sadhu would be returning from the palace before dark and, if we could stay that long he may have some news for us. Immediately Rashvi replied by asking, "If it is permissible, could we stay in your home until we get all the news concerning our next step, whenever that might be."

Rahelani responded affirmatively and expressed her delight that we would consider staying for a couple of days. Once again, the meal was exceptional and very spicy but delicious.

Another storm that afternoon forced us to remain indoors and reminded Rashvi that we were supposed to be past the summer monsoons. Eventually the table talk drifted back to our journey to Jerusalem and the many questions that Merrayum needed to discuss. Actually, we were eager to answer her numerous questions. The most pressing ones were about our time in Jerusalem during the feasts of Seder and Pentecost. Since Simon of Cyrene and I were members of the same family through marriage, she asked me numerous questions about his vision as I had heard it months before the Seder, which he had shared with us in Rahelani's home in Alexandria. Then she inquired about its graphic and accurate fulfillment after the Seder celebration itself. She had heard the story, but she still could not fathom the possibility of its truth. As I shared with her all I knew and experienced with Simon long before we all agreed to travel to Jerusalem, she was overwhelmed by the implications of the possible truth of such miraculous events.

Earlier that morning Rahelani shared her experiences with Merrayum which caused her to evaluate the possibility of truth in what her parents were telling her. It was something which far exceeded her current concepts about the reality of earth and its place in the universe. If she accepted what we were telling her as truth, God had to be more than someone or something our simple, human minds could ever comprehend. He is small enough to enter our brains and place pictures and words from the future into them and immense enough to redefine life and death itself, not only here on earth but throughout the universe. If she were to believe all of what she had been told, then everything she had ever understood about God had to be rethought and eventually redefined.

In India she lived in a vast world of spiritual metaphysics revealed through countless gods which were simply the reflections of human dreams, needs, and desires. But what her family was now telling her, challenged her to rethink everything in her systematic Jewish mind, called her to face the possibility that she must redefine God into a being which is the only true force in the universe. It forced her to accept a reality existing beyond the physical world in which we live. She wasn't sure if she could leave her solid Jewish faith in a God who created all, and ruled all, while taking the giant leap into a universe where the line between mental visions and reality disappear along with the line between life and death. The difficulty accepting what she heard, and still knowing God's part in all of it was beyond her ability to reason. Yet, the more we shared and the more truth and honesty she detected within us, the more she was inclined to consider such extreme possibilities.

Her greatest conundrum was how this all-powerful force of the universe could specifically love her as an individual and have its personal presence dwelling within her. At what point could she let her solid, logic-based understanding of an orderly and stable world be replaced by a faith in an unexplainable counter reality? On one side it seemed so foolish, on the other side so alluring. If this was a more complete understanding of who God was, she knew she had to consider it.

Then Rashvi pulled the stopper out of the bottle when he shared what we all experienced in Jerusalem at the Feast of Weeks, but what Greek speaking Jews in the Empire refer to as the Feast of Pentecost seven weeks after Jesus walked out of his tomb. First, he told Merrayum that all but two of Jesus's disciples were uneducated fishermen or peasants, much like the simple people in their own community of Paravur. That in itself, defied any logic of such men presenting divine revelations and transcendental teachings.

Then Rashvi dropped this boulder of faith into her lap. "While we were in an atmosphere of worship and prayer with the disciples and about a hundred other followers of Jesus, people began to glow like there was a fire within them which was trying to come out of the tops of their heads. For some reason this phenomenon didn't seem to startle any of us, probably because of the extent of God's power which we had already witnessed.

What happened next however, did startle every one of us. I heard the Galilean fisherman next to me praising God and his son, Jesus, in the most beautifully poetic phases . . . in Malayalam, the language of our birth. At the same time a farmer next to your father was praising God and his son in Tamil. Later, after I had been speaking and spent time praising God in a state of ecstatic joy and adoration, Hanno later told me through a translator that I had spoken all of those words not in Malayalam as I thought, but in the most beautifully accented Carthaginian he had ever heard. In fact, his interpreter repeated to me exactly what I had said, but he translated it into Aramaic, even though I was sure I had been praying only in Malayalam. It felt so strange yet glorious. What we heard seemed as though God was telling us to share the love of his son with every nation. Truly, it was an amazing afternoon of pure worship.

"Hostile groups in the city, who had contributed to Jesus' death, were at that time keeping a close watch on his disciples. They also heard the many languages coming from the house. When they discovered who was speaking, they were amazed. This experience persuaded many of them to believe the man they had sent to his death was truly the Messiah, or the Christ as they now say it in Greek, which was the term we are now using to refer to him. We were compelled to believe that God was doing something new and very different for the whole world through Judaism."

Without warning, Merrayum began to weep as she realized that what we had shared had to be true and that God really was personal and loving to all who would believe that he had sent his son to draw us all closer to himself. She definitely had a lot of thinking and praying ahead of her. She had to solve one primary question. Could God really have a son? Or was that term a Euphamisim?

The next day, when Sadhu returned from his meeting with his brother-in-law, the King of Chera, we could tell by the smile on his face that he had good news. The discovery that there was a tie between the king's own Jewish family and a Jewish trading house in the Roman world had truly intrigued His Royal Highness. In fact, he asked Sadhu to help him meet me as soon as possible. Sadhu agreed that I needed Captain Paulus to stand beside me with the king's former servant, Rashvi, and himself. We immediately sent a message to Lucius on the *Triton* asking him to return with the messenger as quickly as possible.

CHAPTER 48

KING ABRAYAMSA – NOVEMBER 12, AD30

The next morning, Rahelani joined us as we left immediately after breakfast for the winter palace in Chendamagalam, located on the Periyar River where it twisted its way out of the hill country. It was only an hour and a half away on horseback. That was easy enough except Hanno and I had never been on a horse in our lives. Sadhu seemed very sympathetic and gave me a gentle old mare who seemed to be content to simply be around people. Unfortunately, Sadhu had no more old mares, so Hanno found himself sitting atop a recently retired stallion war horse which was the largest horse he or I had ever seen. Sadhu assured him that his horse, Lord Vishnu, was supposed to be very obedient. However, he wasn't positive because the king had gifted it to him while he lived in Alexandria. Looking over my shoulder at Hanno, he looked frighteningly massive himself.

As we departed through the gate of their fabulous home, I felt like a foreign emissary going to meet some distant royal potentate. Then it hit me! That was exactly what this teenager was doing. What was I supposed to do, or say? Thankfully, Sadhu came over to check on me when we stopped to give the horses a ten-minute breather. What he told me helped, but I was sweating more than my mare.

Arriving at the palace without incident, I was stunned by its unique beauty built to look as though it was floating on top of the river. As we dismounted, six grooms came out of nowhere to walk the horses in what looked like a parade ground. As our mounts were being cooled, we followed an aged royal aide who treated each of us as though we were old friends, as he led us up the grand flight of stairs into the spectacular palace.

We waited in an anteroom until we were announced and led into the king's private chambers. Rahelani immediately ran to be embraced by her young nephew. Then, the handsome king walked up to Rashvi, his former slave, and embraced him affectionately. Then I thought it strange that Rahelani rather than Sadhu introduced Captain Lucius Paulus, myself as Jacobus BarSirach, and finally Hanno as Rashvi's husband. After making some sort of joke about Rashvi marrying a strong and very handsome bride, the king looked at me rather quizzically and asked my age. I was surprised that he addressed me in perfect Aramaic. When I told him I was fifteen, he laughed and threw his arms around me exclaiming that he was fifteen when his father died, and he was called upon to ascend to the throne of Chera.

He went on to say that many boys never have a chance to enjoy their youth but are obligated to become men long before their time. As I glanced at Lucius, I saw his trademark grin as he caught the gist of what was being said in Aramaic and proudly tipped his head to me.

During the first half hour of our meeting with the king, he wanted to know all about "me," which made me uncomfortably vulnerable. He was intrigued when I told him I was an identical twin and was born in Hispania, a Roman province near the edge of the world. He was also fascinated by the fact that he perceived my family to be much like his own. I then told him that I was adopted to become the brother of my cousin and then I was married to him to become his husband next to his wife and children. When he heard my last statement. he smiled and said my family was much like his own. I couldn't help but wonder if he had a husband too, along with his several royal wives. When he learned that Captain Paulus had been my mentor, he congratulated him on a job well done. Then it was me who grinned and proudly tipped my head. What fascinated me most about the king was that he was near the age of Yacobsa, his nephew back in Aegyptus . . . and he even looked a lot like him, too.

After tea was served, we sat in a circle and began to speak of the business at hand. We started with the rules of trade that would govern all of our dealings. After he and Rahelani spoke extensively in Malayalam, he looked at me and took my hand in his and announced that "I" would be given a twenty-five percent discount on all purchases out of his warehouses. In response I looked at Sadhu to be sure I understood the process in India. He nodded to me, and I committed to the King that any Roman goods he chooses to take in trade or purchase outright would also be valued at a twenty-five percent discount below the price we would charge to all others. With that major business relationship agreed upon, he wrapped both hands around mine and said he was looking forward to a very long and close friendship.

As we completed breaking the ice and establishing our business relationship, the king stood, and we all followed. He placed his arm around my shoulder and invited us to join him for lunch. Leading us into a moderately sized dining hall, he invited us to have a seat in gilded chairs around a surprisingly modest table much like we had in Syracuse. The first thing placed in the center of the table near the king and facing him was a stuffed peacock, exactly the same as the live ones we delivered to Gallia over a year earlier. Captain Paulus also looked startled to see another of those great birds, this time in the center of a formal dining table.

After the remainder of the dishes were set before us, the head chef came in with his assistant and lifted the beautiful bird off the golden platter it had been setting on. To our surprise, we saw a golden brown, roasted peacock on a bed of yellow saffron rice and colorful flower petals. The chef sliced the bird and the king was given the gigantic left breast from over the bird's heart. I wondered how he was ever going to eat all of that meat. To my surprise I was given the right breast. The king smiled and said that he hoped I enjoyed forest peacock. I thanked him and took my first bite. It was wonderful, better than any chicken I had ever eaten. He was obviously pleased with my immediate reaction as he placed his hand on my leg under the table and squeezed, the same way Yacobsa did with Hanno when we first met in his parents' home in Alexandria. I was beginning to think that the Indians were perhaps even bolder than the Romans, at least sexually, if that were possible.

By the end of the meal I agreed, in open consultation with Sadhu and Lucius, that our first order would include half a ship load of black pepper, Roma's most sought-after commodity in India. We would take half of the ivory in the Muziris warehouse, and half of the silk fabrics currently in stock. To reduce our cash payment for those three items, the king agreed to take one third of our top-grade frankincense, all of our Aethiopian emeralds, and all of our red Sicilian coral. Fortunately, Sadhu had shared a flask of our Italian wine with the king the day before, and he agreed to take twenty amphorae, half of what we had, and seven amphorae of our Hispanic olive oil, also half of our stock.

He then assured me, "The neighboring king of the country in the mountains to the east of Chera would want the balance of those products. His kingdom is landlocked, and he doesn't have direct access to the Roman Treasure Ships, therefore he purchases most of what he desires through me. He may also want to trade in kind for things he takes from you. He is my younger cousin, and I will send word that you are here and that you are distantly connected to our family. He often comes down to see me when I know we can strike a profitable arrangement with a Roman merchant. Let's see what he brings with him when he comes . . .and I am sure he will like you"

In one afternoon, we had sold over half of what we had brought with us and purchased two thirds of what we needed to fill our ship's hold, all at healthy margins which Sadhu carefully verified. By the end of the meal, the king had quietly given me his first and second names, Chadra Abrayamsa. He wanted me to always use the second name whenever I was in his presence rather than Your Royal Highness, except before the court or during official business meetings. As we grew closer through the afternoon, he eventually asked if I would like to spend the night, or even a few days, at the palace. What should I do? I went down stairs to check with Sadhu who was in discussion about the movement of goods with Lucius. I decided to ask them both. They agreed it may be good for me to stay at the palace for a few days.

Later that afternoon I affirmed that I could stay at the palace for a few days longer, as Sadhu and Captain Paulus would need the time to coordinate with the king's agents to evaluate and plan the initial transfer of goods and money. Then in false spontaneity, Chadra suggested that we leave first thing in the morning to visit his cousin, King Shikrit of Padyan, rather than wait for him to come to us.

He assured me that it was less than five days journey to his mountain palace up the river by elephant. That did it! If it meant I was going to ride an elephant, I was going. When I relayed that plan to Sadhu and Lucius, I surely received different reactions. Sadhu began to laugh as though he knew something no one else knew, and Lucius' eyes nearly popped out of their sockets because of the elephants. Receiving no negative response, I went back to Abrayamsa and told him our schedule had been cleared. Immediately he called for his personal valet and gave him some instructions. In the meantime, he advised Sadhu that we would need samples of the Frankincense, Italian wine, and Hispanic olive oil. He also asked for a sample of the Aethiopian emeralds and Sicilian red coral which the king had just purchased himself. Captain Paulus wrote out the instructions and sent them with Rashvi and Hanno with an escort to the *Triton* by way of a shortcut directly down river in a special palace barge. They were sure they would be back in the morning, within three hours after sunrise.

That accomplished, I had the remainder of the day and until early morning to be entertained by the charming Abrayamsa. While he was teaching me a game called chess, he casually mentioned his brother in Aegyptus. When I heard that, I nearly dropped my queen. Looking at him directly in the eyes, I asked, "Where in Aegyptus does he live?"

He looked back at me very strangely and replied in a tone of disbelief, "Why, in Alexandria, of course. I was preparing to ask you, where in Alexandria he lives. What is his house like? Especially, how is he doing? I miss Yacobsa very much. He is my twin, not identical like you of course."

At this point I was completely confused. "I thought you were his uncle, and your sister his mother."

"Oh, oh. I suppose I have ruined everything again."

"I don't know. What could you have ruined? Now I feel closer to you then ever!"

"I haven't the slightest idea either. We need a very long talk, but it is now time for supper. When we go down, please don't say anything about this to anyone."

Still confused, I agreed.

We cleaned up and went down to eat with Sadhu, Rahelani, Lucius, and as it turned out, some other members of the Royal Family who were also there to properly meet the King's guests from Roma. It was self-evident that they were from a different branch of the family for their skin was much darker than those members I already knew. I also instinctively knew this was going to be a lot more difficult to untangle than I had originally expected. The meal was also a little more difficult to navigate than it was at noon. None of the darker members of the family spoke Aramaic. It was like there were two totally different dinners going on at the same table.

After we completed our last course of chilled exotic fruit, Abrayamsa excused the two of us as we returned to his private quarters. Sitting in opposing corners of a divan constructed of snow-white marble inlaid with semi-precious stones shaped like birds and flowers, he began to open his heart.

"I miss Yacobsa because I love him. I have never loved anyone more than him. We grew up as lovers. He was the other half of me. He was the perfect brilliant, witty, and handsome prince. When father separated us, I thought I would die. We had recently fought a minor war with a small kingdom to our south and Rashvi was a captured royal eunuch who was put in charge of the royal household here in the palace. He understood immediately that I was slowly dying of a broken heart and decided to help me in any way he could. I had no idea what happened to Yacobsa, all I knew was that he had disappeared.

Then after a year, a beautiful girl was brought into the palace. She was mysteriously placed in the family women's quarters where I lived. All of her face, except for her hauntingly beautiful eyes, was covered by a veil, so I thought she belonged to my father and he was waiting until she was a little older to take her to his bed. She hadn't even been in the palace for a full day before she came to my room holding her finger up to her veiled face asking me to agree to be absolutely silent. When I agreed, she lifted her dress to reveal that she was a he, not a she. Actually, more than a he! That piece of "he" that I saw under her dress I knew like it was my own. That quiet, demure, teenage girl was my dear Yacobsa. The next night Rashvi smuggled him back in and we hid him in my private quarters where he would be undetected, as long he was never seen by anyone, especially Rashvi.

"Rashvi, as a eunuch, understood my frustrated need for love and he always looked the other way, but one day there was no way for him to look other than straight ahead at Yacobsa, and he was forced by his honor to reveal his presence to our father. But first he gave us fifteen minutes to bid one another farewell and Yacobsa time to escape. When the guards arrived, he was long gone, and I swore he had only been there for an hour before Rashvi discovered him. When Yacobsa was finally discovered a few weeks later, it was decided he should be given to our older sister, Rahelani, to finish raising. We have never seen each other since.

"A year later our father died, and the royal council endorsed my father's decree of succession and had me, the older twin, crowned as king. It was then that it became my royal duty to marry two or three princesses and continue the dynasty. That was the most difficult time of my life. I was just a year older than you are now before I was finally man enough to mount one of my wives, but of course nothing came of it. This happened about three or four times a year for about five and a half years. Then, with a lot of loving help from Rashvi, one of my wives announced she was pregnant. My wives at first objected to having two men in bed with them, even if one was a half-man who had no affection for women. Finally, the aged queen mother had a grandson to continue my father's dynasty.

"In the meantime, I had no way to locate my beautiful Yacobsa. It was as though he had totally disappeared. Then I learned he was sent to a Rabbinical School in Persia. My grandfather on my mother's side had been a rabbi and my brother-in-law was a rabbi. That is why so many in the palace speak Aramaic to this day, including my dear Rashvi. It was because of his knowledge of Aramaic that Yacobsa survived in the women's quarters for as long as he did. Two years ago, I learned that he returned to Chera and was once again living with my sister. A few months later I learned that the whole family moved to Alexandria to investigate more favorable trade relations with Roma. Unfortunately, Rahelani never had a child of her own. For that reason, from the first day we were separated she treated Yacobsa as her actual son rather than her brother. If it weren't for her, I would have no idea what could have happened to him."

He looked at me with tears in his eyes as he asked me again, "What has happened to Yacobsa?"

I wasn't able to start anywhere other than a year ago when we first met. "My dear Abrayamsa, I have only known your brother, whom I love very dearly, for sixteen months. Our ship was laid over in Alexandria picking up a cargo of grain for Roma. One evening when our work aboard ship was completed for the day Hanno, my personal slave who is now a freeman and married to Rashvi, walked with me to see the amazing tower of fire which is used to guide ships safely into the harbor even in the middle of the night. Before we could even reach the tower, we encountered Yacobsa and two other Indians doing the same thing we were. I tried to speak with him about trade with India, but he understood none of the major languages of Europa which I spoke. In desperation I finally made a disparaging statement in Aramaic which he responded to with excitement. I was overjoyed because he was one of the most beautiful men I had ever met. It was then that he told me how we could reach you here in Muziris."

I continued for three hours to share my ongoing relationship with his brother and the love we had for each other. I even shared my efforts to overcome his ten-year long inability to become virile until just a few days before we sailed from Aegyptus. I ended by telling him of Yacobsa's beautiful relationship with Timnah deep in the Aegyptian dessert ten years after his separation from Abrayamsa. Then I asked if his name, Abrayamsa, meant the father of Yacobsa in the Torah. When he told me it did, I smiled and told him that my name meant Yacobsa. Crying for joy he wrapped me in his arms and wept repeating the words "thank you" over and over again as he kissed my neck.

The next morning, I awoke naked in the king's arm's, even though we both decided to avoid all sexual activity. He was so much like his brother, it was easy to see their parallel with Josephus and myself. It was then he asked me why I was not circumcised like both himself and Yacobsa. It was then that I shared my childhood with my Josephus, growing up in the home of a non-religious Jew. The whole time he continued to hold me and kiss me until we needed to go downstairs for breakfast.

By midmorning, Rashvi and Hanno had returned to the palace dock with two chests of samples. In front of the palace, six elephants and their mahouts were ready to carry us up the river and then into the ghats until we reached the palace of King Shikrit of Padyan, a kingdom about twice the size of Chera. My greatest excitement came when all the elephants began to make a trumpet sound as we began to move out of the parade ground.

After an hour in the river, I looked back to see the six elephants behind me, including our two pack elephants, and was I surprised . . . or maybe not really surprised . . . to see another twenty elephants with at least three fully armed soldiers on each elephant's back. Each of us sat on a comfortable leather armchair mounted inside a partially enclosed box with a canopy over it to keep out any rain or too much sun. I shouldn't say each of us because the king rode on an immense bull elephant in a much larger open box and was seated on a small throne with a fully armed soldier standing behind him holding a magnificent umbrella. There was no question that riding an elephant was far more comfortable than riding camels, or maybe even horses.

On each side of the frontier between the two kingdoms was a cargo station for customs payments by transporters of goods between the two kingdoms. It also provided a place to stop and rest on the long journey. Each kingdom provided local servants and cooks to make the night a restful one. Nearing the station, the elephants requiring a rest for the night, stepped out of the river onto the coast road coming down from Padyan to the ocean. The next four days were spent on that road going deeper into the forest and higher into the mountains. At the end of the fourth day we arrived at the marble plaza laid out in front of King Shikrit's mountain palace. It was truly beyond magnificent. It had been built by the king's great grandfather from profits from the Greek spice trade. He also owned three gold mines further up in the mountains which brought him a steady stream of wealth in gold, sapphires, and rubies. When I asked Abrayamsa if he had such mines in Chera, he replied "No," but he guaranteed that I would love their beautiful white and black pearls.

After a night of feasting while getting to know King Shikrit, who spoke only Malayalam and Tamil, we adjourned to our rooms to get a good night's sleep. Once again Abrayamsa asked if I would join him in his bed. That night was definitely good for business, even without the dance of love. The king was obviously Yacobsa's twin in so many ways.

The next day was spent in sharing and evaluating the wine, the high-grade Hispanic olive oil for lamps, top grade frankincense, brilliant emeralds, and blood red coral beads more precious than pearls. The king was impressed by the finer quality of each of these items which he knew he could sell to other merchants, his own nobility, and the high cast Brahmin priests of the temples throughout the country of Padyan. He agreed to purchase everything we had left to sell. We agreed to deliver his entire purchase to the Chera cargo station within twenty days, and there it would be guarded by Chera soldiers until his pack elephants arrived to transport it the rest of the way to his mountain palace.

As it turned out, we also made an excellent profit in our exchange for sapphires, rubies, and even a few large diamonds for a large sack of gold coins even after allocating twenty percent as King Abrayamsa's commission. The one thing we always needed to keep before us in times like these was the twenty-five percent customs tax, we needed to pay in gold to the Roman customs agents in Berenike.

On the second morning, after another fabulous night in the arms of the king, we remounted our elephants and headed home to the sound of nature's unique music of twenty-eight elephants blowing their trumpets to the whole world. The remainder of our time in Muziris entailed the use of our longboat and three of Abrayamsa's barges to empty the ship of all its cargo. The first part of it went up the river to the border station for King Shikrit, where a platoon of King Abrayamsa's soldiers was waiting to guard it until his elephants arrived to take it on up to the palace warehouse. On the last elephant up river, King Abrayamsa sent twenty percent of his emeralds and coral he had just purchased. The balance of the ship's cargo was delivered directly to an empty warehouse in Muziris.

Once the ship was totally emptied, Hanno supervised the reloading of everything purchased from the warehouses in Muziris. Because of the double handling of smaller quantities into only four boats at a time, Hanno's job lasted ten days. Once the accounts were settled with Abrayamsa we still had forty-five percent of our gold left and ten percent of our hold was still empty. We either miscalculated the cargo space in the *Triton* or Hanno got his Galatians to pack it much tighter than we expected.

Sitting down with Sadhu we evaluated our purchases and the space we had left. My first impulse was to take the balance of the ivory. After further discussion, we decided to fill the balance of our empty cargo space with beautiful, translucent, green painted, HanChin pottery as delicate as lotus flowers, and any remaining space after that was loaded with very fine HanChin silk and carved jade. That agreed upon, we weighed out the balance of the ivory and put that much gold aside, then got the clearance price from Abrayamsa for the balance of his HanChin pottery and jade. Putting gold aside for that, then on the last day, our final large purchase of silk was finally weighed out and I took that final small chest of gold to King Abrayamsa myself that afternoon.

By that time, we had called in about half of our crew and three of our archers who had opted to spend their time in India with a companion in Muziris. Of course, the three cargo slaves had been required to remain in the hold as guards. Only one of our eunuch sailors had been interested in the upkeep and communication hassles required to have their own cook, clothes washer, and bed companion. The question for them and the rest of us was how long it would be before we pulled anchor and headed home. It was now late December and the earliest northeast monsoons would be hitting South India at any time. We wanted to be ready when they arrived, so we could immediately begin our voyage back to the Sinus Arabicus and Aegyptus. Some of the other captains were mystified by how the last ship to arrive at Muziris was going to be the first to fill its hold, and now be the first to leave for Berenike. What they didn't know was that the buyer on the *Triton* spent the last few days, and nights, with the King of Muziris.

It was the morning of January 3rd, and the wind abruptly began to blow from the northeast indicating either a possible false monsoon or the first day of the longest storm any of us had ever lived through. If it was, it could continue to blow and begin to rain for the next four to five weeks. Some of the old India hands among our archers were thinking it was worth the small risk to prepare for our early departure. They were sure that we should be able to pull anchor within the next forty-eight hours.

Understanding that we would be the first ship in the Muziris flotilla to set sail, Lucius decided to take the risk. Operating on the archers' assumptions, we agreed that Hanno, Rashvi, and Lucius should accept an invitation to a farewell dinner at Sadhu's home and then to spend the night and have a final breakfast together. As the others scrambled into the longboat at the Muziris dock, I rushed down from the Royal Palace, where I spent one last night, and joined them. Near sunset it began to sprinkle for the first time in over two months. By the time we were in the longboat to return to the *Triton* the next morning, the rain was becoming steady but not heavy. Arriving at the *Triton* by noon, we took a final head count, a quick inspection of the ship and the security of its cargo, pulled anchor, and set the sails. We were off toward the coast of Arabia and home . . . soaking wet!

CHAPTER 49

CINNAMON – JANUARY 30, AD30

Sailing west from the mouth of the Periyar River, I looked back over the rail at the *Triton's* stern, thankful that God had brought me to this land of so many wonders and so much beauty. Under the heavy sky and steady rain, I watched as the stunning coast slowly faded from view. Something inside of me was calling me back, as if it were in fact my home. But why? My task was successfully completed, and I was free to return to my family. Was it King Abrayamsa and his stunning reflection of "Prince" Yacobsa who was calling me back? Was it the exotic beauty and simple life that could be lived there? I really couldn't determine what that Siren's voice inside of my head was calling me to. As my struggle turned to reflection, I understood what that call was . . . the voice of God. It was like his hand which led me to Jerusalem that history changing day. Yes, God was calling me back to India for a strange and unknown purpose. My new life's calling was now to learn what that purpose was.

After six days of constant rain we were more unsure then ever of our current bearing without sun or stars. We needed to be heading straight west, but were we? The next morning the sun broke through the clouds shortly after sunrise but disappeared again within an hour.

That was long enough for Captain Paulus to detect that we were definitely off course, but not knowing how long we had been off course, he had to make an adjustment with no accurate assuredness. For the next four days we continued to sail blindly in the direction we thought was true west. Then at midday the clouds opened again, and we began to closely watch the sun to determine which direction it was going, but again we were foiled after an hour. We had the sense that for the second time we were headed slightly south of true west. Again, we made an estimated correction.

Then after four more days under the clouds, we awoke to a breaking sky with slight patches of blue opening overhead. It took us two hours to understand that the ship had again veered to the south and our course needed a third correction.

But how much correction? Captain Paulus had no way of knowing. We had no capability to back up and find the places and times we veered south, so he could only guess the extent of our necessary northward course correction. Once again, he could only pray for the best. On the morning of the third day after the last correction we awoke to a bright sunny sky, with the sun rising directly in line with the center of our stern. Whatever drifting we had experienced we were now squarely sailing to the west.

We had no knowledge of how much our previous drifts altered our probable landfall. All we could do was continue as we were and find out at the first landfall, where we needed to go next to find Point Elephant. We were twenty-three days out of Muziris on a forty-five-day voyage to Berenike, which meant we should arrive there in four more weeks, plus or minus a couple of days. We were, therefore, quite mystified when the plateaus of Aden appeared to our northeast six days early. We knew immediately that we were the victims of a major error. How could we find out how much of an error we had made?

All of our charts were useless. First, we needed to find out where we were. Looking at the charts one more time, Captain Paulus realized there were very few settlements or landmarks on any coastline in the direction we were headed. The only option we had was to find the nearest village and inquire about our location.

Sailing northwest early the next morning, hopefully in the direction of Aden, we came upon a fishing village strung along a flat sandy beach with a dreadfully modest wooden wharf with several Arab dhows moored at one end. Dropping anchor near the vacant end of the wharf, we lowered the longboat and rowed toward a small cluster of buildings. Dragging the boat out of the surf and onto the sand, Captain Paulus, Rashvi, and I walked to the nearest building which showed any sign of life.

Seeing two Nubian men sitting under a palm thatched awning by an open door, we approached them. They stood as they saw us coming and greeted us in a language we didn't understand. Rashvi immediately attempted a response in both Malayalam and Tamil but failed. Then I tried Aramaic but also failed. Then Captain Paulus took a stab with Latin and succeeded . . . partially. When he asked where Aden was the youngest man pointed back northeast up the coast and said something like, "Here Pano. Aden nine day point around."

Then he asked, "Where come?"

Captain Paulus gave the simple answer. "Come India," and pointed east.

Then the Nubian asked. "Want spice? Cinnamon?" Captain Paulus replied, "No money. Gone,"

Then he turned to me. He quickly asked if Rashvi might know the pricing for cinnamon. He replied, "I know it well, because Muziris usually has a good supply but they were sold out by the time we arrived. The best cinnamon grows on the other side of India and beyond the

Kingdom of Padyan, on the island of elephants, sometimes called Taprobane. I know the pricing for it if you want to try for some."

Captain Paulus turned back to the Nubian and asked, "Cinnamon price. Look, taste."

The man replied, "Yes, yes. No more gone. Cheap price. You look, taste." Captain Paulus nodded and said, "Go see, taste."

The basic conversation completed, we followed the man through the doorway and entering a dark room which smelled wonderful. He lit a small lamp and we saw only three bales, evidently of Cinnamon bark. Pointing to them he opened a corner of each, so we could see the cinnamon and taste it. He pulled a stick of bark out of each bale and handed them to us. Captain Paulus and I both deferred to Rashvi for the first taste. He took a bite and slowly nodded and then passed them on to us. Speaking in Aramaic, I asked what the going rate for one of these would be in Muziris. Telling me, I passed it on to Captain Paulus. Smelling and then tasting the sample, he asked the price for the three bales. The Nubian threw out a number which was nearly double the price in Muziris. Hearing that, Captain Paulus handed the cinnamon back to the man and turned to walk out.

Immediately the man ran to stop him and gave another number. Since Captain Paulus already knew the margins, he waved his hand and kept walking. The man kept after him saying it was his best.

Captain Paulus stopped and slowly turned to face him just after walking out the door. With his face beet red from holding his breath, he pointed to Rashvi and yelled back, "He in house of India King Abrayamsa. I also sell to other India King Shikrit. They never send you cinnamon again. Ever. No, like you cheat us. Me buy Aden not you!"

We continued walking to the ship as the Nubian and his friend finally caught up with us and said in sailor's Latin, "You are right, I not give you my best price. Two gold pieces per bale and they yours."

I told Rashvi what his final price was, and he confirmed that it was a good price. Captain Paulus asked him to bring the bales to our longboat and he would give him six gold coins. We purchased three large bales of good quality cinnamon weighing nearly the same as two grown men for six gold coins. Rashvi estimated that on the Alexandrian market we should get fifteen times that much, in Roma much more. As Captain Paulus went to the ship to get six coins, Rashvi and I waited near the dock for the bales. Within two minutes after the bales were brought to us, Captain Paulus arrived back with the money. We carefully inspected each bale as they were loaded into the boat and headed for the *Triton*. While they were loading the cinnamon down into the hold, I suggested that the cargo slaves stack the three bales as a dividing wall between their sleeping area and the black pepper. Everyone thought it was a terrific suggestion to keep the air at the back of the ship more breathable, but the slaves knew I did it to give them a little more privacy.

Once we reopened the sails and were out of sight of the sleepy fishing village Rashvi approached me with an observation that he was sure the cinnamon we just purchased was actually stolen. He also thought we may have prevented them from being caught as the thieves. Then, he stated that he sincerely doubted they knew the true value of what they had. Laughing, I agreed that I also held that same suspicion.

Within twenty minutes the village was out of sight and we were headed northeast toward Cape Elephant. Going against the monsoon, it took five days to sight Cape Elephant and turn into the Mare Arabicus, then sail seven days west to Aden. With the monsoon now steadily at our backs, we were in a celebratory mood when we sighted the Roman outpost just in time to refill several barrels of much needed fresh water.

As we approached the harbor I found myself alone with Rashvi at the stern of the ship. I decided to take the opportunity to thank him for all he did to make our trip to Muziris such an amazing success. Of course, he was gracious, perhaps even a bit dismissive, but I felt he needed to know how I felt. It did entice him to open up a bit and be less proper with me. To begin the process, I asked him if Hanno met his expectations. Immediately he became quite exuberant explaining that Hanno was a dream come true. He had never felt love anywhere, from anyone, like the love Hanno had given to him. He was actually overwhelmed with the fact that Hanno never felt he could do enough for him. He has even worked constantly to learn Aramaic. Laughing he chided me that now they know how to make love without me.

On that, I turned to look directly into his eyes and declared that Hanno was my first true love after my twin brother, and that I would love him until the day I die. Then I ruined my planed joke when my voice began to break with emotion. Rashvi, took my hand and simply stated that he knew the truth about my love from the day he first met me at Sadhu's house in Alexandria and served us tea. Yes, he knew everything when I arranged for him to unite with Hanno at Alexander's home near Jerusalem. He actually felt that I had given Hanno to him as a gift, and Sadhu gave him to Hanno as a gift. He never knew that such love could exist between friends. With feigned sorrow, I asked if the way Hanno was learning Aramaic meant I wouldn't be needed in their bed again. Immediately, as I turned to walk over to talk with Captain Paulus, I heard him shout back, "Don't be so sure of that!" We had truly built an inseparable family.

As the sound of the anchor hitting Aden's water rang in our ears, relief filled all of our hearts.

CHAPTER 50

SINUS ARABICUS – FEBRUARY 11, AD30

After two days in Aden restocking our supplies, we brought the last longboat of sailors and archers aboard and then discovered one Nubian archer was missing. Scanning the shoreline, he couldn't be found. Do we stay and search for him or do we go? Captain Paulus' order had not been followed, therefore he was obliged to call for the anchor to be pulled and the sails opened. As we sailed away from the Aden shore, we all had our eyes glued to the people along the shoreline looking for our one missing archer. He had disappeared into the city never to be seen again.

Within two hours we rounded the cape of Aden and entered the Sinus Arabicus to begin the final leg of our seven-month ocean voyage. Soon our work would really begin. Three days later the cargo slaves complained of a foul odor in the hold which neither the pepper nor cinnamon were able to cover. Because it was an unventilated space, they were unable to trace its origin. Captain Paulus, Hanno, and I descended the ladder and verified we had a serious problem, but where was its source and what was it? Hanno then had one of his great ideas. Take a sliver of frankincense and light it, then walk it throughout the hold until the odor was no longer detectable, then extinguish the incense and wait a few minutes, then walk the entire hold again until we detect the odor reappearing.

Following his suggestion, we found ourselves waiting and then combing through the hold again until one of the cargo slaves shouted that he smelled it again. We all dashed to the bales of pepper and began to sniff for the most potent area. Locating it, we moved four bales to another area, and then we saw him. Our missing Nubian had been murdered and buried in the pepper while everyone was ashore. Quickly we relit the frankincense and pulled his body into the open passage. He obviously had been killed and buried among the pepper bales while everyone was ashore . . . except for the Captain, Hanno, Rashvi, and me. We had seen the Nubian leave in the longboat full of the other archers.

When did he return? Who came aboard with him? More importantly, why?

Wrapping him in a scrap of sail mending canvas, the cargo slaves took him up on deck into the light where we could examine him and then bury him at sea as quickly as possible. The intense heat had caused the body to begin to decompose and drain fluids. In fact, as we examined the body the slaves went below to scrub down the decking and some spots on the bales. The Captain gave them the remainder of the incense sliver and told them to burn it all. Because this ship had two hatches, they were both left open after dark allowing the air movement to help ventilate the hold. Meanwhile Rashvi examined the body as everyone looked on. Rolling him over, we saw the two wounds in his back. It looked like he had been stabled by a sword and not a knife. There were no swords on the ship, so how was he stabbed with a sword? We looked up to Captain Paulus as he whispered, "We have been robbed."

It had to have happened late at night when the four of us were asleep in the cabin and only one sailor was on guard. The Nubian must have been brought on board by the robber to show him where we kept our gold, jewels, or any other valuables that could be easily removed. But what didn't make any sense was that the Nubian didn't know where any of those things were located. The only thing they could have taken from the hold was ivory. Going down to the hold again, we took one of the oil lamps from its normal location and walked to the ivory with the cargo slaves. After rechecking the area where the body was found, they agreed that three small tusks that had been placed against a support brace were missing, but on careful examination they could find nothing else out of order. Going back on deck, we left the cargo slaves to restack the now dry pepper bales.

It became evident that at least two men had to have brought our man aboard while either our guarding sailor or one of us was busy with something else. Beside the one sailor, Hanno, Rashvi, and I took turns at watch that night. We called the sailor over and we all compared our memories of the night in question. I remembered hearing a thud, but on looking around I assumed it was a cross beam hitting the mast in the breeze. Rashvi remembered hearing a splash, but when he looked overboard toward the shore, he had seen nothing. Then the obvious hit Hanno. Standing on the roof of the cabin during night watch, we couldn't see the front hatch because the archers' tent was pitched between the cabin and the hatch and they probably boarded with our Nubian on the seaward side to avoid easy detection. When he couldn't show them where the gold and jewels were kept, they killed him before they grabbed the tusks and fled. As they were leaving, one of them dropped a tusk on the deck. That was probably what I heard, but I could see nothing because of the tent.

The loss of three small tusks was minor, but the death of one of our archers was terrible. His death stunned all of us, especially the other archers. In questioning the archers, we learned that he and another Nubian were brothers- in-law and his wife would be destitute. The captain asked where they lived and learned they lived in Berenike. He had no children unless one was born while he was away. Captain Paulus made a point that he would visit her as soon as we arrived in port.

As we wrapped, bound, and weighted the body with several ballast stones, I asked Hanno if he would do the funeral. He was honored that I asked him, and he agreed. As soon as the body was prepared, it was carried to the stern where I found Hanno speaking to the Nubian brother-in-law through the translation of one of the Aegyptians. He learned that his name was Akko and that this was his third trip to India. Hanno had asked that the Nubians and Aegyptians stand beside him during the funeral and that the funeral would be in Greek, so it could be translated to the Nubian brother-in-law.

Like we had done with Mago's body, we laid Akko's body parallel to the stern so it would be rolled off into the wake of the ship and disappear. The entire crew was present as Hanno addressed them. He told them that the Creator God of the universe loved his wayward child, Akko, and that God's son had received him in death. He then knelt at the head of the body, placed his hand on the head as in a formal blessing and prayed a magnificent prayer asking God to look after Akko's family and protect them in the years to come. Then he nodded to the slaves to roll him into the sea. At this point Rashvi sang a beautiful song in Malayalam, followed by an "amen" by Hanno, who then turned and embraced Akko's brother-in-law.

For the first time we saw this very diverse crew of multiple languages and cultures come together as a single unit. Even the three

Galatian cargo slaves were included. That afternoon the cook prepared a very good meal of rice, lentils, dried fish, dried grapes, dates, and dried Indian fruit. He had a little wine left in the store, so he brought that out, too. It seemed so strange to see a crew bond on the last few weeks of such a long voyage. They had been a great crew, quick to respond to their captain's orders, always helpful and courteous to the passengers, and they always seemed to be patient on the long and boring voyage. I even began to wonder if there were any thoughts about taking some of the crew, or even a slave, to Alexandria and then bring them back in a few months to repeat it all again.

After spending a few days considering the issue of the crew, I approached the captain about his thoughts on the matter. He agreed that the crew was a good one and the slaves seemed exceptional. The crew had followed every order and expectation like they had worked together before, and perhaps some of them had, and I wondered why I had never thought to ask Hanno about them. The slaves also worked very well together. I had never realized they were all Galatians and cousins until we had to deal with the death of our Nubian archer. I began to wonder how they became slaves.

One day, after the midday meal, I asked the Galatians to join Hanno, Rashvi, and me at the stern where we could speak privately. I knew very little about Galatia, so to get them to open up to us I asked them their real names and if they would tell us about their Greek speaking province in central Asia Minor. Why are most Galatians we had met blond and blue eyed, whereas all of the others from Asia Minor we had ever known possessed dark hair and brown eyes? They appeared excited that we really wanted to know about them and their small province.

Collectively they shared their history. "Our people originally came from southern Gallia, just north of Hispania, and settled in the area north of Macedonia about three hundred years ago. Then our three related tribes split from the main body and crossed the Bosporus and conquered their way across Asia Minor until they were stopped by the Greek army of the Seleucid Empire, who used their frightening war elephants they had brought from their Indian provinces. Forcing our armies to retreat, we settled on the Anatolian Plateau around what became our capital of Ancyra. We slowly dropped our Celtic language and adopted Greek as our neighbors had done. About eighty years ago we were absorbed into the Roman Empire as a province culturally distinct and separate from our neighbors."

Then Hanno told them that he had been a slave for most of his life and wanted to know how they became slaves. In response they told a tale we had heard far too often.

"About ten years ago the Roman general who wiped out the last pirates on the Pontus Euxinus to the north of Asia Minor decided he would retire to a great latifundium he created, to raise wheat for sale to Rome. To do this he confiscated land near the Bithynian-Galatian frontier. Then he illegally sent out slave catchers to the provinces around his estate. At the time our family was participating in a local celebration in a town just a few miles south of the estate's boundary. It was his men who caught the three of us, who are cousins, and we became a part of his great Latifundium. We worked there for four years until, for some unknown reason, we were taken to Byzantium and sold to a ship owner. It was then we learned about loading and packing cargo. Fortunately, we were always kept together."

Then Hanno asked his all-important question, "Were you castrated?"

When they replied they hadn't been, he asked if they were eunuchs. The youngest of the three replied in the affirmative while the other two denied it strongly. I couldn't help but wonder how the three got along without conflict, but when the eunuch then dropped his head in shame, I understood. He acted out the female role for the other two. Nodding I told them we understood, and that their arrangement was what it was, for now. I knew I had just found a new personal slave to take Hanno's place. As I looked at Hanno, he nodded his head.

The younger slave was Tectos, the one who always seemed curious about everything. I then decided to have Hanno tell his story from his childhood castration to the present. For nearly half an hour the three slaves sat spellbound as he shared his story and introduced his husband. By this time Rashvi was understanding quite a bit of Greek and smiled as Hanno spoke of him. In Carthaginian I asked him how he procured the slaves. He simply said they had just arrived on a ship from the north with eleven other cargo slaves for sale. He looked them over and purchased them because they looked like a set and would probably work well together. Slapping him on the back I told him he had a good eye.

For the remainder of our voyage to Berenike I made it a point to know Tectos, the younger cousin, in a more personal way, enabling me to discern if he should be taken to Alexandria or even Syracuse. When he found out that I too was an uncut eunuch, he revealed much more of himself to me. In Galatia, on the Latifundium, and in the holds of ships, eunuchs, cut or uncut, were looked at as sub-male and sometimes subhuman. They were there to be used by the real men as sexual outlets. It turned out that Tectos had a Greek education, and a good one at that. The most amazing thing about him were his eyes, as blue as a bright summer sky. His skin was also amazing, because of years in the holds of ships, he had no ruddiness or tanning. His skin was nearly as white as milk. Because his hair was the color of burnished silver, I could barely see it on his chest or legs.

Six days out from Berenike we spotted another Arab dhow approaching us. Once again Hanno pulled out the shields and the arrows wrapped in oil. Within minutes after we stood in formation along the rail with our tall shields to protect us, the dhow dropped its sails and began to turn away. Several of us thought it was probably the same dhow we encountered eight months earlier.

Six mornings later, as the sun rose to our right, we saw the massive row of ships in the distance ahead of us. By early afternoon we found our berth and slowly drifted into place, and the crew secured our moorings. Our sea voyage was finally over, and it was time to sort out all that happened and what we might face ahead.

CHAPTER 51

DOWN THE NILE – MARCH 13, AD30

After lowering the *Triton's* two pairs of loading planks to the dock, Captain Paulus and I were the first to officially disembark to meet with the Roman customs official. After half an hour of presenting cargo manifests, cost statements, and other documentation including the ship's log, we finally received our customs charge which was to be paid in gold before anything could be offloaded. Those captains who could not pay in gold needed to pay in kind, whether it be pepper, silk, rubies, or ivory. Because of the terrific discounts we received for most of our purchases, there was much more gold left on board than we had ever expected. Therefore, our customs tax was able to be paid in full that very hour.

However, we still were unable to begin offloading the cargo because we had no warehouses in Berenike. The *Triton* was our warehouse and we would wait on the arrival of a large camel caravan which would transport everything to the Nile River. That might require over a week and perhaps two or three separate caravans.

The first thing Lucius and I needed to do after paying the crew and archers was to go with Akko's brother-in-law and an Aegyptian translator to visit Akko's wife. Entering the town, we wandered through many narrow alleys and finally came to a courtyard off one of the alleys. As we entered the courtyard, our Nubian archer called out to those inside the house. Suddenly there was a burst of energy and noise as children and adults rushed into the courtyard to greet us. Among them was an attractive young woman whose smiling face quickly turned to pain when she saw three strange, white men standing with her brother. When he looked to her and spoke, she began to wail. Finally, her mother quieted her as our Aegyptian translator spoke to her briefly. Captain Paulus immediately began to speak in short sentences which our Aegyptian was able to translate. First, he told her of her husband's bravery against thieves who tried to rob our ship and do us harm. Then he presented her with her husband's entire wage. Finally, he handed her three additional gold coins to help her through the months ahead. We all bowed to her in respect and left them to grieve alone.

Arriving back at the *Triton*, we saw that Hanno had already found our agent and had brought him to the ship to meet with Captain Paulus. As newcomers to Berenike, we were unfamiliar with the necessary procedures of offloading the ship and then putting the ship into storage until the next season. There were also other questions. How do we hire a caravan to carry the cargo to Kopios on the Nile? When we arrive there, who do we contact to hire barges to Alexandria? Our agent was our salvation in dealing with all of these questions. He knew he would be well paid if he properly expedited these issues for us. He returned the next evening to assure us that the second caravan to arrive in Berenike within the week would be large enough to transport our entire shipment, and it was already assigned to us.

Meanwhile we dismantled the archers' tent and began moving many of the bulky items, such as spice bales, up onto the deck. The next day we finished stacking the bales and had begun bringing up the baskets of delicate HanChin pottery when our caravan of over one-hundred camels eventually arrived loaded down with bales of dried grass from the Nile Delta. This food for the camels was unloaded close to the well near the edge of town. The camels would be kept there within a secure stone enclosure to eat and drink their fill as they waited to be brought to the *Triton*, ten at a time by their specific driver who they knew and trusted. At the ship, the crew would offload the cargo to be re-loaded onto the camels by the drivers. In the meantime, Hanno was working with our cargo slaves to continue pulling more items up on deck. This gave Captain Paulus the opportunity to evaluate how the three of them worked together and with others.

This procedure continued for four more days from sunrise to sunset. Finally, the *Triton* was empty, and the camels were loaded so Captain Paulus asked the caravan captain how many camels he had left for passengers. He checked at the camel pen and discovered there were eleven available. Captain Paulus determined that there would be fourteen men going back to Alexandria. Our agent assured us that if we offered six drivers two silver coins each, they would share three camels among themselves and give us the other three. When Captain Paulus made the offer, we almost instantly obtained our three extra mounts.

After five days of loading, the caravan captain informed us that first thing in the morning they would be preparing to leave and that we should be there early to be introduced to our individual camels and load them with our personal belongings. Everything had already been packed and each of our four chests of gold were already securely hidden among our personal belongings, so we had the evening to rest and share with the crew our trust in them and what their destiny would be as a part of Aetna Shipping. Captain Paulus told Tectos that he was to be assigned to me, and that his two cousins would be assigned together on his next ship. He commended the three of them for jobs well done. He then turned to the seven crewmen and told them he was proud of their near flawless skill and that he also wanted them with him in the future if they wanted to join him. Unanimously they agreed to follow their captain who would continue to have a crew that was predominately eunuch and cargo slaves who weren't. This was an unusual role reversal, but the captain knew that shore leave would be much easier to deal with this way.

At sunrise, care of the *Triton* was turned over to our agent with the assurance he would see us again in June. Then we grabbed the last of our baggage and began our fifteen-minute walk to the staging area. When we arrived, the caravan was in its final stage of assembly formation. As soon as that was completed, our crew was assigned their individual camels and were located at the back of the caravan with several of the drivers who would insure that no cargo came loose and fell to the ground. The remaining four of us and our three slaves were assigned camels near the front. The sun had risen, and we began our march through town, heading toward the mountain pass and into the heart of the Aegyptian desert.

Because we left in midmorning, our entire six-hour journey to the well at Cabalnum was entirely in daylight. This first oasis we would use as a water stop for food and just a little sleep. We spent the remainder of the day resting and sleeping until the stars appeared overhead. That was our signal to begin our regular routine of twelve hours of night travel and the twelve daylight hours for rest, eating, and sleeping. This routine continued uneventfully for eleven more nights until on the final morning we saw the dark line of trees ahead of us along the Nile River.

When we headed out that final night, we expected to reach the river by dawn, but we did not anticipate a sand storm which forced us to stop in our tracts five hours away from the Nile. It was difficult laying against our camels, but they protected us from the cutting sand all night and into the next day. Like so many other things, the storm did not last long and by early afternoon it was over. With only a few hours left to travel, we mounted up and reached Kopios before sunset. We were all exhausted and slept with our camels one last night before addressing the difficult job of loading the barges for Alexandria.

The next morning, Lucius and I walked through the shady trees down to the river docks to hire six large barges to Alexandria. Fortunately, we were introduced to a barge operator who had five barges which we could begin loading immediately while we waited on a sixth which was scheduled to arrive in the morning. Agreeing to his price, we loaded three of the barges by sunset and the next two were loaded by noon the next day. The sixth barge arrived shortly after sunrise and was offloaded shortly after our midday meal. We immediately set about loading our remaining cargo, so we could set sail down the Nile while there was still daylight.

Captain Paulus decided that I should ride in the first barge with my new slave, Tectos. He would ride in the second with his two cargo slaves. Two crewmen should ride in each of the third, fourth, and fifth barges, while Hanno and Rashvi should ride in the sixth with the cook. Our small flotilla was a spectacular sight as each barge's two tenders raised their sails and began gliding down the river, visually reminiscent of the elephants going up the river in India.

On this trip I was not distracted by Yacobsa, although Tectos was becoming more relaxed and inquisitive with me each day as he learned my story. Both of us were in awe of the sites we saw as we floated by them. We looked in admiration at the ancient cities as we passed by each with its spectacular monuments . . . the stunning temples with their gigantic pylons . . . the huge waterwheels which irrigated the massive fields of wheat along the river banks . . . and finally the great pyramids at Giza with the massive sculpted lion with a man's head carved out of the stone hill in front of them. Looking at my companion. I couldn't help but wonder how many slaves and citizen conscripts it took through the centuries to create those magnificent monuments which held our attention hour after hour and day after day. Unfortunately, without their labor, and often their expendable lives, none of this would have been possible.

Even though the Nile is famous for being a lazy river, we were now flowing with the current and our journey was two days shorter than it had been the previous summer. When we approached the lush delta, we once again took the western most estuary which split off from the main river, entering the massive grasslands and forests which grew so lushly in the delta's fertile soil. It was here I saw my first hippopotamus up close. In the wider river the boats always stayed as far away from them as possible because they were known to attack boats and kill people who fell overboard as invaders of their territory. We also saw several Nile crocodiles, both on the banks and in the river. Being in barges, which were the largest boats on the river, helped me to feel safe, but it still didn't calm all of my tension.

We sailed down Alexandria's river channel which emptied into the Mare Otia, the lake on the south side of the city, and pulled up to its wharf. Once the barge was secure, our Aegyptian crew set about dropping our sail and lowering our mast. This prepared us to be towed through the city canals and under bridges to our docks in front of the huge Aetna warehouse at the far end of the harbor.

Now it was time to wait for the other barges to arrive about fifteen minutes apart. Hopefully the tow camel on duty would also arrive soon to pull us through the canals into the harbor. Fortunately, Captain Paulus' barge reached the wharf within fifteen minutes, and I verified with him that I and Tectos should run ahead to the warehouse to give them time to prepare mooring space for all of us. When the first tow camel arrived, Captain Paulus took my place to guide the camel driver as this would be the first to pull up to our dock closest to our warehouse. My responsibility was to approve all the mooring details with our sergeant.

Once my barge reached the entrance to the harbor, Captain Paulus threw the tow rope back to the camel driver who returned to the lake to tow the second barge into the magnificent harbor. The warehouse sergeant had begun to create the mooring spaces for the six large barges. Frantically he set about talking to our other ship captains about moving their ships closer together, enabling some additional space for the barges to dock. One ship had just finished loading and was waiting for the last of its crew to arrive so it could leave for Athens in the morning. The sergeant offered to row his sailors out to him if he would anchor fifty paces out from the dock. Once he did that, we had room to moor three barges before dark.

As they were mooring the first barge, I had Tectos join me as I ran to Yacobsa's house to inform them that we had just arrived complete with crew and cargo slaves. While performing that vital task, the first barge slowly slid into place as both of its boatmen rowed with all of their might and the warehousemen quickly secured it tightly. About thirty minutes later, the second barge came out from the canal where Captain Paulus met it and directed the boatmen into the harbor and toward its mooring position at the dock behind our first barge. As Tectos and I returned, Captain Paulus discussed the things we required with the Sergeant. They decided to go ahead and moor the first three barges to the dock and temporarily tie the last three barges beside the three moored barges so that they would be two barges deep enabling greater security for our cargo and would keep some space open for other ships. Following that plan we had all six barges secured by an hour after nightfall. We could have never completed bringing in the sixth barge if it were not for the bright light coming from the top of the Pharos.

Exhausted, we had warehousemen stay on the barges overnight to help the boatmen protect the cargo. We would bring food in a little over an hour. When everything was settled and secure, we made our way to Yacobsa's house to get a decent meal and some rest. Suddenly it dawned on me that I forgot to tell them how many we brought with us. Yacobsa and Timnah were startled to see fourteen of us walking into the house. We were more than they anticipated. Naturally the cook suddenly became concerned about having enough food for everyone, so Yacobsa told him to simply bring out cold food and we would all do fine. When Rashvi heard that, he told Yacobsa we also needed to take some cold food down to the barges as well.

Halfway through the delicious meal I decided to test the depth of my friendship with Yacobsa by asking a few pointed questions about how things went while we were away.

"How were things with the Persian carpets? Were you able to get all of the paperwork done before you left for Syracuse? Did you get to Roma and how was everything received? Were the sales strong?"

Excitedly he answered in the affirmative on each point. In fact they were selling so well that after the first day Stephen decided to raise the prices by twenty percent. This was the response we all needed to hear as our Aramaic conversation was translated around in Greek and Latin. Then I decided to drop my bombshell and gauge his response because some of his "family" eating with him that night knew exactly "who" he really was.

"Your Royal Highness, your twin brother, King Abrayamsa, asked that we give you his love, and tell you he misses you deeply."

There was a sudden dead silence as Timnah gasped a loud unbelieving, "Huh?"

Quickly, Yacobsa grabbed Timnah's hand and squeezed it, and looked at me in disbelief. He asked apologetically, "How did you find out?"

"It was hard to hide once we began conversations with your brother, and then your sister, Rahelani, filled me in on the details. They never wanted to deceive us, but things progressed so quickly that they could never find the right way or time to tell us the secret. Once we arrived at the palace the disguise was impossible to maintain. They were very sorry, and I assured them that the truth would never change anything between our two families."

To break the tension and suspense, Lucius dropped his own bombshell, "Jacobus, thirty-nine days ago it was the third of February and if my memory serves me right, it was also your sixteenth birthday".

Suddenly I was the one who had nothing to say except, "How did you know?" Yacobsa and I looked at each other and began to laugh.

I got up, walked over to him, and he stood to welcome me. We threw our arms around each other and continued to laugh as everyone, except Lucius, sat there totally confused. When things quieted down, Yacobsa reached down to Timnah who was seated beside him and lifted him to his feet. He proudly announced that if Timnah would still have him, they wanted to be united as soon as the right person to perform the ceremony could be found. He turned to Timnah and asked, "Will you still have me, even though I am not who I told you I was?"

Timnah looked into Yacobsa's smiling eyes and waited for a moment before replying, "Since you were not trying to deceive me, but the whole world . . . and since it was your wonderful family who was trying to hide your true identity . . . and since you are the love of my life and I cannot live my life without you, I can find no reason to throw our love away now." He wrapped his arms tightly around his prince and kissed him.

Of course, our crew and slaves were still totally overwhelmed by one confusing revelation after another. They had no social or cultural tools to help them process what they had just heard and seen. I glanced around and Lucius was grinning as usual, but looking at each of the others I saw questioning expressions which I understood to mean, "What kind of people are these anyway?"

CHAPTER 52

TOGETHER AGAIN – MARCH 21, AD30

It had been a successful day, but I had one more major task to complete before I could really relax for the evening. I must get a report to Stephen, informing him of our arrival in Alexandria and some of the blessings and surprises of our journey. That meant I needed to get a letter to him by way of our ship leaving at sunrise for Syracuse via Athens. The crew and slaves had just left to relax in the back garden, so Lucius, Hanno, and Rashvi remained with me at the dining table.

We victoriously informed Stephen of the details of our cargo and that we returned with a healthy gold surplus, even after paying Roman customs. We all agreed that Stephen should approve that all ships calling on ports in the eastern Mare Internum with only partial loads needed to be rerouted to Alexandria. There they could fill their empty cargo space with portions of Indian goods for delivery to Syracuse. Lucius also wanted to know if the *Dolphin* could be returned to him for five months if Stephen didn't have another task for him to perform. Also, Stephen needed to know that he was now traveling with his own crew and cargo slaves from our India trip.

While I folded the letter for sealing and delivery to the captain of our ship in the harbor, I inserted a note of my own. I then volunteered to take the letter myself while asking if the Captain anchored next to our barges would be sailing to Syracuse from Athens. Before leaving I went to the garden and invited Tectos to join me as an escort.

When we arrived at the warehouse I checked to see if the Sergeant was in his quarters and was informed that he had just taken the last crewmen to the ship anchored on the other side of our barges. Disappointed but not deterred, I was determined not to miss the ship if they chose to pull anchor as soon as the sergeant's boat headed back to shore. Quickly as possible I climbed out onto the outside barge closest to the ship when I saw the Sergeant coming down the rope ladder to his boat. Calling him over to the barge I asked him where the ship was headed after Athens. When he answered it was Syracuse, I asked him to pull alongside so I could hand him a letter to Stephen. He quickly pulled over and took the letter back to the captain who had heard everything and sent a sailor down the ladder to pick it up. Once he had our letter in his hand he waved to me in acknowledgement.

After I thanked the Sergeant for his help I asked Tectos if he had ever enjoyed Alexandria at night. In a serious tone he admitted that being a cargo slave prevented his enjoyment of anything anywhere at night. Remembering Mago and Hanno that first night out of Valentia nearly two years earlier, I suggested that he follow me. Crawling over our covered cargo to the dock, I took his hand and told him we were going to take a walk. We walked over the canal bridges to the peninsula where the Pharos was built. Walking out to its furthest extremity we stood and looked out at the beauty of the harbor at night, its ships, and its buildings in the flickering light from the giant beacon. Looking up at the Pharos he was in awe of its immense size and the amount of light it sent across the harbor, having never dreamed that anything like that could exist.

After another half hour admiring the harbor's beauty, we turned to walk back to the house. As we neared the gate to the Jewish Quarter, I asked Tectos how old he was when he became a slave and how long ago it had happened. I learned he was taken by the slave catchers when he was fifteen, perhaps nine years earlier, but he wasn't sure because he lived in the hold of a ship. The seasons on the Mare Internum were different from the Galatian Plateau and it was confusing from down in the hold. This meant he was probably near the age of Hanno. When I asked if he had been well treated, he became quiet as a stone. I waited a minute and then assured him that I was more than his new master. It was also my duty to be his protector. To illustrate that, I reminded him of Hanno's story and that he grew into manhood being sexually abused daily by his Roman owners. They used him for pleasure whenever they tired of their wives or wanted to avoid the burden of more children of their own. I knew I hit a nerve when I saw him slowly nod his head.

Then I told him, "Hanno learned to trust me and even love me. I learned that the more he loved and admired me, the more I loved and trusted him. I lived with him and his fellow Carthaginian slave, Mago, for over a year in the hold of Captain Paulus' ship. Eventually I trusted him like a brother for he had risked his life for me, and Mago even gave his life to protect me. A few months after that, on his birthday, I freed him, and he has been my loyal servant ever since. In fact, I sent him to Berenike ahead of any of us with a fortune in gold to purchase the ship for our voyage to India. He was also the one who bought and paid for everything in Berenike . . . even you. By the time we arrived he had the *Triton* purchased and ready to sail. Hanno and I are now like brothers."

Looking at him as closely as possible in the dark streets of the Jewish Quarter, I saw the first visual expression of positive emotion since the day he came aboard the *Triton*. It is a fact that slaves don't smile much, and Tectos was proof of that. All I could do was to assure him that he was safe and would be well cared for. All he needed to do was obey.

Reaching the house, we discovered that most of the men had already found their sleeping mats for the night, so I asked him if he was ready for sleep or if he wanted to continue our conversation. When he said he would rather continue, I took him out to the back garden where we sat by the well. Looking up at the stars, I asked him if he ever considered how they came into being and why they never changed. With a tinge of sarcasm, he replied he never considered where anything came from, just whether he would survive. I understood that his scars were deep, and it would take a miracle for him to overcome the last nine years of pain. I was exhausted, but I believed an hour with Tectos would pay huge dividends in the months ahead. When our exhaustion got the best of us, we found two empty mats in a corner of one of the sleeping rooms. Placing our oil lamp on the floor we laid down to get our first good night's sleep in over three weeks. As I began to drift off, a hand gently touched my arm and a whisper came out of the darkness.

"Thank you for caring about me and for allowing me to sleep next to you." When I awoke the next morning, Tectos' hand was still on my arm as he slept peacefully. I thought for a moment and decided to reach across and gently awaken him by rubbing his shoulder. His eyes slowly opened, and I smiled and reminded him that we had a busy day ahead of us. He smiled back until he realized his hand was still on my arm. Suddenly he had a look of panic and then questioning, as he pulled his hand away in fear of some form of reprisal. I continued to smile and watched as he relaxed and began to sit up. My hand on his shoulder kept him down with some gentle pressure. We looked deeply into each other's eyes and I watched him smile back at me. It was the ideal time to tell him who I was.

"Before we get our breakfast there is one other thing I need to tell you. Tectos, I am a eunuch just like you, so I understand some of your fears. Also, the reason Captain Paulus allowed me to take you away from his crew will help you understand many other things that you will see and hear in the days and weeks to come. Not only am I a eunuch, but so is Rashvi and Hanno, Yacobsa and Timnah, and even Captain Paulus. You also need to know that I am married to the man who is the director of Aetna Shipping. Actually, we are cousins and adopted brothers who love each other so much that I became his male spouse who sits beside his female spouse, whose primary duty is to give him his children. . . ."

I froze midsentence. Last night Yacobsa mentioned nothing about Leah and the baby. I needed to find out how they are. Without explanation I bolted off my mat and headed out the door to find Yacobsa. First, I checked his room and then the kitchen. Running through the house I checked the garden, the latrine, and then the bathhouse. Nothing! He was nowhere to be found. Then I ran back to the kitchen to ask the servants if he had already left for the warehouse. They confirmed that he and Timnah had just left, just as Tectos walked into the room. He had a puzzled look on his face. I told him that we needed to get our sandals on and head to the barges. As we ran to the sleeping room to get them, my explanation awoke everybody in the room. He followed me to the docks just as he would be expected to do. The difference was that he showed true concern for me and my failure to make my inquiry sooner.

At the dock, I saw Yacobsa and Timnah aboard our third barge working with the warehouse men to get it offloaded as quickly as possible and sent on its way. This would allow the barge tied to it to be pulled to the dock for its offloading. Once I arrived, Yacobsa sent Timnah back to the house to get the rest of the crew and cargo slaves down to the docks immediately. Captain Paulus was already in the warehouse working with the sergeant getting everything checked in and matched to our customs manifest from Berenike.

I called up to Yacobsa for a work assignment for Tectos, and while we waited for Timnah to return, I boarded the barge to have a quick conference with our Royal Prince. The first thing I asked was, "Is Leah in good health? What about the baby?" I was relieved to learn that Leah was doing very well and is extremely happy. She had delivered a second son to Stephen which made him absolutely ecstatic. I was also excited for he would be like my son just like Aaron. Coming down from my emotional high, I ran into the warehouse to help direct the warehouse men reorganize the floor space so that all the Indian cargo could be placed together in the same section of the warehouse.

Once the balance of the crew arrived the first barge was emptied and sent off, and the barge next to it was pulled to the dock to be offloaded. The warehousemen who began offloading the barge in the early morning could begin to pack the warehouse. With all the help we now had, things really began to happen. By midafternoon the second barge was offloaded and sent on its way. By sunset the third barge was also offloaded and pushed into the harbor as the boatmen rowed it to the canal and met the camel driver to tow them back to the wharf located on the south side of the city, not far from the back wall of the Jewish Quarter. There the Aegyptians could reset their mast and sails enabling them to head back up the river.

The next morning, we ate our breakfast early and headed for the dock once again. With our midday meal delivered to us to save time, we were able to send the sixth barge on its way well before sunset. That gave us time to get the last of the cargo into the warehouse before dark.

We were ready to begin organizing the warehouse the next morning. With everyone working hard the following two days, we knew where everything from India was located and we could begin loading it onto ships headed anywhere near Syracuse. Captain Paulus gave everyone a day off to do what they wished, but they were required to spend the night at "home." The Warehouse Sergeant was expecting a ship from Caesarea and also one from Cyrene at any time. He knew the one from Cyrene was headed to Sidon and the one from Caesarea was headed to Cyrene but was unsure of its port of call after that. I sincerely prayed it would be Syracuse.

The first ship in, came from Cyrene on the day the crew was on leave. It remained in port three days for offloading and loading cargo. On its third day in port, the ship from Caesarea arrived and began offloading by midafternoon. When the captain came ashore, I approached him and introduced myself. After telling him of our trip to India, I asked him what his port of call was to be after Cyrene. He answered it was Corsica and then on to Ostia. I asked how full his hold would be between Alexandria and Cyrene and then from Cyrene to Corsica. He shared that his largest cargos were offloaded in Alexandria with only a small local delivery going to Cyrene, with nothing to pick up there. This meant that the hold would be over a third empty when it left Alexandria. Then I asked if he could stop at his home port in Syracuse on his way to Corsica to deliver a cargo of ivory and spices along with myself and my personal slave. That caught him totally off guard, but he was obliged to do as I asked, especially when I mentioned that I was Stephen's brother.

With our passage cleared, I searched the warehouse for Lucius to tell him what I had done. When he heard, he asked what ship had just pulled in. When told him the *Swallow,* he ran to find the captain. It turned out that they knew each other quite well and he verified my story. The final items of Alexandrian cargo were offloaded from the *Swallow* the next evening, and they were ready for us to load the Indian cargo in the morning. I told the captain that we would bring aboard ten bales of spices, two baskets of Chinese pottery, and fill the rest of the space with ivory and several moderate chests of personal items. With the help of some of our crew to get it on board and with our three cargo slaves helping to pack, it was all loaded before sunset.

The captain informed me that they would be ready to leave Alexandria in the morning, and we could spend the night on board if we desired. I agreed that would be the easy solution. Tectos and I joined everyone at the house for dinner, said our goodbyes, and picked up all of our personal affects and headed back down to the *Swallow*. We arrived on deck twenty minutes later and the captain told Tectos he could join the cargo slaves and I could join the crew in their cabin. Immediately I shocked him when I told him I would sleep in the hold with my slave. This actually caught Tectos even more off guard.

The next sunrise found us sailing out of Alexandria's harbor on our way to Cyrene. In the evening several days later, we sailed into Cyrene's island port of Apollonia. We offloaded our modest cargo in an hour and prepared to depart for Syracuse the next morning after breakfast. Tectos and I had been sleeping in the bow with the three bales of cinnamon and seven bales of black pepper. It proved to be an overpowering fragrance but not terribly unpleasant. We enjoyed our private time together as Tectos grew more relaxed and trusting of me each night. I began to feel that the bonding process for Tectos had progressed very well. I needed him to trust me with his life, so I could then trust him with my own. The Greeks often said that training a personal slave was much like training a horse. Trust was always the key.

Five days out of Cyrene we saw the mountains of Sicilia on the horizon at sunset. The next morning, we would make out the faint outline of Syracuse on the line between mountain and sea. By sunset we were ready to pull into the bay, but the captain decided to wait until morning. I had a restless night unable to wait for the sun to rise which I would not witness buried deep in the hold. When I heard the anchor coming up, I knew it wouldn't be long before I would see my love. Drifting along the dock and watching the bow hand throw the mooring rope ashore, I could hardly wait for the planks to go down. Before they did, however, the Sergeant and some of his men came out to see what unscheduled ship had pulled in so unexpectedly. Immediately upon seeing me, he sent a runner to Stephen as I called out to greet them. I had Tectos go down into the hold and bring our personal items up as the sergeant ran up to greet me as soon as the planks hit the dock.

When our personal items were at my feet, I told Tectos to get the other slaves and some of my friends among the warehouse men to bring up the chests as well, for they would be taken directly to the house. I watched him closely as these unfamiliar orders were immediately executed. I had the warehousemen take it all down to the dock and place them next to the warehouse door. Only then did I let our sergeant know that I had also brought ten bales of spices, two large baskets of green HanChin pottery, three bales of embroidered silks, and over a hundred large tusks of fine ivory. When I told him that it was only a tenth of what was coming, he rolled his eyes laughing that he needed to get busy in the warehouse.

As the spice bales began coming out of the hold, I saw people turning the corner and running down the dock toward us. The first one to reach me was Aaron who jumped up into my arms to kiss and hug me like I was his lost puppy. Then came Stephen, and it was I who stepped into his arms to kiss and hug him like he was my lost puppy.

He was followed by Leah, the girls, and a nurse carrying her new son. Leah also hugged and kissed me, but more like a brother. The baby was six months old and as beautiful as any child created by Stephen. Haji and Rufus were the last, but they were also beside themselves with excitement.

Stephen and I walked up the plank together to greet the captain who I thanked for enabling us to be there. I called down to the Sergeant to let him know they could begin offloading as soon as the cargo slaves brought our many items to the open hatch. Before going home, I wanted to show Stephen exactly what we had down there. When we crawled out of the hold and prepared to head for the dock, I told him that what he saw was only a tenth of what we brought. He was ecstatic! Stephen stopped to greet the Captain againand also thanked him for dropping us off. When no one was looking, he gave him two gold coins as a tip.

At the warehouse door I gave the Sergeant our shipping papers to inspect and asked him for some of his warehousemen to assist us with the chests.

When we walked through the massive wooden doorway, I knew I was finally home, and we were all together again.

CHAPTER 53

HOME – APRIL 17, AD30

I led our porters to the central atrium and had them line up the chests in a specific order, facing the front of the house. After all of the porters except Tectos left to continue offloading the ivory, I called the family into the atrium for a presentation of our voyage's treasure. As I pulled five keys out of my pouch tucked away in the lining of my tunic, I turned to Stephen and declared, "Stephen BarSirach, Director of Aetna Shipping, it is my honor to present to you some of the proceeds of the *Triton's* trading mission to Muziris, India. It was there, with the help of our new trading partners, Rabbi Sadhu, his wife, Her Royal Highness, Princess Rahelani and her brothers, His Royal Highness, Prince Yacobsa, and His Royal Highness, Abrayamsa, King of Chera, we were able to experience the most successful venture imaginable."

With that announcement I waited for the shock to subside. As they began to ask questions about so many royal titles, I assured them we could discuss those details later. First, I wanted them to see what that partnership made possible in such an amazing land.

I handed the first key to the stunning Tectos and he opened the first chest as everyone gasped. It was filled with the world's finest frankincense from the exotic lost island of Socotra. I asked Haji for a knife and a burning lamp, and then I cut a sliver from a ball of frankincense, placed it on the knife's blade, and lit it. The atrium was quickly filled with the most aromatic incense which lingered enchantingly throughout the house.

When Tectos opened the second chest, even Stephen gasped. It was filled with carved and polished jade from the jungles of Chryse across the Sea beyond the kingdom of Yacobsa's cousin, King Shikrit of Pandyan. Each piece that was exquisitely set as stunning jewelry, was mounted in some of the finest worked gold I had ever laid my eyes on.

The contents of the third chest drove them wild. It was filled with cups and plates of solid gold which were subsequently filled with hundreds of rubies and sapphires, both uncut and cut, from the mines of King Shikrit. Many of these magnificent gems were also fashioned into beautiful pieces of jewelry, also set in gold.

The fourth chest was a great surprise, for it was half filled with gold coins and setting on top of the gold was a small chest. It was a thrill to explain that this was the gold we had left after buying the *Triton*, fitting it out, paying the crew, buying slaves, hiring nine archers, renting six Nile barges, and paying our twenty-five percent Roman customs charge.

Then I asked Tectos to open the little chest setting on the gold. Everyone was speechless for it contained five large cut diamonds which were given to us by King Abrayamsa and his cousin King Shikrit. They were setting on a deep bed of large strung white and black pearls, a gift from King Abrayamsa.

When Tectos opened the fifth but smaller chest everyone remained quiet until Stephen finally asked, "Where did all of THIS gold come from?" Smiling, I replied, "This was the twenty to thirty percent discounts we didn't have to pay for our purchases. So, rather than buying one hundred elephants like Hannibal, we just brought it back home again." Everyone went wild for that was the same as a double profit . . . paid up front. Considering our ship, deeply filled with an amazing cargo of fabulous treasure, it seemed unreasonably excessive!

As everyone gathered around the open chests to admire the vast treasure, I pulled Stephen aside. While holding his hand I asked how we did with the carpets from Persia. He kissed me passionately and assured me that they made a fortune for Aetna Shipping. I grabbed him and squeezed with all my might as I exclaimed that I knew we could do it.

Since it would be another four hours before our evening meal, I asked if my slave, Tectos, and I could have a small meal of lunch leftovers to hold us over until dinner. Immediately Haji had the cook begin to make up two massive plates of food for us.

Before I could get to Tectos, who was standing behind the chests watching me, Stephen asked who he was. I told him that after Hanno purchased the *Triton,* he also hired a fabulous crew and some very helpful archers. Then the day before we left for India, he brought aboard three slaves he had purchased earlier for use in the hold. They were cousins from Galatia who had worked together in the holds of ships for nine years. He told me he bought them because they seemed like a "perfect set," and he was right. Once we got to India, I realized I was going to need someone at my side to help me with details, so I watched this one's performance closely. Then when we returned to Berenike, I decided it was time to get to know him and for him to know me. First, we traveled together across the desert and then on the same barge down the Nile. By the time we arrived in Alexandria, I really had the opportunity to watch how he followed orders and how seriously he took the tasks assigned to him. Then I told him who I was and what I needed in a personal slave . . . which seemed to frighten him until we took a night time walk around the harbor. That night I told him that Aetna's working agent who bought our ship, bought him, and arranged most of our details was our former cargo slave who proved his loyalty and abilities to us. At that point his fear of me as a master disappeared and I began to see ever growing signs of his trust and hope for a better life.

As I finished telling Stephen many reports of our missions' success, Stephen asked Haji to escort the young slave to us for a meeting. As Haji left, Stephen turned and commented that the slave looked like a beautiful Greek god carved in the finest white marble. We were still laughing as Haji approached us with a very nervous Tectos. Before Haji said a word, he bowed deeply, as he often does when he wants to appear formal. Following his lead, Tectos did the same while keeping his eyes on me. I think he was still recovering from what was in the five chests I had him open. It finally hit me that he probably never thought there could be that much treasure anywhere outside of the Emperor's palace. I looked into his eyes as he straightened up and continued his gaze. Then I realized he was probably in shock after discovering that he had been sleeping with that treasure for months.

To set him at ease as much I knew how, I stepped over to him and placed my arm around his shoulder as I turned to face Stephen. "Stephen, I would like you to meet my valued servant, Tectos of Galatia. He has performed excellently throughout our entire voyage and has never resisted any request that I know of from myself or anyone else. Tectos, this is your supreme master, Stephen BarSirach, Director of Aetna Shipping, my cousin, my brother, and my husband. I am sure you will find him to be the greatest master in the Empire. All he asks is that you always do your job to the very best of your ability and answer his questions honestly and without fear of consequences."

As standard procedure, Stephen simply welcomed Tectos into his home and assured him that he would be safe within its walls. Then he panicked Tectos in the same way he does most slaves. He extended his hand in friendship. As Tectos quickly glanced at me, I nodded my head in affirmation. Extending his hand to Stephen he then experienced an emotional breakdown. As Stephen released Tectos' hand and put an arm around his shoulder, he led us into the dining room for a great lunch, perhaps the best Tectos had ever eaten. As we began our meal Stephen left us alone to sort out Tectos' new life. And he had a lot of sorting to do! He was beginning to comprehend that his life as a slave would never be the same as it was before Hanno bought him from the itinerant slave trader who sailed into Berenike six months earlier. We all knew it would take time, but he appeared to have the right disposition to adjust to this new life quicker than most.

Finishing our meal, we returned to the atrium to work out some important details with Haji. He would serve as Tectos' guide through the hidden traps slaves often face when they move from a ship or latifundium into an elegant residence. The advantage Tectos had was that he spoke an educated form of Greek and had a rudimentary knowledge of Latin from his four years working on the latifundium, and as I had just recently learned, his father was a provincial king who Tectos had watched as he held court. It was becoming more evident every day that there were many things about this slave I needed to know, especially why his hair, skin, and eyes were fairer than his cousins, but first things first.

With Tectos off with Haji, I returned to the atrium to relock each chest for storage in Stephen's office, a task which Festus and Tectos could complete after dinner. But my important task was to spend a few hours alone with Stephen in our room. The second I walked in I knew I was truly home. The bedclothes were pulled back, the shutters to the atrium were secured, and two oil lamps were burning on stands on each side of the bed. Best of all, Stephen was laying in the center of the bed, ready and waiting. Removing my clothes as quickly as possible, I climbed into his arms while praising God for his goodness to me. It was an unbelievable afternoon in the arms of the man at the center of my very existence. The fragrance of his body after nearly seven months of separation was almost more than I could handle. Every minute, every second, was burned into my memory. His gentleness and his power, his romance and his dominance, but most of all his love carried me away to the gates of paradise. The five hours we had together seemed more like five minutes, and soon Haji gently rapped on the door announcing we had fifteen minutes until dinner.

After a grueling afternoon with Haji, Tectos looked exhausted yet happy when he was brought to dinner to sit beside me, dressed in a new tunic. Actually Haji looked a little too happy as well. Then when Festus walked in following an afternoon helping at the warehouse, I understood why starry-eyed grins were evident on both their faces. Then, in bolted my little shadow whom I loved dearly. Before settling into his chair beside Tectos, Aaron crawled into my lap and kissed me so intensely that I was forced to push him away to avoid an altercation with his mother. Looking over to her I was surprised to see a genuine smile on her face, indicating she knew that I was her son's "adult" idol.

Once we were all seated, Leah lit the candles and Stephen recited a prayer in Hebrew. At the word *Amen*, the servants entered with a true celebratory feast, which totally baffled Tectos, and that which caused me to ask everyone to speak in Greek rather than Aramaic. During dinner I was bombarded with scores of questions about India. When I told them about the elegance of Yacobsa's brother and that they were twins like my brother and I, they declared that was too improbable.

As unlikely as it seemed I finally convinced them with a string of anecdotes. Then when I told them that Prince Yacobsa had studied at a Rabbinical School in Persia like his father, the shouts of impossible rang out again. Then when I told them that Sadhu's carpet contact in Persia was as good as gold, it hit them. The carpet merchants were also a part of the Jewish Diaspora network, and apparently very close and solid with Sadhu and Yacobsa. Sadhu had also assured me that they saw us as a part of their diaspora network and that was why our prices were so much better than anyone else's.

Then I mentioned that I had a record of all our Indian costs packed in my personal belongings which I would use to create a spread sheet, so we could take Sadhu their share of the profits next summer. It was exciting for me to share how unbelievable they were as our agents, even on the mysterious island of Socotra where we made our purchase of the superior frankincense. Because of Sadhu and Rahelani, we filled our ship to the brim in a little over a month. In fact, we were the last of twelve ships to arrive in Muziris and the first to leave, in less than a hundred-twenty days. We rode in on the tail of the southwestern monsoon and rode out on the second morning of the northeastern monsoon. Actually, because of the ferocity of the monsoon we became lost and landed south of Cape Elephant in Pano, where we think we bought the last three bales of stolen cinnamon at ten to twenty percent of the price we would have paid in Aden.

Our only disaster occurred in Aden where one of our archers, who we hired to fight off pirates, was kidnapped when all but three of us were ashore for the night. He was then brought back to the ship to lead his abductors to our treasure hidden in the ship's hold, which he could not do because he had no idea where it was. They then killed him, buried him in the bales of pepper, took three small tusks, and rowed their small boat back to the city. It was Tectos who discovered his body three days later and ascertained that their only booty was the three small tusks. Hanno performed his third funeral at sea . . . and he did it as fine as any rabbi. The ceremony was followed by a beautiful funeral song by his husband, Rashvi.

With that simple revelation about Hanno and Rashvi, I was hit by questions from both Leah and Haji. Looking over to Stephen my eyes must have told it all, and he promptly shared that part of the story about the marriage of Hanno and Rashvi which took place in Jerusalem in the home of Leah's nephew, Alexander. Naturally that caused more questions. I was more than thankful that Stephen was there, for he handled it much better with Leah than I ever could.

As the dinner continued, I kept an eye on Tectos, attempting to evaluate his manner of eating a real meal. The longer I watched him the more I understood something I really didn't expect. It was becoming obvious that he was adjusting much quicker than a simple cargo slave could ever be expected to adjust. I was becoming more certain that there was more to this man than I had been led to believe. I needed to learn more before he joined me on our first trip to Rome. The more I thought about it, the clearer the solution to my challenge became. Looking back at the time I spent with Hanno and Mago, I realized that there had to be a great deal of personal time invested with Tectos. But how could this be done with the family all around us?

After a wonderful night with Stephen, I awoke feeling refreshed and ready to face the many tasks I had ahead of me. First, I needed to take Tectos to the warehouse and begin organizing our shipment before another load arrived from Alexandria, which could happen at any time. That would depend on when the ships left Alexandria, and the number of ports of call between there and Syracuse. The more I contemplated the potential congestion ahead on the dock, the more I realized I could not put it off another day. Speaking with Stephen, he agreed and said it would be a wonderful way for Tectos to learn our systems, especially since he already knew the cargo. I agreed to speak with Tectos immediately, before breakfast.

Running to Haji's room I knocked on his door and waited. Hearing voices inside I knew he was there, so I waited a minute more before knocking again. Just as I lifted my hand the door opened slightly, and Haji stuck his head out. When I asked if he could tell me which room he had given to Tectos, he turned a deep red and opened the door. Walking in, I saw Festus and Tectos laying in Haji's large bed. All I could do was laugh and shake my head. Standing next to me in an aroused state Haji simply stated that he felt sorry for Tectos and was just trying to help him feel welcome. By the look of things, he was obviously feeling very welcome. Then before Haji or I could say another word Tectos spoke up without waiting to be asked. When I looked at him in surprise that he, a slave, had the courage to cut his master off, he blushed and apologized.

With that corrected, I nodded for him to continue. With the assurance of my nod, he threw back the sheet that was over him and Festus, stood up and came to me and bowed his head and asked if he could explain. Reaching out to lift his chin so that his eyes could look directly into my own and see that there was no anger, but only my compassion as I studied his stunning white body highlighted with a few beautifully placed soft dabs of pink. Bringing my eyes back up to his own, I asked him to continue.

"When I was fifteen my cousins and I were out hunting rabbits about two miles from the town where our parents were officiating at a festival. We were still on Galatian land controlled by my father, and I knew the area very well and entered a small wood and located a brush fort we had maintained every year at this time when we came for the festival. It was a refuge from prying eyes. We had removed our tunics and began playing soldiers. Being the youngest, my cousins were the Roman legionnaires and I was the vanquished Gallian. Playing our roles properly, I was the one who was always sexually vanquished by the Romans. I was also being verbally degraded by my cousins as one mounted me from behind, and I satisfied the other with my mouth. We were so into what we were doing, we didn't hear the slave catchers who were creeping through the brush to find the source of all the noise. By the time we saw them, it was too late. The only consolation was that I watched as two of the men raped my cousins, just as they liked to "pretend" they were doing to me.

"What happened after that is irrelevant, except that from then on we were always on the bottom because of our youth. Once we were sold as cargo slaves in Byzantium, things went back the way they were in our brush fort, with me being the one who was actually raped. This continued even in the hold of the *Triton*. I might as well be a woman as far as they were concerned. It wasn't until the day we left Berenike for Alexandria that the rapes stopped, thanks to you, my new master. Your kindness and concern for me caused me to fall in love with you, and I cannot stop myself nor apologize for it. When I met Haji yesterday afternoon, he somehow already sensed that I was a eunuch and that I had a serious problem with abuse. After conversing for about half an hour, he finally asked me if I had ever been treated like a man. When I told him that I had always been treated like a woman, he asked if I would like to know what it felt like to make love to someone as a man. When I answered yes, he taught me for the rest of the afternoon. It was unimaginable! Then last night Haji asked if I would like to spend the night with Festus and him. So, here we are. Now I finally know what it is like to be a man.

"Master, I am very sorry if I have violated your trust in me."

With that last statement I could not contain my tears for another second. Walking up to him, I put my arms around his stunning nakedness and kissed him full on the lips for nearly a minute. Then I felt his manhood come alive, immediately stopping me. Happy beyond words I gave him a giant hug and told him to never address me as master again and to get dressed for we were going to spend the day in the warehouse. While he was rushing to dress, I walked over to Haji to kiss him and extend a gigantic thank you for what he and Festus had done for Tectos.

Knowing my handsome slave loved me, we ran to the kitchen for a quick breakfast before we headed for the docks.

CHAPTER 54

SPREADSHEETS – MAY 15, AD30

Arriving at the docks we discovered men running everywhere in an effort to remove all of our cargo from the *Swallow's* hold, so they could set sail for Corsica. There were piles of tusks and bales of pepper scattered along the dock waiting for space to be found in the warehouse, which increased our risk for theft. Walking into the warehouse, I left Tectos to watch the ivory while I went in search of the sergeant. It suddenly became obvious what the problem was that they were having. The Sergeant was meticulously reorganizing the warehouse as we did the year before to store and price the Persian carpets and Sadhu's own shipment from India. There was a strong chance that we would once again need Stephen's younger cousins to help with the paperwork, but first it was imperative that I ascertain Tectos' writing and math skills. To my delight I soon discovered that he had an exquisite hand to write Greek and could cypher numbers in his head as quickly as Josephus. He would definitely be our lifesaver.

In my desperation, I suddenly realized this year's shipment would be totally different because of the large quantity of bulk items. Therefore, we simply needed to get the cargo moved into the warehouse where it would be much easier to deal with. Also, I needed Tectos to go back into the hold to assure that everything from India was already pulled out.

As I addressed the space issues with the Sergeant. Tectos took a thorough appraisal of the cargo on the dock and then everything that had been placed in the warehouse by sunset the day before. He quickly ran up on deck to check what was up there, and then to the hold to check if there was anything that remained down there. Having lived in the hold with the cargo for ten days he was familiar with all that was down there. Everything seemed to have been removed until he checked the remaining cargo going to Corsica. Behind a stack of cedar timbers from Sidon he spotted a medium sized tusk wrapped in a large piece of red silk which was used as packing in the baskets of HanChin pottery.

He left it where it was and dashed to the warehouse to call the Sergeant and me.

Just as we entered the hold, we saw a crewman moving the silk wrapped tusk to another hiding place. The Sergeant immediately called him to halt, which he was obliged to do since he couldn't escape. Tectos grabbed the thief by the back of his tunic and called up through the hatch to reach the Captain. At the same time the thief dropped the tusk on his bare foot. Standing on one foot he was screaming while Tectos still held him by his tunic. I came back into the hold with the Captain and I saw who the thief was. He had tried to befriend me many times on our way from Alexandria, asking questions about our voyage and what we brought back from India. He also had tried to seduce me twice.

I began to call him out by his name, Horse, while challenging his sanity. He had evidently thought I was simply delivering freight to Syracuse, not realizing that both the freight and the ship he was on was owned by my family. Obviously Tectos knew him, too, and was very angry, perhaps vindictive. But it was the Captain who was really livid. Coming down the ladder he was a witness firsthand, to Tectos' struggle with a thief. This made him look very bad . . . harboring a thief in his crew without knowing it. The Captain told him to get up on deck. While he tried, he continued screaming about his broken foot. Finally, losing his patience the Captain took off his belt and began to lash the thief who finally crawled up the ladder and fell face down on the deck, screaming in pain.

While everyone ran up the plank to see what was going on, Tectos slid back down the ladder and retrieved the tusk and its silk wrapping and took it into the warehouse. He returned to reenter the hold and while he was down there the Captain demanded the thief tell him if he had hidden any more of his master's cargo. Our felon sobbed loudly and nodded his head. The Captain demanded what and where it was hidden. The Captain lashed him one more time which caused him to scream, "Some pottery" just as Tectos climbed out of the hold carrying two very fine pieces of HanChin pottery bowls beautifully covered with paintings of exotic birds.

The Captain lashed him again and repeated the question. This time Horse sobbed and then screamed that he didn't take anything else. Furious, the Captain rolled him over on his back and looked at his crushed foot and ordered his first mate to go into his cabin and bring back his wood chopping ax. While the mate was gone, he told the thief that he had brought judgment upon himself for his foot was beyond repair and needed to be removed NOW. If it wasn't, he would die a slow agonizing death as it began to rot.

When the first mate returned with the ax, he ordered a seaman to bring a scrap board from the repair box. Returning with the board, the Captain ordered him to place it under the thief's ankle. He then ordered his mate to chop the foot off above the ankle and throw it into the sea for the fish. With a soul wrenching scream the foot was off and into the sea. Turning to me he apologized for the incident and promised no one in his crew would ever try to steal from anyone ever again.

Feeling sick, I left the ship and went into the warehouse to recover for a few minutes on a sack of wheat. Tectos instantly wiped my forehead with a wet cloth as I lifted my head from my hands, He knelt before me and asked if I was sick or just in shock. I looked at him and smiled, thanked him for his help, and told him I was feeling much better.

When Tectos went back aboard the *Swallow* to double check the hold and bring in the two bowls, I tried to stand a few times, but the persistent dizziness forced me to remain on my makeshift stool. Soon Tectos returned and assured me that everything was out of the hold and announced he would be back in a few minutes. While he was gone, I walked around the warehouse to regain my senses. The Sergeant and our warehousemen entered and continued sorting the existing freight and bringing in the remainder of the tusks from the deck and stacking them in the far corner where we had stacked Sadhu's ivory the year before.

After twenty minutes Tectos returned and apologized for taking so long. He had been with the Captain to learn what he was going to do with the thief. It seemed they were going to bind his leg and then take him to the center of the city where he could beg for the rest of his life, however long that might be. I reached into my tunic and brought out three copper coins and a silver one and handed them to Tectos. I told him, "Go with the crewmen and find out where they put Horse. Give him these coins and then come right back for I need you in the warehouse."

The warehousemen and I had been stacking the ivory, when it dawned on me that I should ask the Sergeant about mounting the giant pair of tusks taken from a rouge bull in rut who had killed at least two villagers. Telling him that I wanted them for behind Stephen's desk, he enthusiastically informed me that there was a skilled craftsman in town who could complete the job in less than two weeks. When Tectos walked in the door I asked him to coordinate the project with the Sergeant.

At that point there were only nine bales of pepper, one bale of cinnamon, and two baskets of Han pottery left to stack and all would be complete . . . for now. Thanking everyone an hour later for their help, I told them I would be back in the morning to help them prepare for the next ship, whether it was bringing our cargo or not. I then took Tectos with me to visit the Captain of the *Swallow* before they pulled out with the tide in a few hours.

When I came aboard, visit the Captain was extremely apologetic about the incident earlier and asked that I assure Stephen that everything had been taken care of. I sincerely thanked him for helping us, but I also wanted to know more about the thief. I learned he was from Thracia and had been with the *Swallow* for less than a year. His Thracian name was too difficult to pronounce so the crew had just called him Horse. As far as anyone knew, he had a wife someplace, but no one knew for sure where. He had been a constant trouble maker on shore leaves, especially in the brothels where he would often rent a woman and a young man together. In the morning when he would come back to the ship, he was often followed by the brothel owner, who demanded more money because Horse would usually leave the young man he had rented unusable for several days. He never seemed to damage the women, but he was ruthless in his use of the young men. After I thanked him for his help, I went ashore and followed Tectos as he led me to the spot where Horse had been dumped.

We found Horse lying against a crumbling wall leading to a narrow alley in the city center. He was crying as he held the cloth wrapped around the stump of his leg. He had his face buried in the sheet the crewmen brought him in. Tectos immediately observed that his stump was still bleeding heavily. Horse heard us speaking and looked up in sheer terror. Finally, I was able to calm him down and reassured him that he had been punished enough. While I spoke, Tectos opened the bloody rag around his leg and told me the end of the leg bone was shattered as the ax cut through it. He needed to tie a tourniquet around his leg, or he would bleed to death by morning. Tearing off a strip of the cloth he was laying on, I gave it to Tectos as he finished picking out pieces of bone from the stump. He quickly tied the strip of cloth around the stump as tightly as he could. Then he tore a larger piece from the sheet and rewrapped the stump. As Tectos finished dressing his stump I ran to the nearest street vender and bought a small flask of wine, a loaf of bread, and a chunk of cheese. Giving them to Horse, I assured him that we would return in the morning to check on him again.

We returned to the warehouse as the loading planks for the *Swallow* were being hoisted aboard, and I called to the captain to see if he was ready to cast off. Hearing his affirmative reply, I walked over to the bow line to release his mooring and cast him off. Within minutes the bow sail was opened, and he gave me the signal to throw the rope aboard as Tectos did the same at the stern. Taking a pole, I pushed her off and she started to become a dark memory.

As I walked into the warehouse, I checked our cargo and asked the sergeant when the next few ships were scheduled to arrive from the east. Checking his board, he said one could arrive in the morning from

Corinth and another from Alexandria in three days. I requested he also inform us in the future of each scheduled arrival. Then we headed home to begin setting up our cost and profit spreadsheets patterned after the ones we had developed for our last shipment of Indian goods.

With each day, Tectos revealed a sliver of light into his life and heart so I could know how to better understand him. The way he would care for Horse was amazing. Even though he didn't like him, he visited him twice a day to feed him, check his leg, take him a bowl to urinate and defecate into, and even wash him when he was soiled. I found it amazing that a slave would show such compassion to someone he disliked. Occasionally someone would drop a coin on his sheet, but otherwise Tectos would ask for a coin every few days to keep him fed. Through all of this we learned why the crew called him Horse, and it truly bothered Tectos that a man gifted with such a physical asset could turn out to be such a self-centered and destructive idiot.

I watched his compassion and his natural ability to take control of a situation as difficult as Horse. I asked him what made him that way. He shrugged his shoulders and remained silent. Then one morning we were sitting on the dock watching the fish swim at our feet while waiting for the arrival of our ship from Alexandria. Without warning he opened up to me. What I learned made me feel proud and ashamed simultaneously. Without apology or hesitation, he took my hand in his and began to share how Hanno helped him adjust to the long and boring voyage to India.

"Hanno shared your experiences in Jerusalem last year and how that changed his life. He shared how both of you were attracted to Jesus and how moved you were as you watched Jesus being lowered to the ground from the cross the Romans had nailed him to. He spoke of your emotions as you watched his beloved John hold his legs as the nails were pulled out of his hands. He assured me of the great impossibility when he arose from the dead and walked out of his tomb and continued to teach his followers for more than forty days until he was carried into the sky and disappeared. He also told me what happened when the spirit of God came upon many of you as you worshipped Him one afternoon and many began to praise God in languages they had never learned. He claimed that day had totally changed his life and Rashvi's too."

I was suddenly compelled to squeeze Tectos' hand and began to weep. Tectos was truly a jewel! I asked him what he thought about the things Hanno shared with him. Instantly he responded with a forceful, "I saw the truth in his words and accepted them. The voyage to India changed my life. I no longer felt like a slave, but a messenger for God."

Turning to face Tectos, I felt compelled to kiss him. I laid my head on his shoulder and wept. He caressed my hair and kissed my forehead. What had God been doing all around me while I never recognized it? I wiped the tears from my eyes and looked straight at Tectos and whispered, "I can never again think of you as my slave. You are my lost brother and I always want you at my side. I love you." I felt his body heave against me as he cried profusely.

Sensing that someone was behind us, I turned to see Haji standing about two paces away. He was also weeping. Finally, he spoke to tell us that he knew God was with our family, and that he was happy that he also had gained a new brother. After looking out onto the bay he remembered to announce that the ship from Alexandria was two hours away and lunch would be served in ten minutes. Smiling we got to our feet and began the walk home with me between them.

We were at another beautiful meal with our fabulous family, and I felt compelled to announce that Hanno had introduced Tectos to

Jesus and to God's love, and he had joined us as another member of The Way. He was the first person any of us had known, who followed the teaching of Jesus and was not first a Jew. This good news really called for a celebration, and Leah vowed we would have it, but first it was time for me to share what Tectos had been doing the past week.

I began by sharing what had not been made public about the attempted robbery on the *Swallow.* "Tectos had not only stopped the thief, but he had found each item the thief wanted to steal and their hiding places. When the thief was apprehended by Tectos, in the thief's struggle he dropped a large tusk on his foot and crushed it. The Captain then lashed the thief a few times and then turned him over to get a better look at his foot. It was beyond repair, so the Captain decided the thief had been punished enough, but his foot must be removed immediately, or he would never survive. After his foot was chopped off, crewmen took the thief to the city center where he would live his remaining days as a beggar. Tectos followed them, cleaned his wound, and applied a tourniquet to stop the bleeding. Every morning and evening since then he returned to feed him, remove his waste, bathe him if he had soiled himself, and dressed his wound. He did all this for an evil man who he had found repulsive ever since meeting him in Alexandria. As Peter told us nearly a year ago, we should be the hand of Jesus extended to the poor. This is what Tectos has been doing for he takes his new faith very seriously."

Tectos had kept his head bowed the entire time I spoke, fearful I would say too much. I suppose I may have done what he feared, but everyone needed to see the measure of the man they have accepted into their family. I for one, was proud to have him among us and as I looked at the others, I would say they were proud, too. As a reward, Stephen declared that he shall no longer sleep in the servant quarters but in his own room in the male section of the house, next to our room.

Tectos' head jerked up in disbelief. That meant he was to be treated as an equal and not as a slave. Not only was he to be taken seriously, but his ideas and values were to be respected also.

As soon as lunch was finished, we needed to excuse ourselves to meet the ship sailing into port from Alexandria. Stephen joined us and as we reached the docks, we were relieved that we beat the ship by ten minutes. That gave me time to get my customs documents from the sergeant, so I could begin my walk through the hold before dark to get a quick idea of what we would be dealing with in the warehouse. We still had nearly an hour of sunlight to get an accurate overview, so we could prepare the warehouse. Walking through the hold which was half full of our cargo, mostly spices and pottery, we realized the task ahead in keeping the warehouse organized really would not be so difficult after all. It was obvious that our shipment from India was more monolithic than the three hundred distinctly different carpets from Persia that we had to keep track of.

Aside from the gems and frankincense in Stephen's office, the only cost/price challenges were the individual tusks which needed to be weighed, and the distinctly unique pieces of HanChin pottery. With the shipments coming in smaller sizes, Tectos and I would be able to easily keep pace with it.

Because of the merchandise we already had on hand, we were able to construct spreadsheets for pepper, cinnamon, HanChin pottery, silks, and ivory. We would work on each of the merchandise groups in Stephen's office at night. Using the customs manifest we were able to lay out the spreadsheets by category, but we were still required to fill in the data for each item. The most critical parts of our job would be to identify the individual cost for each item, calculate our market price, and then mark it. By the time the next ship arrived from Alexandria each tusk had been weighed, numbered, and entered on its own line, as were the pepper and cinnamon bales which would later be priced out in portions for sale in smaller lots. Even though the many different sizes and degrees of workmanship on the HanChin pottery combined with their esthetic beauty had us bogged down, we felt we were as ready as possible for the current delivery. By evening everything was offloaded into a vacant corner of the warehouse. This would be a snap. That evening we also began work on the chest of frankincense and in two nights we should begin on the jade.

This continued for over a month as ship after ship coming through Alexandria delivered Indian cargo, keeping Tectos and me extremely busy. When the last ship arrived, I was startled to discover that it was under the command of Lucius and his Briton crew. Stephen had them take over the *Swallow* for three months to make grain deliveries between Alexandria and Ostia. On his first delivery to Ostia they stopped in Syracuse to deliver the last of the ivory and the last two bales of pepper. We would be ready to begin sales on his next trip to Ostia.

A side benefit of this strategy was that Tectos was able to see his cousins again for a day. Stephen's plan was to use the *Swallow* for the next few months to make small deliveries of Indian goods to Ostia for the Roman market while also making his grain deliveries.

Going aboard when the loading planks were lowered, Tectos and I were delighted to see Hanno and Rashvi. Rashvi was especially needed to help us with our sales in Roma, and it was a great relief to see him here. Then out of the cabin came Prince Yacobsa in all his finery with Timnah at his side! Stephen had brought us all together to get this year's cargo sold as quickly as possible while working to collect what we needed to take to India for trade in late summer. This included going to Massalia twice on his return to Alexandria to pick up loads of the finest wine of Gallia. One load would be sold to our customer in Alexandria and the other would be warehoused there for transshipment to Kings Abrayamsa and Shikrit in India.

As Tectos' cousins brought the cargo up on deck, they saw him for the first time and bowed deeply before he checked off each item on the nearly completed spreadsheets. In all the excitement of the morning, Tectos forgot to go into the city to take care of Horse. As soon as he had everything checked in, he slipped away to take him some food for the day and take care of his other needs. When he returned an hour later, he was ashen faced, and it was evident he had been crying. Sometime after Tectos had visited Horse the night before he had died, and the civil authorities were removing his body just as Tectos arrived. Horse had survived his wound for nearly two months and was regaining his strength, but suddenly he died from a fever which he contracted only two days earlier. Tectos was devastated and was blaming himself for his own negligence.

Thankfully, he eventually realized that he had done everything he could. He had even introduced Horse to the God of creation and the love and compassion of his son. He was getting morally stronger and for the first time since Tectos had met him, Horse was thinking of others. He had been sharing his food with the other beggars in the city center, and even gave his cherished silver coin to an old beggar woman he had befriended. Tectos believed that the last two months of Horse's life had totally made up for everything he had done before. But he was still pained by Horse's loss. I told Lucius what had happened, and then I took Tectos to the beach where I had enjoyed many great times in the past, just to give his grief my undivided attention.

When we reached the cove I always found to be picturesque whenever I needed to be alone, I asked him if he would like to join me for a swim. Stripping down we ran for the modest surf and spent a wonderful hour talking as we swam and laughed. I saw a new side

I had rarely had the slightest glimpse of. He was laughing! In fact, he even felt free and happy enough to grab me and try to push me under. I found we were bonding in ways we had always resisted. Then, after one riotous game of tag I kissed him as we laughed. He froze and just stared into my eyes as he reached to touch my face. There were tears in his sky-blue eyes as he whispered something in his mother tongue. Then he returned my kiss as a charge of energy ran through my body. It was then I realized he really did love me and that he really had given himself to me those months ago in Alexandria while we slept beside one another with his hand on my arm. He really had become my new Hanno.

I could not help myself as I responded to that revelation. Throwing my arms tightly around his beautiful body, I kissed him again while sharing my heart with him. Hanno would always be a part of my life, but over the last year, as he found his life's love and partner, I knew that even though he was always there for me, his first obligation was to Rashvi. Yes, that made me lonely at times, especially when I was separated from Stephen. But Hanno was always there for me and I knew he loved me. Suddenly I was sensing something frighteningly different and totally new. Our bodies were instantly responding to what our hearts were feeling, and this time I didn't want to pull away. All I could do was hold him and relish this new and beautiful experience. It was then that he began kissing me everywhere, always telling me he loved me except when he went under water to kiss me there. As he looked into my eyes again, he kissed with all the passion within him. In doing so I experienced a massive thrill charging through my entire body without being touched anywhere below my chest.

Whatever it was that happened that day, I can truthfully say it lasted a life time. Tectos and I would never be separated.

CHAPTER 55

PRINCE YACOBSA – MAY 18, AD30

After two hours in the surf we returned to the *Swallow* just as the last of the family baggage was taken home from the warehouse. This allowed us enough time for Tectos to spend an hour with his cousins and for me to spend an hour with Lucius before we headed home to join our expanded family for lunch. During my time with Lucius, we discussed what we would face ahead, both in our trading in Roma and with our trading with India. He was scheduled to leave in a few hours and I needed to feel that I understood each phase of our strategic plan. He was preparing to deliver the grain in Ostia and then proceed on to Massalia to pick up the wine for delivery to Alexandria, and then repeat the cycle again, except he would pick up cargo for Roma while in Syracuse rather than deliver it.

I also asked what happened to the captain and crew of the *Sparrow*. He knew of the attempted theft but knew no more. A few weeks ago, he received two letters from Stephen, one addressed to the captain of the *Sparrow* and one to him, ordering that he prepare to take over the *Sparrow* when she arrived in Alexandria. He knew nothing about the former captain and crew other than they were still in Alexandria when he set sail to Syracuse. I was left with only one option, to ask Stephen when we returned for lunch. Checking the sun, I knew we had better hurry and get Tectos home before they ate without us.

As we turned the corner to home, we saw Haji step out the door to call us to lunch. The three of us dashed in as quickly as possible, walking through the empty dining room, straight into the atrium. Yacobsa, Timnah, Hanno, and Rashvi were sitting with Stephen and Aaron as they shared their experiences of the last six months in Alexandria and India. We only had about ten minutes with them before lunch was served, but I was startled by Aaron's incisive questions about India. He had already learned a great deal from Tectos and me, but he had taken that information and processed it into sound knowledge. Having recently turned nine, he was truly becoming articulate and a beautiful youngster.

When Leah called us into the dining room, I was curious to see how Stephen would seat us. Naturally he kept each couple together, including Tectos and me, even though we weren't a true couple. He had Hanno seated directly across from me with Rashvi at his side. Yacobsa and Timnah were next to them. Next to Tectos was Haji with Festus, which pleased Haji immensely. This would allow the four-people sitting closest to Stephen to be the voyagers from the *Triton*.

After Stephen prayed, and before the questions began, I told the family that Horse had died during the night and that Tectos was taking it pretty hard. Those who were not fluent in Greek, Rashvi and Yacobsa, thought that Tectos had a horse which died. After seeing the confusion, I explained the story to them in Aramaic, emphasizing that Tectos had led the thief to faith in God and his son, Jesus, just as Hanno had done with him. Everyone was silent for a moment, then Rashvi asked a surprising question in Aramaic which Tectos did not understand.

"This morning, when Tectos' cousins came out of the hold and saw him for the first time, I noticed that they instantly bowed to him and he accepted their bow as he continued with his work. On our voyage they always seemed to dominate him because of their older age, but now they treat him like a master. What has happened?"

I remembered the incident as well, so I explained the question to Tectos in Greek. He knew Rashvi had been talking about him but was totally unprepared for his question. He bowed his head for a moment and then, looking straight at Rashvi and Yacobsa while taking my hand under the table, he shared the story of his life before his capture while I translated.

"Our legends have it that the Galatian tribes began their migrations east at the beginning of the Punic Wars between Carthage and Roma as they fought for control of our lands in Southern Gallia near the Hispanic border. The Galatian people in central Asia Minor are made up of three of those Celtic tribes which arrived in Asia Minor nearly three hundred years ago. Of those tribes, the one who controlled the other two and dominated the highland plains around our capital of Ancyra is the Tectosages. Under the Romans my grandfather was the traditional king of that tribe when I was captured. My father was his heir and is probably the king today. I was given the best Greek education and was raised to be king. However, as long as I was a slave without status, like my older cousins who were born of a foreign concubine, they treated me as their slave. When they saw me this morning, dressed in a new tunic and checking in the ship's cargo, they realized I once again had status over them and they became frightened, perhaps fearing for their lives. What they don't know is that I will never be king. This is now my family and I will never leave it, especially Jacobus."

What surprised me was that the four men across from me understood and agreed with him. Stephen reached out and took the hand beside my plate and held it tightly. At sixteen, I felt like the most fortunate man in the empire. I loved all the men around me and they loved me. What more could a born eunuch ask for?

As the lunch progressed, the questions about India and Alexandria became even more involved and exciting. There were many great things ahead for this family, but I needed to get back to the *Swallow* before she shoved off for Ostia. Once again reaching for Tectos' hand, I told him we needed to go. We told everyone we would see them in a few hours, in time for Shabbat.

We reached the dock just as Lucius was signing off on the cargo papers in the sergeant's office. I said farewell to him there as he kissed me for the first time. It felt strange to be kissed by the rugged man who had taught me so much through the years and who I admired more than anyone except Stephen. Tectos and I took our stations at the mooring ropes and awaited his order to cast off. As we waived goodbye to Lucius and his crew, I put my arm around Tectos' waist so that his cousins could really see that he did have status. When I knew they were watching us, I turned and kissed him. Even Tectos was happy I had done something so brash.

As they sailed out into the bay, Tectos and I reentered the warehouse and did what we could to complete the last entries on our spreadsheets. We only had two entries left when Haji entered the warehouse with Aaron at his side. He agreed that we had time to finish those entries before we left. In the meantime, Aaron spotted the tusks stacked up in the far corner and was fascinated with them. Having never seen an elephant, he could not imagine how any animal could have teeth so huge. As I told him of our elephant ride up the Periyar River with some of the elephants of the king carrying as many as five men, his eyes nearly popped out in disbelief. He found a matching pair of small tusks laying alongside the major tusks. While he was rubbing them and admiring their beauty, I found the Sergeant and asked him to put them aside for Aaron's birthday. Smiling broadly, he said he would have them ready to pick up in a week.

When Tectos finished his last entry, we followed Haji back to the house with Aaron between Tectos and me holding our hands while asking more questions about elephants. When we entered the house, Haji led us straight to the mikvah where Stephen was waiting. He already had his towel around his waist and waited as we disrobed. Even though this was not Tectos' first Shabbat, I gave him a sponge bath while I repeated the purpose of the mikvah in Jewish tradition, along with the Shabbat meal to follow on all Friday nights.

Once Haji dried us, we stood naked in front of Stephen who obviously loved what he saw. Then He proceeded into the tank and submerged himself in the required manner and quickly exited. Then it was my turn to follow his lead as I always did. As I exited and took my towel from Haji, Tectos did exactly what we had done and then exited the tank to receive his towel from Haji. When we were all dried, Haji led us to Stephen's and my room where clothes for the three of us were already laid out. As we stood in a circle facing one another, Haji removed our towels and began to dress Stephen. As Tectos watched, I could see that he was nearly overwhelmed by the masculine beauty before him. I was surprised that when it was my turn, Tectos actually became excited, a fact which was not lost on Stephen. Then as Haji dressed Tectos in "his" Shabbat robes, both Stephen and I kept our eyes glued on him, in his excited state which actually made him feel quite awkward.

Finally dressed, Haji led us to the atrium as he dashed to his own room to quickly complete his preparations. Within five minutes we were all in the dining room standing at our same chairs we had at lunch. As Leah lit the candles the Shabbat ritual began, complete with songs and prayers. As we were seated, Stephen remained standing.

Once the room was quiet he began a speech honoring Tectos, not only for what he did to protect our cargo, capturing the thief, but then nursing the thief through the love of God. Then he came to his main point, the celebration of his birth into the family of God. As he completed the speech, he turned and picked up a scroll from off his chair and held it up to me saying, "This deed of ownership for the slave known as Tectos is relinquished by Aetna Shipping to Jacobus BarSirach granting him all rights and privileges over said slave for as long as he lives or until this deed is transferred or terminated."

As everyone applauded, I jumped to my feet to accept the deed and then pulled Tectos to his feet so I could unashamedly kiss him to seal our personal bond to one another in front of the entire family. Tectos was shaking with uncontrollable excitement about officially being a part of the family, and not the business, and especially a part of me. As we kissed, everyone stood to their feet to applaud, this time for the two of us. Before we sat down again, I stepped around the table to kiss Stephen, who also had tears in his eyes. I wept as I thanked him for his trust. Looking at me strangely he held my face in his hands as he kissed me in return with overt passion.

As we settled back into our seats the platters of exquisite foods were brought in celebration of Tectos' following of The Way as a *Goy* without becoming a Jew first. The meal was amazing as was the loving mood expressed by everyone. At the end of the meal Stephen stood again to make another family speech, this time about Yacobsa. It was his intention to assign Yacobsa the responsibility of acting as the head of our trading delegation in Roma which would include all three couples. Timnah would act as his personal second. Hanno would handle all logistics with Rashvi as his second. I would act as the technical director with Tectos as my personal second. In public everyone was to defer to Prince Yacobsa or myself, the family's representative. We would take at least four separate trips to Roma, as we accumulated enough merchandize stored in our Ostia warehouse to make the trip practical.

Yacobsa would always be dressed as the prince he is, while I would be dressed as a young aristocratic merchant, and Hanno would be dressed as our wealthy Phoenician advisor. We needed to attract attention to ourselves as well as our merchandise. Our customers must see us as influential direct importers of the highest quality Eastern goods into Rome . . . especially the Ivory, gems, HanChin pottery, silks, spices, and frankincense. They had already learned that about our Persian Carpets five months earlier.

It would be about three weeks before the *Swallow* would arrive to pick up our first partial load of cargo for the warehouse in Ostia. Now that all our merchandize was listed on the spreadsheets, Tectos and I needed to sit down and compute our actual costs for each item and then record our standard selling prices. This was the part I always feared, but with Tectos' math skills I knew we could have that all completed in less than a week. Once again Leah agreed to visit her favorite shopkeepers and our other local customers in Syracuse to get things started by letting us know their reactions.

That night as we prepared to go to our separate rooms, Stephen asked if I would like Tectos to join us now that he was my personal slave. I was shocked because I had never considered doing that before. When I told him that, he looked deeply into my eyes and asked if that was what I meant when I said, "Thank you for trusting me." I nodded in the affirmative. Then he asked if I was celibate the whole time we were apart. I told him I was except for a few weeks in Alexandria, the Aegyptian desert, and finally Berenike when I needed to do some sexual role playing with Yacobsa to get him through ten years of flaccid manhood. We never actually had sex, I needed to get him over his fears, so he could make love to the man of his dreams when he met him. We were only in Berenike for ten minutes when he saw Timnah again. I'm not sure, but I don't think he's been flaccid since. Stephen laughed and thanked me for the sincerity of my love. Then he asked me again if I would like Tectos to sleep with us. I still felt uncomfortable with the idea, but I knew it was my right for he was now my slave. I decided to ask him . . . not tell him, even though I already knew he was desperately in love with me.

Going to the next room, I knocked on the door and waited. Soon a near naked Tectos stuck his head out the door and was surprised to see me . . . I think he was waiting for Haji and Festus. That gave me the courage to ask, "Tectos, now that you are legally mine would you like to spend tonight with Stephen and me?"

At first, he hesitated in fear of the thought of Stephen seeing us together for the first time. Once I assured him that Stephen loved and respected him as a man, not as a slave, and that he would not be touched by Stephen unless it was something he wanted, he immediately grabbed his tunic and closed the door behind him as he almost pushed me to our room. Walking into the room, Tectos saw Stephen laying on the bed but he turned his attention immediately to me. Asking if I needed him to remove my clothes, I nodded in the affirmative. After removing my clothes, he dropped his small towel. I then took his hand and lead him to the bed where he laid down beside me, just as Hanno used to do. Laying there with Stephen on one side and Tectos on the other I felt like the angels had just called me to heaven.

Yes, there were times of ecstatic passion that night, but most of all there were such deep feelings and beautiful words and acts of love that I am still at a loss to describe what I felt that night as Tectos possessed me for the first time. It had to be the most beautiful night of my life, and I believe my two men who I loved with all my heart both felt the same way.

THE TWO PRINCES – JULY 11, AD30

After two round trips to Roma, Massalia, and Alexandria, the *Swallow* arrived in Syracuse four days after we completed all of our costing and pricing for both our individual and bulk items we planned to sell in Roma. As the weeks slipped by, it became imperative that we also begin to think of all the other items and tasks we needed to complete in preparation for our departure for India in six weeks.

The following day was spent separating everything designated for our first full shipment of Indian treasures destined for Roma while at the same time identifying the Roman commodities we planned to ship with our gold to India. Fortunately, anything that we wouldn't sell on our first trip to Roma would be held over in the Ostia warehouse until it was sold. Also, Stephen had once again arranged for our lodging at the home of his old friend, Antonius Junius Balearius. His friend had also arranged to host a business dinner in the home of the Emperor's cousin before we departed Roma.

Upon the Swallow's arrival, we began loading cargo for our departure in three days. On the morning of the third day, the crew worked diligently to pitch a large, very luxurious, and colorful tent on the center of the deck between the hatch and the mast. By the time all of our personal baggage was loaded into the tent by Haji and Festus the *Swallow* looked like Cleopatra's royal barge with streamers and flags flowing in the wind and a golden sail mounted to the mast. Our entire crew of Briton eunuchs were clean-shaven and dressed in brightly colored uniforms, and Captain Paulus was dressed in an Indian silk uniform complete with a gold turban with a peacock feather in front. Even Tectos' cousins wore bright blue tunics with red head bands. We had known that Stephen wanted us to put on a show when we entered Roma, but this was over the top!

After lunch, we put on our extravagant attire to wear for boarding the ship. Stephen told us that we should always wear our formal clothes until our second day out from Roma on our way home. Approaching the dock, I was surprised to see all of the extended Jewish family, both young and old. standing in front of the warehouse to see us off. As we followed Stephen up the loading planks to commend Captain Paulus for a spectacular job of showmanship, the entire crew bowed low to us in practice for Roma. I smiled as Tectos' cousins bowed, almost in fear of him, and in a regal gesture he touched their heads as he past.

Standing next to the captain by the boarding planks, Stephen turned to at least twenty of his peers and family in Aetna Shipping to thank them for supporting his ventures in Persia and India. He was pleased to remind them that they now had family ties with two kings who considered the members of Aetna Shipping as extensions of their own families. That being said, he walked down the planks and turned to join the others as they waved us farewell while the planks were pulled aboard, and the mooring ropes were tossed up to the two cousins.

We felt the excitement, when we opened the golden sail entering the bay, to the sound of cheers and applause carrying across the water to the *Swallow*. It was exciting to watch everyone remaining frozen to the dock until our view of them disappeared behind the harbor barrier. Looking around at all those standing on the deck, it finally sunk in that some of us were going to play roles that were very foreign to us, but we all had the same objective, show Roma that it could only get the best from Aetna Shipping.

The word was already out in Alexandria that the best Gallic wines were from Aetna . . . Lucius had more than doubled our money in last week's transaction alone. Now, with a shipment of Roma's favorite spice, greatly discounted black pepper, we knew our name would continue to resonate and become synonymous with fair pricing. After all, the poor were demanding pepper as much as the rich, and cinnamon was right behind in its demand, and that was certainly discounted, too.

On the evening of our third full day at sea, we approached the mouth of the Tiberis and waited to catch the next incoming tide which would carry us to our warehouse door in Ostia. While waiting, the splendor of our ship, crew, and passengers began to attract the attention of people on the shore as well as on the ships around us. It already appeared that Stephen's idea to recreate the pageantry of the colosseums and hippodromes of Roma to attract customers might have been a very wise move. By the time the tide brought us into the Tiberis, and we were moored to the dock in front of our warehouse by the magnificently liveried cousins, Captain Paulus disappeared into his private sleeping cabin. A few minutes later, he emerged with a huge Indian processional umbrella created from deep blue silk with trim and decorations of gold. Sadhu had given it to him in Muziris, assuring Lucius that we would need it for his brother-in-law when he was in Roma.

As everyone was waiving back at the crowd on the dock, Lucius called Timnah over to the cabin where he showed him the immense umbrella. He quickly explained that it was a symbol of royalty, and as he opened it, he "ordered" Timnah to go immediately and stand behind Yacobsa with it shading him at all times. Understanding the captain's purpose, he dashed to his station to the surprise and awe of everyone, especially Yacobsa who also played the role by waiving to everyone on the dock. As the cousins lowered the loading planks, the Sergeant followed his instincts and boarded the ship to first welcome Yacobsa, then Captain Paulus to Roma.

News of our dazzling arrival spread up the river and into the City like wild fire. Stephen had informed Antonius that we would be arriving within the week with great pomp and asked him to send a servant to guide me, Hanno, and the Prince to his villa as soon as a messenger from the warehouse reached him. I am not sure if it was the great pomp or the thought of seeing Hanno again that compelled him to gather up his elegant Nubian and a man servant to dash down to the dock in his most lavish attire. The crowd had begun to thin when Antonius reached the ship and he lit up like a candle upon laying his eyes on Hanno once again. Hanno immediately leaned over to warn Rashvi before it was too late. As quickly as possible I stepped in and made the required introductions.

Amid all the "Pomp," Antonius took on his natural airs to welcome us as an official representative of the imperial family of his cousin, the Emperor Tiberius. By that time, not only were the Galatian cousins completely dazzled, but so was Lucius and everyone else who had begun to regather around the *Swallow* to watch. Within half an hour Antonius' cart arrived to transport not only our personal baggage, but also a full selection of our most spectacular Indian and HanChin treasures which were selected to stimulate our host's extravagant taste.

It took less than an hour to reach Antonius' stunning villa, secluded in a lush grove of trees looking down on his mother's small but exquisite palace perched on a cliff above a sandy beach. As the door was swung open to us, we entered the grand fountain filled atrium which captured the cool breezes that blew in through the forest from the sea below. Antonius directed his Nubian man servant to show us to our rooms for a little relaxation before his friends arrived to meet us later in the afternoon. In his normal coy manner, he mentioned that we each had a private room. Knowing his game, I decided to play it as well. I told him that only three rooms were required. Clapping his hands, he asked if we have had some more weddings.

Flippantly I replied, "We have had only one, but we will have two more very soon." Bouncing back, he asked who the lucky couple was. Finding out it was Hanno and Rashvi, he feigned the role of a lover scorned. Then looking at me he asked who the other two couples were.

Immediately I countered, "Prince Yacobsa and his aide, Timnah. Then there will be me and my aide, Tectos." Silence.

Then in just three seconds, we heard a very startled, "What?!"

Laughing, I dashed over to Tectos and wrapped my arms around him as I shouted to all in the room that I wanted to spend the rest of my life with him. Then he whispered, "What about Stephen?"

I simply replied, "Instead of two wives, he has one wife and one husband, and I will have two husbands, Stephen and my wonderful Tectos, because I don't require children."

The time was imminent for Antonius to jump in, "First, you take Stephen away from me, and then Stephen takes you away from me. Now you are saying I can't have the enchanting Tectos either. If it weren't for the fact you are making me a rich man with my many commissions, I would require you to sleep alone in the forest tonight." As everyone who understood Greek laughed at his satirical humor we began to disperse to our rooms.

For the next hour it was necessary for me to spend it with Tectos in our room. My sudden announcement proved far too much for him to absorb in so short a period. A few years ago, he was an agricultural slave, beaten and abused. Just a few months ago he was a cargo slave confined to the hold of a ship where he was sexually abused every night. Then he became my personal slave and assistant, and he was trusted with everything I had. Suddenly he was faced with the new reality that I loved him above all others. It was beyond anything he could have dreamed for himself, but it was also a love beyond what I could have dreamed . . . even from my wonderful Stephen.

On top of everything else, he had discovered a new faith that suddenly gave him a life which took him beyond a life of servitude and into a life of service and the helping of others. The cause of that change was still difficult for him to fully understand. All he knew was that he had begun to feel different inside about the value of his own life and the lives of others. If his future held out hope for himself, it only seemed natural to hold out hope for others. Where this entire social, psychological, marital, financial, and political structure of Roman law got turned on its head, was the undeniable fact that he was a slave . . . property to be used and disposed of at the desire and whim of the property's owner.

The question I suddenly needed to address was what to do about Antonius. He was a Roman aristocrat who was culturally against everything my love for the slave Tectos stood for. I had to think of something to say and do as quickly as possible, or I may have singlehandedly destroyed years of work by Stephen. As Tectos and I returned to the gathering in the atrium, I knew I needed to act quickly.

Almost instantaneously the candles flickered on in my brain and I began to set about my task. Watching as Antonius roamed about the room trying to settle in his own mind what his reaction to my childish stupidity should be, I jumped into action and called to him out loud.

"Antonius, this get together with your friends today is a great time for me to announce my upcoming marriage to Tectos, the Crown Prince of Galatia." Smiling at my own wit, I continued, "His father, the King of Galatia, will be traumatized to learn that his precious son has married a citizen of the dreaded Roma . . . and to another man at that!"

As the whole room broke out into peals of laughter, I glided over to Tectos and threw my arms around him again, just waiting for a bull elephant to step on me and squash me like an Indian coconut. As I turned to kiss him, his face became red with a mixture of embarrassment and pure rage.

In a very controlled voice he asked, "How can you call me, a slave, a Crown Prince?"

"Your father is a king, isn't he?" "Yes, I suppose."

"You are his oldest heir, aren't you?" "Yes, of course!"

"Doesn't that mean you are a Crown Prince?" "But I am a slave of Roma!"

"Only for a little while longer, Tectos, only for a little while longer." "What?"

"Just be patient my beloved."

By this time Antonius had begun to approach us, so I was ready to turn to him and throw my arms around him and ask him to do us a favor. When he agreed, I asked him if this evening after everyone arrived, we could celebrate the planned marriage of the two princes.

He spontaneously agreed and indicated he would let his mother know immediately. As he dashed off, I was able to spend a few more minutes with Tectos, which he desperately required. He agreed to accept the fact that we were getting married, perhaps at the same time as Yacobsa and Timnah. I promised him that we would begin working out the details immediately upon our return to Syracuse.

By the time Antonius' guests began to arrive we were all in our full regalia, except for Tectos, of course, because Yacobsa and I were having great fun searching for jewels and silks to make his attire appear more royal. When he was finally properly clothed, I went out and told Antonius the time had come when he could introduce the princes to his guests. With all the pomp and ceremony, he and his staff could muster, he waived his arms dramatically and introduced His Royal Highness, Prince Yacobsa of the Kingdom of Muziris and Chera, and also His Royal Highness, Crown Prince Tectos of the Kingdom of Galatia, now proudly a semi-autonomous Province of Roma in the east.

Spontaneously the guests began to applaud with a degree of enthusiasm, which triggered a degree of my own embarrassment catching even myself totally off guard. Then with Rashvi and Hanno at Yacobsa's side and Timnah and me at Tectos' side we began to hold an impromptu royal court which thrilled Antonius to no end.

As the platters of food and cups of wine came out from the kitchen, I felt a great sense of reward as I watched the second love my life begin to assimilate into his hereditary role which was cruelly forfeited with his Roman capture. Standing next to the dark and elegant Indian, my Galatian took on the aura of a precious pearl shimmering in the light of a room filled with burning oil lamps. I was amazed at how perfectly he took to his lessons from Yacobsa.

Just as I approached the two and placed an arm around each waist, Antonius announced the room's newest arrival, his mother, the cousin of Emperor Tiberius. As a powerful force in Roma's Julio-Claudian Dynasty, I immediately tipped my royals as to her superior status, which the guests acknowledge with proper grace and ceremony as Antonius presented them to her. It created the perfect impression for Antonius' guests to receive. But the best was yet to come. As she greeted me personally by name, she thanked me for all the treasures she had purchased the year before and asked what wonderful things I had for her to see this time.

Turning to Yacobsa I asked him if he had her gift from his brother the King of Muziris and Chera. Nodding his acknowledgement, he reached into his robe and pulled out an ivory box which he presented to her with impeccable ceremony. As I made a small speech on the part of Aetna Shipping, I encouraged her to open it. Suddenly there was a gasp from both her and Antonius. Stephen had decided to present her with the largest of the five diamonds we brought home as gifts and her delight was more than evident.

"This is the most beautiful gem I have ever seen. Please, both of you, give your brothers my sincerest thanks." With that, she stepped forward and gave me a kiss on the cheek as everyone applauded in wonder.

Looking at Antonius with a grand smile I asked Yacobsa if he had his gift from his cousin the King of Padyan. Once again, he acknowledged by reaching into the other side of his robe and extracted another ivory box which he now presented to Antonius, who by this time was bubbling over with anticipation. Naturally Antonius required no encouragement and opened his box immediately, followed by a scream. He slowly extracted a flawless pigeon blood ruby the size of a hen's egg. He began to weep with joy as he thanked Yacobsa and me for the love we had shown him.

With the gifts presented, Rashvi, Hanno, and Timnah withdrew to my room and began to bring out chests of gold mounted jewelry, cut stones, sheep skin thin HanChin pottery glazed in brilliant colors, carved jade and ivory, arm loads of sensuous silks . . . many embroidered with gold threads, nuggets of the finest frankincense, and one pair of giant ivory tusks mounted with silver. By the time the evening was over, Tectos and I sold the entire cartload which we had brought up from the ship.

We knew it would be a short night for we had to leave first thing in the morning to retrieve another cartload of treasure. But Tectos and I still had no private time together to express the excitement we both felt for our future marriage which included Tectos' emancipation from slavery. In some ways he was as eager as a child, in others he was as terrified as a prisoner being dragged to his cross. We enjoyed a wonderful night of new emotions and expressions of love. The knowledge that he would soon be a freedman and the hell that the slave catchers had sentenced his life to would soon be shattered and over, infused him with unexpected bursts of energy throughout the night. By sunrise I was exhausted and craving several hours of additional sleep. But I had no hope of even a brief nap.

After a quick breakfast we were on our way to pick up our most valuable load of merchandise of the season, for its presentation later that evening at the home of the emperor's cousin. Arriving at the warehouse we were greeted by a lavishly costumed Lucius Paulus anxious to learn all the news. Before I told him anything else, I told him about Tectos and myself, which caused him a greater expression of genuine joy than I had ever seen from him in two years. He totally forgot about the night's events as he inquired about every detail of our decision and how it would create a change in Tectos' slavery status. What we hadn't yet thought of was how this news was going to affect

Tectos' cousins. Lucius assured us that he would inform them after we left with the cart.

Lucius already had the cousins separate the second load as per Stephen's instructions and had them load it up as quickly as possible. As they did, they noticed that Tectos was no longer dressed as my assistant, but as a person of much higher status than myself. As they were finishing up, I pulled Lucius aside and told him about Tectos' reinstatement by Aetna Shipping as the Crown Prince of Galatia and how it stimulated the guests' enthusiasm. Obviously, I was not too sure about how this, along with the future marriage would sit with the cousins. The captain's judgement of character would be critical in this matter. Giving me a giant hug, he assured me of his support and assistance. We then boarded the cart beside the driver and headed off up the river road.

When we arrived at Antonius' villa, he had the driver take the cart down to his mother's modest palace as we all followed behind. Her home was abuzz with servants as they began the preparations for the evening's fete. Since his mother was nowhere in sight, Antonius went about showing us where to place the chests and other items where they would be secure until after our dinner. With Tectos and me getting hungrier by the minute, we all headed back up the hill to have our midday meal.

After the meal, I shared with Tectos about the care with which Lucius would be watching and evaluating his cousins as they learned more about his quickly changing status. Sensing his concern for their welfare, I assured him that Lucius was the best man in the empire to evaluate men. Also, any recommendations he might make would not be acted upon without Tectos' own personal approval.

Feeling a little more at ease, he leaned over and kissed me as he told me once again that he could not believe these things were really happening to him. I then reminded him of his selfless care for Horse as he sat beside the street begger day after day. "God used you to share his love with a violent thief. You didn't have to wash him when he defecated on himself. You didn't have to feed him and share your faith with him, but you did. Perhaps God saw that he could trust you with greater things. Now he is trusting you with me, and I am very proud of you and honored to have you in my life."

We were finally blessed with a few free hours to rest in the hopes of taking a well needed nap. I was amazed at how thoroughly bonded Tectos had become to me since our journey down the Nile. I was at a loss to explain my own feelings toward him. I knew the sexual element in our relationship would always be there, but there was something else happening to me . . . a connection deeper than I had ever felt, even with my twin, Josephus. Josephus! I hadn't really thought of him since the Nile. I must have finally become a man. Perhaps that is what this is all about . . . now I truly see myself as a mature man.

As my eyes slowly cracked open to the faint sounds of movement, I saw Tectos already dressing in all of his finery, checking everything so it would all be perfect. Turning to see me looking at him, he bent over to give me a kiss and told me he was now ready to dress me for our big night. I let him continue his role as my personal slave, not because he was, but because he was the love of my life. Within thirty minutes we were out the door, meeting with the four others in our delegation as we compared notes among ourselves.

We were ready. For what . . . we weren't really sure. All we could do was to trust God to open the door for our meeting of Roma's rich and powerful. Suddenly it hit me . . . who did we think we were. This whole thing was my responsibility and in spite of what was happening with Tectos, I was still just a teenager. Then it began to sink in. Over the past two and a half years I had quickly become a rich and powerful person in my own right. I was no longer thinking like a child, but I was also taking responsibilities that were not necessarily given to me. I was being prepared to make a difference, but I still had no concept of what that might mean.

Returning to Antonius' villa, later that night, I was certain that something gigantic was on the horizon and Tectos was a part of it. Everything we took down to the palace that afternoon was sold, and people were placing orders against what we had in Syracuse. What surprised me most was that Antonius had begun treating me as a younger brother and I was beginning to get the feeling that his mother was looking after me like I was a young son. I wasn't sure about these phenomena until I mentioned it to Tectos as he was undressing me for bed later that night. He replied that he had noted the same things and felt we need to speak to Stephen about it as soon as we returned to Syracuse.

The next day Antonius' big brother demeanor became stronger than ever as we visited the high-end shops of Roma selling the remainder of our warehoused merchandise at very strong margins. In two more days, the entire shipload was sold, and the gold deposited in the hold of the ship. The *Swallow* had already been loaded for our return voyage to Syracuse, allowing us to drop our moorings and drift down the Tiberis on the receding tide by midmorning the next day. With the wind at our backs we should be home in three days.

Sailing smoothly on the open sea our pretentious clothes were finally replaced with more sensible attire. Yes, it was a bit of a letdown as we suddenly looked rather shoddy, but we were surely more comfortable.

CHAPTER 57

THE APOSTLE – AUGUST 2, AD30

Upon our return to Syracuse, we immediately began selecting the merchandize for our next delivery to Roma. As soon as the cargo from our Ostia warehouse was offloaded, the process of packing the second load of Indian goods into the hold began. Our goal was to sell two more ship loads of Indian goods in Roma before we loaded up with wine, olive oil, iron and silver ingots, and finally gold coins. We needed to be in Alexandria before the end of August, so we would have time to complete preparations for our departure up the Nile. In the meantime, Hanno and Rashvi would leave immediately on our next ship to Alexandria and then follow their previous route down the Sinus Arabicus on horseback to prepare the *Triton* for departure in late September, over a month later than the previous year. However, the more I weighed the schedule, the more I felt we needed to take only one more shipload to Roma before leaving for Alexandria much sooner and taking Hanno and Rashvi with us.

When we moored in Syracuse, I needed to sit down with Stephen and discuss our personal relationship before I could do anything else. Fortunately, he was at the dock waiting for us and greeted me with open arms and his spectacular kisses as I left Tectos on deck. Seeing a tall nine-year-old Aaron running down the dock behind him shouting my name, my heart forced me to break loose from his father and grab him up into my arms, laughing and crying with joy. Settling my emotions as best I could, I kissed both father and son with an open loving soul. My conflict was before me and only I could deal with it . . . hopefully with Stephen's help.

While Stephen and I walked home hand in hand, Aaron took my free hand and marched along with us. As I shared our over anticipated success, due to his cleaver planning, I found myself more and more animated as I recalled event after event to his anticipating ears. Each report caused him to smile broader than the last. Then I told him I literally presented Tectos to Antonius and his mother as the Crown Prince of Galatia, and that we suddenly had twice the fire power at the two dinners which hosted Roma's rich and powerful. It was inevitable. Stephen came to a halting standstill as the consequences of what I just said fully sank in and he painfully looked at me as though I had committed a capital offense.

After I assured him that Yacobsa was constantly at his side, tutoring him flawlessly, he finally asked if it was really possible. Then I reminded him that Tectos really was his father's heir, he really did sit at his grandfather's knee as he held court, and he really was of royal blood. It was then that Stephen began to see the humor of it all, especially when I shared that a very frightened Tectos had to be reminded of these same things while he was my slave. To the people of Roma, he really was the Crown Prince of Galatia, not a cargo slave who was raped every night by his own cousins.

We turned and continued our walk home with silent Aaron listening to every word and, I am sure, remembering every word. It was now time to address the matter of Tectos' slavery and all that needed to be done, and why. Fortunately, it was Stephen who instigated that part of our discussion . . ..

"You love him, don't you?" "Yes, very much."

"More than you did Hanno?" "Yes."

"Are you planning to free him?" "Yes, I must."

"Does he love you as deeply as you love him?" "Yes, I am sure of it."

"Does he understand that you and I are married?" "Yes. He also knows my love for you is unbreakable."

"Do you think he would accept being a concubine?"

"His uncle had a concubine and her sons raped him daily."

"He does want a permanent binding relationship?"

"Yes, but he refuses to stand between you and me . . . He loves you more than you could ever imagine."

"Would he accept you taking him as a second spouse, as I did with you?" "I am sure of it."

"Jacobus Didymus BarSirach, in your youth you have demonstrated your intellect, wisdom, and determination to succeed in all that you do. Plus, even though you may not realize it, you are also a man of great wealth. Therefore, as your older brother, I approve your request to take a second spouse."

"Stephen, in all honesty and sincerity I don't know what to say or how to say it the best I can, and give you my thanks and my endless and passionate love."

"That is all I could ever ask for. Now you must make Tectos a freeman at our evening meal."

Spontaneously Aaron threw up his hands and cheered, "Now I will have three Dads!"

Fortunately, we had just arrived at our front door and I bent down so we were eye to eye and asked Aaron to promise not to tell anyone about this except Grandfather Sirach up in heaven. As my nine-year-old nephew threw his arms around my neck and kissed me on my lips, he promised on his love for me and his father to honor my trust.

Since it would be another hour before our mid-day meal, I asked Stephen if I could send Haji and Festus to help Tectos escort our chests of profits back to the house.

Laughing as he wrapped his arms tightly around me, pulling our bodies together so I could feel how intensely happy he was to have me home, he said, "Do as you wish. You have every right in our house and on our ships."

Stunned at the implications of his words, I called for Haji and gave him an errand to perform with Festus, which may take an hour to complete. After calling Festus to join Haji, Stephen took me by the hand and led me to our room for fifteen minutes of excitement, passion, praise, and pure love. When we finally emerged to the sound of Haji opening the front door and men walking back to Stephen's office, we ran to join them just as Haji turned his key in the office lock.

Stephen told Festus and Tectos where to set their chest, and the wide-eyed cousins were to put theirs's right beside it. Saying there were three more, Festus left Haji behind as he and the three slaves dashed back down to the dock. While they were gone, I opened both chests to reveal the contents. Each was filled with silk which shocked Haji as he commented that this had to be the heaviest silk in all of Roma and India. Asking Haji to join me, we bent over and lifted out two arms full of silk revealing half a chest of gold coins. Closing the lid, we opened and removed the silk from the second chest as well.

Haji quickly took the silk and began to stack it in a storage room. Just as I closed the lid of the second chest and all the silk was hidden away, there was a resounding knock at the door. Haji wiped his forehead and ran to admit the next two chests. After positioning them alongside the others, I told Festus he could remain while Tectos escorted his cousins back to retrieve the last chest. Once Festus returned from sending the slaves away, he was met by a laughing Haji who asked him to help empty the third chest. Reaching in, they each extracted another arm full of fine silk. Looking into the chest as he was turning away, he, too, began to laugh. Upon returning from the storage room they removed the silk from the fourth chest and stored it away just as Tectos knocked on the front door. Haji led them in, and the cousins set the fifth chest next to the line of four, and I instructed them to follow Festus back to the ship. Starring at the row of chests with a totally confused look of awe, the cousins did as they were told.

Now it was Tectos' turn to be in awe as Stephen reached out to take his hand and pull him into his arms to embrace him closely and kiss him as though he were a long-lost lover. Gasping for air, he looked first at me and then back at Stephen in total disoriented confusion. He had a wonderful time playing a great charade while in Roma, but this was reality, and once again he was just a slave. Was this very powerful man preparing to rape, or at best, seduce him, or worse, to keep him for himself? But then I reached out to him and did the same. Slowly he began to weep as it began to sink in. His life was changing forever . . . and doing it very quickly.

Haji walked up beside him and addressed him as brother as he gave him a brotherly kiss and asked Tectos to assist him emptying the silk from the fifth chest. Once again, we all burst out into peals of laughter. Looking down he saw even more gold than he had seen that night at Yacobsa's home in Alexandria. In shock, he heard Stephen simply say, "Welcome to the family."

Stephen closed and locked the fifth chest, as he announced that our mid-day meal would be on the table in minutes. Then we would have an hour to ourselves before we needed to begin the work of the day down at the warehouse. Haji and Tectos dashed out to the storeroom to deposit the last of the silk before the dinner bell rang.

The mid-day meal was sumptuous as usual, but this time Aaron insisted, as only a extremely precocious nine-year-old can, that he sit between Tectos and me. Giving in, I knew how excited he was, and I was pleased he shared my joy without a trace of jealousy. Tectos knew nothing of the events to come. Before his prayer, Stephen formally welcomed us both home and thanked us for a job well done in both Roma and India. Of course, Tectos found the India comments misdirected, as all he did in India was to get raped twice a night for the sake of duty. Knowing this truth Stephen kept an eye on him to judge his response. He noticed that Tectos revealed evidence to the training of his youth, as he looked over to me and smiled graciously. Then as Stephen began his prayer Aaron grabbed my hand and held it tightly. Glancing down I saw he was also holding Tectos' hand. He really was accepting the new man in my life.

After an hour of passion and exhausted rest with Tectos, Haji rapped at our door calling us to meet Stephen in the garden atrium. Upon our arrival he pointed to five bales of silk we needed to return to the ship. With the help of Haji and Festus we each carried a bale as we went to meet with Captain Paulus. Upon our arrival everyone stopped to perform a proper bow to Stephen and then continued with their work. Tectos' cousins were working the hold, much to his relief, but he still noticed the broad smile on the faces of our crew of eunuch Britons, which he couldn't help but return blushing as he did. It seemed they had a way of knowing, or at least suspecting, everything. They knew what the cousins had done to Tectos every night. They also knew his status had skyrocketed since they first arrived in Syracuse, but they weren't sure why. Was it because his master had taken him as a lover, or did it have something to do with the giant charade in Roma? Whatever it was, Tectos was way below his masters' league, so he still needed to stay beyond the reach of his lecherous cousins.

By sunset, with the help of all extra hands, the entire next shipment to Roma was verified and nearly loaded. With all looking good we might be able to depart with the next afternoon tide. Preparing to return home for supper, we were joined by Hanno and Rashvi, Yacobsa and Timnah, and finally Captain Paulus. It was a joyous procession that made its way home that evening. Only Stephen knew what lay ahead, and he was planning to surprise everyone, even Leah and the children.

Reaching the house, the door was swung open by Haji dressed in his most formal attire and greeting us with elaborate ceremony. I should have suspected something, but as Grandfather once noted, "Unless there was danger in the air, I should suspect no one's evil." As Haji led us to the dining room, Leah and the children were already finding their places, and each of us were shown to our own places individually. Once again, Aaron was already seated where he could hold the hands of "Father number two and Father Number three." Stephen was smiling as I looked up at him with my own knowing smile in return.

Once again, we were welcomed formally by Stephen and he then prayed over our gathering. Through the course of the meal he made several comments about the amazing tasks we had performed and how he could not be prouder of the example we were setting for all of Aetna Shipping. Then as the sweets were brought in to signal the final course of our meal, Stephen stood to make some announcements.

First, he asked me to join him, "I wish to commend the courage, excellent judgment, unwavering obedience, and loyalty of Tectos of Galatia as shown to his legal master Jacobus Didymus BarSirach. In response, his master in accordance with the customs of this family now presents this certificate of emancipation to Tectos BarSirach which is valid for the rest of his natural life."

The room burst into wild applause as Tectos put his face in his hands and wept. As I picked up his certificate to present to him, I was already beaten to his seat by Aaron who was already smothering him with kisses. My former slave Hanno who was cheering like he was watching a chariot race. It took at least five minutes for the applause and shouting to settle down enough for Stephen to begin to establish the slightest form of order. When we were all seated and quiet again, he announced, "I now have the distinct honor to present two other certificates which still require the signature of the senior rabbi of Syracuse in the morning. The first is to legalize the marriage of Yacobsa, Prince of Chera to Timnah of Judea. The second is for the marriage of Jacobus Didymus BarSirach to his second husband Tectos BarSirach of Galatia. Let's all congratulate the happy couples." Once again Aaron beat me to the lips of my beloved, but how could I spoil his fun? By my estimation, Tectos had no idea who was kissing him anyway . . . he was in total shock.

We all then adjourned to the garden atrium to celebrate with more wine and sweets as Lucius gave out his orders in preparation for the next day's departure for Roma. Of course, he allowed us all until mid-morning to get there in our wedding clothes, so we could change into our elaborate Royal attire before the tide changed.

Everyone but the captain, spent the night at Stephen's home. Stephen suggested that Tectos and I spend the night in one of the guest rooms, so we could focus completely on each other. As it turned out, the three couples stayed up to speak of how becoming a part of Aetna Shipping had totally changed our lives. We decided that when a person works with Stephen, things can happen very expeditiously.

I had already spoken to Stephen that morning about the *Sparrow* departing for Alexandria immediately after our return from Roma taking all of our cash proceeds with us. I was hoping that after his analysis of the proceeds from our first trip he would think it possible for us to make an early departure. He already had all of Sadhu's money put away in a separate chest for us to deliver or reinvest for him in India. Stephen agreed that the sooner we set sail from Berenike the greater our chances of success. We had decided in consultation with Lucius that we should have enough cash reserve by the time we depart to pay the custom tax upon our return to Aegyptus. If we sailed out too late, we would have very little to pay taxes on. It was less than a perfect situation.

In the morning before we left for the synagogue, I asked Stephen about Sadhu's contact with the Jewish carpet merchants in Persia. "If they could still acquire quality carpets from north Persia, Scythia, the Caucasus, and others from the vast steppes of the north, we may be able to collect another large shipment in Sidon before the year is out and be able to hit the Roman carpet market for a second successful season. Besides there is no heavy customs tax in Sidon."

I assured him that I would immediately ask Sadhu to contact his man directly upon my arrival. On second thought I realized we might have a way to cut six months' time off the transaction. Talking to Yacobsa I discovered he knew his "father's" contact through his time at the rabbinical school in Persia. He could send a letter off to him directly through the Persian rabbi scholar at the Alexandrian library. We would assure him that we would have his full payment in gold waiting at our Sidon warehouse at the time his caravan delivered them from Ecbatana.

Our second trip to Roma was every bit as lucrative as the first. We were well received again by Antonius and his mother who had additional friends, both private and commercial who were disappointed they missed us on our earlier visit. They even had a few who we had just sold to who wanted to purchase more. Right away we decided to add twenty percent to every price because we only had one more ship load left. We sold out in four days and we were on our way home with six chests of gold, much of it on deposit for products we still had in Syracuse.

Arriving home from our second trip to Roma, Stephen told us to begin the reloading of the *Swallow* for Alexandria immediately. We already had a vast quantity stocked and ready to ship in the warehouse, including fabulous Roman glass and two Archimedes clocks for King Abrayamsa and King Shikrit. Now it would only take two days to load everything on board to depart Syracuse and head for Alexandria.

The winds were perfect, and the sea was smooth, so we reached that beautiful harbor in seven days. It was mid-day when we dropped our moorings at our warehouse near the entrance to the Jewish quarter. After a night's rest Hanno and Rashvi headed east on horseback with two saddle bags of gold. Once again, they were headed for the northern tip of the Sinus Arabicus where they would then head south to Berenike. After their departure I set out to hire two very large river barges to take us upriver to Kopios. Finally, I located two at dusk. I told the owner where we needed to have them in the morning to begin loading from our warehouse for Kopios. In the days that followed Captain Paulus emptied the *Sparrow* for its return to its former captain and crew. He then moved with his Britons and the cousins into Yacobsa's house in the Jewish Quarter.

The next morning was Shabbat in the Jewish Quarter, so I decided to take Tectos for worship. He enjoyed the ceremony of our wedding with all the spiritual lessons, but he was curious of what a Jewish sermon would be like, and so was I. We arrived about thirty minutes early, so we stood in the courtyard and watched Jews from all over the world gathering for worship. We were just about ready to enter when I thought I saw a familiar man near the entry gate. Walking up to the man, I tapped him on the shoulder. As he turned, we immediately through our arms around each other and called out the other's name. Reaching for Tectos, I introduced him to Thomas, one of the twelve disciples of Jesus. It was nearly time for the service to begin, but we all agreed it was more important to meet with each other than hear the Torah read.

Walking back to Yacobsa's, I learned that Thomas had just returned from upriver after sharing the message of Jesus with the Jewish community in Aethiopia. He spent a year with them after receiving an invitation from the queen's treasurer who was in Jerusalem when Jesus was killed. While there he saw the number of both Jewish and Goy . . . non-Jewish believers . . . increase every week. Unfortunately, he confessed that he was unaware of the locations of any of the other disciples, but he was thinking of now going to the Jewish community in Persia. By the time we had reached Yacobsa's home, a very radical idea had begun to form in my head. As Yacobsa opened the door at home, he cried out, "Thomas!" The rest became history.

As tea was prepared, I shared the news that Hanno and Rashvi had just left the morning before for Berenike on the Aegyptian coast of Sinus Arabicus, to prepare our ship for its coming return to India. Then I took the leap of faith and asked Thomas if he had ever heard the voice of God in his heart calling him to India. He looked at me with intense eyes which began to fill with tears, and he whispered, "Every day."

By midafternoon we took him down to the warehouse to meet the Sergeant and see if he had heard from the owner of the barges. Learning that the barge owner had not contacted the warehouse, I began to feel a little tense. Thomas just placed his hand on my leg, and I immediately relaxed with the assurance the barges were on their way. As we walked back to the house, Tectos ran up behind us to tell us the barges had just come out of the canal and into the harbor.

I knew I had a confession I needed to share with Thomas as we turned back to the warehouse. "The first thing I wanted to do when I saw you this morning was to offer you free passage to India enabling you to meet with the Jewish community there. The synagogue in Yacobsa's home town seats a couple hundred people, and many have already heard about The Way of Jesus. Also, the senior rabbi was at the crucifixion of our Lord, and you might remember seeing him at the feast of Pentecost."

"Could that be the one who I called the Holy Rabbi, Sadhu?" Affirming that it was the same man he remembered, I turned to Yacobsa.

"Thomas, this is Sadhu's nephew, Prince Yacobsa of Chera. He too, is a follower of The Way. Now I must confess that the other reason I was so tense was because you are a holy man anointed by God and we are all eunuchs. Many religious people feel we are unclean because we cannot or will not procreate children and have no desire or ability to marry or even lay with women. Therefore, we often seek romantic relationships with other men."

Taking both my hand and Yacobsa's, Thomas promised, "God loves you more than you could ever imagine. He brought you to the execution of his Son, and he rejoiced with you as he flooded you with His spirit at the great feast of Pentecost. Now you are touching people all over the world because you have learned how to follow Him. You should also know that the royal treasurer who invited me to the Aethiopian royal court was also a eunuch."

At that moment, I thought of my precious Tectos and the dying thief, Horse. God really had moved in Horse, and it was directly through Tectos. Thomas continued as though he was reading my thoughts. "We will never be what the religious leaders told Jesus we had to be in order to experience the love of God. No man, not even God's Son was good enough in their judgment. For many years my question had been, 'are these men really good enough for God to accept . . . or is that even the issue?' In fact, Jacobus, I remember your slave, Hanno. His master cut off his balls and made him a eunuch when he was just a child. Several years ago, I dedicated myself to God as a third type eunuch . . . a eunuch by my own choice, to abstain from the love of women forever and therefore, I also will never produce children for Israel.

"Yes, the heart of each man is what calls God to himself. Jesus assured us that he would never turn away one of his children who thought he did not deserve God's love, but who still trusted in God and not in his own attempts at holiness. This is the dilemma of the rabbi wrapped in his own spotless robes. He must remember, the loving rabbi who rents his robes apart and weeps with the eunuch who is ridiculed for his sin. That rabbi is a true man of God."

CHAPTER 58

PASSAGE TO INDIA – OCTOBER 20, AD30

As we moored the barges to our dock and began to bring the cargo out of the warehouse to load, Thomas asked me directly if I was serious about leaving for India as soon as the barges were packed, and when everyone was prepared to take him with us. I looked at him and said with as much sincerity as I knew how to express, "Yes, I am very serious. We should be ready to pull away from our dock by tomorrow afternoon. If you feel God is leading you to India, be here tomorrow before midday."

Thomas looked directly into my eyes and replied, "Some have said I wouldn't excel as a disciple because I was never really sure about God's voice when he spoke to me. They said that I was always too indecisive. Well, I'll tell you right now, I'm going to India tomorrow! I'll be here in the morning."

When I saw the glimmer in his eyes I couldn't help but laugh. When I finally caught my breath, I asked where he was staying and if he would honor us by staying at Yacobsa's house for a night with all of us, including the crew. I even assured him of some terrific Indian food. By that time his excitement level was running pretty high, and he claimed, "I am compelled to accept your hospitality." He left immediately to collect his few belongings, and he promised to see us before dinner.

I was delighted when in midafternoon I saw a smiling Thomas walking through the gate of the Jewish Quarter carrying a small bundle of assorted items tied up in a grimy piece of scrap cloth. He walked up to me, held up his bundle. and asked if we would have enough room aboard one of the barges to squeeze in all of his worldly goods. Seeing the look on my face, he stated simply that he travels light, and he can take all his belongings anywhere. With a chuckle in my voice I told him to bring them along to Yacobsa's.

Walking to Yacobsa's, I learned that Thomas knew nothing about India . . . its customs, climate, or its Jewish community. I knew we would have plenty of time to discuss these things during our voyage, but I felt compelled to share some points of interest with him before we left. Entering the front door as one of the servants showed us in, I put his bundle in the main room and asked him to join me in the small garden where we could sit and talk. We had about three hours before dinner, and I took every minute of that to orient him to what was ahead. The more we shared the more convinced he seemed to become that God was directing him to India. By dinner he was as assured of that, as he was that the sun would rise in the morning.

I felt comfortable with that, and led him into the main room when everyone arrived for dinner. Most of them seemed surprised when I introduced the Galilean as a passenger who would be traveling to India with us. Those who knew him from our time in Jerusalem were more than excited to have a disciple of Jesus among us. Sitting down to dinner, everyone's excitement increased as Thomas spoke of his years with Jesus and his time spent in the royal court of Aethiopia. By the time the meal was over, all of us were sure that Thomas was going to make our trip much more meaningful as he shared his understanding of God with each of us.

Even though it turned out to be a late night, we were all ready to finish loading in the morning and have the barges towed through the city's canals to the Nile wharfs by sunset the next day. We left our Briton sailors on the barges while the rest of us went back to the house to get our final night's sleep. First it seemed a little selfish, but soon I remembered the Britons enjoyed sleeping under the stars.

Our major complication was that Tectos and his cousins were going to be together much longer than I thought the cousins would want. If the cousins weren't such a great team, I would probably suggest exchanging them for two cargo slaves from the warehouse. However, it was a fact they knew the Indian products better than anyone I could hope to replace them with, so I might as well accept the reality that I, or someone, might need to become a peacemaker.

Our second complication was that Yacobsa wanted to take Timnah to meet all of the family in India. The Sergeant had reassured us that he could handle the possible arrival of the Persian Carpets from Alexandria, Syria if they beat us home from India. I prayed he could because he had only worked with carpets once before;

The crews' first night on the Nile docks turned out to be a beautiful one. Everyone else, especially Tectose and me, as we slept that last night alone in a room at Yacobsa's house. Knowing it would be the last time for us to have any degree of privacy, it was a time for passion and loving, even though it turned out to be a terrible night for sleeping. The next morning Tectos and I got up with the sun and went directly to the warehouse with Yacobsa and Timnah to say farewell to the Sergeant and to collect our Captain who spent the night in the warehouse with the Sergeant. I realized for the first time how long these voyages must be for him, and the loneliness he must feel. I told the Sergeant that we would see him next year. As they shared a final embrace, we turned and headed for the barges on the lake behind the city.

By the time we arrived, everyone from the house was already there and prepared to push us off as soon as the Aegyptian pilots finished mounting the masts. When we were all in our preassigned places, the sails were raised, and the ropes released from the wharf and we began to cross the lake. Traveling through the estuary with twelve hours of daylight ahead of us we saw more wildlife than on our past trips. This time I also noticed many more birds, most of which I had never seen anywhere else. At one point a hippopotamus came disturbingly close to our lead barge. Knowing their ability to capsize a boat kept all of us on the lookout. After wiggling its ears at us and opening its cavernous mouth to roar at us, it slowly sank and the Aegyptians began to panic and Thomas began to pray. It seemed likely that he swam off to find his mate.

On our fourteenth day we reached Kopios and I hired sixty camels, significantly more than the year before, but we had more people and more trade goods . . . also more gold, including Sadhu's. It took a day and a half with everyone working, to get all the camels loaded by the end of the second day. It wasn't over yet! We all had to mount up and ride through the night until we reached our first well and then we had a chance to sleep through the day. The next evening, we ate a filling breakfast and mounted up to again travel through the night. Finally, reaching the last well eleven days later, everyone was eager to strike out the next evening to reach Berenike before lunch,

Going down the mountain trail into Berenike we noticed there were only a handful of ships still in port. Fortunately, we already had our crew with us, so all we had to do was load the *Triton* and be on our way. We looked for a familiar face as the camels began walking down along the docks. Finally arriving at the second ship from the end we heard a familiar voice coming from the very last ship. Immediately Hanno and Rashvi climbed over the side and ran to meet us.

In minutes they saw Yacobsa and Timnah while they began to inquire about their reason for being with us. Yacobsa assured them that our Sergeant had everything under control in Alexandria and they decided to join us and take the opportunity to introduce his new husband to the family. Meanwhile, our same Aegyptian and Nubian archers appeared out of the hatches to see what all the commotion was about. We stripped the riding camels of our baggage before they were led to the corral in groups of five. Then everybody began offloading the freight camels and getting the cargo on board before nightfall. Fortunately, we didn't have to get it down into the hold until morning. Security required that we only needed to get it off the camels and onto the ship.

The next morning Hanno and I went to meet with our agent to verify that we had paid for everything necessary. The crew got most of the major items below deck where the cousins were working in the desperate heat to get everything secured. Later I couldn't find Tectos, and Lucius told me that he had been working all morning in the hold with his cousins. With that I decided that if he could do it, so could I, after all my specialty was filling up the tight spaces.

An hour after dark everything was below deck, and Hanno said the tide should be going out in two hours. By sunrise, Berenike was beyond our wake as we headed for Aden down the Sinus Arabicus. Walking around the *Triton* I was once again amazed at how massive and beautiful she was. Everything was perfect, and her sails were full. I could only pray they would continue that way as we were among the last to make the crossing to Muziris that season. We made it to Aden without seeing a single dhow trying to cross our bow. We filled up on fresh water and headed straight for the far tip of the giant island of Socotra.

There we picked up another chest of fine frankincense while making a toothless old man very happy. As I walked away from his hut and looked around, I began to wonder what he does with all his money. When I mentioned my observation to Thomas, he told me to look closely at the fishing village on the beach below. As I did, I saw people sitting around doing nothing, not even fishing. He asked if I saw it. I had to answer that I saw nothing. Thomas smiled, "That's it exactly. The old man is the head man of the village and he sells frankincense to buy food for the villagers from Arab traders. This part of the island is a desert. All they have is fresh water, ocean fish, and frankincense. They have become totally dependent on the frankincense trade."

So far, we had cut off two days from the last years' time. Captain Paulus confidently assured us that he understood the chart much better this year, and with precision he was hoping to cut another two days off by arriving much closer to Muziris than we had last year. It was a challenge, but we felt like we needed to do it because of our late departure and the uncertainty over the number of days the winds would continue in our favor. Checking with Rashvi and Yacobsa they assured us that they would recognize the topography of the coast no matter where we made first landfall. The real comfort was that Thomas maintained his seat at the bow where he prayed during the many boring hours of the ocean's sameness.

One day, about five days before our anticipated arrival in Muziris, our watchman spotted another Roman trader on the horizon far to the north. Lucius presumed that it was headed for Muziris as well, but it was following the course on the map which we followed the year before. We all prayed he was right.

In three days we began seeing shore birds who were fishing rather than migrating. We had to be within a couple days of land. Suddenly it started to cloud up and rain very hard. Fortunately, it didn't last more than half a day, but it wasn't until late that night that Lucius was able to verify our position by identifying the new star he had been following in a straight east direction. Learning what these new stars represented was another important thing he discovered from the year before. He felt confident that one of the next two mornings would put us within sight of our destination.

The next morning Tectos and I were at the bow when the sun rose straight ahead of us. Once the glare diminished as the sun continued to rise, we saw them . . . the ghats. By noon Yacobsa Identified the unique contour of the mountains as placing us about an hour north of the Periyar River. Our plan was to drop anchor in the mouth of the river within four hours . . . if there was room left for us. This would allow us to go ashore at sunup and arrive at Sadhu's by midmorning. Yacobsa almost wanted to dive in and swim ashore now. He really was homesick, and he was dying to introduce Timnah to everyone. Finding a good anchorage, both Timnah and Thomas joined Yacobsa and me as he watched the shoreline for an hour looking for light somewhere along the beach or up the river. We only spotted a couple of torches about half a mile down the beach . . . probably fishermen or turtle hunters.

Before the sun came up over the horizon, we were all up on deck ready to eat a light breakfast and see India again. As the sun came over the ghats, we all gasped at the lushness of the shore and the river banks. Of course, that was a real mystery to those who didn't realize Muziris was not a city, but a trading post hidden in the forest. Within minutes the cook was out with bread, dates, some dried meat, and a jug of wine. As we finished, a pair of the Britons moved quickly to lower the longboat. Because they were the fastest to get to the boat, they were first to claim the right to row us ashore. It was obvious they were also excited about being back in India. Once they were settled in and on the water, our delegation climbed down the rope ladder and took our places. Captain Paulus called down from the deck that he would join us later.

Looking over at Thomas before we pushed off from the ship, I saw tears running down his beard as his head was bowed in prayer. This was a great beginning.

CHAPTER 59

THE TORAH – OCTOBER 27, AD30

Rowing to Muziris, was the most exciting event we had experienced in over a month. To see the flowers in the trees and hear the peacocks screaming in the early morning light was like a welcome home from India herself. It was a spiritual experience, just to watch the expressions of joy on Thomas' face. He counted the minutes until he would embrace his great Indian rabbi. When I had the courage to break into his quiet personal revelry, I asked him how he felt. With the joy of a child all over his face, he simply said, "I'm home Jacobus! Home! Thank you!"

Finally arriving at the wharf, I instructed our Britons to pull the longboat ashore and join us on our long walk past the warehouses and into the city of Paravur and its spectacular Hindu temples. Reaching the far side of the city, we took Thomas to see Sadhu's synagogue which he had heard so much about. After walking nearly an hour and a half we reached the massive walls surrounding Sadhu and Princess Rahelani's beautiful home.

Standing in front of the great door of his former home, with only Timnah at his side, Yacobsa pulled the bronze chain and rang the bell.

The rest of us were standing back to one side, holding our breath with anticipation. When the door cracked open and the face of the old servant woman from Alexandria peeked out, there was suddenly one of the loudest screams I had ever heard. Throwing the door wide open, she bent to kiss Yacobsa's hands with tears in her eyes as others began to come streaming out from the house.

Poor Timnah was wanting to disappear, but he didn't have a chance. Everyone knew he belonged to Prince Yacobsa and began to express their love for him as well. Soon Rahelani and the sadhu arrived at the door and all the servants parted so they could greet their son. After their ecstatic welcome, Sadhu looked past his son and saw me standing with one of our Galatian cargo slaves who seemed rather finely dressed for a slave. Coming to greet me, he froze in his tracks when he recognized Thomas as the other man standing next to me. Immediately he began to weep for joy at such a gift from God. The apostle and the rabbi were locked in a hug that even Rahelani couldn't break into . . . and would never try to.

After about fifteen minutes of loving Indian chaos, Rahelani regained her dignity, or at least as much as she could on such short notice and invited all of us to come in off the street and into their beautiful garden. Instantly the servants dashed into the house to prepare tea and an early lunch for us. In the meantime, I was still trying to control my simultaneous laughter and tears, especially when Rahelani saw her former slave, Rashvi, standing next to his amazing Hanno. More hugs and kisses. At this point, I decided it was time to introduce Tectos to Sadhu. When I introduced him as my second husband, Sadhu got the most peculiar look on his face. He asked if Abrayamsa with his several wives had influenced me. Knowing how he meant it, I grinned and replied that it was the best advice the king had ever given me. Laughing with me, he called Rahelani over and she began to make over me like the mother I never had. In the meantime, Tectos was not understanding a word of the frantic Aramaic which was flying around with Malayalam and even a little Tamil thrown in now and then.

Soon enough Tectos became the center of attention for most of the servants. None of them had ever seen a man who was so white with such silvery, gold hair and such sky-blue eyes. It was like seeing an elephant in Syracuse, and Tectos was not too sure if he liked being the sideshow. However, the true celebrity among the Indians was definitely Thomas. It was as if God had just dropped him out of the sky to help Sadhu at the synagogue and his ministry throughout the kingdom.

As the servants were preparing the lunch, Rahelani lead us into the dining room to recline on the cushions and have some tea. In the meantime, Sadhu pulled himself away from Thomas long enough to send a messenger on horseback to the palace informing King Abrayamsa of our arrival and the arrival of his brother, Yacobsa. Within half an hour the food started to come out, and then came out some more. By that time Yacobsa's sister, Merrayum, had arrived with her husband and children. The reunion was truly familial as the children were introduced to their Uncle Yacobsa. When Sadhu told his daughter that one of Jesus' disciples was sitting across the room, she hastily got up and asked her father to introduce them. Thomas didn't have much of a chance to receive nourishment that morning as Merrayum basically sat at his feet asking questions for at least two hours and listening to his retelling of many principals that were taught to him by the Master.

After lunch, I asked the Britons to return to the ship and bring Captain Paulus back to the house if he could get away. They were gone in a dash, happy to do whatever I asked. Having been with Lucius for over fourteen months, I could see their tremendous loyalty to him and to Aetna. I wondered if they had yet discovered that their Captain was a born eunuch just like themselves.

It was midafternoon when we heard a large group of people at the outer door. Sadhu's manservant ran out to see what the noise was all about. With the door opened we saw the king on his horse with five accompanying guards! Immediately he closed the door and opened the giant gate for the horsemen to enter. As King Abrayamsa dismounted, he instantly asked to see his brother. Following Sadhu's servant into the house, he was led to where we were all seated and the servant announced, "The King!"

We all scrambled to our feet, with most of us totally disoriented. Abrayamsa made a dash for Yacobsa, throwing his arms around him and kissing all over his face. When they finally, ran out of kisses, King Abrayamsa turned to see the rest of us and began to laugh. I was pleased that he came to me first and also kissed me, then to Rashvi, his father's loyal slave, and finally Hanno. Looking at the others he didn't know, I saw that it was probably my responsibility to introduce everyone to the king.

"Your Royal Highness may I introduce Timnah of Judea . . . your new brother-in-law, Yacobsa's husband. Next is my new husband, the heir to the throne of Galatia, Crown Prince Tectos. Lastly, it gives me great pleasure to introduce Thomas of Galilee and Judea, friend and admirer of your brother-in-law, the sadhu and your newest subject who is taking up permanent residence in your beautiful country. Your Royal Highness will also be glad to know that our Captain Lucius Paulus though delayed with tasks aboard ship will be here in a few hours."

Laughing in his typical way, he slapped me on the back and responded to my formality by saying it sounded like I brought a delegation of ambassadors to his humble kingdom. Suddenly I remembered Antonius' greeting and became even more formal proclaiming, "Regrettably I brought no credentialed ambassadors, but I did bring sincerest greetings from members of Roma's imperial family of Tiberius Claudius Nero Caesar, Emperor of Roma. They asked specifically that I thank you for the gifts we gave to them in the name of King Abrayamsa of Chera."

Everyone dropped their jaws and stood silently staring at me. I suppose I took it a little over the top, but it was absolutely accurate, so I continued. "Those gifts were carried to an imperial family gathering in our honor at a seaside palace outside of Roma by your twin brother, Yacobsa, who as a Royal Prince of Chera, represented your kingdom." As King Abrayamsa looked over to Yacobsa, he saw the biggest smile any of us could have imagined. With tears in his eyes, the king took his brother in his arms again as they both wept. The love between them was rekindled once again.

Sadhu and Rahelani knew we had contacts with the emperor's cousin but had not dreamed that it could have been formalized in such a way, and so quickly. In fact, as I looked back and thought of Stephen's reaction when we returned to Syracuse, the whole thing did seem like a fantasy.

As a result of the recent rain and gentle breezes, the afternoon seemed much cooler than it had been mid-ocean. Rahelani decided we should retire to the garden and claim the comfortable chairs while enjoying the breeze under the trees. Looking up into the branches, I reminded Tectos that the beauty of the mosses and orchids on those great branches were something he could have never seen looking up in the hold of a ship. Taking my hand tightly in his own he whispered, "I never saw anything while looking up in the hold of a ship . . . except the face of one of my cousins while he was raping me."

Tectos wasn't trying to chide me, but to make a point. He continued, "Life in the hold of a ship did not have much of a view of our world and the lives we are living. That life is a sealed tomb inside of me." His words crushed me as I reached out to hug him in apology as everyone seemed to look on. I can't deny that I could not understand his years of pain, just as I could not understand Hanno's. Just thinking that this man I loved so much was representative of one quarter of the empire's population who are held in slavery, really troubled me. Suddenly it crashed down on me that good fortune like ours was the cause of so much of their pain.

Embarrassed, I turned and walked silently into a dense and secluded sector of the garden and sat on a bench with my head in my hands. How could I have said something so insensitive to a man I loved so much? I should have shared the excitement of his new life . . . not reminded him of the pain of the one he left behind. I needed his tenderness and gentleness more than anything else. Then I felt his touch on my shoulder as I looked up into his beautiful sky-blue eyes. I had so much to learn about the tenderness of love.

Walking back arm in arm to join the others, the moss and the orchids overhead looked even more beautiful than ever. Immediately Rahelani came up and put her arms around both of us, sensing our brokenness and our new adventure in the world of love. To cheer us up she happily informed us that her little brother was going to plan a royal dinner and reception at the palace within two weeks for everyone, including our crew. As she took my free hand and led us to Abrayamsa, I thanked him for his hospitality and for giving us such a high honor. Laughing, he waived his hands in denial, following typical Indian fashion as he replied, "No, no, dearest young friend, I must thank you for making me a very rich man!" The humorous truth of his statement struck us all.

Suddenly I remembered Sadhu's gold! Rushing over to him with Tectos at my side I apologized for not bringing his payment from Stephen with me when we left the *Triton*. We left the ship in such a rush I totally forgot about it. Then it was his turn to waive his hands in denial and say, "No, no, I am not worried, my friend. Now I must thank you for also making me a very rich man!" Once again everyone began to laugh as Abrayamsa stepped over and slapped his brother-in-law on his back and shouted at the top of his voice, "Isn't it wonderful to have a young friend in Roma!!!" In the ruckus I heard a soft sweet voice whisper in my ear, "Yes, it is, and I love him."

Later that evening as we were preparing to enter the dining room, we heard the brass bell at the gate ringing loudly. Sadhu's manservant dashed out the door to see who it could be at that hour and returned a few minutes later followed by a properly attired Captain Paulus and our Breton rowers dressed in fine tunics looking as proud as young Jewish boys on their wedding day. They were carrying a beautifully carved chest between them. Lucius apologized for being late, but he couldn't find where I hid the key, commenting that there are thousands of places to hide a small key on a large ship. With that he bowed and handed me the key.

Since everyone was still standing, I suggested they gather around behind me because we had a very important presentation to make. Then I called Sadhu and Rahelani to stand beside me as I gave the key to Tectos and asked him to open the chest for our wonderful hosts. Bowing, he turned toward the chest and inserted the key and turned it. Waiting a few seconds for suspense, he lifted the lid as everyone gasped, not because the chest was filled with gold but because on top of the gold was an ancient, giant, synagogue scroll. At that point I turned and proclaimed, "Sadhu, your dear friend, Stephen, acquired this ancient Torah in Jerusalem with the help of your special friend and admirer, Nicodemus. It was written many centuries ago in Babylon where your family has its roots. Over the centuries, this scroll has been at the heart of more than three synagogues. This is Aetna Shipping's gift to the rabbi of the great synagogue in Paravur. It is a true gift of love from us to you."

Everyone stood silent as Sadhu reverently stepped forward and knelt to first touch the scroll gently, bent forward and kissed it, and then he picked it up and held it tightly. When he stood, he cradled it in his arms next to his heart. Rahelani began to clap and sing something in Hebrew as all the Indians joined along . . . including King Abrayamsa. As Sadhu walked around the room with the scroll still in his arms, they all danced along behind him. Absolutely no one even cast the slightest glance at the fortune in gold in the middle of the floor, so I motioned Tectos to close the lid and lock it. When he offered to return the key to me, I told him to keep it and present it to Sadhu at the beginning of dinner.

During the Torah celebration, the servants in the kitchen were expanding our dinner into a banquet, and Rahelani asked the two Bretons to join us. Then Sadhu asked the Captain, "Did you walk through the forest and then the city with that priceless Torah without an escort?"

Lucius replied, "There are six Aegyptian archers outside and the king has an escort of eight Cavalry Guards who are in the garden as well."

Sadhu laughed and told him, "I can't invite the horses in to eat my grass, but I must invite the soldiers, for they are more than welcome and so are your guards from Aegyptus."

Tectos quickly joined Sadhu's manservant and called all fourteen men into the house.

When the eating area for the soldiers, archers, and sailors was being prepared Sadhu asked Thomas and me to sit on each side of him. Abrayamsa sat next to me and Rahelani next to Thomas. The dinner was greater than fabulous. It was truly memorable, especially for Tectos who was seated next to the King who insisted on caressing his beautiful white leg all evening. It was quite late when the dinner ended and Abrayamsa and his escort left for the palace.

Rahelani then had the dilemma of finding a place for the rest of us to spend the night. Starting with six Aegyptians and two Britons, she had a large sleeping room in the servants' quarters which was ideal. Tectos and I were given my usual room, Captain Paulus was also given his old room, Yacobsa and Timnah were given the one next to that, and Hanno and Rashvi were given the room next to that. Thomas was placed in the elegant room which was usually reserved for Abrayamsa on his occasional escapes from the palace.

When she got it all sorted out, Rahelani announced to all of us, as she bid us all a good night, that the world was sleeping all over her house . . . six Aegyptians, two Britons, one Hispanic Jew, one Galatian, one Carthaginian, one Judean, one Roman, and one Galilean recently arrived from Aethiopia. She began to laugh hysterically the more she thought about it. Then, still laughing, she threw her hands up and shouted "Goodnight" in every language she could think of. When she joined Sadhu in her own room, she asked him if he thought she had forgotten anyone. Looking at her with a very sad face he replied, "Yes, me in Malayalam!" With that, she punched his arm and pulled him into bed . . . still laughing.

The next morning, when we left Rahelani's beautiful home, our Britons and Aegyptians couldn't stop talking about dinning with a king in the home of a princess who invited them to spend the night. It was also something we all marveled at as well. Captain Paulus proudly told all of us as we passed through the gate, "Remember . . . Great things can happen when you work for Aetna Shipping." With that we all agreed.

The next week was spent working out further details of that season's trading, even though all the terms were basically the same as the year before. Of course, the biggest sensation was the extremely accurate clocks that Stephen purchased in Alexandria for Kings Abrayamsa and Shikrit. King Abrayamsa promised me he would keep the clock a secret until King Shikrit was presented with his own clock the night of the royal dinner.

My head was still spinning days later with what King Abrayamsa told me that night at dinner. "When King Shikrit comes down for our celebration, he committed to bring an immense elephant pack train which would deliver everything you purchased last year and more, especially in gems, fine silks, and rare and unique spices . . . plus several loads of forest ivory. King Shikrit also promised to bring a special gift for Aetna Shipping to use as a symbol for your trade with India."

The greatest item going to Roma with every shipment from Muziris was still black pepper. The crew was loading about three longboats of pepper and other spices a day into the hold of the *Triton*. Also, Abrayamsa had his warehouse restrict the amount of ivory for sale to other Roman merchants so that we would have about fifteen percent more than in the previous shipment. Then as we continued the difficult task of emptying the far corners of the ship while it was simultaneously being loaded, we reached the area where many small items had been stored. We located three large straw packed baskets of fine Roman glass vases and bowls which were intricately carved through one or two layers of different colors of glass creating a miraculous interplay of light and color. Fragile as they were they became cherished possessions for each of the royal cousins.

The final new group of products that we brought was an assortment of Roman armaments including fine iron swords, shields, and horseshoes. For a novelty we also brought two baskets of ostrich feathers for processions and royal decorations. We also had many other small or useful items that Rahelani had mentioned the previous year including carved cameo broaches, rings, and necklaces carved from conch shells. Each piece had an image of a portrait, animal, or flower carved with exquisite craftsmanship. Also, in the small items was the red Sicilian coral beads always popular in India. We also had more of the fine Gallian wine which both kings wanted to have in reserve for palace use. The olive oil and frankincense also brought us high profits. As the bow was now empty, filling the entire hold could proceed without delay.

CHAPTER 60

A ROYAL FEAST – OCTOBER 31, AD30

The day of the royal feast finally arrived, and our entire delegation, except the cargo slaves, went to Abrayamsa's palace tense with excitement. All but the sailors and archers spent the night at Sadhu and Rahelani's home in preparation to greet King Shikrit when he arrived at the palace. His scheduled arrival was to be midday, but he surprised everyone by arriving on horseback three hours early . . . rather than by elephant. He apologized to King Abrayamsa, stating that his entire stable of elephants was being used to bring the baggage, retainers, and his items for trade. In fact, the reception had to be delayed by several hours because his retinue would not arrive at the palace until midafternoon.

I wondered about how all this confusion would affect Abrayamsa's plans for a pomp and ceremony reception. Milling about on the palace parade ground, rather than lined up the stairs at the palace entrance, we left the Vizier with a hasty change of plans since the guest of honor was visiting with the guests below. I think the dozen horses were a major distraction for most of our seafarers, and Abrayamsa was obliged to come down the steps to greet all of us in the middle of that chaos. Fortunately, his important guests were all friends or relatives, and the horses were soon taken to the stables. I thought the confusion cleared when we all followed the two kings up to be introduced to Abrayamsa's Vizier, who had been left standing alone at the top of the stairs with the royal honor guard.

After all the ceremonial bowing and formal cordiality, Abrayamsa eventually invited us into the palace where we were each formally received by the two kings. The still flustered Vizier then escorted us into the large Assembly Hall where we encountered clusters of chairs everywhere along with the king's three wives and their retainers. The Vizier evidently realized he was defeated as the day's chief of protocol. Shortly after my entry I noticed that he wisely decided to sit down and chat with King Shikrit's Vizier who seemed to be having the same problem.

Faced with having caused an informal gathering, King Shikrit was placed in a bit of a disadvantage. He would have preferred a reception like he had for us the previous year. The root of his problem was that his mother tongue was Tamil his second language was Malayalam and he had no more than a weak knowledge of Aramaic from his childhood days with his Jewish mother, the sister of King Abrayamsa's mother. Consequently, he constantly found himself looking for a translator to help him until Abrayamsa finally sent Rashvi and Hanno over to help.

Tectos, who was at least Greek educated and had learned Latin as a slave, was able to pass some information on to our Britons and Aegyptians who were totally overwhelmed by everything they saw and heard. However, the one who enjoyed the chaos most was Thomas, whose Greek was limited and very idiomatic, but his native Aramaic was among the best in the room. King Abrayamsa's youngest sister, Princess Merrayum, wanted to spend most of her time with Thomas anyway, making their connection very productive. She was disappointed that she had only a limited opportunity to spend quality time with Thomas while at her parent's home nearly two weeks prior. After the usual small talk which she agreed to translate for Thomas, she held him by the hand and poured her heart out. She loved God with all of her entire being, but she was struggling between the Law of the Torah and the simplicity of Jesus' message which her brother-in-law, Sadhu, told her was a fulfillment of the Torah. It sounded like a contradiction which Sadhu helped her with significantly, but she still had many questions. This was exactly what Thomas had encountered among the Jews in Aethiopia. Leading her to an arrangement of unoccupied chairs at the far end of the Hall, he invited her to visit with him for a while.

Thomas was never aggressive but always gentle. Looking at Yacobsa's sister he sensed her need. "Merrayum, Jesus did not want to replace the Torah and the other great messages and lessons delivered by God to our forefathers. His purpose was to fulfill them. The laws of the Torah were meant to guide us not rule us. The love of God in our hearts is what should govern us. It is not what we do or don't do that matters. It is how we reveal the true love of God to others that really matters. Tonight, if there is pork, or serpent, or horse on the banquet table, as a child of God I will feel free to eat it. I am sure it will be delicious. My purpose is not to intimidate my host and look down at the king because I am a better Jew, but to thank him and praise God that I have been brought into his life to reveal God through me.

"Another illustration of this would be your beautiful brother and his loving Judean husband. Many rabbis would say that Moses stated that Yacobsa's love is evil when he wrote about the great evil of a man laying with another man. Jesus turned that upside-down when he told us that a born eunuch, like your brother, should not marry a woman therefore making two people miserable. Neither should eunuchs like

Hanno or Rashvi who have been emasculated. Nor should eunuchs like me, who have vowed to abstain from the love of women to avoid the many family distractions from what God has called me to do. Moses needed tens of thousands of children who would grow up to be warriors who would defeat the armies of Canaan . . . and he only had forty years to get them. God now needs men who will not be distracted from the individual tasks of sharing his love and grace which he has chosen for them to do. Men like Yacobsa, Jacobus, Hanno, Rashvi, and myself . . . we all have a purpose. So do you my dear Merrayum. Love God with all your heart and love your neighbor like you love yourself. That is the greatest commandment now. Since I have been here in India, we have a unique problem . . . the Avarna, or the Untouchables. That is India's bigger dilemma for God's people.

"Today we call this understanding of God's love 'The Way.' It is the way we are to live like God would have us live. We are not to be other people's judges, but to be other people's advocates before God. 'The Way' is love, and I see so very much of that in your heart. Follow your heart, and you will find the understanding you seek."

Shortly after Thomas completed his time with Princess Merrayum, the Vizier called all of us to King Abrayamsa's Throne Room where two thrones were set up side by side, as they would be at an international council. As King Shikrit was shown his throne by his cousin, we all gathered around to hear a short speech of welcome by the Vizier. Bowing we acknowledged his position and waited for King Abrayamsa to take the proceedings to the next level. At his signal, I approached his throne and bowed again as I began to address both kings in a formal greeting, giving them thanks for opening their kingdoms to us.

Following a nod from King Abrayamsa, Hanno left the room to bring in the gilded Greek clock from Alexandria and place it at the feet of King Shikrit, and Rashvi did the same for his former master. As they simultaneously backed away and bowed, I explained that these very rare gifts were clocks which accurately tell the time of day all the way through the night. They were invented by a Greek scholar in Alexandria and rulers from many nations are commissioning them for their own governments. Then I informed them that Rashvi would instruct them in their proper operation and maintenance later.

Even though Abrayamsa knew all the details of our mission, I went through everything again for King Shikrit. Upon completing that critical formality, I asked King Abrayamsa for the privilege of introducing our delegation. Once again, I introduced Tectos as the Crown Prince of Galatia and Lucius as our Captain. At that point I once more formally gave them greetings from the Imperial Family in Roma who thanked them for their gifts of a magnificent diamond from King Abrayamsa and a stunning and vibrant Ruby from King Shikrit. The last formality was to review the terms of our dealings with them, exactly as they were the year before.

Bowing in proper Indian fashion the Vizier announced that our meeting was over, and it was time to adjourn to the Dining Hall. Following the kings, we watched as they sat side by side at the far end of the table. Then the Vizier began taking each of us to our assigned seats. Once we were all seated King Abrayamsa thanked King Shikrit for honoring us with his presence. Then he stood and offered a blessing prayer in Hebrew which totally caught each of us off guard. With his amen, the staff began bringing in enough food for an army . . . only an army would have no idea what they were eating or how to eat it. To my delight they started with three peacocks in full plumage set down on the center line of the table. Each peacock was setting on a large mound of gold nested on a silver platter studded with brilliant blue sapphires.

I reached over and took Tectos' hand, for he nearly passed out when he saw the magnificent giant birds of a hundred colors and immense open fanned tails as they stared at us as though they were daring us to attempt eating them. Breaking our trance, other unbelievable dishes were brought in followed by premium wine from our amphora of Gallian vintage which was poured out to everyone. Immediately three chefs entered and lifted the hollow peacocks from their immense mounds of gold and began to carve the roasted peacocks which up until now had been hidden from view. After the meat was served, the staff scooped out large spoons full of gold leafed rice. Then we each helped ourselves to as many of the other wonderful delicacies before us as we would like to try. Looking around the table I noticed that other than Tectos it was Thomas who was most uncomfortable by the excesses of the menu, especially the eating of real gold as though it were no more than bread.

Before a dessert of fruit that had been chilled in a deep well of very cold spring water, topped with sweet yogurt was served, we were informed by the Vizier that King Shikrit's caravan had begun its decent down the great hill east of the palace. Tectos was about to see his first elephant! He had seen their teeth and even slept with them, but he still couldn't visualize an animal with teeth that size which could be treated like a family pet.

He was one of the first out the front entry of the palace and into the courtyard as he heard the thunderous trumpeting of their call to announce their arrival. As a giant bull led the others that were piled high with bales of pepper, spices, silks and scores of other commodities the Romans want, Tectos had to rub his eyes in disbelief. The rider of the lead elephant was nearly hidden behind the giant animal's head and ears, but the animal was completely free of any reins or any other human assistance to guide it other than hearing the rider talk to him or poke his ears with his bare feet. Tectos now understood why his ancestors fled to the high plateaus of Galatia when they encountered the Greek armies coming out of Persia on creatures like these.

Hearing the trumpeting, the palace livery staff came from every direction bringing ladders and ropes to assist in the offloading of dozens of these giant beasts. Then the most amazing thing happened. When King Shikrit came down the stairs to appear before the caravan, in unison every elephant bowed down on one knee while raising its long trunk, to silently greet their king. No one in Galatia or Roma would ever believe what Tectos was seeing. As the animals began to settle down on their stomachs side by side around the courtyard, the livery staff leaned the ladders against the animal's sides and began to untie and remove their cargo. As strange as it seemed, the elephants looked as though they enjoyed all of the sudden attention . . . and also getting those heavy loads off their backs.

While they were unloading, King Shikrit surprised everyone by taking my hand and asking King Abrayamsa to join us as we reviewed his elephants. After we walked past each animal, we continued to the far side of the courtyard where the military road came out of the mountains. There stood a six-year-old female elephant covered with a blue silk blanket with an elephant and a double-sailed Roman ship emblazoned in gold on each side of the young and beautiful animal. Standing next to her was a handsome young man my own age who was her trainer. As I walked up to pet her, Shikrit stated the unbelievable. "Jacobus, little Estara is my personal gift to you for your willingness to see our people as equals to your own, and for taking many of us into your extended family. My mother was the Jewish sister of the Jewish mother of King Abrayamsa and we have all sensed your Jewish kinship to ourselves. We also wish to thank you for bringing us another rabbi to aid our sadhu. Now my cousin also has a gift for you."

Turning to Abrayamsa I saw the same glow in his smile that attracted me the first day I met him. "My dear Jacobus, Estara, like all of us has few friends which she really loves. Her mother died a few weeks after she was born, and the ten-year-old son of one of my mahouts wanted to go to Shikrit's stables to be her brother. Jaya has been Estara's brother ever since. You might say they were raised together with Estara's aunts always there to look after them. Since it would be cruel to separate brother and sister at this age, and knowing your personal love for your own servants, I give Jaya to you as well. You can leave them to be nurtured in my stables or you can take them to Europa with you now or at any time in the future. For the time being your family in India is even larger. The Blue blanket draped over Estara is actually two banners which we encourage you to raise on your ship whenever you personally sail into a port, especially Roma.

As everyone else returned to the Assembly Hall, Tectos and I stayed with Estera and Jaya. Yacobsa and Rashvi remained behind to verify the cargo as it was delivered into one of the king's barns around the side of the palace near the stables and the river where it could be easily loaded onto the royal barges for delivery to the *Triton* for shipment.

Returning to the Assembly Hall, we were superbly entertained by a full-bodied orchestra which created sounds and rhythms I had never heard in my entire life. Then with a clang from an immense cymbal, a troupe of spectacularly attired dancers and vocalists appeared to dance out stories of ancient legends. Those from the Ramayana seemed hauntingly sad, and those from the Panchatantra were obviously boisterous and humorous. Their final numbers were deep statements of faith from the ancient Hindu Upanishads, "The One God" and "God Is Within You." None of us had ever seen or heard anything like this anywhere in the world in which we had extensively traveled. I could see that Thomas was deeply moved by the translated narrative provided by the sadhu.

It was late into the night when we finally mounted our horses and headed back to Paravur to spend the night. Sadhu, Rashvi, Hanno, Lucius, Tectos, and I would return to the palace the next day to complete a day of business. Prior to leaving we had a wonderful breakfast with all our delegation. To a person everyone thanked us for allowing them to experience a day that none of them would ever forget. In fact, many of them complained they would have no one to tell about it because no one would believe them. We said our goodbye as our sailors and archers left to return to the *Triton*. The remaining six of us who were needed at the palace mounted our horses and headed out.

When we arrived at the Palace, we were greeted properly by the Vizier who told us that Shikrit's trade items were in the barn by the river. His trade director was already there to help Sadhu, Rashvi, Hanno, and Lucius sort everything out. It would take a full day to get it all identified and ready to float down the river to the *Triton*.

The Vizier informed Tectos and me that we were welcome to join their Royal Highnesses on the back terrace overlooking the river. Taking him up on his suggestion we followed him through the palace to a beautifully pavilioned terrace of shinning marble. It covered nearly two full sides of the palace rising directly out of a bend in the river as it encountered a moderately forest-covered cliff which altered the rivers course.

Turning the terrace corner, we came upon the two naked kings performing breathing and muscle exercises which they called Yoga. They happily welcomed us as though they were in their royal robes, but as eunuchs we admittedly had a difficult time remaining focused. Eventually they completed their exercise routine and wrapped themselves in brightly colored, calf-length cloth that they referred to as sarongs, which were popular with the Malay traders from the Spice Islands. After visiting with us about Rome and Jerusalem for an hour, the kings excused themselves to get dressed.

As we waited Abrayamsa's manservant appeared with a silver tray with two cups of chilled yogurt whipped to a froth with sweet fruit juices. Tectos commented that for some reason the breezes blowing up the river from the ocean and through the trees and along the cool, shaded rock face seemed to reach the terrace significantly cooler than the breeze on the other side of the palace. We discussed the genius of Indian architecture and the environments in which they place their buildings. We began to see our Greek and Roman methods as inferior, though grander in many aspects. By the time we had redesigned the city of Roma, the kings returned in their proper, informal attire.

Joining our discussion, they emphasized the fact that south India has only two climates, hot and dry, and very warm and wet. Because of those realities, Indian architecture is never concerned with cold and seldom concerned with cool drafts except in locations like some very mountainous terrain as in some portions of Shikrit's realm. There, braziers may be occasionally required at night. We quickly found it easy to understand why HanChin silk fabrics were so popular in India among all but the poorest of people.

By evening the inventory was verified in Aramaic and a copy given to me to approve. I was actually stunned by the variety of the shipment and the reasonable total cost in gold coins we were required to pay for it. Of course, over the next two days we would discuss the items Shikrit desired to take in trade and the gold value of those trades. Tectos, Rashvi, and I had some tedious work ahead of us, with Sadhu's valuable help. By the time we were finished, both Shikrit and I detected an even closer bond than we had the previous year.

CHAPTER 61

WHERE'S MY HEART – DECEMBER 29, AD30

The next weeks were filled with hard work, as the crew and cargo slaves continued the heavy loading and packing of more bales of spices and tusks from King Shikrit which completed the packing of bulk items. Then came the myriad of baskets of HanChin pottery, jewelry, and silk. Every day as we waited on the monsoon, someone would bring us something special to pack. If the monsoon came later in January, we wouldn't have enough space to pack our barrels of fresh water. Those last days were also our final opportunity to pack dried fruits, melons, coconuts, and cured, salted, and dried meats plus a few sacks of flour for flat bread to go with every meal.

Our final preparations for departure, now carried the sense of urgency we faced a few days earlier. Knowing our departure would take place at any time, we spent many of our daylight hours with our Indian friends. In the process we created even tighter relationships with one another. As each day passed, I saw Sadhu more as my spiritual father and less as a business partner. He also realized that my love for his adoptive son, Yacobsa, was strong and unrelentingly eternal.

With Tectos at my side, I could easily remain in India until I died, but I also had that other half of me in Syracuse. Stephen was the most amazing man on earth, and he loved me dearly, and I him. However, I spent less than one month of nights with him per year, and many of those were with Tectos on the other side of the bed. The amazing Hanno, my first true love, was seriously considering a permanent life in India with Rashvi and his extended family there. He was slowly learning Malayalam from his life tutor and in his spare time he was even working with Sadhu and Thomas, both in the Jewish community and among the Hindus. That six-year-old orphaned sex slave had truly grown up to be a sensitive and awesome man of God who everyone, Roman or Indian alike, loved and respected.

Nearing the end of the year, we knew the time to sail home would be upon us soon, and decisions needed to be made within a month. I was leaving much of the technical wrap up to Rashvi and Tectos who were both extremely capable. As the days passed, the pain of parting from some of my dearest friends began to plague me. Yacobsa and Timnah were seriously considering building a home near the palace of Abrayamsa, while also thinking of the possibility of joining the palace staff. Considering the speed that Timnah was learning Malayalam, he would become a great asset to us in India. The one person we all new would remain in India was Thomas. He was very sure that he was right where God wanted him to be, and sincerely felt his life was complete in India.

I was prepared to return to Syracuse in all areas of my thinking except one, Estera. How do you say farewell to an elephant? Yes, she was calling me the loudest. She was the most amazing creature I had ever encountered. However, with Jaya's assurances she had accepted me as a part of her family within a week of meeting me. On the slow days, following the hectic times of project completions and establishing costs, I would head for the royal stables and spend as much time with her as my obligations would permit. Being with her was like my years with Josephus when we had no cares in the world and could play with our dog and monkey every day. Whenever she saw me entering the stable, Estera would call to me wanting me to just come and be with her for talking or petting. She loved it when Jaya and I would lay down with her and just talk to each other in limited Aramaic or directly to her in any language. In early December Jaya encouraged me to take her for a walk on my own. As frightening as it first seemed, each time she caressed me with her trunk she helped me feel more confident. Eventually Jaya asked me a logical question. "If she decided to run away, where would she run to? She knew the elephant stable was her home so where else would she want to go?"

Eventually Estera convinced me herself. When we unfastened her leash, she would begin to push me out of her stall. Within minutes she had me out and walking in the elephant exercise yard. After half an hour running off in every direction, she would always run back and try to talk with me or push me to go here or there. But it always seemed like a sudden impulse when she decided to run down to the river and take a bath. Jaya assured me she had planned that move all along.

Then one day Jaya called from the stable and told me to take my clothes off and join Estera in the river, or at least that is what I thought he said. When she saw me take my clothes off, she knew she had won and began to swing back and forth and call me. As soon as I got to the river bank, she was in all the way and slapping the water with her trunk like Aaron used to do with his arms. Suddenly, she would stop and look at me and finally shake her head until I bent over and began to cup my hands and splash water at her in return.

By that time, Jaya was at the bank taking his clothes off to join us. Estara really became excited seeing him remove his clothes. Actually, it got me a little excited, too. She knew it was going to be a fun time and she had won the communication game. Beautiful Jaya dashed in and threw himself over her back, causing her to slosh around trying to push him off with her trunk. After a few more pranks she stopped and looked directly at me, dropped to her knees, and rolled over on her side to get Jaya to slide off her back. All this was accompanied by our laughter and her loud squeaking. Then she just laid there and looked at us as she splashed the water with her trunk. Soon Jaya said that she wanted a massage, so side by side we rubbed her side, belly, and legs. As soon as we stopped, she began splashing water on us again until we began to splash water at her and then continued her massage.

After half an hour of rough play by the three of us, Jaya suggested we calm her down and get out. That afternoon swim became an everyday occurrence until the *Triton's* departure. The three of us became increasingly knitted together each day. It soon became obvious that the monsoon would begin any day and our time together would have to end. Not only was I deeply attached to Estara but to Jaya as well. During those final days I would wrap my arms around him whenever possible and he would always do the same with me. We would just hold each other, and not say a word for fear of saying something too personal or intimate.

Our good-bye was going to be difficult for each of the three of us, but as our departure approached I was sure there would be others besides Thomas who choose to stay. Yacobsa and Timnah were seriously thinking about it as was Hanno and Rashvi. As the first cloud blew across the sky from the northeast, I waited to hear of any stay behinds among us. Finally, it came. Yacobsa and Timnah came to me as soon as they saw that first cloud, to tell me they had made their final decision to stay. So much had changed in India since Yacobsa left years ago to find his fortune, first as a rabbinical student in Persia and then as an Indian merchant in Aegyptus. He had become whole since his return, not just because of his family's acceptance but because of the unconditional love he received every minute of the day from Timnah. He would still work this end of the Indo-Roman trade with Timnah's help. Timnah the camel boy even volunteered to assist Jaya with Estara. He had been spending a lot of time with her, and Jaya was sure he would understand how elephant's think just like he was able to do with camels.

That last night at Sadhu's house I assured Yacobsa and Timnah that I would miss them very much, but we would still be together for about four months each year. Rahelani reminded me that I was one of her boys and if something tragic ever happened in Roma, I always had my room upstairs. That night I went back to the ship and put together a saddlebag of gold for my two friends to use as needed for Aetna's business, and then I decided to fill a second bag, so they could build their new home next to the palace. Meeting them at the warehouses in the morning, just as it was beginning to sprinkle, I gave them their bags of gold and put my arms around them both and suddenly began to weep. Over and over I kept thinking of our time in the desert when I truly connected with my beautiful Prince.

Getting back into the longboat and rowing as fast as we could, we got to the *Triton* before the rain really began to come down in torrents and the wind picked up. Climbing aboard, Lucius saw my pain and took me into his arms and kissed me with greater tenderness and compassion than I had felt since I left Syracuse. Then Tectos took my hand and led me into our tent and laid down beside me. I felt his love reaching out to me as we felt the wind begin to fill our sails.

We were going home, but we would be back.

CHAPTER 62

MANUCHER – SEPTEMBER 19, AD31

Departing Alexandria, in route to India for the third time, we needed a replacement for Yacobsa. Having no one available in Syracuse or Alexandria who spoke both Aramaic and Malayalam, we began looking for someone who spoke any of India's major languages. Just six weeks before we were scheduled to sail up the Nile, we discovered that our contact representative for the Persian rugs in Sidon spoke Hindi, a language closely related to his Persian mother language, Farsi. Stephen and I took our next ship sailing to the western coast of Asia to discuss the possibility of him joining our team going to India.

Almost immediately, we knew he would be a great fit. He was twenty years old, just two years older than me. His family was taken to Babylon from Jerusalem over six-hundred years ago and never looked back. Manucher had known Yacobsa for only a few months in the Rabbinical School of Ecbatana before Yacobsa went home and then on to Alexandria. Returning with us to Syracuse, Manucher was eager to prove himself to me as an able component with Aetna Shipping.

He worked hard and skillfully preparing our Roman inventory for shipment and continually verifying the accuracy of our paper work.

When Captain Paulus arrived with the *Dolphin* two weeks before our scheduled departure, Manucher worked excellently with captain, crew, and cargo slaves as they packed the hold and checked each spreadsheet. Both the crew and cargo slaves admired his gentleness, which in the process, we learned that his Greek was impeccable with only a slight Macedonian accent.

When the day arrived for our departure, once again the entire extended family stood at the dock to cheer us on our way. Fortunately, the northeasterly winds were exactly what we needed to arrive in Alexandria. We had two days to spare, to consider any last-minute details, especially in the purchase of dried fruit, dates, fish, and other nonperishable foods. Our last task was to load the two large Aegyptian barges and have them ready to head up the Nile.

Manucher was also eager to prove himself to me as an able component in Aetna Shipping during our journey up the Nile together. Once again Hanno and Rashvi were central to our mission as they traveled together down the eastern coast of Aegyptus to reach Berenike about ten days ahead of us. This time Captain Paulus and his Breton crew and Galatian cargo slaves traveled with us up the river.

It was our third year in the India trade, and we began considering the future of the cousins who were developing into valuable assets to Aetna. Stephen and I decided to make them freemen if their excellent record continued until we returned to Syracuse the next winter. As soon as we arrived in Berenike the cousins were the first aboard the ship, along with Hanno, to inspect the hold and the storage area for our provisions and three barrels of water and one amphora of Italian wine.

After nineteen days on the water we finally reached the small hamlet of Erhor at the eastern tip of the mysterious island of Socotra. As we dropped anchor about two-hundred paces from shore, Lucius, Manucher, Hanno, Tectos, and I were welcomed by about fifty people more than happy to see their years' entire harvest of frankincense get hauled off to Roma and India by their mystery benefactor. Once again, the old man in the stone hovel was more than happy to accept a sack full of silver coins for his people in exchange for the fruit of his labor. Because we kept our word to him and returned every season, he never once attempted to raise the price on his frankincense. Climbing back into our longboat with two more barrels of cool spring water, and another chest full of top-quality frankincense we rowed to our ship and prepared ourselves for the last leg of our long voyage to India.

On three occasions while crossing the Mare Erythraean, Manucher awoke in the middle of the night to watch Tectos and me making love in our cozy, little tent pitched near the bow of the ship. We also shared the tent with Hanno and Rashvi, so when I mentioned it in passing to Hanno, he chuckled and whispered that they had noticed him doing the same with them probably five times. In Response, I asked him if he thought it was cruel to awaken him and basically tempt him beyond any viral young man's ability to resist such a floor show, especially when we had a full moon.

Three days later I went down the front hatch into the hold to get some small dried fish for a snack back in the stern. Half way to my goal I heard familiar soft whispers. Peaking over some baskets it was clear that Manucher had a thing for one of the cousins as they sat there holding hands. Was love in the air? I had no way of knowing, but they sure seemed to be attracted to each other. I decided that in the future it may be wise to let them have some discreet time together . . . but I thought the cousins were not eunuchs. Only time would tell.

At sunrise three weeks later, we noticed that bumpy gray line on the horizon. We would be in Muziris in a day and a half. Arriving at the mouth of the Periyar River we noticed only three ships anchored in the bay. That meant we were early enough to pick the finest qualities of most warehouse items. The excitement was affecting every one of us. Even Manucher, who had never been to South India was churning with pent up excitement.

On our arrival in Muziris, we experienced the warmest welcome any of us could have hoped for, especially from my little girl, Estera, and her increasingly handsome playmate, Jaya. I was stunned that she had grown to nearly my exact height and was now only half my age. It was Sadhu whose welcome was among the most touching. He wrapped his arms around me and exclaimed, "I thank God every day for compelling you to go to Synagogue that day in Alexandria where you met the Apostle. He has become the most tireless man I have ever known. He still carries his small cloth bag with him everywhere he goes, and he is going endlessly."

Sadhu brought me to tears of laughter when he proclaimed that King Abrayamsa had finally procreated another heir to the throne and was now considering the wisdom of retiring from that difficult vocation.

King Shikrit asked Tectos and me to join him for two weeks in his mountain palace. As I expected, our recreational time was spent primarily in his apartments. We did have a great time and it wasn't as sensuous as we had initially expected. However, I did often think of the temple dedicated to pleasure in Paravur. One thing I must say about the king is that he worked very hard to honor us as a married couple.

By the time of our fall departure to Berenike, it had become obvious that Manucher and the youngest Galatian cousin, Amyntas, were smitten with one another. That was not a problem for anyone on board, because they were both performing their duties flawlessly. However, it was a bit of an irritation for Tectos.

As the days passed, I knew I needed to bring the romance up and talk it over with him. When I did, it turned out that he wasn't upset about his cousin's happiness, but that he couldn't imagine his cousin in a true loving relationship. He always perceived Amyntas as an exploiter. Tectos' uncle named him after an ancient Galatian king which Tectos felt went to his head and made him very dominating in all of his friendships. When I pressed him on that point, he admitted that he really didn't want to see him happy, which was so unlike Tectos. Immediately I discovered I had another job. Tectos and I needed to spend more time with Manucher and Amyntas during our forty-five days isolated in the middle of a giant ocean.

Within an hour, Tectos approached me from behind, put his arms around me and apologized. Tectos never was a social person, but rather withdrawn with other people besides me. I was proud of him by the time we reached Berenike. He always liked Manucher and through that he learned to reach out to his cousin and actually see him for what he was, a eunuch in denial trying to be as masculine as his older brother. Suddenly he didn't have to pretend any longer, just show the man that he loved that he knew how to love.

By the time we reached Berenike and chose our camels for the journey to the Nile, the four of us were nearly inseparable. When we all arrived in Syracuse three weeks late, Amyntas was ready for his emancipation and eventual union with his Persian dream, Manucher. Fortunately, Amyntas older brother, Candor, seemed to hold no grudge, so he would also receive his emancipation.

Once again, when we returned to Syracuse our ship's hold was bursting with Roma's addictions. Our profits over those few seasons enabled Stephen to have four additional ships built for the Mare Internum trade and a large two mast ship like the *Triton* to work the Oceanus Atlanticus trade, calling on Brittania and northern and western Gallia. Aetna Shipping had worked its way up to be the fourth largest shipping company in the Mare Internum . . . and we weren't even Romans by birth or heritage.

CHAPTER 63

NOSTALGIA – OCTOBER 3, AD71

Aetna's pattern of growth and expansion continued until my wonderful Stephen died after we had over forty years together. That night Tectos spent sleeping on Stephen's left side and me on his right. I awoke out of a foggy dream to hear deep sobbing next to me. I quickly got my eyes open and saw Tectos laying across Stephen's chest sobbing uncontrollably. Reaching out to Stephen and touching his side I suddenly understood. Our beautiful Stephen had died in his sleep. I was in a state of shock and tried to pull Tectos off the man who had given him everything . . . even me. Stephen was already cold and a pale white near the color of the body sobbing on top of him. Getting up I ran to tell Aaron and his husband of his father's death, and to assist me with my grief stricken Tectos. It was as if Tectos wanted to die with his former owner and master. Once they extricated him from Stephen's chest, we saw in death, a still virile man who was the image of male strength and power even in his seventies. Yes, he was still the most beautiful man I had ever seen. A few days later, the entire Aetna family joined us as we placed him in the family tomb below his father, Sirach.

Ten days later we placed my beautiful Tectos next to him, after he died of a broken heart.

It was May and I decided that I needed to spend one more year or maybe two in India with my family there, to recover from my own grief. Josephus had died before we were twenty when he fell overboard in a storm. I had only seen him twice after I left Valentia. I had no one else but Hanno, and he was in India, also alone after the sudden death of his elegant Rashvi. Of course, I had my loving 'son' Aaron, but he and his Judean husband were running the third largest shipping business in the Mare Internum, second largest if we included India and our now strong presence in the Oceanus Atlanticus. They ran it all with the assurity of his father. We had made a terrific team for the last few decades, but it was time for me to go my way. Aaron slept with me about every other night and he was a compassionate comfort to me as a loving solace since the death of my husbands. Aaron was always the son this eunuch could never biologically have.

Brimming over with healing anticipation, I was in Alexandria by the second week in June to help prepare for the voyage to India. Yacobsa still owned the house which we used frequently, and the staff helped and encouraged me tremendously. By this point in my life I was extremely wealthy and wanted to take a small chest of gold for Thomas and his work among the poor and the Avarna.

We soon set sail up the Nile with a full contingent from Aetna Shipping. Within a reasonable time, we reached Berenike and I was comfortable enough to aid in our final preparations prior to our departure. I must admit it was exhilarating to walk up to the *Triton* and still see her beauty that Hanno had seen decades earlier when he purchased her. Her name emblazoned on the bow and stern looked freshly painted in brilliant colors. It also looked like she had fresh sails ready to be dropped to begin our long voyage.

Going to the captain's cabin, I introduced myself to a young man with piercing black, no nonsense, eyes. He estimated that we would be sailing down the Sinus Arabicus in three to four days. Then he mentioned that he seldom had passengers aboard. Trying to understand the reason for his dismissive comment, I mentioned that I often carried as many as eight passengers on the Triton, but she was a much younger ship in those days. Continuing, I mentioned she had made me a very rich man but now I needed to visit my elephant at the Royal Palace in Muziris for a few months, before going up to visit some of our partners in Persia. With that I walked off leaving him to think. I vowed to never address him first until we arrived in Muziris.

While eating breakfast on deck the day we were scheduled to depart, eleven additional loaded camels arrived at our loading planks supervised by an elderly man about ten years my senior. Somehow, he looked distantly familiar as he boarded the ship to greet the captain. But before he reached the captain, he stopped and stared at me and asked if I was Jacobus BarSirach. I nodded and smiled asking who I had the pleasure of meeting. Laughing ecstatically, he said he was Tectos' cousin, Candor, who I had freed from slavery about thirty-five years earlier. Wonderful! Now I had someone to talk to and learn from during the long voyage ahead.

First, I wanted to be sure he knew his cousin had died just two months earlier. As he nodded his head, I realized that the entire Aetna family would have heard of my two husbands' deaths through the shipping communication system. The evidence of his own sorrow for the death of his cousin was very evident on his face.

The next morning as the sails were dropped, I turned to admire the golden coloring of the fabric. It was then that I noticed after many years, that the *Triton's* trading colors were emblazoned on each sail ... a blue elephant with raised trunk over a blue double mast

Roman trading ship mounted on a blue band of water. Seeing our logo designed by King Shikrit so many decades earlier was like a personal sign welcoming me back to India.

Standing at the bow of the *Triton* forty-six days later, I felt exhilarated as I looked out over the tranquil river to the forests of Muziris . . . and we were only two days late. Asking my Galatian relative if he would like to join me at the Royal Palace when we go ashore in the morning, he turned to the captain who simply nodded. Once we left the longboat and its oarsmen at the wharf and there was no one else around to overhear, I had to ask what it was with the captain. He shook his head and simply said, "He is new from one of our competitors. Our regular captain was checking out the ship after getting it out of storage when he slipped, fell over the rail backwards, cracked his head and died. I can't help but pray that we haven't selected this new captain in error."

Entering the city of Paravur we first arrived at the synagogue and I stopped to walk in to see if the new rabbi might be available. He wasn't, so we continued walking to Sadhu's home where I stopped to ring the bell to see if any of the family was still there. When the servant opened the door, I asked for Prince Yacobsa thinking he would be my best chance. The old servant looked at me strangely and told me that he was 'now' in the palace. I thanked him and asked Candor to join me as I went on toward the palace. Arriving at the front parade ground, I decided to go around to the stables. Not knowing what to expect, I began walking around the elephant stalls when suddenly there was a ruckus down toward the far end. Continuing to walk I found Estara waiving her trunk with pure excitement. She was now nearly three times my height and had already given birth twice. Walking into her stall she began touching me and smelling me all over. It had been nearly ten years since I was last here to spend some time with her, but she treated me like it was only yesterday.

Looking for Jaya, I walked around the corner to the horses. There he was as handsome as ever, grooming a beautiful stallion. When he heard me approaching, he turned and shouted my name as he bowed deeply. I reached out, grabbed him, and pulled him to me, being as happy as he appeared to be. Holding Jaya in my arms was the best I had felt since the death of Tectos. I couldn't help myself, so I kissed him on his neck as I continued to hold him tightly. Then I detected him sobbing and I pulled back to look at him. Tears were running down his face uncontrollably. Without warning I kissed him on his lips and told him I missed him. Then he smiled and told me that he dreamed of me every night.

Walking back to a very anxious elephant, she ran her trunk all over both of us in sheer joy. She had her family again. Candor, who had followed me, had never witnessed anything like this and was literally stunned. Then I realized that Jaya and I had been holding hands the whole time. So what, we were old men and could do whatever we liked. With a gleeful smile spread across my face, I held his hand even tighter. Then I asked him about Abrayamsa, and he became very sad. With his head bowed, he reported that the king was killed by a leopard deep in the forest. Then I asked if one of his sons was now king. Jaya shook his head slowly while looking to the ground. They both had died from some terrible sickness. Giving up, I asked who the present king was. Then Jaya smiled as he lifted his head and shouted, "Yacobsa!"

Of course, Candor still understood none of what happened or what was said in Aramaic, so I told him that one of my oldest friends was now the King of Chera. Still holding Jaya's hand, we walked back around to the front of the palace and up the stairs to where the guards were standing. I asked Jaya to tell them I am King Yacobsa's old friend, Jacobus, from Roma who has come to meet with him. Hearing that, they looked at us strangely as one of them went inside. About five minutes later the door swung open and there stood my beautiful Prince.

Running out to the landing, he swept me into his arms and kissed me over and over. The guards and Candor were more than a little confused, but Jaya was laughing happily to see the king loving his master as much as he did. Seeing the happiness on Jaya's face, Yacobsa stopped and turned me to face Jaya. Then he said in a very matter of fact voice that Jaya loved me more than life itself, ever since that afternoon when he was presented to me with my elephant. After a brief moment's thought, I took Jaya's face in my hands and kissed his soft lips with all the love and passion I had been needing to share for months. When we finally came up for air, Yacobsa asked about the confused looking man standing off to the side. I simply answered that he was a cousin-in-law. The three of us laughed but Candor continued to stand there trying to understand what was happening.

King Yacobsa led us into the Palace, and I was struck with so many memories . . . and questions. Immediately I asked about Timnah. With a gleaming smile he replied that Timnah makes such an elegant queen. Seeing my confusion, he called a footman to find Timnah. After a few minutes she arrived. I gasped! Yes, he did make a stunning queen but what was going on.

Laughing and waiving his hands he attempted an explanation that made sense, "When Abrayamsa was killed we had a royal crisis. With my nephews also deceased the royal council wanted me to marry one of Abrayamsa's widows. That was never going to happen. First, I wouldn't. Second, I couldn't. You are familiar with my condition. If they put me in bed with one of those widows, I would not get aroused again for twenty years. So, I told them I already had a wife. At first the family was horrified that I would tell them that, but then they realized there was no alternative.

"My husband had to become my wife. In other words, my prince became my queen! The council keeps waiting for a pregnancy announcement, but there is none. We are thinking that when I die the crown may have to pass to my cousin Shikrit's grandson and then marry him off to one of my nieces . . . one of Merrayum's granddaughters. In the meantime, we have the beautiful and elegant Queen Timnah of Judea who has turned out to be some woman, and she is still trying desperately to conceive. Actually, I think the council is beginning to realize that she is now too old to bear children."

Looking at Queen Timnah I could see her as the hostess of an elegant state dinner, with the grace and beauty of any of India's queens. Fortunately, Timnah never truly matured as a man and still had skin as smooth as a baby's. One thing for sure though, if she ever entered a camel race she would win hands down.

CHAPTER 64

FINAL FAREWELL – MARCH 18, AD72

With my age at fifty-eight, I had spent a wonderful year and a half with my new manservant, Jaya, in the palace of the King and Queen of Chera. It had been a fabulous escape from the pressured reality of forty-four years of working with Aetna Shipping, most in the Indo-Roman trade. My acquaintance with the many children of my old friends had proved to be one of my greatest joys of my extended stay, living in India. These are the new leaders of tomorrow, not only in the palaces but in the temples, synagogues, churches, and schools of India. Queen Timnah had become as fluent in Malayalam as she was in Aramaic. After two decades with Rashvi, the love of his life, Hanno now spoke Malayalam and Tamil with the fluency of his Greek and Carthaginian. Still better for me, the precious love of my old age, Jaya, now speaks flawless Aramaic and even a little Latin.

With technical and political advances, it has become a smaller world, but the more I have learned about it, the bigger I realize it really is. Roma has become smaller as it has conquered more nations, for now, we know there are many more nations living beyond our frontiers who are growing ever more powerful each year. The giant HanChin Empire far to the east of India could prove to be an unsuspected rival to Roma, and as these empires grow stronger, the many nations between them will need to get out of their way. But where can they go? Or more accurately, where will they go?

Since the death of Jesus, the Judeans have been agitating for more freedom from Roman control. Eventually, there will be more provinces that will follow suit, of that I am very sure. Empires like Roma and Macedonia can only be held together with another nations' blood. I have been told that the HanChin in the far east are growing stronger every year and soon they will begin pushing their neighbors to the west out of their homelands. Then those nations will push their neighbors further to the west until vast armies flow across our borders from out of nowhere to destroy what Roma has built through the centuries with its spilling of so much blood.

The legendary Indian non-port of Muziris was still making monarchs and trading families very wealthy, but it is sucking the life out of Roma through the removal of its gold to feed its growing addictions which my family at Aetna Shipping helped create. As the Greek philosophers of centuries past warned, "For every event, there is a subsequent effect in the form of an unintended consequence." The greater the events the greater the consequences.

For instance, the more Judea irritates the power of Rome and presses to manipulate its conqueror, the greater the consequences they will bring upon themselves. They will crush themselves from within, leaving Roma with the job of cleaning up the mess afterward. The more the Roman state takes similar actions of force against other provinces, the weaker she will subsequently become. Then the cycle of birth and destruction will expand from one society to the next. It happened in the past with Macedonia and Carthage. I feel as though

I will see it in the future if I just live a little longer. However, it may take a couple hundred years, but eventually Roma will go broke, then suddenly, die, and disappear like everyone else before her.

Since living in India, I have learned to live for today and today only. The politicians in Roma and Jerusalem are doomed. It is just a matter of time. People like me have all the time in the world, and the world is still beautiful. Meanwhile, I have my wonderful Estara and my beautiful Jaya. Perhaps my elephant and her mahout are enough for now . . . and maybe forever.

Hanno had been working with the Apostle Thomas whenever he returned to the Malabar Coast. Occasionally he would join Thomas on a longer trip to share the truth of God's love with everyone, even the eunuchs. He did just that before I arrived back in India, when he joined Thomas in the Tamil city of Mylapor over the mountains on the east side of India. When Hanno explained the growing danger that they were facing in that region from the leaders of a very militaristic Hindu sect, I urgently encouraged them to stay in the western kingdoms of India. Predictably, Thomas returned to Mylapor while Hanno stayed behind to spend quality time with Jaya and me.

Hanno was my first adult love as the eunuch slave who guided me into my own eunuch adulthood from the time I was fourteen. I had been discussing with him my thoughts of taking Estara and Jaya up the coast of India to Persia and then maybe beyond as far as Syrian Alexandria or maybe even Sidon where we might catch one of our ships to Syracuse. I was also intrigued by the thought of traveling further down the east coast of the Mare Internum to the house in Alexandria, Aegyptus.

My biggest problem would be the need to take adequate amounts of food along to maintain Estara's diet. I knew there were some desert coasts along the way which could cause us a problem. I had also been speaking with the commander of the Royal Elephant Corps about the best way to achieve my goal. He was definitely helpful, especially when he suggested I talk to some of the Indian traders who visit Muziris during the monsoons after the Romans have all left. Using that simple resource taught me a great deal.

One day as Jaya and I were putting our plans together, Hanno came running to see us at the stables. He looked devastated and had obviously been weeping. Yacobsa had just received word from the King of Padyan that Thomas had been murdered by a militaristic Hindu priest who threw a spear into his back. Rather than the usual cremation, his local followers buried him and are erecting a monument over his grave. Yacobsa assured Hanno that the people of The Way in Mylapor were taking care of everything and he should not consider going there.

Now Hanno had to make some decisions about his own future. With Rashvi dead for sixteen years, Hanno had developed some strong skills for maintaining his independence, but he was nearly a decade my senior and his hard life had truly worn him down. The more he thought about it, the more he felt sure that he should travel back to Alexandria with me and move into the old house. Understanding his quandary, I asked him to sleep with Jaya and myself for a few weeks to help him sooth his loneliness and then decide if that was what he really wanted to do.

In spite of his age and harsh life, Hanno was still a very powerful man, and I knew that he might intimidate the delicate Jaya. But after his first night curled up around Jaya like a loving protector, I told him he had just discovered his new call in life. In fact, after a month with us, knowing most of his other friends had died or returned to Rome, he volunteered to drive a horse cart full of fodder and our baggage ahead of Estara on our trip to the Mare Internum. It was comforting to know that the love between us had never waned through the decades.

He continually promised he would always be there when I needed him, and he never stopped believing in me. He had journeyed from a castrated six-year-old sex slave to one of the greatest loves of my life, all the while showing the love and grace of God wherever he went.

Discussing our plans with Yacobsa, he reminded me that he had the good fortune of traveling to Ecbatana and back when he attended the Rabbinical School in Sadhu's hopes that he could assist him in Chera's synagogues This gave us some comfort knowing the king had made the journey twice before. He also offered to help make our journey a little easier by giving us some letters of introduction. Because of the Indo-Roman trade networks he had relations with several kingdoms up the coast as far as the mighty Indus River. From there the number of Jewish settlements would begin to increase as we entered Persia. Once we crossed over into the Roman province of Assyria at the western end of the Sinus Persicus, we would only need to follow the Euphrates River northwest to Babylon and then on the ancient King's Highway toward Edessa, then straight west to Syrian Alexandria and the Mare Internum. We all felt the journey was possible and that Estara could easily make it if we reached the Persian coast in the spring when there would be more grass for her to eat.

We eventually decided it would be best to leave just after the northeast monsoons lost most of their power, when travel up the coast would be more comfortable. That gave us about three months to plan any details necessary and send some correspondence to a few kings along our route. Yacobsa's stables prepared everything we needed, including a large cart and a recently retired war horse who was still blessed with adequate stamina, and who was already well acquainted with Estara and Jaya.

As the day of our departure drew near, the palace leather smith completed a padded collar for Estara which could hold several hundred gold coins for emergencies plus a baggage platform for on her back which we would need to remove and place in the cart for a few days each month to prevent any sores caused by the rubbing of its straps. Naturally we had planned to stop every few days, so we could all have a bath and some fun. Yacobsa even presented Estera with all her royal parade trappings which she had worn for decades at all official occasions and royal processions. She looked magnificent in her formal attire, and everyone would know she was a special royal elephant and not a working animal. He also gave Jaya his royal livery so he, too, could look the part when we reached a border or a royal city.

The day before our scheduled departure, King Yacobsa hosted a great banquet for our many friends and family to join in bidding us farewell. The gracious Queen Timnah saw to it that everything was perfect. She was amazing! Princess Rahelani taught her fabulously well. In fact, that last night, as I watched her hostess our farewell, I saw Rahelani in her every move and gesture she made. She certainly loved Yacobsa to have totally altered her personal gender identity to remain at his side every minute of every day . . . and night. As she kissed me farewell the next morning, I was truly kissed by a great queen. Her people had sincerely grown to love her, even if she was born a Jew. After all, they had had a Jewish queen in the past.

CHAPTER 65

REFLECTIONS – SEPTEMBER 25, AD73

Before we left the palace courtyard, we took Estara to bid farewell to her two adult children, her several grandchildren, and her one remaining old aunt who had helped raise her. Estera seemed to sense that it would be her last time with her family, but she also sensed it would be a special day and her excitement was evident in everything she did. As we left later that morning, we paraded through Paravur and were greeted by everyone we passed. Knowing that we were coming, some even threw flowers or handed us strings of flowers to wear around our necks. It was the most beautiful and most sincere farewell I had ever experienced. Most of these people had never met me, but they all seemed to know Hanno.

Walking down the road, as we entered the beautiful forest on our way to the Periyar River, I began to reflect on the unbelievable life God had granted me. I was a spoiled egocentric child in a wealthy family who didn't want to grow up . . . if I couldn't do it my own way. I knew that I could never like girls. My twin brother was a great lover, and I knew I could never find any girl who was better than him. After reaching legal adulthood at fourteen, I was contractually sold to my father's uncle to serve as an apprentice on one of my family's ships. It was there I lived with two slaves who were adult men ten years my senior. These men were truly sent from God, for they introduced me to the true meaning of love, charity, and compassion. I learned to love them passionately, as they loved me. One even died protecting my life, while the other lived to protect my future life. Still, the three of us learned together what love and trust was. Without their tenderness I could have never opened my life to God. We were three eunuchs, two created by the cruelty of the knife and the third created a eunuch by the grace of God. Being anything other than a born eunuch was beyond my capacity to imagine.

That afternoon, as we reached the Periyar River we took all the royal trappings off Estara and the rest of us to pack them away. I hired a ferry barge to take the cart and our belongings across the river, and then all of us . . . including Hanno's big warhorse . . . took a swim across the river together and got settled on the north bank. Fun loving elephants tend to keep us young in our old age just as children do. Even so, we only played for a short time. Then Hanno hooked up the cart to begin our journey north. As usual, Estara liked it best when I rode on her shoulders directly behind Jaya . . . which was my choice, too. Holding onto his tight waist was very invigorating. We always made a point to stop at midday in a grove of trees or a grassy meadow so Estara could have a brief meal before we stopped for the night. On some occasions we came upon rivers that had no barges or fords to use for crossing, so we would follow the road for an extra couple of days up the river until we reached a crossing of some sort. We had plenty of time to enjoy one another's company, as I frequently got down and rode with my best friend, Hanno.

Often when riding with Hanno, I would gaze across the water and listen to the surf pounding the beach as I reflected about how God had used Hanno everywhere he went. Even though he had had "man sex" at least seven thousand times before the day God knocked on his heart's door, he had been sharing God's love ever since that day. To me, the amazing thing was how quickly he discovered the difference between sex and love. Hanno had gone from a man with no concept of love, to becoming a man who demonstrated love everywhere he went, to everyone he met. The amazing thing was that everyone seemed to love him back . . . even our local Hindu priests. The truth is that I became a better man because I was loved by him.

Coming back from my mental distraction I had to admit that much of the territory we passed through was some of the most beautiful landscapes I had ever seen, and so were many of the cities. Every royal city we passed through with our introduction from King Yacobsa welcomed us diplomatically, so we all made a point to wear our king's livery, especially Estara when entering a royal city. Having a royal elephant several months journey from her king was a true sensation, even among some of the kings we visited. Of course, the farther north we went the more difficult it was to find people who understood Malayalam or Tamil. We were very fortunate to have had a Hindi speaking scribe in Yacobsa's court who wrote several letters for us in that northern language.

Over forty-five years earlier, that night when I first met my Prince on the promenade in Alexandria changed my life forever. I had never imagined that a man as beautiful and elegant as Yacobsa could even exist. He took my breath away that night, just as he did the morning he kissed me good-bye in front of his palace. Those days in the desert spent in his arms while resting in the shade of our camels can never be forgotten. As much as I wanted to give myself to him, we knew our love was to be given to another. The next day, arriving at the *Triton* for his first time, he found the man of his dreams, Queen Timnah of Chera, the Judean camel driver.

Arriving back in the land of the camels, we approached the major Indo-Arab seaport city of Braganza, located on an immense bay that extended several days journey into the Indian heartland, there we needed to make a decision. Did we want to continue for about ten days traveling around the massive peninsula that formed the bay or cut overland on a royal road to the northwest, which would take only about four days? This would mean that Estara would need to forgo her daily bath. We were obviously not in a rush so Estara's vote carried the day. Actually, we all enjoyed the afternoon romps in the surf. Once we reached the large estuary at the northeast end of the gigantic peninsula, our course would take us northwest toward Persia.

Traveling northwest for eighteen days, along the shores of the Mare Arabicus we eventually reached the last of India's great rivers, the Indus, where Alexander established the eastern edge of his Greek empire. Fortunately, we found a large ferry crossing just one day's journey up river, which was far enough away from the marshy flood plain to provide a high and dry road for the horse and cart. Once again, we traveled along the coast for another week within the former territories of the Greeks. Eventually we encountered the small Roman trading outpost of Barbaricum, which maintained a massive caravan route along the southern coast of Persia to the Roman province of Assyria in the west. We were beginning the last and most difficult leg of our adventure.

Stopping to enjoy some well-earned rest for man and beast, we set up a small encampment on the edge of a grassy meadow on the beach just beyond the nearby town. Laying back under the date palms, it was the perfect location for reflection. Looking south across shimmering water I was reminded of the silver-gold hair of my beloved Tectos, the brilliant slave, born a prince. I neglected to really notice him until after our first journey to India on the *Triton* was completed. In all my hours of subsequent reflection I could never understand how I could have neglected noticing that most beautiful pearl shut away in our hold full of treasures. He was always quick to respond to orders or even simple observable needs, and his degree of curiosity was beyond anything I had observed in any slave. I sincerely believe that if I could have seen that precious pearl in the *Triton's* oyster-like hold, I could have saved him from over a hundred rapes. Finally, my blindness fell away, and I discovered the love of my life sleeping in the darkness below my feet. I thank God, I noticed him before it was too late. Thinking of his death. I realized how fortunate I was to have two husbands in love with each other as fully as I loved them. But as I entered my senior years, to discover our patriarch, Stephen, dead between us, and then Tectos' death by sorrow shortly after, was nearly more than I could handle. Returning to India to visit my two remaining loves, Hanno and Yacobsa, was the medicine Aaron recommended. Now I have Hanno sleeping beside me again, as my sorrow ebbs further away each night.

After a few days rest and conversations with the commanders of the small Roman garrison at Barbarica, we prepared ourselves for the journey on the trading road along the desert coast of Baluchia. The temperatures were beginning to cool as the breezes began blowing from the north, but we knew fresh water would be vital for someone as thirsty as Estara. We were assured by the locals that every few days travel we would find a village or a spring of fresh water.

In thirteen days after departing Barbarica we reached the small Roman trading outpost of Oraea where we rested for two days. In another ten days we reached the beautiful agricultural region of Ommana which was famous for its wine and dates. After resting here for another day, we traveled through many farming and fishing villages until we reached the mouth of the Sinus Persicus.

From this point forward, we traveled a hilly coast road at the foot of snow-caped mountains which, because of the cooler weather, provided adequate fodder for Estara. She enjoyed the novelty of cool weather but still got excited each time we stripped her for her anticipated bath in the surf. Throughout our time on the road, Jaya would often lead our war horse into a gentle surf on a sandy beach where Estara would want to play with him. Every one of us still seemed happy and healthy, especially Estara, who loved having us play with her continually. In this less populated region I was able to spend more intimate time in the cart with Hanno. We had memories of the thousands of tender nights when we had the opportunity to share our hearts and bodies with one another, especially after the murder of Mago. There were times I would spend a whole afternoon sharing my love with him as our horse just followed the big elephant ahead of him. I was so thankful that, in our old age, God had brought us together again to be comforts for one another after our numerous losses.

This sparsely populated region continued for a month more of easy travel along the north shore of the Sinus Persicus. Eventually, the mountains to our north got smaller and smaller until they finally disappeared. We found ourselves on a dry salt plain and I became very concerned about food for our animals. The road we were on was still well traveled, in fact more so, therefore encouraging us to continue to the northwest and hope for the best. Then we saw it, a true Roman town larger than the small Persian hamlets we had passed through in the last month. We had reached the border of Rome's province of Assyria. Stopping to pay the usual Roman border tax, we were kindly informed of the best route to travel with an elephant who loved to take baths.

Continuing on in the following days, we found more agriculture in this fertile land, interspersed with small marshes and canals as we traveled on. Six or seven days of water, reeds, and marshy grasses were all we could see to our west which delighted Estara to no end. We had just successfully traveled the route that the Seleucid Greek armies used to resupply their forces with Indian war elephants. Thinking of those ancient times I couldn't help but reflect on my wonderful Tectos again and the fear his ancestors felt when the Greek war elephants would charge their Galatian foot soldiers and cavalry. Now here we were with peaceful, fun loving Estara, our playful elephant.

The marshes finally ended, and we could make our way west to the mighty rivers of ancient Babylon. In the cool waters of the Tigris River, which was fed by the streams coming down from the Zagros Mountains to our east, was where sweet Estara loved to bathe and drink every evening at sunset. Following the Tigris for about two weeks, we came upon a city which used large barges to move armies and livestock across the Tigris to the Euphrates River and the ancient city of Babylon to the west.

For days I had wondered why the Romans, or anyone before them, seemed to have never built major bridges across these great rivers. They did it everywhere else they went. Why not here? Finally, after passing through countless villages and cities since beginning our journey north along the Euphrates on the ancient Kings Highway, the reason slowly became obvious. I saw no buildings built of stone or timber! Everything was made of bricks of dried mud or fired clay. In this terrain, even Rome had to bend to conform to the world around her.

After a month and a half of walking along the beautiful river, we saw mountains to our north, the indicator that we would soon have to turn west again following the ancient Kings Highway which connected Babylon with Aegyptus. We were finally on the last leg of our journey as we traveled west from the city of synagogues, Edessa, towards Syrian Alexandria on the shore of the Mare Internum. Recalling that Stephen brought me there the first time, caused me to weep. It was there, two weeks after the crucifixion, that we first met a young Manucher and our extended family of Persian Jews who became our steady supply of beautiful carpets from Persia and the countries to the north. Those nights spent exclusively with Stephen were the dreams of any young eunuch come true . . . especially mine. Falling asleep in his arms every night gave me the assurance that all was well, even after the terror we had just lived through during that never to be forgotten Seder in Jerusalem decades earlier. The more I remembered of those nights of passion and love the more I wanted to weep, but also the more I found myself rejoicing for God having given me such a wonderful man for so many years.

Before arriving at Syrian Alexandria, the ancient Kings Highway turned straight south heading through the Syrian breadbasket to Damascus. There we learned that the highway would divide again to form the Coast Highway heading southwest. The Coast Highway went around a large snow-covered mountain and followed the Upper Jordan River south to the large lake in Galilee where Jesus had once lived. From there it was an easy journey to Alexandria on the Nile. We decided to stay on the Coast Highway.

Traveling southwest out of Damascus for a few days, we noticed several contingents of military personnel along the road marching toward Damascus. The soldiers looked exhausted and among them we would see an occasional wagon of wounded. As startling and bizarre as they looked to us, I was sure we looked even more so to them. Since our arrival in Damascus, and noting a military presence there, we decided to dress our animals and ourselves in the royal livery of Chera. Seeing us coming down the road toward them, I knew we were the last thing they expected to see. At one point, where the highway followed the Upper Jordan River down into Galilee, we were stopped by an officer who "needed" to inquire about our presence in the Galilean mountains. Gracefully Estara kneeled to the ground as I dismounted and approached the officer's horse, handing him a letter of introduction in both Greek and Latin signed by King Yacobsa, King of Chera. He looked at me like I was a talking Aethiopian baboon and asked how in the world I got to Galilee from India. Pointing to dark skinned Jaya I replied that we had traveled for nearly a year after leaving my ship and crew to sail back to Rome with our Indian treasure, but without us. Now we wanted to tour the extremities of the Empire. Seeing him stare at Hanno in the cart, I simply said, "He is my loyal Carthaginian servant since I was fourteen years old and he goes with me everywhere."

Shaking his head in puzzled disbelief, he returned my letter of introduction and waived us on. As Estara was assisting me while remounting her, he advised me to go directly to Caesarea from Galilee as they were having some difficulties in Judea. Thanking him for the information and courtesy, Estara gave him and his soldiers a parting blast of her trumpet as though she wanted to be a part of their military procession. The next day we arrived in Capernaum and let Estara play in the cool waters of the lake until evening. The next day, we continued down the highway toward Caesarea, but as the highway forked again, we turned south to Aegyptus, still encountering an occasional Roman platoon, but no one else.

On our third day of traveling south to Aegyptus, we reached the old camel caravan road from Jerusalem which wandered down out of the hills to merge with the highway north to Caesarea and south to Aegyptus. Looking up in the direction of the small village of Timnah, the birth place of the Queen of Chera, we knew that Jerusalem was just a day's journey beyond. I called back to Hanno and asked if he would like to go to Jerusalem. Laughing, he said he would love to. Turning east we began our climb into the Judean highlands anticipating a great reunion, but things seemed strange. There was no traffic on the road! Stopping to spend the night at an old camel camp, we found everything strangely quiet. Not even a Roman soldier could be seen or heard.

Setting up camp we remained ill at ease. The only sounds were a few barking stray dogs and perhaps a jackal or two. Spending a restless night, we were all looking forward to dawn, especially our animals.

CHAPTER 66

DAY OF TERROR – OCTOBER 3, AD73

The next day, as the morning breeze came down the hills from the east, both animals became agitated. We noticed it, too! There was a faint foul odor in the air resembling Rome's burning garbage pits. We had smelled the garbage burning in Jerusalem's Kedron Valley before, but this was more rancid than that. Hurriedly we packed up and dressed in our royal livery and headed into the hills toward Jerusalem. The further we traveled into the afternoon, the worse the odor became. Eventually, it became putrid and Estara, not being a war elephant, had to be urged to continue. Finally, cresting the last hill we saw it!

There, less than a mile away, were giant piles of stone and rubble surrounded by decomposing naked corpses hanging from hundreds of crosses. Where the gate to the city once stood, piles of corpses were dumped against the base of what was left of the city wall. There they lay, some burning like an overcooked roast right where they landed when they jumped or were pushed from the top of the wall before it was pulled down from the other side. Even the Temple Mount was missing . . . just a pile of rubble and smoke which still drifted up into the gentle breeze blowing toward the sea.

What happened to our many younger friends? Could our family have survived just an hour away? Up on the ridge at Bethphage there were many places to run and hide before the Romans got there. All we could do was pray that they got away and fled north along the Jordan River or south across the desert to Alexandria. The wonderful men I had loved . . . gone, especially the courageously beautiful Aaron BarHanno. He was one of the bravest men I had ever met, surviving the butchering of his stomach and genitals to go on and proclaim God's goodness by taking the name Aaron, God's messenger. I prayed with all my heart that he was alive somewhere.

It was over. The stubborn Judeans of my heritage finally went too far, and Rome had had enough. For three years the prophet had told them how God wanted them to live, but they wouldn't listen. Instead they crucified him and today thousands of Judeans had been crucified, too! Why did they have to be so stubborn? God had so much for them to accomplish. He had unified the world under Rome and given us the opportunity to make a difference with our witness of God's love. Hanno sat weeping in the cart just asking over and over, "Why wouldn't you listen?" It was their golden opportunity to change, not just themselves, but also the world around them. They insisted on doing it their own way, even fighting among themselves. Now they were wiped from the face of the earth. Those few of us who are left must accept the task to share God's love and grace with the same people who did this to us.

It was September 25, AD73 and three very broken and devastated eunuchs left Jerusalem that day, vowing to make a difference ourselves.

We had also seen great suffering inflicted on eunuchs by the righteous and powerful of both Rome and Judea, but we always persevered. Whether we were born eunuchs like myself, made eunuchs like Hanno, or chose the life of a eunuch like Thomas, Jesus told Thomas and the others that it was proper for us to not marry and have a family. We were always different, and others often didn't like us unless they could use or manipulate us to their advantage.

What will the future hold for us now that Jesus and his message of love and mercy has been taken from us? We had already heard that some in Damascus have said that eunuchs should live without intimacy and love. Instead we should close ourselves in cells or desert caves and be penitent for our sins. There we should stay without the loving touch of another human and live our entire lives like an unclean leper. Does God intend us to be imprisoned in our own bodies without ever feeling any source of human love or touch? If that is so, mankind doesn't need such a God. But God created eunuchs to live for love and intimacy just like everyone else.

That night, as we left Jerusalem, I thanked God for giving me and the castrated slave, Hanno, the gift of love. God had protected me from a life of black and white rigidity, where everyone believes that they are the only ones who can be right, and they will fight to the death to prove it. Yes, leaving Jerusalem after seeing the terror caused by such a need to be perfect without consideration of others, we continued down the highway to Alexandria, stopping only to eat what our stomachs could hold down. On the second night we felt far enough from the evil to stop and rest. Going about two hundred paces to seclude ourselves behind a grove of olive trees we set up camp protected by a cart, a horse, and an elephant. There Jaya, Hanno and I laid down in one another's arms. We were thankful that God had blessed us with each other's love . . . especially Jaya who chose to wait nearly forty years until I considered him of value to me.

Actually, our exhaustion could not overtake us that night. We seemed driven to share our love with one another throughout the night. By morning our emotional tiredness was equaled only by our physical exhaustion, so we agreed to sleep on until midday under the shade of the olive trees. Later in the day, in the brilliance of daylight, we noticed that periodically along the road there were bundles of clothing or valuables scattered everywhere along the roadside. There were obviously survivors who did escape out of the hills. With each mile we traveled there were increasingly more items scattered beside the road. In the late afternoon we saw our first body. It was an old woman who bore no evidence of having been killed, but rather died of her own exhaustion. Until nightfall, we saw only one other body. This must have been a valid escape route.

The next afternoon we came upon the Hebron Road which came down out of the hills, three days journey south of Jerusalem. It was also littered with personal belongings which became less important the further they had to carry them. The next morning the coastal city of Gaza was cited on the horizon, so we halted for a while to bring out our royal trappings before we continued toward the city. Arriving near the city walls we encountered hundreds of people huddled around small cooking fires, most with few belongings with them. Sadly, we noticed that most were men, but there were very few children. Choosing to continue on the road to see what was happening in Alexandria, we came upon a young man who was severely beaten, limping along the side of the road. When I heard Hanno call from behind I asked Jaya to stop Estara. After a few minutes he came up beside us with the young man and said he felt impressed to stop and talk with him. He was from Bethphage!

I told Hanno in Carthaginian to put him in the cart beside him, clean his wounds, give him some food and water, then learn what he could from him as we continued on our way to a satisfactory campsite before sunset. Later as Jaya prepared our evening meal Hanno told us that the young man's name was Aaron BarJoseph. "He also said he was named after Aaron BarHanno who led his family to an understanding of The Way. When I told him that I am the Hanno who led Aaron, my fellow Carthaginian, to an understanding of The Way, he grabbed me, wouldn't let go, and wept. He believes that Rufus and the rest of his household escaped the night before he did. He was sure they were heading to Alexandria."

Sitting around the fire for two more hours we learned many wonderful things about our Bethphage family. The only truly sad news was that both Alexander and Eli had died recently. Aaron was sure that everyone had headed for Alexandria in the night that Jerusalem began to burn.

When it was time to get some sleep, Hanno suggested that Jaya and I sleep with him as usual and he would give Aaron a blanket to sleep nearby. Giving Aaron his blanket the young man asked if it would acceptable if he slept next us. I then cautioned him that we were eunuchs and that he may feel uncomfortable next to us. Looking down into his lap he confessed he was also a eunuch. By the time the sun came up over the eastern desert both Hanno and Aaron were sound asleep under the same blanket. As we finally got up and dressed, Hanno confessed that he felt like Aaron's grandfather.

As the days progressed Hanno became more closely attached to our young man knowing that God had guided us to him for a very important reason. Soon we arrived at the river crossing near Memphis where we lined up with other Judean refugees to board a barge to be ferried to the western bank of the Nile. By this time Aaron had become extremely attached to Estara, as she became very trusting of him. Whenever we stopped for a break he would lean against one of her magnificent tusks and rub her trunk. One morning while passing workers in a vegetable field next to an irrigation canal, Jaya called down for Hanno to buy a sack of vegetables for Aaron to feed to Estara. Being asked to feed Estara when we stopped for lunch truly made Aaron's day, and Estara's as well. She was beginning to bond with a young man again.

On our fifth day walking down the western estuary the Pharos became visible over a grove of low growing trees. That night as the four of us laid together a short distance from the eastern gate, looking at the giant beacon I couldn't help but share the details of the night I met the beautiful man who is now the King of Chera. When I told him that I also got to know his husband here and eventually introduced them, Aaron obviously became confused. How could a king have a husband? With that we all chuckled as I shared the story of the Jerusalem camel driver who actually married the future king one day at the house we were planning to stay at in Alexandria. He couldn't believe it. Telling him that his husband had to become his wife when he became king totally pushed my credibility over a cliff. Then as I referred to her as Queen Timnah of Chera he challenged me for telling him a children's fairytale. Laughing we all swore it was true, but it seemed too far outside the realm of possibility for him to accept.

At the break of dawn, we were four eager men anxious to enter Alexandria's eastern gate ahead of all the refugees we had passed on the road on the day before. Once again, we were dressed in our finest livery, including Aaron who we festooned up beautifully. We began our parade to the eastern entry to the Jewish quarter where we stopped and prayed. Dismounting as we entered the gate I led the way to Yacobsa's house. I knocked on the door and waited. I prepared to knock again just as it opened.